By David Liss

The Day of Atonement

The Day of Atonement

A Novel

DAVID LISS

Random House
New York

Copyright © 2014 by David Liss

Published in the United States by Random House, an imprint and division of Random House LLC, a Penguin Random House Company, New York.

RANDOM HOUSE and the HOUSE colophon are registered trademarks of Random House LLC.

LIBRARY OF CONGRESS CATALOGING-IN-PUBLICATION DATA

Liss, David.
The day of atonement : a novel / David Liss.
pages cm
ISBN 978-1-4000-6897-5
eBook ISBN 978-1-5883-6963-5
1. Inquisition—Fiction. I. Title.
PS3562.I7814D39 2014 813'.54—dc23 2013049206

Printed in the United States of America on acid-free paper

www.atrandom.com

987654321

First Edition

Book design by Virginia Norey

For Eleanor and Simon

The Day of Atonement

Prologue

Lisbon, 1745

When I was a boy, there were days when I was out-rageously, deliriously happy, even while I knew such happiness to be a mistake. Perhaps it is merely the way memory works, but over the decade that followed, I came to believe that the day of my greatest happiness was also the last time I knew of any happiness at all.

I recall running along Chiado Hill, moving with the grace and speed possessed only by the young, winding through streets crowded and so narrow I could have reached out and touched the houses on opposing sides. Seven years before that day, when I had been only six years old, my uncle had been trampled to death by a care-less *fidalgo* on horseback not far from the very spot where I ran. My mother often reminded me of the dangers, but I knew better than she—or, I presumed, my late uncle—how to avoid them. I was an expert at dodging beggars and peddlers, avoiding the notice of judgmental priests, and leaping over piles of donkey turds. I knew how to place my feet to avoid slipping upon the street stones, uneven and loose. I made myself an engine of propulsion, as methodical and unwavering in my purpose as the distant windmills on the hills beyond Lisbon.

That day I ran with perhaps a bit more caution than was my usual. I was thirteen years old, and had the sense of invulnerability of all boys that age, but I was also a Portuguese New Christian, and therefore well attuned to the ways in which the universe's clockwork mechanism produced irony and misery in equal measure. I'd seen men taken by the Inquisition on the same day they were to be married or had witnessed the birth of a child. Both of my grandfathers and one of my grandmothers had died in the dungeons below the Palace of the Inquisition. My mother often said that too bright an outlook invited bad luck, and I knew she was right. But that did not mean she had to be right today.

Over and over again, I put my hand inside my pocket to make certain it was still there—the necklace I had bought, just that morning, from Old Paolo, the peddler. I clutched it and felt the cool of the silver, which somehow reminded me of the softness of Gabriela's skin. The necklace was for her, and so it seemed to me almost a part of her already, and touching it felt intimate and exciting and forbidden. I also wanted to make certain a pickpocket hadn't taken it, for to travel five minutes out of doors with silver on your person was to invite theft.

I had lived all my years in fear and uncertainty, for that was the lot of my kind, but that day, at that moment, all was different. I had decided I was in love, and though she had not said so, I was sure Gabriela loved me in return. Earlier that afternoon, we had kissed for the first time, and I knew, right then, how I wanted my life to unfold. I knew how it *must* unfold because we would not be in Lisbon forever, nor even for long. Soon, we would no longer live in fear. It seemed simple and inevitable.

I was not supposed to know any of this, but I had a habit of eavesdropping. This was surely my father's fault. If he did not send me out of the room when he discussed matters of importance, I would not have to resort to listening in secret. If he were willing to share with me the family business, I would never have had to teach myself how to unseal and reseal notes without leaving a mark on the wax. I knew he had his reasons. In Lisbon, secrets could be deadly. Perhaps he was right not to trust a boy my age, but someday he would realize how much faith he could put in me. Until then, I would take matters into my own hands.

I never said a word of what I knew, though I ached to tell this secret to Gabriela. By law, New Christians could never leave Portugal, but my father had money secreted away, and he intended to bribe soldiers and customs agents and sailors. He had friends among the colony of English merchants, that confederation of traders called the Factory. I had read the letters, written in code, that my father had sent to his friend the Englishman Charles Settwell. Our family and Gabriela and her father were going to leave. The five of us would flee to England or the Netherlands or France or another country beyond the Inquisition's reach.

Perhaps it would not be this month, or even this season, but plans were in motion, and they could not be stopped. My father would soon have the money he required, and in Lisbon, the power of money dwarfed the power of the law, the crown, and sometimes, if luck was with you, even the Inquisition.

No, I could not tell Gabriela about any of this, but I could show her what she meant to me. For now, that would have to be enough.

I emerged from a series of dark and winding alleys and onto my own street, wider and brighter, with attached houses covered with glittering tiles. All through the city, bells rang, as they always did, loud and clear and bright. They were the sound of home. I ran past a trio of New Christian traders, friends of my father, clustered in serious conversation, and if they paused to look up at me as I sped past, I thought nothing of it. I offered the men a wave and moved on. I ran past a cluster of dark-robed Jesuits, and if their eyes fell upon me, I hardly cared. I even ran past the very worst of that species, the Jesuit Pedro Azinheiro, an Inquisitor who was said to hate Englishmen even more than New Christians. The man was a dandy, a womanizer, a mockery of a priest, and there was no one more feared among the city's merchants. Even so, I waved at him as well. I was merely running, and even the Inquisition would not make a crime out of that.

The hill grew steeper yet, and I began to run short of breath, but it hardly mattered. I stopped and leaned forward for a moment, breathing hard, feeling the sweat drip down my back. My shirt, under my waistcoat, clung to my body. It was May, and already as hot as summer. I knew it would be cooler wherever my father chose to take us. That would be a nice change.

I found her where she said she would be, only a few streets over from our houses, outside the church of São Roque. She sat on the low stone wall, her legs dangling beneath her long brown skirts. She wore a bonnet that covered most of her inky hair, but the sight of a few wayward strands escaping their bondage excited me in ways I did not yet entirely understand.

Gabriela was lovely, and I was by no means the only one who thought so. Grown men stopped to look at her. That buffoon Eusebio Nobreza often attempted to strike up halting conversations with her, but if I was around, we children would start giggling, and Eusebio would storm off, infuriated.

Now neither of us giggled. I walked over to her, still winded from my run, taking in deep breaths as I let the sight of her wash over me. I tried to be subtle even as I stared at her big, dark eyes, her round face, her sharp nose, slightly flat at the bridge. All of her perfections and imperfections cast a spell, and I found that, for a moment, I could not speak.

"You're late," Gabriela said, pursing her lips into a knot. "I told you to meet me here *before* the bells rang."

Just like that, I was no longer apprehensive. Why should I have been? This was Gabriela, not a stranger. I had no memory of anything before I knew her. We had almost no secrets from each other. She knew the whole of who I was, and knowing that, she had chosen to kiss me that very morning.

"I'm only seconds late," I told her as I pushed myself up on the wall to sit next to her.

"Still," she said with a smile both wicked and shy, "you shouldn't keep a lady waiting."

"Then I won't," I said. "Never again." I reached into my coat pocket and pulled out the necklace. "I brought you something," I told her, holding it up for her inspection. What I wanted, more than anything, was to put it on her. I wanted to reach out, placing both hands behind her neck, and gently brush her skin with my fingers as I fastened the hooks. The thought of doing it made my heart pound, and so I hesitated, and that instant became several seconds while I remained frozen, holding up the silver. Gabriela's eyes went wide and then narrow and finally wide again. What did it mean? I tried to interpret her expression like a Gypsy sorting through tea leaves. As I did, a hand reached out, fast as a rabbit, and pulled the necklace from my grasp. My gift to Gabriela had been stolen.

Once again, I was running, this time downhill, which was both easier and more dangerous. I nearly caught up with the thief just a few streets away. The fugitive was small and quick, but his legs were not as long as mine, and as much as he wanted to escape with the necklace, I wanted it back more. He was greedy, but my need was greater.

I was perhaps ten feet behind the thief when he went flying

through the air in an awkward, flailing tumble. His arms were splayed, and his mouth formed an O of terror and surprise. He landed hard, managing to keep his face up, but his chest slammed into the paving stones. I heard his sudden exhalation of pain.

The thief had been tripped. My friend Inácio had apparently witnessed my pursuit from a doorstep, and thrust his foot out just in time. Now Inácio sauntered over to the thief, who remained immobile. He reached down, placing his massive hand over the thief's slender fist. He forced the fingers apart and took the necklace.

He held it up as I approached. His grin was equal measure pleasure in his conquest and for the opportunity to tease me. "For me?"

I held out my hand. "Of course not. It's pretty, but not nearly pretty enough for you."

Inácio hesitated, not because he wanted to take the necklace, I knew, but because it was his nature. He did not need to know whom the silver belonged to, only that it was an object of power, fought over by two people, and that made it interesting. He was from an Old Christian laboring family. His father did work for mine, and while we were an unlikely pair, we rarely passed a day without seeing each other. He was a dangerous boy, though never dangerous to me, and I trusted him completely.

"It's a gift," I told him, meeting his gaze, showing him no embarrassment.

A grin erupted under his large, hawkish nose. "Ah," he said, and dropped the necklace into my hand. "She will like it, I think."

The two of us now looked down at the thief, who had not yet risen. A few curious passersby had gathered to watch, but most people merely glanced at us as they continued on their way. A thief in Lisbon was hardly remarkable.

I had known the thief was small, certainly not older than me, but only now did I see that he was a Moorish child, eight or nine years old, wearing a tattered robe that had perhaps once been blue. He was hollow-eyed and shockingly thin, with sharp bones pressing out from beneath his skin. He looked up at us with his huge, sunken eyes and managed to raise his arms to protect his face. "Don't hurt me."

Inácio kicked him in the stomach. It was more to assert his authority than cause him pain or keep him on the ground. Boys on their own in Lisbon had to know how to protect themselves, and I liked to think I was good with my fists, but Inácio was another matter entirely. I'd seen him make a boy vomit blood after a single kick.

"Stop," I told him.

Inácio shrugged. "Just letting him know what we think of thieves."

"Why did you take it?" I asked.

"Because he's a thieving Gypsy," Inácio said. "What other reason did you imagine?"

"I was hungry." The boy pressed his bloody hands to the stones and managed, slowly, to get to his feet. "I thought I could sell it. Please don't call the soldiers. They will hang me."

"Hanging's what you deserve," Inácio told him. To me, he said, "You can't let his sad story sway you, Sebastião. Of course he claims to be hungry, but he'll deliver the silver to his father or his master and they'll feast tonight. They all claim to be starving."

They all claim it, but often enough it was true. In this case, I believed it was. I'd seen starving children all my life. I had never seen a rich thief.

"I won't call the soldiers," I told him. I then reached into my pocket to retrieve my purse, but remembered it was empty. I had spent the whole of my money on the necklace. It had seemed so important, and yet I knew that if I brought it back to Gabriela now it would feel tainted. It would feel selfish and greedy, and I did not want to associate her with anything shameful.

I held out the necklace to the Moor. "Take it, and may Christ bless you."

Inácio stepped between me and the young boy. "No," he said. "You bought that for Gabriela. You can't just give it away to a thief because he wants it."

"It's what I choose to do," I said.

Inácio put a hand on my shoulder, not unkindly. It was more as though he wished to give me counsel—make me the beneficiary of his hard-won wisdom. "Where is your anger?"

I laughed and shoved him out of the way. "I don't like being angry."

The Moor took the necklace and dropped to his knees. He bowed low, touching his head to the street. Then he sprang up and ran, casting a wary look back not at me but at Inácio.

Inácio shook his head. "If I steal from you, do you promise to let me keep what I take?"

"Only if you tell me a very sad story."

Gabriela was still sitting on the wall when I went back for her. She narrowed her eyes and cocked her head at me. "So. Where is my necklace?"

"The thief took it. I wasn't fast enough." I sat next to her, slumping down, performing frustration.

"That's bad news." She shook her head at the unpleasant turn of events. "I can't kiss you unless there is an exchange of gifts."

I tried to say something, but I had no idea what it would have been if I had been able to make my throat work.

"Although," Gabriela said, looking upward thoughtfully, "I suppose if I gave you something instead, that would answer." She unpinned the blue scarf that encircled her bonnet, and pressed it into my hand. "It was a pretty necklace, and I should have liked to wear it," her voice now much lower.

"I'm sorry," I managed.

"I liked it so much that I followed you," she said. "I wish I could wear it, but there are things I like better than jewelry. I am very fond of kindness."

She leaned in to kiss me, and relief and love and dizziness swam about my head in equal measures. This, I decided, is what happiness feels like, pure and unalloyed, and I wished the moment could last forever.

But our lips never touched. As I moved toward her, I felt a hand on my shoulder. I started and turned to see my mother. Her face was pale, and lined, as though she wore the mask of a much older woman. Her eyes were red from weeping.

"We must go," she said. "The Inquisition has taken your father."

My mother gripped my wrist and twisted until my skin burned, and she pulled me down the hill toward the quays. She had been crying, but now she was calm and controlled, her face as sharp and unmoving as stone. I had seen her like this before. When terrible things befell her, she could easily be consumed by her grief, but if there were responsibilities that required attention, she locked her sadness away. She had business, and she was tending to it.

"Tell me what happened," I said. "I need to know."

"It was the Jesuit who has been asking questions. Pedro Azinheiro," she said, her voice flat and empty, as though reading a letter written in a language she did not understand. "He came with the Inquisition soldiers. If I had not been outside, talking to Senhora Paquda, they would have taken me as well."

Pedro Azinheiro. I had *waved* at him like a fool. Better I should have killed him. I wished I could go back and make it all unfold differently. I could have wrapped that silver chain around his neck and choked the life out of him. Instead, my father was gone, arrested. He would be put to the question. He would be made to confess a thousand things he had never done. They would make him say he had lit the candles on Friday night, that he shunned pork, that he fasted on Jewish holy days, that he studied forbidden books and spoke in evil languages. Then, when he at last admitted to all these things, he would be made to say which of his neighbors and business associates had done it with him. He would resist all of this at first, but in the end, everyone said what the Inquisitors wanted them to say. Everyone broke. We all knew it. My father would break too.

There had been no public burnings for many years, but when my father finally emerged, a year or more from now, he would be emaciated and old. He would be impoverished and humiliated. And they had asked about my mother too. They would come for her soon enough. They were coming for all of us.

This was what we had feared, every day, almost every hour. It had happened. Part of me felt like perhaps this should be a relief—we no longer must wait for it. That much was true, but it was no comfort. This was the end of everything I knew.

We would never leave now. We would never escape to another country. All of that was gone. My family, my hopes, my life with Gabriela. It had vanished.

"What are we going to do?" I asked. I was trying not to cry. I wanted to be like my mother. I wanted to be about goals and tasks.

"We are doing what your father wanted," she said. "What we both wanted. It is what we planned for."

"Will they arrest us too?" I asked.

"I won't let them have you," my mother said. "Your father and I agreed on that."

"But what about you?" I demanded. I sounded like a whiny child, and I hated it.

Her hazel eyes vanished into slits, and she turned her hard-set, oval face away from me.

She pulled me onto the quays belonging to the Factory. Beyond the swarming chaos of the piers were the great ships moored out on the massive expanse of the Tagus, like floating palaces. Smaller barges moved back and forth, perpetually bringing goods to and from the shore. We stood in the thick of English laborers, English sailors, English factors. They moved around us like ants around a stone. We remained still until one of them approached.

I knew him. He was a handsome and bewigged man, perhaps forty years of age. Charles Settwell, one of my father's most important business contacts and his closest friend among the English.

He took off his hat and bowed at my mother. "Senhora Raposa," he said in reasonable Portuguese, "I cannot express the depths of my sorrow at this terrible news."

"Thank you, senhor," she answered, her voice stiff and formal. "There is little time for sentiment, however. When does the packet leave?"

"With the tide. Soon."

She nodded and swallowed hard. "Then there is some good fortune here, at least."

"Of a dark kind, yes," Mr. Settwell agreed.

"What is happening?" I demanded.

My mother lowered herself to look directly in my eyes. She was a tall woman, and I had not yet come into my full height. When she put her hands on my shoulders and crouched down like this, it made me feel like a child. Sometimes I hated it. Now, I craved it.

"They will come for me," she told me. "They will come for you too. That you are so young will not stop them. You know that. Senhor Settwell has always been willing to help us. He will put you on the English packet, and you will go to England, where they can never harm you."

"No," I said. "You must come with me. We must get Papa, and we'll all go."

"It is too late for that," my mother said. "It can only be you. They can smuggle a boy, not a woman. They cannot take the risk of me being caught. They risk enough with you."

"I can't go," I said. "I won't go without you."

She began to cry then. I could see she was struggling not to, but the tears began to flow fast and hard. Her eyes were red, and her lips trembled. "Please, Sebastião. You must do what I say. You can't know how I want to hold on to you, but if you don't leave they will hurt you. They will make you scream, and they will make us listen to it, until we give them every name they want. Do you understand? They will use you to destroy us, and nothing you say will stop them. We could tell them everything we know, but they don't care about what is true. They will hurt you to make us bend to their will. I know you want to help us, but the only thing you can do is be safe and free. That is how you will help me and your father."

I was crying openly now. Under any other circumstances, I would have been furious with myself for weeping, but now I didn't care. "But I won't see you again," I said. "I won't even have the chance to say goodbye to Papa."

"I cannot say what will happen. I pray to the saints we will find each other." She crossed herself, and then stood and looked at the Englishman. "Take him."

"No, Mama," I said, but I knew the words were empty. She had made it so I could not stay. She had made it clear that to do anything but get on the barge would be a betrayal of both her and my father. To be loyal to my family, I must abandon them to the Inquisition.

I threw my arms around my mother and felt hers around me. I took in her familiar scent, and for the briefest of moments I felt safe with her. I forgot, for that second, that the future was fixed and immutable. I allowed myself to believe that things might somehow go back to how they were before.

Then the Englishman put his hand on my shoulder. "If we are to go, we must go now," he said.

My mother pushed me away, firmly but with such warmth I felt my heart breaking anew. "I love you, my sweet boy," she said. "We both love you. Be well, and don't forget us."

"No," I whispered. "Not yet."

She was already turning away, losing herself in the crowd. I moved to run after her, but the Englishman grabbed my arm hard.

"I know you want to," he said, lowering himself to speak directly to me. "You'd be a wretch if you didn't want to, but you cannot go after her. You must honor their wishes. Getting you to safety is the only power they have over the Inquisition. It is all they have left, and it will be all they will have to sustain them in the months ahead. If you love them, you will not take away that shred of comfort."

I looked up at Mr. Settwell and saw that he too was weeping. Then I reached into my pocket and felt something. It was Gabriela's blue scarf. I ran my fingers around and over it and I closed my eyes. I would never see her again either.

I could never say what happened in the minutes afterward. Did I later will myself to forget the moment when I chose to abandon my parents? Did I expunge from my memory the decision to escape rather than stay with Gabriela? I don't know why I can't recall those moments, but I am grateful that it is so.

London, 1755

It was a cold night in a rainy winter. The streets were full of melting snow and horse shit. The thief had fled through the alley, and I ran after him because that was what I did. I was a thief taker, and I was acting in accordance with my duties.

That was what I told myself: but the man in question was not really a thief. He had, however, tried to take something from me. No, that wasn't quite true either.

He had flirted with a woman I was courting. Yes. That was certainly correct. He had tried to steal from me the woman I loved.

But again—that wasn't right. I did *not* love Leonora, however deserving she might be. I had been courting her because my patron, Mr. Weaver, thought it would be good for me to seek a wife. He thought a kind woman would prove a calming influence. It was not turning out to be the case. Mr. Weaver was rarely mistaken, but this time, he had erred significantly.

I shook off my hesitation as I ran. This thief was called Harry Nunes. His ancestors were Portuguese Jews, but he had lived his whole life in England. He knew nothing about betrayal, and so he thought it was a game to take what belonged to another man. He also clearly knew nothing about the Portuguese spirit. You did not attempt to steal another man's woman unless you were prepared to pay the price. I knew that even before I understood why a man might want to steal a woman, or to keep one.

I had heard, from children on my street—that's how I discovered it!—that Nunes had visited Leonora. He had brought her a gift of flowers and cakes, and he had stayed for hours, visiting with her and her parents. There had, I am certain, been laughing within her home, for Nunes was a merry fellow. I was not.

Nunes was no fighter, but he was swift. When he saw me as he left his father's silversmithing shop, he had known at once, and he fled. He leapt over stone and crate and broken barrel. He was as graceful as a deer, but every man's luck runs short sooner or later, and he tripped over nothing at all—his own feet got in the way—and flew forward, sliding face-first through the muck in the alleyway.

I was on him in the span of three breaths, turning Nunes over to make sure he didn't drown in the growing puddle. I would not have him drowning before I was done with him. The rain was coming down hard now, and lightning was slicing through the gray covering of clouds. I would have liked to think I resembled a spirit of righteous vengeance. In truth I knew what I looked like—a jealous madman.

Nunes's lips quivered, and he formed words only after several unsuccessful attempts. "Sir," he said. "I never meant to offer offense."

"Then you should not have called upon Miss DeCosta," I shouted at him.

He tried to scramble away, but my grip on his collar was tight. "She told me she did not think you were serious in your interest in her," he said. His eyes were wide, darting back and forth, as though some escape were just outside his range of vision. "She says you do not love her."

Of course I did not love her. I was not made for such feelings, but I did not like the reminder, coming from Nunes. I struck him in the face, feeling the warm pain of flesh against knuckles. I knew how to hit hard without doing myself too much damage. I struck him again, this time in the stomach. I was lost to my fury, but some part of me, some distant voice, did not want me to disfigure the poor fellow, to break his nose or knock loose his teeth. I raised my fist once more. The thunder and lightning seemed to be coming from within me, a product of my anger.

"Stop it, Mr. Foxx."

I froze, but I did not turn to look. Not at first. Chasing Nunes through the wet London streets had required not a moment's thought, but looking to see who spoke required all the courage I could muster. It was, of course, Leonora DeCosta, standing in the storm. As I came to myself, I realized where Nunes had been running—to the DeCosta home, looming above us. A tall footman held his own coat over Leonora's head to protect her from the rain, and he was mostly successful. It was no easy task, for Miss DeCosta was tall herself, shapely and beautiful. She was also clever and witty, precisely the sort of woman who ought to have found a way into my heart.

"Miss DeCosta," I said, dropping Nunes and straightening up. I spoke as though it were a chance encounter upon the street, as if I had been doing nothing more shameful than taking a stroll.

"Why would you do this?" she asked.

I could say nothing. It suddenly seemed too absurd. He had brought her cakes. He had sat in her parlor. There had, perhaps, been laughter.

"I'm sorry," I said to her.

Despite the footman's best efforts, water trickled down her face. It was rain, not tears. "I had heard," she said, her voice hard and icy, "that you destroy everything you touch. I see now it is so." She looked at her footman. "I shall survive a little water. Help Mr. Nunes."

The footman appeared momentarily confused, unsure if he should obey, abandoning his mistress to the elements. She glowered at him, and he moved.

I turned away. I wanted to help Nunes myself, to apologize to him, but he would not want me. I recognized that.

The anger had been upon me, chasing and beating Nunes. I knew it well. It had been my companion for years, for almost as long as I had been in England. It was the only thing that eclipsed the grief, and that was why I had allowed it in, reveled in it.

I began to walk in the rain, not toward my home. Not toward anything. Leonora's words stung me. I destroy everything I touch, she had said. And it was true. I thought about the friends I had made, the women I had known. They all left me soon enough. Only Mr. Weaver remained loyal. He shook his head when he heard about the things I did. He tried to talk to me, to encourage me to find other ways to vent my passions, but then I would feel the rage again, and I would do something else, and another person would be unable to forgive me.

I walked, making no effort to protect myself from the cold or from the water that poured down. I liked how it felt. I liked that it was un-comfortable and miserable. "I must do something," I said aloud. The thought of poor Nunes running from me, as though I were a mon-ster, filled me with shame. I remembered that day, ten years before, when I'd chased a thief through the Lisbon streets and allowed him to keep what he had stolen. I had not been a monster then. How had I become a person that my former self would have despised?

"I must do something," I said again, though I had no idea what it could be.

Then, at once, I did know. It came to me, unbidden and fully real-ized. I knew how I was going to purge myself of all this anger. I was going to be someone other than a brute who beats helpless men in the rain. The answer was clear and welcoming.

I was going to have to kill someone who deserved death before I killed someone who did not.

Chapter 1

Lisbon, 1755

I am not a kind person. That much, I believe, I have established in the previous account of enraged rival-pummeling. If I am a monster, however, then I am monster made, not born.

Indeed, I was made by men such as the priest who stood before me.

A man might live in London all his life, might upon a daily basis risk encounters with cutpurses and toughs, *renegados* who would slit a stranger's throat for no reason but the thrill of murder, and for all that never cross paths with anyone as dangerous as a Portuguese priest. Here was the real devil.

Standing in the gloom on the Falmouth packet ship, I watched his movements, the half-laugh and calculated smile as he peered through my cabin door. The priest's expression revealed nothing, for deception was the way of his kind, as natural to him as lying down at day's end is to you. But it could be my way too. I had not come to Lisbon to kill this particular priest, but I would kill him all the same if the need arose and not regret it. I'd never killed anyone in my life, but I knew I could. Refraining from murder, not the murder itself, had always been the difficult part.

The priest was not five feet in height, and so plump that he looked like a ball for a child's fairground game. His eyes were wide and bloodshot; his nose large and red from, I supposed, a healthy appreciation of Portuguese wine; and his ears comically massive and hairy. It was impossible to conceive of a countenance less threatening than that of this stunted man with his fleshy fingers, thick as carrot stubs, wiggling as though he played upon an invisible pianoforte. The priest's masters had chosen him for his task precisely because he seemed harmless and bumbling, the very thing to soften the Englishman's fear of papists, a mistrust bred into his roast-beef heart since the days of Bloody Mary.

The ship upon which I had arrived had been at anchor only a few hours now, and it was necessary to undergo this little dance with the priest before I could set foot on dry land. I made no complaint. I was not yet ready to leave, though I had watched from the deck as we approached the City of Seven Hills, as Lisbon styled itself. (The claim, of course, was rubbish. There were far more than seven hills, but the great men of the capital liked to shave off a few insignificant mounds of earth, all the better to suggest a similarity to imperial Rome. Rather like suggesting a monkey resembles a lion because they both have tails, but of the city's many crimes, an inclination to boast was among the more forgivable.)

First the packet had anchored by the stout watchtower at Belém so the health inspector might take a cursory tour through the small ship, looking into our eyes and mouths, making certain we were not spotted or vomiting or covered with boils. There we had been treated to a bit of theater. Act I: the health inspector finds much in the crew's appearance to alarm him—sallow complexions, coughing here and there, some alarming smells from the chamber pots. These sailors, he concludes, must never be allowed to spread their contagion ashore. Act II: The captain presses into the inspector's hands a purse bursting with silver. Act III: The inspector, upon closer examination, decides that the crew is healthy indeed, and the packet is given permission to continue. The curtain falls, and all applaud.

As we continued on our way, I had watched as the distant palaces and monasteries and cathedrals glittered into view. Then, as we had moved east into the Tagus, came my first glimpse of the white stone and blue tiles and red terracotta roofs. There were the clusters of poor hovels in the Baixa and the Alfama. There were the flashes of green from the juniper and Mediterranean oaks and olive and lemon trees. There was the distant sound of a thousand churches ringing their bells at once.

The August sun had warmed my face as the ship sliced through the sapphire water toward this city, so strange and so familiar. In my memory, Lisbon was a place of looming dusk, its sky forever domed by sooty clouds. It was a land cast in gloom eternal, where shadows had more substance than men. Now the sunlight and the swirl of color, the indifferent beauty of the city and the sea, struck me as a species of mockery, one more deception from Lisbon's endless supply. That was well enough. This time, I had a few deceptions of my own.

Even for the wary, a category that describes nearly every Englishman who arrives in Portugal, the city exuded its charms. Lisbon had seduced its share of pinch-faced and scornful Anglicans, come to spend a year or two, but who remained for as many decades. Poverty and despair and injustice were hidden from this distance. They were not on the skin of the beast, but in its lifeblood, flowing through secret channels and arteries, so that from the Tagus the eye fell only upon beauty paid for with Brazilian gold and diamonds. Domes and towers and arches jutted forth to announce that here was greatness, here was power. This was the story the Portuguese liked to tell themselves. If they spoke the words often enough, perhaps they could shout down the truth.

These last brooding thoughts I had indulged in from my cabin. I had already seen enough of Lisbon at a distance that morning, and I was not yet ready to return to the place I had lived for the first thirteen years of my life. Lisbon had been my home and my cruel master. Lisbon had taken my parents and stolen from me my friends. Now, I would soon walk its streets. I wished I had not hidden away Gabriela's scarf, saved all these years, for I wanted to hold it. That ragged bit of cloth had become the sole monument to all I had lost, and I thought it would, at the very least, fire my determination.

The priest was but the first test, the first coin to deposit at a long and ever greedier series of tollhouses. He had appeared outside my open cabin door in his black coat and white cravat, grinning cheerfully and knocking with a lively flick of the wrist as though he were an old friend come to call. I turned to face him, and it was at that moment that I truly understood, perhaps for the first time, that I had placed myself in an impossibly dangerous situation. This thought cheered me.

"Now then, you must be Sebastian Foxx," the priest said in native English. His voice contained only warmth. Like his appearance, it was meant to announce that this was a harmless man, jolly and good-hearted, no one to fear. This was no agent of a corrupt and degenerate institution, its maw set on devouring good Protestants and shitting out papist turds. No, no, he was just a jolly fat man, and who doesn't love one of those?

"I am Foxx." I stooped slightly as I spoke, for I am tall, and the cabin's ceiling was low enough to brush my wig. A typical Englishman, on his way to Lisbon to engage in trade, might think of the cabin as a prison cell, and the beckoning city outside as freedom. I knew the precise opposite to be true.

The priest stepped into the gloomy chamber and reached out to take my hand, which he clasped with familiar warmth. His skin was sweaty and not at all pleasant to the touch. I wished I had put on my gloves. I would make a point never again to touch a priest without them.

"I am delighted to meet all newly arrived Englishmen," he assured me, "but as you are the only one on this packet, today I am especially delighted to meet you. You have rescued me from a very dull afternoon."

I had seen priests in London—many of them and regularly—though these were generally of the Church of England. From time to time I had also spied clerics of the Romish church, but upon English soil such men were utterly impotent, deprived of rights and privileges, and more despised than Jews. They were frightened, skittish things, prone at any time to be struck with dead rats hurled by gleeful children raised not to understand entirely the difference between a Catholic priest and Satan. Here, in Portugal, it was another matter. This affable man could have anyone he pleased arrested upon suspicion of any crime, or, if he chose, no crime at all. A stranger upon the street whom the priest cared mark with a jab of his thick finger would find himself clapped in chains and dragged to the dungeons of the Palace of the Inquisition. The Inquisitions of France and Italy, even the notorious Inquisition of Spain—they were all dead or toothless. In Portugal, the Inquisition continued unabated, deadly and pervasive and merciless.

I laughed nervously, for I did not wish to appear at my ease. My long apprenticeship under the great thief taker, Benjamin Weaver, had given me many skills. Most of them could be best witnessed as I thrashed a defenseless man in a London alley, but there were skills of a subtler nature too. For example, I knew how to pretend to be someone I was not, and this was more than simply making claims about oneself. A man's nature was conveyed by a thousand means, by movements of hands and eyes and mouth, by how he stood or sat, by what he looked at and looked like. I little doubted my ability to make the priest believe I was what I wished him to see.

I returned the priest's handshake, though my hand threatened to slip from his well-greased grip. "I very much doubt I shall relieve you from dullness, for I've little to say that will prove entertaining."

"That's where you are wrong, my son," the priest said. "I love nothing above meeting new gentlemen." Then he released my hand, and I was glad of it.

I invited the priest to sit in one of the rough wooden chairs bolted to the floor. The vessel had not been built for the comfort of its passengers. The packet's chief purpose was to convey goods and mail from Lisbon to Falmouth and back again on behalf of the English Factory. Sometimes the packet carried many voyagers, sometimes but one or two, and none of these enjoyed any particular luxury. My cabin contained only two chairs, a table, a bed, and a trunk for storing a few articles of clothing. When upon the seas, it was near impossible to move without knocking into the furnishings, and my shins bore bruises from unsteady efforts to dress or use the privy.

"Now then. Sebastian Foxx," the priest said, consulting a little book full of notes written in a dense hand, each stroke neat and fully articulated. "This is your first voyage to Lisbon, I see."

I said nothing for several long seconds as I scratched at crystallized salt upon the splintering arm of my chair. It was something an anxious man might do. Indeed, it was something I ought to do in earnest, for what I planned to do was madness. I ought to be *terribly* anxious.

"Forgive me," I said, affecting mild embarrassment. "I was surprised to hear you are an Englishman, or you speak as one at the very least."

"Henry Winston, originally of Marylebone," the little man said with an easy smile and a new round of spasmodic finger wiggling. "And now I am here, in Lisbon. It is the place for an Englishman of my religion."

"It is what I have heard. Indeed, I ought not to be surprised to meet you, but it is one thing to be told there are English priests in Lisbon and quite another to encounter one."

"Most Englishmen regard my religion as a form of plague," said Winston. "They do not wish to get too close for fear I shall infect them with my Romishness." His laugh sounded decidedly practiced.

"It seems foolish to recoil from Catholics in Lisbon," I noted, like a man trying to ingratiate himself. "They are everywhere. Or so I am made to understand."

"It is a devout city, and with no small share of priests, true enough. And we must do our duty." The ship pitched a bit upon a wave, and Winston lashed out to take hold of his chair. He looked positively abashed an instant later. "You must think little of me, but even anchored upon the river, I do not much care for the feel of a ship upon the water."

It was admittedly a bit choppy, but I had grown used to movement of the seas. The weather had been much rougher on the passage from Falmouth. Once we had come upon a summer storm and there had been general fear of foundering. Ill content to cower in my cabin and hope we remained afloat, I had joined with the sailors in securing the deck. While my attention had been fixed upon loose riggings that whipped around with strength enough to snap a man's bones, a great wave had collided with the ship, sweeping torrents of blood-warm water across the deck. I had grabbed a rope an instant before the water slammed into me, blasting my body twenty feet into the air. The wind screamed in my ears. Lightning flashed, illuminating the frantic efforts of the seamen below. For a moment I was aloft, flapping like a standard. It seemed I might be up there forever or might as easily let go, losing myself in the tempest, merging with it, not in truth dying, but simply changing form to wind and rain and lightning. My hands were raw, and bursts of light illuminated the blood-stained rope. I could not hold on much longer, so perhaps I should choose the moment rather than leaving it to uncaring chance. Was there not some merit in making the decision myself? Was there not honor in surrendering to the elements?

Then, for no more than a heartbeat, the wind paused, and I fell, colliding against the wet wood of the deck. I was briefly insensible, but I soon awoke with a dull ache down one side of my body and the taste of blood in my mouth, my hands stinging. The pain was nothing but distant noise compared to the spiteful satisfaction of knowing the wave and the wind were gone, and I yet remained.

To the priest I said, "In time, a man grows used to the waves."

"I am not a sailing man. I made the voyage here once, and shall never return."

I nodded slowly, showing the priest the unease and caution he would expect, and then a bit more beside. About now he would begin to suspect that I had something to hide. I would appear to do my best to make conversation, but not chat easily. I would affect comfort, but my actions would betray a man unskilled at keeping secrets. If he was a perceptive fellow, and they would have no other kind in this role, he would see it all.

He clapped his hands together. "To business then. Portugal is a Roman Catholic kingdom, as you are aware. The open practice of other religions is not tolerated. You may not bring Protestant prayer books or Bibles into the country. You may not discuss your religion with anyone not already a declared Protestant, and then only within a private residence, and never upon the streets or within a public building. You must show respect for all members of the Church, all processionals and displays of faith, even when they are not led by a representative of the Church. Failure to do so will be to invite the attention of the Inquisition, which you wish to avoid. The Inquisition has the power to arrest anyone on Portuguese soil for any reason it may choose. Being English or wealthy offers no immunity if you are guilty of heresy."

I knew all of this very well, but did not, of course, indicate the depth of my understanding. Instead I told him that the captain had explained these details previously.

The priest then smiled, perhaps to soften his message. "It is by no means a difficult thing for an Englishman to spend his time here unmolested by the Inquisition, but respect for our ways and a willingness to be forthcoming are necessary. So, to begin, you must tell me why you have come to Lisbon."

"I am to engage in business," I answered, letting the prepared lie roll off my tongue, savoring this first course. "I have come into an inheritance and now wish to establish myself as a factor, perhaps to work my way into the Factory."

"A young man like you, so very industrious. I am made to understand you are but three and twenty, but you conduct yourself as a man older and wiser. I admire that, sir. Tell me the truth. Have you brought any illegal books here, Mr. Foxx?"

"Certainly not," I said. The discomfort in my voice was feigned and had nothing to do with the illegal book I had indeed brought with me. The volume I had hidden away was, in fact, far more shocking than anything the priest might suppose me to own.

The priest leaned forward and smiled, perhaps warmly, perhaps malevolently. It was hard to say. "You are certain?"

"I have no wish to begin my career in Lisbon by running afoul of the law," I assured him.

The priest leaned back and studied me with the particular attention of a man well practiced at detecting liars. He squinted slightly as he examined my face. For in my dark eyes and strong features, I believe Winston recognized something not entirely English, something strangely familiar. "I know how attached the English can be to their sacred books. We will, of course, search your possessions."

I did not doubt it. It was why I had not chanced bringing a wide array of weapons with me and had come on the ship unarmed but for a single blade. One dagger of sentimental value would raise no suspicions. Of course, I would have to procure more blades, and perhaps firearms as well. Some grenados, if I could find them, might come in handy. If not, a few barrels of gunpowder could be of service. I was not quite sure what I would need, but it would be better to have more than I required than less. I'd been known to enjoy making things explode from time to time, and what better place than this to indulge? I would rather level the entire city than let the man I sought escape.

"Come, sir," the priest continued. "It is wise to tell us now, for possessing illegal books is not a crime while you are still on the ship."

Having lost myself in a reverie of gunpowder, I returned my attention to the priest's concern about the rather less explosive power of the Book of Common Prayer. "I chose not to bring what I could not keep."

"I will take you at your word, sir, for the time being. Tell me, what is your religion? Are you Church of England, or a member of one of the colorful dissenting sects?"

I did not answer, and this time my hesitation was genuine. I had prepared my response, practiced it in the silence of my cabin every day since leaving England. It was the first step down a path that, even now, I was not certain I wished to take. I might still retreat. I might choose a safer, less permanent course, but then the image came to my mind again. The man in the alley, Mr. Nunes, his face distorted in pain, his head knocked hard against stone, his eyes wide with terror at this beast that had set upon him. Behind him, Leonora DeCosta, witness to it all.

That memory had brought me this far, and it would take me along the rest of this journey. There were but two options before me now. I could remain the thing I had become, or I could cleanse myself in the very fires that had forged me. If I but said the words, I would inevitably draw out the man I wanted—the man who was said to loathe Englishmen above all else. Pedro Azinheiro. I depended upon my recollection of the man, that he could not resist the bait I was prepared to dangle.

The priest attempted to put me at my ease. "You are in no danger. We do not expect Englishmen to share our views—at first, at any rate. Ha-ha! You need only answer the question."

I remained silent. Winston must work for his answer so that when he received the gift, it would be all the more believable.

The priest leaned forward until his face was close to mine. His breath smelled of onions and fish, and his body reeked of old sweat. "I am beginning to lose my patience, sir."

I wanted him to stoke the fires of his expectation, to create the tension of the unfulfilled, the way a good playwright makes the audience long for the murder or the marriage that is all but inevitable. When I said the words, it would be like uttering an enchantment in a child's story. Portals to other worlds would open. The gate to hell itself would swing wide.

My voice was hardly more than a whisper as I spoke the lie. "I am a Roman Catholic."

The priest said nothing for a long moment. He stared as though looking at something impossible, a prodigy or a vision. He worked his lips like a man doing sums in his head. Then, at last, he stood and walked over to the cabin door with deliberate steps. Pressing the door closed, he turned back to me. The room was now considerably gloomier, and it filled rapidly with the priest's unwashed odor. "It says in my account that you are a member of the national church. We ask as a matter of form, but we know things, Mr. Foxx. We always know. Why do we not know this?"

I closed my eyes for an instant too long for it to be a blink. "I have deceived people all my life." I sighed and lowered my gaze. "A man of the Roman church can get nowhere in England. My parents were very careful to hide their religion, that we might cleave to the Church and yet not suffer for it. I came here to Lisbon in an attempt to estab-

lish myself in trade, but I will fail before I can begin if my countrymen discover my true religion. You must know that."

"And yet you tell me the truth?" the priest said.

"I do not wish to lie to a priest," I said. "That would be a sin."

"A *terrible* sin," he agreed. Nevertheless, his voice remained skepti-
cal. He was like a man who finds a diamond in a dung heap. He cannot believe his good fortune, and so he tries, again and again, to prove
the diamond nothing more than a piece of glass.

"Convince me," said the priest, his words now hard and clipped.
"Say the Ave Maria."

I did. Upon command I also said the Paternoster and the Anima
Christi. The words were ashes in my mouth, but I spoke them from
rote. I had, after all, spent my first thirteen years a faithful adherent
of the Church. His faith had been my own.

The priest walked to the door of the cabin and then back again. It
was but a few steps, but he was too full of energy to remain still. "You
need not worry. You may be sure we know how to value our friends."
The air of jollity had returned.

"I am glad to hear you say so." I removed a handkerchief from my
pocket and began to wipe my brow.

"And," said the priest, "our friends must know how to value us."

The priest's meaning was clear. An Englishman, secretly Catholic,
within the circle of the Factory—this was a prize the Inquisition must
claim.

"I seek only to engage in trade," I told him, still wiping at my forehead, my nose, even running the handkerchief under my wig, moving it askew so I looked disordered and, I felt sure, slightly deranged.
More importantly, I looked vulnerable. "I have no desire to be caught
in intrigues."

"No intrigues," the priest said. "Certainly not. Never an intrigue.
We would never do anything to harm the prospects of a gentleman
if he is of use to us." The priest nodded as he spoke, as if urging me
to agree. "I shall report what I know to my superiors, and you must

understand the flow of power here in Portugal. Priests and English-men talk, and if the wrong man whispers in the wrong ear, secrets might be difficult to contain. If, on the other hand, you were to de-clare your willingness to aid the Church, that would be a different thing entirely. A favor done for the Church now and again could help you rise quite rapidly, I assure you."

I stared ahead blankly, like a man who had wandered mistakenly into a forest darker and more tangled than he had imagined. I al-lowed nothing of my real thoughts to show, but I considered how this news would move through certain channels in the Palace of the Inquisition. The Inquisitors would whisper and wonder and specu-late how this new Englishman might be of use. One priest would speak of it to another until the news came to the man I sought, and he would look up. His eyes would grow wide. He would smirk, never suspecting that it was a trap that scented the air.

Only a few hours in Lisbon, without even setting foot on land, and I had set things in motion. These people—my enemies—already danced upon my string. Unless I dangled upon their rope. That was also a possibility.

I put my face in my hands as though I were overwhelmed, con-fused, full of regret. Only three and twenty, and I was in waters well out of my depth! I knew not what to do, and wished—oh, how I wished—someone would save me! "Might we not forget this conver-sation ever took place?" I begged.

"That cannot happen," the priest told me as he opened the cabin door. Halfway out, he turned back. "Go about your business. You will be contacted when it is convenient, but until that time you may take comfort in the knowledge that you will have the blessing of the Church." Then he closed the door behind him with dramatic finality.

With the priest gone, I let my false expression fall away, a burnt egg sliding from a pan. I was now in danger, and I welcomed it. The expectation thrummed through me. My skin tingled with the thought of it. All those priests and Inquisitors swarming about me, looking to squeeze me like a lemon, filled me with eagerness and a kind of calm expectation and, indeed, gratitude.

Gratitude, I decided, was most appropriate. Keeping my voice just above a whisper, I spoke the words of the *Shehecheyanu,* the ancient prayer of thankfulness at auspicious times. In London, I had become a Jew in truth, converting, learning the ancient rites of my people. I had not done so out of devotion, but out of defiance. Always, in the back of my mind, I had dreamed of this moment, when I would do what had been forbidden to my ancestors and forgotten by my parents. How long, I wondered, since Hebrew had been spoken aloud in Lisbon? Perhaps this was the first time in twenty or thirty or forty years. What ghosts did I raise with these words breathed into the musty darkness? The act of defiance, secret and small though it was, pleased me.

Lisbon was the last place upon the whole of the earth I should be, but here I was, and there was no undoing what I had set in motion. I began to gather my things in preparation to leave. There was nothing to do now but to remove myself from the protection of Englishmen and find my way in a city full of villains. They had tried to destroy me once, and they would certainly attempt to do so again. Let them make their best effort. The priests and the Inquisitors, the factors and the traders—they would all discover the man to be much more dangerous than the boy. This time the schemes and the plots and the secrets were mine.

Chapter 2

Ten years earlier, I made the bleak journey from Lisbon to Falmouth. Once the ship sailed out of Portuguese waters, the captain himself had fetched me from my hiding place in the hold and delivered me to one of the smallest cabins. He ordered that meals were to be sent to the room every day, but I was otherwise left to mourn in solitude. That was a mercy. I craved no company and no conversation. I wanted no one to see my tears. I lay upon the thin and scratchy mattress that smelled of mold and sweat, and I tried to dwell upon nothing but the rolling of the ship. I didn't want to think about those I had left behind, those I had abandoned. I felt alone and desperate and terrified and nauseated with guilt. I wanted to feel nothing at all.

Everyone I knew was gone. Perhaps my parents might be executed or they might be set free to live in poverty and want. Regardless, I would never see them again. Nor would I ever see my friends. How would my days pass without wily Inácio by my side? How could I imagine wanting to live without Gabriela? Only in being torn apart from her had I understood the depth of what I felt. Now that was a raw wound, gaping and unable to heal. Even if I could someday return to her, she would no doubt be married. I still had her scarf, and I clutched it, pressed it to my face as I tried to recover the faint floral scent of her skin. Life in Lisbon had been cruel, but it was the only life I had ever known, and it was finished.

After we reached England, I continued the journey with one of the ship's officers, a thin man with a limp, a blotchy complexion, and a perpetual reddish stubble upon his chin. Mr. Hastings, as he was called, had business in London, and before the ship had departed Lisbon, he accepted payment from Charles Settwell to see me from Falmouth to the capital. He was not a friendly man and spoke to me only to introduce himself and to say he did not much relish the company of children. He said this several times in the course of no more than five minutes, so I suspected it must be true. I nodded when he talked, but said nothing, and that was evidently to his liking.

Mr. Hastings fulfilled his responsibilities perhaps with less scrupulousness than desired, but with more than might have been expected. He made certain I had a place to sleep and enough to eat. If Hastings dined on beef and beer while I made do with hard cheese and brown bread, it was of no consequence. I ate little and that without relish. It was true that sometimes I was sent to pass the night in the stables while Hastings took a room, but I little cared for comforts. In any case, the stables were preferable when Hastings brought a woman back to our lodgings, although the sounds of his rutting were always mercifully brief. That Hastings had me pay, from my own purse rather than the funds Settwell had provided, for our room and food and, occasionally, his female companionship, was unsurprising. I could not expect him to care for me out of kindness. He was an Englishman, and I understood that most Englishmen did nothing if they did not see profit in it.

Hastings and I passed our days riding in silence in a bouncing coach alongside a curious admixture of passengers—people belonging to classes and representing occupations whose existence I had never previously suspected. England, I understood at once, was as unlike Portugal as China or India. It was not merely different, but deeply alien. Servants upbraided their masters. Women dressed down their husbands in public. Customers were at the mercy of the shopkeepers from whom they wished to buy. The journey to England from Lisbon was less like crossing an ocean and more like venturing into the land of fairies.

Before I had ever set eyes on it, I supposed London to be a city like Lisbon, but when it came into view, the size and the filth and the congestion confounded my imagination. It was spring, but still cold, and the air was thick with black smoke belched out from countless chimneys. Everything I touched was coated with a brown and oily scum. Two or three breaths of London air made my lungs ache. From a distance I saw both its massive buildings and the sprawl of lesser structures made of stone and brick and decaying wood. From the coach's window, I observed not only beggars but whores too, who plied their trade openly and without shame. There were also other kinds of women upon the street—noblewomen and fashionable ladies without veils to cover their faces and in gowns that exposed no small part of their bosoms. There were merchants and peddlers and gentlemen and the poor. I saw no priests, no monks, and no nuns. The coach paused in the streets for the passage of drunks and defiant laborers and pigs and cows and sheep herded by their scowling minders, but never for a traveling relic or holy procession.

Once we reached the center of the city, Mr. Hastings took a portion of my remaining funds and hired another coach, giving the driver a particular destination. During this last part of the voyage, Mr. Hastings wrung his hands as he looked out the window. "I'm almost free of ye," he said. "I hope you'll report I treated you kind."

I nodded. I did not like to speak anymore—not with these strange people in this strange country. I hated the way words felt in my throat, dry and rough as though moving against a tender grain. I understood Hastings wanted some assurance I would not complain about him, and I was willing to give it. I supposed I might have been treated better, but I did not much care, and I saw no reason to make trouble upon first arriving in a foreign land whose laws were a mystery and whose customs were a riddle.

At last we arrived at a street full of people who looked, for the most part, impoverished. We left the coach and walked past innumerable peddlers, men and women selling food and clothes and trinkets, all shouting their wares at once. There were odd-looking men with beards and long coats. I heard English and a strange sort of Portuguese and a language that sounded like German. The air smelled of bread and cabbage and fish. Brisk business was conducted everywhere.

Suspecting the answer, I spoke my first unsolicited words to Mr. Hastings. "What are these men?"

Hastings wrinkled his nose. "Jews," he said, keeping his voice low as if this were a secret.

But it was not a secret. I could see that much. Jews. Actual Jews. Not New Christians, but my ancestral people, undisguised and undiluted, out in the street and speaking their own languages. There were men with long beards, who held books written in a strange script I knew must be Hebrew, though I had never before seen the letters. I had heard that Jews lived openly in England, but knowing and seeing were two different things.

Hastings, oblivious to my wonder, asked for directions and then led us to a large house off the main street. Here things were less chaotic and the poverty less oppressive. The officer knocked and a serving woman of middle years answered the door. Hastings briefly explained his business, and we were ushered inside, directed to a sitting room, and told we would have to wait. The woman said that the master of the house was out and would return in an hour or two.

Hastings handed her a letter for her master and accepted, in return, an offer of wine. I asked for nothing and refused all offers with the fewest words good manners would allow.

The room was unlike anything I had ever seen, even in the houses of English merchants in Lisbon. There were no tiles upon the walls, no gilt or silver-plated ornamentations. There was only a settee and a few padded chairs upon a fine-looking rug, a cabinet with some china inside, and a few paintings upon the papered walls. The room did not appear poor, but it did strike me as plain and utterly without the desire to impress.

We waited for only three-quarters of an hour. I heard the front door open and a deep voice and some whispers. Then, after a few minutes, a tall man in fine English gentlemen's clothes entered the room and bowed to Mr. Hastings. He held the open letter in one hand. This man was quite old—at least fifty—but he was fit and broad in the shoulders and carried himself with energy. When he shook Hastings's hand, his forearm, thick and coiled with muscle, protruded from his coat sleeve. Unlike most English gentlemen, he wore his own hair, which was dusty brown, streaked with gray, and pulled back in the style of a cue wig. He had a distinguished face that had aged well, with a square jaw and intense dark eyes. Despite his many years, there was something commanding about him. It wasn't the authority of station but something else entirely, a kind of easy confidence, and I found it instantly fascinating.

After exchanging a few pleasantries with Hastings, the man extended his hand to me. *"Olá, Senhor Raposa. Eu sou Benjamin Weaver, e eu sou amigo do Senhor Settwell. Bem-vindo à minha casa."* His Portuguese was strangely accented but I understood him.

I took the man's hand without enthusiasm. "Sir, I speak English."

Benjamin Weaver smiled thinly. "Quite well, too." He turned to Hastings. "My thanks to you for seeing the boy here safely."

Hastings tugged at the lapels of his jacket. "It weren't trouble.

Nothing out of the way, that is. The boy don't talk much and didn't make a nuisance of himself, which is all one can ask of children."

"And the funds Mr. Settwell provided for you proved sufficient?" Mr. Weaver asked. His voice was full of good cheer, except there was something else there too, and it made me glad it was not me whom he addressed.

Mr. Hastings glanced at the window. "We got by tolerably, I should say. A bit of a pinch here and there, but I shan't complain."

Mr. Weaver looked at me. "Mr. Raposa, did you advance any of your own coin to Mr. Hastings?"

I looked away. I did not wish to say anything. I bore Hastings no ill will for the money he had taken. And this Mr. Weaver, who meant only to help, was presumably a Jew. Yes, he appeared to be a Jew of some means, but Hastings was an Englishman, and I did not want Mr. Weaver to face any difficulties on my behalf by making accusations against a Christian. I searched for the right words, but I could think of none, and so I remained mute.

Hastings, however, had no difficulties expressing his sentiments. "Just a moment," he cried. "Boys, as is well known, are none the most truthful of creatures."

Mr. Weaver held up a hand, and I understood that it would take considerable courage to disregard the implied threat. Mr. Hastings, the Christian and the Englishman, was silenced by the Jew. It was remarkable.

"Yes," I now said. I was apprehensive about what all this might mean and where it might lead, but I was curious too. "Mr. Hastings asked for money to pay our expenses, and I gave it to him."

"How much?"

I shrugged. "I did not keep accounts. I paid as he asked."

"May I see your purse?"

I handed it to Mr. Weaver, who emptied the coins into one of his large and calloused hands. He counted the money, returned the coins to the sack, and then turned to Mr. Hastings, whose red face and intertwining fingers betrayed his discomfort. "You have served the Factory long?"

"I am not a member, but I have worked for Factory men these five years." Seeming to find some courage, he added, "I am well known and regarded, and I am fortunate enough to have many powerful friends."

"Indeed," said Mr. Weaver. "A man so experienced and handsomely connected must know that fast riders are sent from Falmouth to London as soon as the packet docks. These riders dispatch their letters many days before a man traveling the same distance by coach could hope to see London. As the same packet that brought you from Lisbon also contained a letter to me from Mr. Charles Settwell, I know precisely how much money the boy ought to have in his purse, and yet quite a bit of it is unaccounted for."

"You must speak to the boy, then," said Mr. Hastings with a forced laugh. "I need not tell you how ill equipped they are to hang on to their coin. An indulgence or sweetmeat here and there—why, they add up quickly."

"You suggest it was this grieving boy who spent the money?" Mr. Weaver said.

"If you think to accuse me—" But he stopped himself. Mr. Weaver's dark eyes were fixed on him, hard and sure, and Hastings could bring himself to say not another word. I saw nothing in Mr. Weaver's expression or posture or manner that overtly suggested violence, and yet he held himself like a predator poised to spring, like the jaws of a trap, ready to shut fast and fatally.

Hastings staggered backwards. Retrieving his own purse from his belt, he counted out some coins with unsteady fingers and handed them to Mr. Weaver.

Mr. Weaver, however, would not take them. "They're not mine," he said.

Unwilling to humiliate himself by giving money to a foreign child, Hastings set the coins down on the table.

Now Mr. Weaver glanced at them. "You have overpaid by seven pence, but I'll warrant the boy shall keep the money as a token of your good wishes. Good afternoon, Mr. Hastings."

The Englishman bowed in a clumsy and frightened spasm. "Despite any slight discrepancies in the trivial matter of accounts, I have made every effort to look after the boy. I hope you will speak kindly of me to my friends at the Factory."

"I shall speak the truth," said Mr. Weaver. "I see no reason to do otherwise."

Hastings left without another word. Meanwhile, Mr. Weaver slid the coins into the purse and handed it to me. "I know a cheat when I see one, and while you are under my protection, I shall not let a man such as he have the better of you."

For all the menace he had projected when speaking to Hastings, he now seemed to me genuinely kind. It was not the false and sugary solicitude I had endured from innkeepers' wives and servants and Hastings's whores. This kindness was more subtle, for it was unaffected.

Mr. Weaver invited me to sit, and I did so.

Across from me, the older man leaned forward and sighed. "Mr. Settwell has described your circumstances, so I know you have endured much. I shall ask nothing of you until you have had some time to mourn and adjust to the many changes in your circumstances. For the present, you will live here with me and my wife and my daughter. When you are ready, we shall figure out what to do with you. You are a bit old to be put out as an apprentice, but that should not signify. Every Jew of the nation will vie for the opportunity to stand as patron to a young man who has escaped the Inquisition."

I did not wish to speak. My loss and my grief and my misery were so raw, so poorly contained, I feared even the most trivial of words might break the fragile dam I had erected, and I did not want to cry before a stranger. Nevertheless, my curiosity overcame my reluctance. "Why should the Jews wish to help me?"

The man raised his eyebrows as though the question surprised him. "This neighborhood is full of men whose families escaped the Inquisition long ago. They fled to France or the Levant or the Low-lands, as mine did, before coming to this country. These are men whose lives have not been directly touched by the Inquisition in several generations, but the anger runs deep. You defied our greatest oppressors, and that makes you a hero to them and to me."

I looked away. I had abandoned my father in the Inquisition prison. I had left my mother alone. Survival was not, in itself, heroic. The mere suggestion made me angry, and to my surprise I found myself embracing the anger. It was the first time since I had hidden in the hold of the packet ship that I had felt anything other than fear or sadness. I wanted to hold on to that anger, to nurse it like the spark that becomes a flame, because maybe it would burn away everything else.

"Tell me," Mr. Weaver said. "What skills have you?"

"My father is a merchant," I said. "I have learned much of his business."

"You can read and write? Have you a good hand? Perhaps you can be set up as a merchant's clerk."

I shook my head. Making money for its own sake did not appeal to me. As a New Christian, my father had been forced into a merchant's life—trade was considered too debased for Old Christians. I would not, if given the option, choose for myself what had so long been thrust upon my family. "I will do that if it is what you wish. I must do as you say. I know that."

"You must do as *you* wish," Mr. Weaver told me, keeping his voice quiet and calm. "Or as near to it as we can arrange. I do not see that you need to pursue a trade that does not suit you." He stood and put a friendly hand upon my shoulder. "Perhaps we ought not to speak of it at all. You are tired from your journey. I'll have you shown to your room. You may sleep or rest, and when you are ready, we can discuss your future."

I looked at Mr. Weaver's big hand. Even at his advanced age, he was the sort of man no one would dare to trouble. I wished to be like that. I wished to be someone other men feared. "What is your trade?" I asked.

"I am a thief taker," he said. Seeing the look of confusion on my face, he added, "I am paid to find people and items."

"What manner of people and items?"

"Lost or stolen items," Mr. Weaver said. "People who are missing for reasons good or ill."

"But you're called 'thief taker,' so you must find lawless men," I said. "Do you find people who have done bad things?"

"Yes," Mr. Weaver said. "That is part of what I do."

"Do you hurt such men?" I asked.

"If it cannot be helped," Mr. Weaver admitted, somewhat abashedly, I thought. "I never seek to do violence, but I am prepared if violence is unavoidable."

I thought about that. The idea of finding someone who had done evil—and striking him, lashing him with a whip, running him through with a blade, or firing a pistol into his chest. All of these things had an undeniable appeal. I had seen how Mr. Weaver sniffed out Hastings's crimes and then humbled him with but words and glances. It must be a wonderful thing to feel something other than powerless. London was a strange city, where Jews walked about openly and could demand justice of Christians. I did not know if I would ever grow accustomed to it, and I told myself I did not want to, that I did not want to let go of my anger. Yet part of me understood that I had come to a place where I might find it possible to live.

Six months later I received a letter from Mr. Settwell. Illness had spread through the prisons. Many of the prisoners died, including my parents. They were gone.

I retreated to my room, and Mr. Weaver did not trouble me. I remained alone for four days. Sometimes I ate and drank. Sometimes I did not.

On the fifth day, I appeared in Mr. Weaver's study. I was thin and ill rested, but I set my face in determination.

"I want to be a thief taker, like you," I said. "I want to learn to hurt people."

"Hurting people will not change what has happened," Mr. Weaver said.

"I know."

"Then I will begin your training tomorrow," he said.

Mr. Weaver proved to be correct. Hurting people never made me feel better, but sometimes, when I punched or tackled or kicked, it made me forget to feel at all, and that, at least, was some relief.

Chapter 3

My trunks would have to be cleared through the customs house, and it might be a day or more before they were delivered. So, with my business aboard the ship complete, I took my leave.

The Tagus is massive at Lisbon. Called by locals the *Mar da Palha*, the Sea of Straw, it was perhaps a mile across to Almada. Vessels of all sizes, from titan East Indiamen to single-sail fishing boats, crowded the huge expanse of water. The quays were used primarily for unloading and loading barges, as the river was quite deep in its center, but too shallow near the shores for the great ships to dock. I took passage on a barge commissioned by the Factory and powered by a dozen hollow-eyed African galley slaves.

I kept my eyes on the water, taking in the range of mighty vessels and opulent barges with their red velvet canopies and gold tassels. They belonged to wealthy *fidalgos*, minor nobility, or perhaps even to the royal family itself. The packet had anchored directly in front of the *Terreiro do Paço*, the Palace Square, and the barge veered westward, past the royal shipyards that rang with the pounding of hammers and the sawing of wood, to a small set of quays at the foot of Chaido Hill. It was all industry and growth and trade here, as goods from all over the world were unloaded and set on carts that rolled toward the warehouses. Silks and furs to dress the rich, and meats and cheeses and grains to feed them.

When I first arrived in England ten years before, I had been shocked to discover that the greatest men in the kingdom took pride in their farmlands. Their properties fed and clothed the nation, and while they might not soil their own hands with labor, they nevertheless understood themselves to be physically bound to the land. An English gentleman always took pride in serving the foods cultivated upon his own estates. In Portugal, a *fidalgo* would imagine himself diminished if he were to bring the fruits of his holdings to market, and so the country could offer its citizens little in the way of meat or produce. The waters were teeming with fish, and peasants and small men and ships from other nations worked them, but no gentleman would tarnish his name by being called a fisherman. I watched, as I came to shore, barrels of salted fish from England being unloaded down the quays. It was but one way in which Portuguese pride made Englishmen rich.

Without ceremony, I stepped upon the quay and began to shoulder my way through the crowd of sweat-stinking slaves and laborers. It was but a short distance to my new lodgings, the Duke's Arms, one of a mass of inexpensive inns and taverns serving the English. I had not chosen the most reputable of such establishments, and my inquiries suggested that a man wishing to make the best possible impression would have stayed elsewhere. I, however, was not looking to make the best possible impression. Far better to appear to be a man who little knows his best interests. Far better to appear to be lost and uncertain in this dangerous city. That was what would get me closest to the Inquisitor I sought.

Naturally, I could not have predicted the day of my arrival—travel from England ranged from as little as eight days to three weeks or longer, should bad weather or pirates intervene—but I had written ahead to tell the innkeeper of my ship's name and its departure date. The inn would know of the packet's arrival and ready my room accordingly.

I considered these details as I walked, keeping my head down, feeling the sun beat upon my neck, smelling rosemary and fish and the sour stink of laborers who passed close. I turned away from all I did not need to see, but there was no blocking out the sounds of the city—the cries of street vendors, hawking their goods in Portuguese and English; the snatches of Arabic and African and Brazilian languages; the strumming of guitars and mandolins, and the pounding of drums. I did not raise my head, and I looked no farther before me than navigating the street demanded. I did not want to see Lisbon. Not yet. It was one thing to gaze at the city from a distant vantage point upon the Tagus, quite another to see it from the streets—to be upon those streets.

For a moment, I was near dizzy with regret. I wanted to be back in London. Not that London was home—not anymore. I had burned my bridges there. I had not so much as told Mr. Weaver I was leaving, let alone explained where I was going—though I left him a letter, revealing all. In the weeks before my departure, I quietly sold all I had of worth. I gathered all the money I had saved over the years and traveled by coach to Falmouth to board the next Factory packet. All my life, events had pushed me from one place to another. In this, I had chosen my way, made my own terrible choice. It was what I said to myself, and yet, as I had boarded the packet, I had felt as though the course I was on had always been inevitable.

The inn was at the intersection of two unmarked streets, sitting astride the hill so the ramshackle wooden building looked as though it might, at any moment, give way and topple face forward into the street like a drunkard. And inside, the common room was full of sots who appeared as though they might, at any moment, topple face forward onto the floor. They were, to a man, British—almost all English, with a few Scotch voices thrown in and one accent decidedly Cornish. None were Portuguese, and that, no doubt, was how the patrons liked it. The British in Lisbon wanted a place to be away from their hosts and their papist ways and the unceasing scrutiny of the Inquisition. Even so, there would be familiars of the Inquisition within the tavern, and every man there knew it. The Inquisition had many powers, but first among these was ubiquity. Inquisitors had the coin to buy agents in any walk of life. Some men went more willingly than others, but in the end no one refused to serve. Anyone who drew the attention of the Inquisition did its will, either outside the Palace dungeon or within it. Most chose to earn gold rather than lashes.

I crossed the warped wooden floors, strewn with sawdust, past English laborers—not a Factory man among them—and approached the counter. I pretended not to notice I was the only gentleman present, the only man in wig and waistcoat, the only man with silver buttons and buckles. The only man who troubled to wave his hands at the buzzing clouds of mosquitoes. The other patrons, however, appeared entirely indifferent to my presence. Indeed, they demonstrated the same indifference to their own lives.

Behind the bar stood a huge man, unusually tall, whose massive frame was composed of broad shoulders and muscular arms, but also an enormous belly that protruded out over his breeches. Like his patrons, he went wigless, and the stubble on his scalp suggested he shaved his head as protection against lice. He dressed in the common Portuguese manner—simple and rough and inexpensive. And like a Portuguese, he was bearded, though his ginger facial hair came in rough patches. The round, too-wide face surrounding his unkempt whiskers was red and blotchy and deeply creased. Humming rather loudly to himself, he kept his gaze deliberately down as he washed out tankards with an oily cloth.

I watched as the heavy man left streaks of grease inside the tankards. My expression must have betrayed revulsion, because the man stopped and met my gaze with a steely look of contempt.

I knew him.

The coincidence ought not to have surprised me. Probably fewer than a thousand Englishmen lived in Lisbon, and I fully expected to see men I recalled from my childhood, but not so quickly, and not where I intended to lodge. When I last saw the man behind the bar, Kingsley Franklin had been ten years younger, quite a bit less corpulent, and far better dressed. He'd been a factor then, and a successful one, a man with whom my father had done frequent business.

For a moment, I feared recognition, but of course that was foolish. He last knew me as a thirteen-year-old boy, hardly worth the notice of a merchant. Even if, for some inexplicable reason, the man recalled the son of a New Christian business associate, if he had clear memories of him and discussed him often with his friends, he would not now perceive the child in the face of a bewigged English gentleman fresh off the packet ship.

His dark expression certainly betrayed no recognition. "Something not to your liking? Not the finery you'd hoped for?" Franklin asked. He narrowed his eyes at me for a moment, daring me to look away, and then returned to the important work of wiping out mugs.

Were this London, I would have taken very unkindly to his rudeness. To best communicate my displeasure, I might well have grabbed his hand, twisted back his wrist until he fell to his knees. I did not enjoy being treated poorly. I chose to let the matter pass, however, for I had not come all this way to teach innkeepers how to conduct themselves, and though he was ill-mannered now, long ago Franklin had dealt fairly with my father.

I said, "I beg your pardon. I meant no offense. I wrote ahead about a room. I am Mr. Sebastian Foxx."

Evidently, he did not care for my efforts to ingratiate myself. "Young fellow like you? I was expecting *Mr. Sebastian Foxx*"—he recited the name with not a little mockery—"to be a man of business. I wasn't expecting a lad making a stop on his grand tour."

If that was the game, I would play it. "I assure you, I am here upon business, and I am three and twenty. Not so very young for a man who wishes to live by his own labor."

Franklin grinned, warming to the banter. "Aye, that's true enough, if you are not still upon your mama's teat."

"I am not." I leaned forward slightly to meet the man's gaze. "Were you a younger man, I might quip that I've actually been upon *your* mama's teat, but given your own advanced age, that would be not a little unsavory."

Franklin stared at me. His mouth quivered, but he said nothing, and I wondered if I had gone too far. Mr. Weaver had taught me that it was easier to get what you wanted from a man if you could convince him he had not been bested.

"Now, shall we discuss my room," I inquired, "or shall we further explore the subject of teats?"

Franklin remained motionless for another moment, then he erupted in a guffaw, showing off a mouth of large and generally intact teeth. "You've got spirit for a popinjay, I'll warrant." He thrust out his hand. "Kingsley Franklin."

I took his hand and shook as though he were a long lost friend, and, in truth, he was close enough. "I believe we shall do together quite amiably."

"As to your lodgings, I think we have what will answer." All hostility had now been erased from our history. "I reckon you'll be glad to sleep upon dry land after all that churning about on the packet. And once you've seen your rooms, perhaps some food and drink will answer."

"Nothing presently, but I assure you, I will want refreshment later, and I shall let you know if it is convenient." I had already informed Franklin I was not easily frightened. Now it was time to assure him I would be a source of coin.

"We aim to please," Franklin replied brightly, having received the message, "provided it ain't much trouble."

With a lazy wave of his hand, Franklin led me through the common room and toward a dark staircase so steep it seemed designed specifically to encourage drunk men to fall to their deaths. Indeed, Franklin's height and girth made the stairs a particular challenge, and as we ascended his breathing grew pronounced and ragged. I watched the man hurling himself upward, and I shook my head at the wonder of it all. I was staying in an inn belonging to *Kingsley Franklin*—a man who had dined at my father's house, whose errands I had run as a child.

The stairs twisted up to a windowless corridor, and Franklin led me through the darkness until we reached a door with the number eight written on it in chalk. He paused and put one hand to the wall while he caught his breath. "Here we are, Mr. Foxx. Not so very bad, I'll wager."

It was not so very bad at all. I opened the door and saw a bright room with a view of the river and the Palace in the far distance. It caught a pleasant breeze, and the furnishings were spare but sufficient. In the front room, a writing table and several chairs and a servant's bed near a fireplace. In the back a clean-looking bed with fresh linens. The room smelled not of sweat or piss, a prospect that seemed all too likely, but of fresh-cut flowers and citrus, sea air and a distant hint of cinnamon and baking bread.

Franklin stood by the threshold, watching me inspect my new lodgings. "My daughter used to help about here until she ran off with a sailor, so I'm a bit shorthanded at the moment. Anything you want, I'll have it for you—me or one of these Portuguese I pay. They're cheap as dirt, and almost as useful."

"I shall keep that in mind."

"And if it's some company you desire, you need only give me the nod," he said with a wink. "I know the best ladies in town, English and natives. Some men, newly arrived, have an inkling to try the blacks, and I know a few places where they are clean and lovely both."

"Should the need arise," I said, "I shall inform you anon."

Franklin held up his hands in protest. "If you're the puritanical sort, sir, I meant no offense. You need not swive a whore to be estimable in my eyes."

"Your disposition is most liberal," I said, making no effort to disguise the weariness in my voice.

Franklin clapped his hands together. "I'll be off and leave you to your settling in." He turned to the door, and had gone so far as to set one foot into the hallway before he turned back around. "If I may be bold, Mr. Foxx, I'll give you a bit of advice—some that I wish was given me. You've come to make your fortune, and I've no doubt you will. Earn your riches, then, and welcome to them, but return home, quick as you can. Men who stay too long do so at their peril."

"And what is it they risk?" I asked. English merchants had always appeared privileged when I was a boy. They could come and go as they pleased, and they had no fear of the Inquisition so long as they did nothing foolish, but Kingsley Franklin, once a successful Factory man, now stood behind the counter of a second-rate inn.

"A man who stays too long risks everything he has," Franklin said, his melancholy undisguised. "A good man was ruined, and I was ruined along with him. I lost all I valued, sir: my fortune; my wife, who left me; and finally my daughter, who'd had her fill of being a poor English girl in a city full of rich Englishmen. Don't wait until you have more than enough. When it's merely enough, it is time to leave."

A great man? Did Franklin's fortunes decline with my father's arrest?

"You must tell me your history, Mr. Franklin, but another time, if you please. I fear I am not a fit audience."

The tremendous sphere of a man had now taken out a handkerchief and was wiping his eyes. "The very devil," Franklin swore softly. "I don't often lose myself like that, but I find myself suddenly in a reflective turn of mind." He started toward the door and then—I could scarcely believe it!—he turned back yet again. Would he never leave the deuced room? "Be mindful to always dress as you are now, in the English manner. Don't think to don the native clothing, as some visitors like to do."

"Why ever not?" I asked.

Franklin squinted. "With your coloring, sir, you could well be taken for a New Christian, and the last thing you want is the Inquisition looking at you twice." So saying, he stepped out of the room and closed the door.

Franklin was going to be a problem.

It might well be that he would never see my resemblance to my father, though I saw it with unavoidable clarity whenever I gazed into a glass. Even so, I must be prepared to deal with the innkeeper.

That was a matter to be resolved later. Now was the time for considering how best to proceed. I breathed in the floral air, laced with the sea scent of the Tagus. Then I decided I would no longer try to spare myself. I approached the window and looked outside, taking it all in: the river and its many ships, the glittering jewel of the Palace, the commotion of the quays.

Then I reached into my waistcoat and tore at the lining, removing two items, setting them both down on the table near the window. The first was Gabriela's scarf, the indigo dye faded now to a dull sky blue, the embroidery spotty and the edges fringed with wear. I held it to my nose and breathed in the perfume with which I refreshed it from time to time. It no longer smelled of Gabriela—her scent was long forgotten—but I imagined that the perfume contained something of her essence. This thing, this one artifact, remained of her, but maybe there would be more soon. When I first decided to return to Lisbon, I told myself not to hope she would be here, in the city, unmarried, free to join me. Yet I did hope, and now that I was here, I knew I would seek her out. There was more than one ghost for me to search for in the city.

The other item was a duodecimo volume of Hebrew prayers. I considered, with some amusement, my conversation with the priest who had sought to make certain I smuggled no Protestant texts. What would he have done if he had suspected the truth, that I was an escaped New Christian, returned as a Jew? The irony would have been lost on him, of course. I had been raised Catholic, as had my father. Perhaps my father's father or grandfather had cleaved to Jewish practices, observed in secret, but over time the knowledge and commitment had decayed. As a child I knew no faith but that of the Church, and so it was the Inquisition that had, however circuitously, returned me to my people.

Centuries before, Jews had prospered in Portugal. It had been the country to which persecuted Jews had fled. Once, thousands of voices would have risen up to recite the afternoon prayers, the *mincha*. Those voices had long ago fallen silent. Though hardly the most observant of Jews back in London, I was now prepared to rekindle a tiny spark of that stifled flame. There would be one who dared pray, if only in a whisper. My voice breathy and trembling, not from fear but from anger, I read, and every syllable was a blow of defiance.

Chapter 4

T he idea of killing the priest had come to me that night in the alley, but returning to Lisbon had been on my mind for months before that. It had begun in the Bevis Marks Synagogue, on Yom Kippur, the Day of Atonement. I had heard the words every year since my relocation to London. It was part of the liturgy taken from the Mishnah. *For sins against God,* the liturgy says, *the Day of Atonement atones, but for sins of one man against another, the Day of Atonement does not atone until they have made peace with each other.*

How could I make peace with the dead? How could I atone for leaving my parents behind to be tortured and die in their prison cells? It had been a strange jumble of ideas. I was not even sure they made sense to me, but I had begun to sense that I needed to leave London and come to Lisbon. I needed to restore order to my broken life, and that could only happen in the city that had broken me. And now here I was. I had left my friend and mentor; I had abandoned everyone and everything in London. I was alone and vulnerable and in danger.

I was glad I had come.

I slept for nearly eight hours. When I awoke, I immediately regretted the lack of a servant. Acquiring one would be among my first tasks. For now, I dressed myself and then emerged to the common room to order food. Earlier the tavern had been crowded, but now there were only a half dozen or so haggard-looking men, all residing in the inn itself, I supposed.

While most of Lisbon was unsafe after sunset, the English streets were not, for they were well lit and patrolled. Even so, it was quickly apparent the Duke's Arms was not a popular destination beyond the bustle of daylight hours. The food, I discovered, was indifferent, the drink well watered. None of it was appallingly bad, but neither was it particularly good. Mosquitoes hovered about the patrons, and enormous flies gathered in clouds above the dishes. It was an inn for those who could ill afford to bring their business elsewhere.

I sat alone by the fire, eating cold chicken and crusty Portuguese bread, washing it down with thin porter. The other men in the room were older, with fraying wigs or no wigs at all, several days of beard growth, eyes and noses and cheeks red with lack of sleep and too much drink. In the fine homes and estates of the Bario Alto were those who had played Lisbon's mercantile lottery and won. These were the men who had lost. None of them showed any interest in talking to the new man, and I was content to return the indifference.

After I ate and called for a second pot of porter, Kingsley Franklin set down his rag and walked over on stiff legs.

"All to your liking?" Franklin lowered himself into a chair, grunting and grimacing as he did so.

"The food could be better," I said.

"Couldn't be worse. But at least there's plenty of it, eh?"

"Better a full stomach than a pleased palate," I opined, saluting my host with my drink.

"A man after my own heart," Franklin said with evident pleasure. "Tell me, sir, if I may be so bold as to ask. How do you mean to begin your business here?" He sounded less like he was prying and more like he wished to offer advice.

"Have you something to suggest?"

"I know a thing or two." He shrugged. "You're used to London and its great size, but Lisbon is a small city. A man can't help but know his fellows' business, and what is true for your ordinary João is twice as true for us English. There's not so many of us that we miss knowing one another, and some keep a better eye upon opportunity than others."

There was no reason not to jump in, then. Both feet. No point looking down. "Do you know a man named Charles Settwell?" I had written to my father's old friend care of the Factory, and Settwell had written back, but our communication had been necessarily guarded.

Franklin looked as though he'd just bitten into something rancid. "What can you want with him?"

I felt my pulse begin to race. That was not the reaction I wished to hear when the man who had saved my life was mentioned. "His name was given to me as a merchant of note."

Franklin shook his head. "He was once, true enough. But he's fallen on hard times."

"How so?" I asked, making every effort to appear indifferent.

Franklin shrugged. "I can't say I know the details, but I can tell you he sold his house in the Bario Alto and now lives in some wretched place on Madeleine Street, on the cusp of the Alfama, the very worst part of the city. Full of Gypsies and escaped slaves and cutthroat Moors, over there. If you want to advance in Lisbon, you'll need better friends than Settwell. Who you know makes all the difference, and if you make the wrong contacts from the first, you'll never recover."

"My information is clearly not current," I said, making certain I appeared only vaguely disappointed. It took no small effort. Every instinct I had urged me to rise from my seat and rush to the Rua Madalena. Charles Settwell had risked everything to smuggle me out of Lisbon. Perhaps there was nothing I could do for him, but if I sought to rebalance the world's scales, I knew that before anything else, I would have to call upon this man and, at the very least, assess the situation.

The next day, I began my work. In the busy streets outside the inn, it was not hard to find a boy willing to run an errand. I handed him a note: for Charles Settwell, I told him, on the Rua Madalena. It was a big enough street, but there would not be many Englishmen upon it. The residents would know him.

The note was spare, saying only that I had arrived and would like to meet. Settwell wrote back with equal reserve, agreeing that he would like to discuss our business, and giving a time and directions.

Having settled that matter, I decided I had already gone unarmed in Lisbon far too long. There was no more delaying it, and so I left the inn and headed into the very heart of Lisbon.

I did not fear discovery. I knew what I looked like—a young Englishman, perhaps with more money than sense. I wore a fine white wig, well powdered, a handsome velvet coat with silver buttons, and black shoes with glittering buckles. I was a gentleman, almost—but not quite—a dandy. No one took more notice of me than my appearance warranted.

The city of hills smelled of the sea and fish and herbs and filth. The streets, as I recalled, rang with the sound of church bells and the sight of clergy—men and women—swarming like beetles in the many colors of their orders. Franciscan browns and Jesuitical black, of course, but also men in reds and blues and yellows and whites, and nuns in their wimples and robes. And among these clusters of clerics were workmen in their plain browns and Gypsies in their ragged finery. Mules and sheep and cattle had their run of the streets, which ran thick with their dung. Unlike in London, few carriages were to be seen—certainly not away from the palaces—and only slightly more people on horse. Here and there, however, were great men or women of the city within palanquins, drawn by heavily muscled Negroes whose owners treated them no better than beasts.

There were beggars—the sick and the wounded, the legless and the armless. There was a bearded man, his face almost fully encased in hair, entirely without limbs, ministered to by an emaciated girl not ten years of age. I had seen all this and worse in London, but here the destitute and desperate were more plentiful and more pitiful, the meat of the city's stew rather than the swirling grease. Here too were lepers with their tattered robes and tinny bells, shunned by all, sometimes pelted with stones by children or holy fools. Many of the beggars were soldiers, still in the king's service, who had gone years without wages while rivers of gold and mountains of diamonds came from Brazil to pay for palaces and cathedrals.

None were so desperate or crippled that they refused to clear the roads when a holy procession passed. It happened twice on my brief walk. The most wretched and wicked men fell to their knees, providing they had knees upon which to fall. Once as a dozen monks transported a communion host in a great monstrance of gold to the home of an ailing *fidalgo*. Another time as a diamond-encrusted casket containing the skull and pelvic bone of a saint was moved from one church to another. Like the rest of the crowd, I removed my hat and kneeled. I felt no remorse or hypocrisy. I was maintaining my disguise, as Mr. Weaver had taught me. In London, the ability to blend in meant success. Here it meant survival. Every bow, every removed hat, every sign of deference, brought me closer to my goal as I ventured upward, ever upward, to the fringes of the Alfama, past the old castle, to where the city began to fade into country.

There, on a dirt road populated mostly by farmers selling produce from baskets, I found the man precisely where he had been a decade before, when he'd sold a thirteen-year-old boy a necklace. I approached the stall and remarked how Old Paolo appeared precisely as I recalled him, tall and thin, with strands of brittle white hair plastered to a wrinkled scalp.

Then, as I grew closer, I saw Old Paolo had in fact changed. The old man's eyes were red and heavy with bags, the skin loose about his face, and his arm shook as he lifted it in greeting.

"Englishman, you have a need," Old Paolo said in broken English. His words whistled through missing teeth. "I see it. What can I sell you?"

I said, "Old Paolo, I need weapons."

When I last lived in Lisbon, Charles Settwell resided in one of the fine detached houses in the Bario Alto, on a street favored by successful factors. The Rua Madalena, however, bordered the dank alleys of the Alfama. Running more or less perpendicular, in a winding sort of way, to the Tagus, the narrow street served as a downhill sewer, and I had to keep close to the walls to minimize the damage to my shoes. The houses here had a decayed look to them, with cracked stone, broken tiles, and rotted wood, warped by time and neglect. Gypsies loitered nearby in the street's shadows, as did Moors, mulattoes, and other dark-skinned men who were perhaps freed slaves, but had more likely escaped. At one house, a pair of Negro women peered out an open door and beckoned me inside. One pulled down the neckline of her tattered gown to expose a chest so gaunt her ribs protruded more than her breasts. I bowed and removed my hat, and the women giggled. Playing the fool was best. Even starving African whores might be Inquisition informers.

I soon came to Settwell's house, close enough to the Street of Tanners that the air was heavy with the scents of dung and offal and lime. I knocked and was met at once by an elderly mulatto woman who beckoned me inside and then reached out for my coat with a trembling hand. Apparently she knew no English and presumed that I, like most Englishmen, knew little enough Portuguese. I was in no hurry to tip my hand, so I contented myself with communicating in exaggerated pantomime and speaking Settwell's name loudly and slowly.

Inside, the house was cramped and narrow, with low ceilings as if it had been made for dwarves. I tarried in a small room, smelling of mildew, that served as Settwell's parlor. There were portraits and Turkish rugs, though these were faded. The paint upon the plaster was chipped, and the paper on the walls peeling. The paintings—none the finest to begin with—were flaking and offered bare patches of canvas. The furnishings were sturdy, but old and battered. The cushion upon my chair belched feathers when I sat.

I waited no more than two minutes before Settwell came in. He was now in his midfifties, thinner than I recalled, and, like his environs, a faded version of his former self. His skin was pale, his wig shedding, his clothes stained and threadbare in places. I remembered him as a vigorous man, tall and commanding in his posture, the sort whom the ladies followed with their eyes and for whom men parted when he entered a room. Now he was stooped, his brown eyes haggard. Nevertheless, Settwell gave every impression of being unaware of, or indifferent to, these deficiencies. He grinned widely. For a moment his old countenance appeared to superimpose itself upon the new, but it passed quickly.

"My dear boy. Sebastião Raposa!" He took me in an embrace, and though I did not generally care for such intimacies, I endured this one without complaint. Settwell was one of the few men to have earned my gratitude.

After an instant he moved away but held on to my shoulders, notably higher than his own. "You've grown quite a bit, haven't you? You were a skinny boy when last I saw you, but you are quite altered."

I clasped one of Settwell's hands. "I am called Sebastian Foxx now."

"Of course you are. Your letter indicated as much. Forgive me. Your arrival has left me feeling quite keenly the passage of years. So much has happened, and so much time has fled, but it seems but a year or two since you were a child."

Settwell hurried across the room and, with jerky movements that suggested a great eagerness, poured Madeira into crystal goblets with chipped stems. We sat in opposing armchairs, faded and tattered.

Our conversation began as the sort to be expected between people who have not seen each other for ten years. I spoke of the thanks I had been unable to express years before, but I did not belabor the point because Settwell clearly did not wish to dwell upon it. Instead he directed the conversation toward his own particulars.

Shortly after I had escaped the country, Settwell had married a Portuguese woman named Mariana, and their daughter of the same name was now seven years old. To satisfy his bride, Settwell had converted to the Catholic religion. He was not a devotee to any church, and at the time it had seemed a small enough concession to affect devotion to one religion rather than another. Soon he discovered that his conversion was not viewed so liberally by fellow English merchants, who immediately treated him as a pariah. Trade opportunities vanished and men with whom he'd done business for years found excuses to avoid his company. The English might trade with the Portuguese, but to worship with them was unforgivable.

After they had been married for five happy years, Mariana died of a sudden fever. She had been well in the morning, delirious by nightfall, and dead two days later without having regained her senses. Settwell had been raising his daughter on his own since.

When he finished his tale, Settwell refilled our glasses. "We are but a pair of survivors, then, are we not, Mr. Foxx? We have been assaulted by all life has to throw at us, but we are not yet done."

I raised my glass. "I should like to think we are far from done."

* * *

Settwell had his servant bring down his daughter to meet me. The girl was a delightful creature with black hair and green eyes, and there could be no doubt that she would grow to be a beauty. I often felt more at ease around children than adults, perhaps because I knew it was less likely they would give me cause to break their bones. Quite charmed, I kneeled before the girl and shook her hand. "It is a great pleasure to meet you, senhorita," I said in Portuguese.

"And it is a pleasure to meet you, Mr. Foxx," she answered in English. "Your accent is very good."

I laughed. "As is yours." Observing that she held a wooden doll in her hand, I said, "And who is your friend?"

"This is Senhorita Catarina," the girl said very earnestly. "She's only a doll, though. She's not real, but my mother gave her to me. My mother is dead, you know. Is yours?"

"Mariana!" Settwell snapped. "Such questions are impolite."

I met the girl's gaze. "My mother is dead, and so is my father. But your father is a great friend to me and very much like family."

"Then I am like family too," the girl said cheerfully.

I stood up again and stroked my chin. "You may be right. I suppose I shall have to buy you something on your birthday, then."

"You don't have to buy me anything if you will only visit," she said.

"I should like the liberty to do both," I told her.

Settwell sighed. "You are very indulgent, sir. I thank you." He took his daughter's hand and led her back to the mulatto serving woman. "Mr. Foxx and I must talk business now."

"How dull," the girl said.

"Terribly dull." Settwell kissed her head and shooed her from the room. When he turned back, concern was plainly written upon his face. It had something to do with the girl, I was certain, but I would not press the matter. Not yet. Settwell would tell me what he wished me to know in due time.

We retired to a dining room, which could have used a few more candles in the sconces and upon the low-hanging chandelier. The table was unsteady, and tilted precariously at one end. The food was served by the same mulatto. In Lisbon, where servants and slaves were extraordinarily cheap by London standards, and even middling people employed several, Settwell appeared to have been reduced to but one.

The wine poured freely, though mainly into Settwell's goblet. I drank enough to avoid the appearance of abstemiousness, for a man with a mind to drink can take offense when his companion desires sobriety.

"Your letter from London was vague to the extreme," Settwell said at last, "and while I understood you meant to visit Lisbon, I could not glean your reasons."

I dared not risk being direct in writing, but now, face-to-face, there was no point obfuscating my purpose. "I've come to find the priest responsible for the deaths of my parents and to kill him."

Settwell said nothing for a long moment. He took another long drink of his wine and looked up at me, measuring my seriousness. "Gad, you mean it. Why should you attempt such a thing? You escaped! You did what so few can ever hope to do, and now you come back on some foolish quest. You will never leave the country alive."

"I left my parents behind, and they died here," I said. "I have an obligation."

"No!" Settwell hit the table. Knives and goblets danced. The man's face had quickly grown red with drink or fury or both. "I shall not have it! Your father knew his ruin at the hands of the Inquisition was a risk, and he begged me to make you safe should the worst happen. I did so because he was my friend and it was what he wanted. Do you think you honor him by returning here to throw your life away?"

I took a breath and leaned back. I wanted to explain myself, if only to this one man. "Everything that my parents did to save me, that *you* did to save me, was intended to give me a better life, but the life I have is broken. *I* am broken. I have become something my parents would have despised."

"I can never believe that Weaver would have raised you up to be something so terrible."

"Mr. Weaver did his best for me, I assure you. I have never blamed him. For a long time, I blamed myself, but of late I've come to understand that it is not my fault either. I have this anger inside me, and it burns every moment. It leads me to do awful things. This dark seed was planted by the Inquisition. I cannot destroy the institution, so I must destroy the man. Then, perhaps, the sacrifices made by my parents and by you will not have been wasted."

Settwell studied me for a long time. "Is there nothing I can say to dissuade you from this course?"

"No."

Settwell sighed. "Then there is something you should know. If you have come to address old wrongs, then you will want to hear of it."

"Is this something to do with my father?"

Settwell nodded, and then fortified himself with a gulp of wine. "You have seen how it is with me now. I am ruined, my boy. There have been reversals, and not honest ones either. Yes, my fortunes suffered with my conversion, but I believe I have been deliberately ruined because I began to ask questions about your father. There were rumors about him—rumors that his arrest was not what it seemed."

"Explain," I said. No matter how quickly Settwell spoke, it would not be quickly enough.

"In the space of but a few months, I heard the same rumor twice—from two unrelated and unconnected sources. It concerns your father and the fact that he may have been betrayed."

I breathed a sigh of relief. This was nothing. Settwell, in his comfortable world of English merchants, could never know what it meant to be a New Christian. "The Inquisition has made betrayal as much a part of life as breathing. I do not wish to know who informed against my father. How can I hate a man who had to choose between my father's life and his family? It is the Inquisition's fault, not its victims'."

"You are a wise young man, and I will not dispute what you say, but I learned that your father was not simply a victim of the Inquisition. There were others, outside the New Christian community, who manipulated him. The Inquisition never found his money. Your father was not betrayed by a neighbor who gave up a name in order to preserve himself. No, I fear he was the victim of a plot to take his wealth and throw him to the dogs that he might not expose the crime."

There were, Settwell said, two sources. One was a merchant, a member of the Factory, who had mentioned, in passing, that he had heard it was possible to deceive a New Christian into bringing hidden money—converted into a foreign currency and stored elsewhere—back into the country and then to steal it just before the Inquisition takes the man. This merchant had not done it himself, but he had heard rumors of past success, and thought it a remarkably clever exploitation of the natural order. "He'd said that as it was inevitable the New Christians were going to be arrested and have their property seized, it was better we should get the money than the Inquisition."

I said nothing of this logic. It had no bearing upon the matter at hand. "The other source?"

"An overheard snippet of conversation between two Inquisitors. One was the priest you have come here to kill, the Jesuit Pedro Azinheiro. He spoke of money that had never been recovered, how it rankled him still. The name he spoke was Raposa."

I said nothing for some moments. I did not trust myself to speak, for if I were to let one thing out, how could I stop the flow of words, end the tumult of thought. Better to stay bottled up than to erupt. At last, when I felt I could control myself, I said, "It was an Englishman who betrayed him?"

"It seems so, though I cannot be certain."

"You inquired into this?"

Settwell held out his hands, gesturing toward the room. "I made the attempt, and you see the results around you. It is true that I had suffered some ill fortune before this, but once I began asking questions, my enemies moved in for the final blow."

"You said the Factory men did not care," I observed.

"The leadership," he corrected. "But there are people within its protection who were willing to pounce upon me when they believed me vulnerable. I was ill used, and yet I cannot have my grievances redressed. I find myself penniless and without influence simply because I asked the wrong questions about your father."

I did not know what to think about this intelligence. Everything buzzed inside my head like a thousand mosquitoes. I had come here with a simple goal: to kill one man. Now, it appeared things were to be far more complicated.

"I wish I could help you learn more, Mr. Foxx, but I cannot even help myself. Worse, I cannot help my daughter. I have not enough money to flee Lisbon, and flee I must. Mariana is now seven years old, the age of religious consent in the Catholic Church. Priests have already come to see me with questions about the manner in which I raise her, for in truth, I am a poor Catholic. I fear they will take her from me, and if they do, I will never see her again. They will tell me she has chosen to live with a devout family, and I will have no recourse. None. More influential Englishmen than myself have had children spirited away by the Church, and once they are taken, they are gone forever."

I swallowed. Here, at least, was something I could do. "How much do you need? I will find you the money to flee Lisbon. I'll shake it out of Jesuits on the street if I must."

Settwell rose and embraced me, throwing too much weight upon me as he did so. He blasted sour breath in my face. Drink had made him unsteady and sentimental, and his eyes glistened in the candle-light. "I hardly know what to say. That my daughter might be made safe would mean more to me than I can say. I shall not forget this generosity."

"Only tell me what you need, and when you need it."

"I'll not have you robbing Jesuits, of course."

"I spoke figuratively," I said. "Such money as you might need is already in my possession." In truth, I had little enough for my own ventures, but I would find what money he needed if his wants exceeded my supply. The option of stealing from Jesuits was certainly not to be eliminated. In fact, it was to be embraced.

"I must have some time, perhaps a few weeks, to settle my affairs. Of course, I will have to be very subtle. If the Inquisition should suspect I plan to leave, they might come for Mariana."

"If you believe her to be in any danger, you must put her in my care. I shall defend her with my life."

"I do believe you mean it, sir."

"Do not doubt it."

Our meeting over, I took Settwell's hand. "You've been most generous, but now it is time to take my leave."

Settwell stepped forward too quickly for a man who had been drinking without restraint. He nearly fell over, and reached out to the wall to steady himself. "You'll go nowhere. You can see it's dark outside. 'Tis no trouble for you to stay here until morning."

I bowed. "I should very much prefer to sleep at the inn, though I thank you for your hospitality."

Settwell laughed indulgently. "You have been away a long time, so I remind you that this is not London. A man does not walk the streets at night. Honest Portuguese remain within doors after the sun goes down, and there is no one about but Gypsies and escaped slaves and *renegados*—if you are lucky. If you are not, it will be a pack of drunken *fidalgos,* who will slit your nose for the delight in watching you bleed. You'll not go ten feet before you are assaulted."

"I well recall the dangers of the city," I said, heading toward the door. "Ten feet is a bit of an exaggeration."

Settwell followed after me, catching his foot upon a threadbare rug and stumbling two or three steps. "Then fifty feet. A hundred. Regardless, there is little chance of you returning to your inn unmolested." He flushed. "I know my house is none the best, but we are hard by the Alfama, and this street is unsafe once the sun goes down."

I turned to Settwell. "Do not think I refuse to stay because your hospitality is insufficient. Such a suggestion insults me."

Settwell bowed. "You are quite correct. I apologize."

Honor was satisfied, and no more needed be said on the subject. "Then I shall go. I have affairs to which I must attend."

"You can hardly have any affairs on these streets at this hour. In fact, I shall not let you go. I am your elder, and I forbid you to—"

"You have a daughter," I said quietly. "If the Inquisition comes for you, you must tell them whatever they wish, because your first duty is to protect her. Therefore the less you know about how I do my business, the better off we both shall be."

Settwell swallowed and nodded. The heat had gone out of his argument. "Your point is well taken, but even so, damn it. Do you know what you are doing, going out in the black of night? Are you truly aware of what awaits you?"

I had listened to stories about how my father had been sold to the Inquisition for profit, and how a kind man had been ruined simply for inquiring into the truth of it. My muscles were coiled and tight, and I could feel my rage, like a living thing, pulsing in my veins. I did not fear that thieves might set upon me. I craved it.

"I know what's out there," I said. "Indeed, I mean to find it."

Chapter 5

For a man who is patient and careful, it is entirely possible to remain invisible in a city at night. I knew how to cling to shadow, how to walk without making a sound, how to vanish into darkness and silence. Many London streets are lit with lanterns and patrolled by parish watchmen, which could make remaining unseen occasionally difficult, but Lisbon, by comparison, posed little in the way of a challenge. Outside of the English neighborhoods, most men did not visit public houses or taverns to pass the night in drink and companionship. Such businesses closed their doors at nightfall. There were no pleasure gardens or theaters or outdoor concerts or firework displays or other nighttime amusements of any variety. The streets belonged to the poor and luckless, the drunk and the thieves who preyed upon them, and the well-armed privileged of the city who targeted all. For the unfortunates who could not escape indoors, night was a time of violence and hunger, of desperate struggle.

Those who chose to venture out upon the streets for

sport took pleasure in that struggle. Noblemen patrolled the city in packs like wolves, stalking thieves for amusement and hunting one another in contests of bravado. I vanished into shadows as one such group passed, too drunk and boisterous to notice me even if I had stood in the open, arms wide. This group had dressed entirely in white, no doubt a taunt to a rival band of *fidalgos*. These grudge matches often ended in disfiguration or death. Sometimes these parties would stumble upon a Gypsy or mulatto who had strayed from his fellows, and they would set upon him mercilessly, offering no more quarter than do huntsmen when they corner the fox. Other times a nobleman would fall behind only to become prey himself. Settwell had not exaggerated the dangers that awaited the unwary.

Nowhere was this more true than in the Alfama, the oldest and poorest part of the city. Here, the streets were so narrow that two men upon opposing balconies could share a bottle of wine without difficulty. Every passageway was winding, steep, and labyrinthine, often encased in tunnels or ending abruptly. A wrong turn could mean a dead end, quite literally.

I ignored the *fidalgos* who stumbled past me. I had no use for them. I continued my patrol, and within an hour I found what I sought in a brutally inclining alley behind the massive gothic cathedral of Santa Maria Maior. There were four of them, dressed in the loose and brightly colored shirts of Gypsies. Four if you didn't count the boy—perhaps thirteen or fourteen at the most, dark-skinned, with wide eyes. It was the boy who interested me. He was with them, but I did not believe he was one of them.

Off to the side, wearing ragged breeches and a vest cut out of a burlap bag, was the group's evident leader. He was tall, thickly muscled in the arms and broad in the belly, and perhaps he had earned his swagger. To me he appeared a buffoon, drinking from his bottle of wine as he strode boisterously along the street, like a child's rendering of a hero. Occasionally he raised his bottle in a toast to a woman he called his Beatrice, whom he credited as the finest whore in the

city. I suspected the pool from which he chose was none the best, and
the lack of leprosy was apt to elevate a woman into the highest rank-
ing.

I moved swiftly to place myself perhaps thirty paces in front of the
Gypsies, and then slowed, coughed, and allowed my boots to scrape
the ground. In response the thieves grew suddenly quiet. I heard
them moving to the sides of the street, pressing themselves against
the buildings, and then falling in behind me. They likely imagined
they were being stealthy, and perhaps they were, but I followed their
every movement. Using nothing but the noise they made to guide
my hand, I could have tossed a knife and had a reasonable chance of
striking one of them.

The men did not long hesitate. To do so would have been foolish.
Their victim was alone and evidently drunk. If they waited, another
band of thieves might appear and claim me for themselves. Within
minutes of making myself known, the thieves rushed at me. I felt a
hand upon my shoulder whip me around. A man grabbed my arms,
and the leader stepped out of the darkness, his wine forgotten. He
now held a long knife almost casually, letting it half dangle and catch
the light of the handful of stars that peered through the clouds.

He stood in front of me, claiming the higher ground on the steep
hill. He had, at least, the sense to do that. Shifting the knife from
hand to hand, he grinned, and in the dim light, there was no mistak-
ing the pleasure upon his face. This was the sort of man who relishes
power over the helpless. He was imposing in his person, no doubt
used to giving orders and having them obeyed, and wore the groomed
oiled beard of a *fidalgo*. I supposed he imagined he belonged to a kind
of royalty among his tribe, and that sort of prominence set him outside the laws of man and God.

In addition to the leader, and the man who held me in place, there
were the two other thieves. They stood back and watched, passing a
bottle back and forth. I ignored them. What little fight they had was
weakened with every swallow of wine. Near those two stood the boy,

who looked at the other men with the cautious gaze of a dog regularly beaten by his master.

It took but a glance to know his story, or at least a reasonably accurate version of it. He was an orphan of the streets, taken in by the thieves as their slave and their amusement, to be used as they wished. If he was loyal and obedient and of some service, and if he lived so long, he might eventually become one of their number. The boy would not wish for it now, but someday it would become the only life he could imagine. Perhaps long ago he had dreamed of escape, but there was no escape for such as he, and at his age he would know that. His eyes set upon me, and he watched with wary interest, taking no pleasure in my capture, merely assessing the situation for how it might help or hurt his station. I knew then that he was desperate, but he was not broken. Not yet.

How many such boys were there in Lisbon? Hundreds certainly. Perhaps thousands. I could not save them all, but I could save this one, as someone had once saved me. Whatever else I did in the city, whatever crimes I contemplated, I would do some good here and now.

"What have we here?" the leader of the thieves said in a singsong voice of heavily accented English. "A Factory man out upon the street at night? It is not wisest."

Perhaps I should have been afraid. I was outnumbered quite significantly, and while I was confident in my abilities, I knew nothing of these men. Each of them might have been my match or more. I felt no fear, however, merely the excitement of the moment and the promise of violence. Once, long ago, in such moments, I had searched for fear, as a sign that I was yet unbroken, but I had long since stopped looking. I was what I was, what circumstances had made me. I wished to change all that, but not just yet. For the moment, I was content with my advantages.

"You say nothing, Factory man?" the Gypsy said, clucking his tongue like a disappointed grandmother.

"I'm not with the Factory." I slurred my words and struck a note of hesitant bravado. "I've just arrived in the city."

"And no one warned you for Lisbon night? Perhaps you've make for you enemies, but I assure, I am not one of them. My name is Antonio Alface de Dordia e Zilhão, and I am the enemy of no man who wants be my friend."

"I am an Englishman," I said, with too much pride and volume, "and if you wish to be my friend, I suggest you release me. You walk a dangerous path, I promise you."

"Perhaps we make a mistake," Dordia e Zilhão said. He pressed one hand to his heart and bowed. "Perhaps we should fear you."

"Do not mock me," I said. "I merely tell you that an Englishman is not to be troubled as he goes about his business."

"Hmm." Dordia e Zilhão ran a hand over his mustaches. "You have given me many ideas to think on. Now, shall I tell you what to think on?"

"If you have terms, I shall hear them," I said, standing up a little straighter.

"Remove your clothes."

"What?" I exclaimed. "What is your meaning?"

"I might cut your throat," Dordia e Zilhão said, "but then the clothes would be stained with your blood, making them have for no value. Hand me your purse and your clothes of your back, and perhaps we allow you live. If you can make it to home, naked, without much troubled, you will learn for you a lesson about Lisbon for which you will owe me thanks."

"And if I refuse?" I asked.

"Then you will have learned a different lesson, but I fear for you it will do no good."

If I complied, did he mean to let me live? I could not say. I did not think even he knew yet what he would do. Such men are often creatures of caprice and whim.

I hung my head, as if in defeat. "I cannot accept your terms. You have made a mistake in taking me, for I suffer from a terrible illness."

"What illness?" Dordia e Zilhão pretended toward bravado, but his tone became slightly more shrill.

I spoke again, running together a string of garbled nonsense.

"What? Speak, English fool."

I mumbled once more, but this time I met the eye of the boy and held it for an instant, hoping he would understand the significance.

Dordia e Zilhão stepped closer and put his head near my own. "Damn you, what are you talking about?"

I lurched forward and struck Dordia e Zilhão hard in the face with my forehead. The blow was sure and staggering. I felt the man's nose pop like an egg, and I heard the satisfying crunch of bone and the warm spray of blood against my forehead as the Gypsy crumpled, coughing up a garbled, gurgling scream. He pitched forward, and the incline of the hill did the rest for me as he tumbled.

The man holding me did not let go in surprise, as I had hoped. Instead, he tightened his grip, perhaps believing that one of the two remaining men would set upon the prisoner. I chose not to wait. I rotated my forearms with a sudden burst of strength, and the thief's grip loosened, if only for an instant. I drove the heel of my boot into his shin, and feeling his hands slip away, I struck the Gypsy in the face with my elbow. I caught him in the teeth, and felt at least two come unmoored. The man dropped and rolled down the steep incline of the street and into the murky dark.

I turned to face the remaining two men, but they had already fled into the night. It was all for the good, and it made my task easier. Though I had dispatched the first two men with relative ease, I could not depend upon my luck holding.

The fight had been short and brutal. My elbow throbbed, as did my knuckles and my forehead. I hadn't noticed the pain in the heat of the action—I rarely did—but now it washed over me. If anything, it was a comfort. I stepped over the groaning body of Dordia e Zilhão and approached the lad, the only one who remained present and conscious.

The light was dim, but I could see the boy was tawny in color and had the high forehead of a Brazilian native, although his other features appeared more European. He was the sort of half-caste that Englishmen would have found shocking but was common enough in a Portuguese port city.

"How old are you?" I asked the boy in Portuguese.

"Fifteen, my master," he answered, keeping his eyes cast down. He was thin, and his filthy clothes hung loose upon his frame. These things contributed to his look of terror, though no doubt he was frightened enough. Still, I detected that he was alert and ready to flee or, perhaps, spring upon an opportunity if one should appear. He was a creature of the streets, and so prepared to endure risk for the chance of reward.

"Small for your age. What is your name?"

"I am called Enéas."

"Well, Enéas, what is the largest sum of money you have ever held in your hands as your own to spend?"

The boy took a moment to consider the question. "One real."

I put a purse in the boy's hands. "Here's ten. It is yours to keep regardless of what you choose. However, I am in need of a servant, one who knows the streets and who can get me information. Is that something you can do?"

Enéas nodded eagerly, swallowing hard, perhaps at the thought of the food ten reais would buy. The boy's muscles were still tense. He was clearly prepared to run, money in hand, should things go badly, but he was not leaving yet. Not until he heard more.

"I can do all that and more," he said, now sounding brighter. "There is no one who knows Lisbon better than I. I know every street and every vendor in every stall. I know every whore and every drunk.

You need but say to me, 'Enéas, fetch me the French whore who used to be a seamstress,' and I shall know who you mean and run to her that very instant."

"I shall certainly keep that in mind. Here is what I propose. Come with me, and I shall not mistreat you or give you cause to complain, and in exchange I ask only for diligent labor and loyalty. If anyone offers you money to betray me, you must tell me, and I shall make it more profitable to reject that offer. If you should choose to betray me regardless, I can promise you a swift death. Is this a bargain you care to make?"

The boy cocked his head as he considered the offer. "Will there be buggery?"

"I shan't indulge," I said, "but you may pursue your own interests when you are not otherwise engaged."

Enéas snorted out a laugh. "I accept your offer. I was a slave to those men, and never earned a coin for my labor or my sorrow. It is said that the English treat their servants well."

"Some do, and some do not," I said. "I do. You will return to my inn and sleep in my front room there. You will eat upon my bill, and rest until dawn. And then I shall put you to work."

"What manner of work, my master?"

"Seeking information and not being detected."

The boy nodded and grinned as though this were the very thing of which he had always dreamed.

Chapter 6

The next morning, I took a leisurely breakfast of bread and cheese. Enéas had settled into his new position with wonderful alacrity, waking early, preparing hot water and fetching my food. Naturally, I watched him for signs that he was merely biding his time, waiting to steal something of value and flee, but Enéas seemed to appreciate that fate had thrown an inexplicably good opportunity in his path, and he was not about to spurn it. Some men are born to cut purses and throats, and some to draw baths and pour tea. Enéas, I felt certain, was of the latter category.

If anything, I would have to work on making certain he was not overly solicitous. I did not want him reordering my trunk or folding my clothes or dusting my desk. I explained to the boy that his task was to run errands, deliver messages, and bring my meals when I had chosen to eat in private. Otherwise, he was at his leisure. This concept confounded the boy. Leisure in his life among the Gypsies, I supposed, had been the time Enéas awaited his next torment.

Having finished the last of his bread, I now looked at the boy, who appeared to have no other business at the moment than staring at me with his huge brown eyes, full of equal measures of fear and expectation. "You have eaten already?" I asked him.

"Please forgive me!" Enéas cried, throwing his hands in the air. "You said last night that I might eat upon your bill, and so I took a portion for myself. If this was wrong, I beg you will work me day and night to make amends."

"You are of no use to me if you don't eat," I answered, perhaps a little sharply. I understood that half of this performance was genuine, the other half masquerade, and I found both parts equally tiresome. "Take your fill, and think no more of it. But eat no more than you require." This last I added lest too much kindness make the boy mistrust me.

"I shall be no glutton!" Enéas said. "I swear by all the saints."

I leaned forward. "Then you are ready to work?"

Enéas clapped his hands together. "You must but tell me what to do."

"I need you to find someone for me. I will tell you what I know of him, but it is many years since I've seen him, so I cannot say the task will be easy, particularly because I wish you to be subtle. Ask no more than you have to of no people but those you must. Use your eyes and ears, and whenever possible, hold your tongue. Do you understand?"

Enéas nodded. "My old master had me perform such tasks when looking for, well, certain things."

"Victims to rob?" I suggested.

Enéas nodded. "Oh, yes. Victims to rob, children to abduct, functionaries to bribe. He had a great interest in such things, and I was very good at finding them." He paused for a moment and looked at me. "I took no pleasure in doing evil, of course."

"Yes, well, this is nothing of that sort. I am looking for someone."

More than anything, I wanted to send the boy in search of Gabriela. The idea that I might see her, that I might see her soon, even in a matter of hours, made me feel drunk with excitement. After all these years, to look upon her again. And perhaps more? When I thought of being reunited with her, I thought of taking her in my arms, of holding her, of having the touch of her skin against mine drive away all that had changed me.

I could not, however, send a Gypsy boy poking around New Christian business. Enéas would draw notice and would likely be arrested. He might cause Gabriela to be arrested too. Instead, I chose to send him after someone else from my past.

"I'm looking for an old friend, one I haven't seen in ten years, but I knew him well when I was a boy."

Enéas nodded. "Tell me what you can of him, and I shall find him. There is no place in Lisbon he can hide from my ever-watchful gaze."

I narrowed my eyes.

"That is to say," the boy corrected, "I shall do my best."

"His name is Inácio Arouca. His father worked as a factotum for various New Christians in the city, but he also owned a small fleet of fishing boats. He was an enterprising sort, as I recall, and it is likely his son joined the family trade or took it over if the father is not alive. Do you think that is enough information for you to begin with?"

"Yes, my master," Enéas said, now nodding eagerly. "That is your first task. Now you must think of a second task for me."

"Perhaps you should complete the first before you begin on the second."

"I have already completed it," Enéas said. "I can take you to Inácio Arouca anytime you like. Right now, if you wish."

I sat up straight. "What? You know him?"

"How should I not know him? Everyone knows him," said Enéas.

"At least men such as my old master. Thieves and cutthroats and poor slaves like myself. He may be your old friend, and I know you would have scorned him in your youth had he not been a good person. Now, however, Inácio Arouca is a terrible man."

We met when we were both eleven, and we became friends at once. Inácio was the son of João Arouca, a hard-bitten Old Christian whom my father had hired as a general agent, a man meant to smooth over rougher business transactions, especially with other Old Christian laborers and small merchants and dockworkers. It helped to have a tough-minded man like Arouca, who could make easy conversation and clarify misunderstandings, and perhaps use stronger tactics when necessary. A New Christian had to be on his guard at all times not to offend, and that was not always easy for a merchant. A disgruntled worker or trader might vent his anger, sharpened with a few embellishing falsehoods, to the Inquisition. Arouca therefore stood as my father's proxy, using a glib tongue or a strong arm as was required.

Arouca came to meet with my father one afternoon and brought Inácio in tow. In the way of boys, I sensed at once the presence of another child in the house. Though my English-born tutor was not present, I—ever diligent—had been at my studies for hours, writing a Latin essay in the style of Cicero. I had applied myself most of the day, but now I wanted to be outside. I wanted to run and climb and kick and throw. I crept down the stairs and saw him. There was something I liked at once about the boy. He had a hawkish nose and curious eyes, and he moved like a predator. Even at eleven, Inácio appeared muscular and powerful, whereas I was as thin as a stray dog. Watching him, I had the undeniable feeling that this Old Christian would be a good friend to have.

I watched the boy, still unseen by him, as he reached out toward a dagger resting upon a stand in the hallway. It had a silver handle, laced with gold and encrusted with rubies, and had been in the family for many years. I was not permitted to touch the blade, and I understood the boy's fascination.

"You are Arouca's son?" I asked.

The boy started and took a step back. "I wasn't going to steal it. I only wanted to hold it." He met my gaze, and though his words had been apologetic, his expression spoke of defiance.

"I'm not allowed to touch it either." I grinned, trying to put the boy at his ease. "But, once in a while, I like to hold it anyway."

Inácio looked relieved. No doubt he had not expected to be believed. He had imagined this son of a rich merchant would assume he was a thief. "You will not tell my father?"

"Tell him what?" I asked. "That you looked at a dagger? That would make me sound foolish."

The boy laughed. "I thought that because you are rich you must be cruel."

"It is a reasonable conclusion," I said, "but we're not *that* rich."

I walked with Enéas, and the boy prattled on endlessly about what he knew of Inácio—what everyone knew of him. He was a smuggler, and a successful one. He had bought a series of houses built up against the old seawall. During high tide, the river rose up to the outer wall of the property, and a false door there allowed Inácio's boats to move in and out with ease, eluding the customs men. He was said to own a dozen or more—which meant he likely had no more than four or five—which he used to bring in goods from Spain.

That, however, was only part of his business. He did not himself lend money or pimp or run gambling houses, but he took money from those who did, allegedly providing protection from interference, though the interference was more likely to come from Inácio himself than any other source. Every petty criminal in the city, including Enéas's old master, had had dealings with Inácio, and they were never pleasant.

I had less difficulty than I would have liked reconciling Enéas's description of a violent enforcer with my memories of my friend. Inácio had never shied away from a fight, and he always had his eye out for a chance to make a few coins. Inácio's father had tied his fortunes to my father's, and when a New Christian fell, as Settwell had learned, he often took his friends with him. Inácio may have found himself without money or an honest means of getting it, and I knew all too well how one desperate choice could lead to another.

We walked east, past the Palace and then the fine shops, gated off so that *fidalgos* and government functionaries might buy their clothes and furnishings without having to come in contact with the poor. Then we made our way into the winding alleys of the Alfama, keeping close to the river. Finally Enéas led us up a narrow staircase, covered and nighttime dark, and stinking of the unwashed men and women who had slept there the night before. Beyond that was a small courtyard of uneven buildings made of warped wood and bricks stained by soot and overturned chamber pots. From there we followed another path down, back toward the river, until we came to a set of nondescript doors.

"Here," Enéas said.

I knocked.

A young man, hardly more than a boy, with a wispy beard, opened the door a crack. The smell of the river exploded from behind him. "What do you want?" he asked.

"I seek Inácio," I said, straining to see past the man. My efforts yielded nothing.

The man snorted. "Many men seek Inácio."

"Then they may knock on this door when it suits them," I said. "It is I who knocks now."

"They may knock," the young man said, "but they shan't be admitted. What makes you think you deserve more than they?"

"Do many Englishmen seek him?" I asked.

The man at the door appeared puzzled.

"That's what makes me think I deserve more," I said. "I'm English, and all Englishmen deserve whatever they desire. Surely you know that."

"Inácio does not see someone simply because he knocks upon the door," the young man said. "English or otherwise."

The burden of refraining from violence began to tire me. "He will see me. Tell him his old friend Sebastião is here."

The man considered this. He scratched at the thin strands of his beard with a bony hand. "You know him, you say?"

"It is what I say. I have just said it. I can say it again if you think it will help you to understand."

Having come to a decision, the man said, "He's not here."

"Why did you not tell us this before?"

"I am telling you now. He is at the Velha Baleia."

The old whale? "Is that a *taberna?*"

The man studied him. "You speak Portuguese well, particularly for an Englishman, but you evidently don't know the Alfama. That makes me doubt you are truly Inácio's friend. Are you certain you wish to find him?"

"I know the place," Enéas volunteered before I could answer. He drew me further into the winding streets full of craftsmen plying their trades; fish-sellers walking about barefoot, massive baskets on their heads; and cartmen pushing their wares through the narrow alleys. Vendors cried out to me in broken English or, more optimistically, in Portuguese. Enéas made it his mission to shoo them all away.

Everything smelled rank, from the filth that ran openly to the unwashed bodies to the odors of food from the homes of Africans and Brazilians and Saracens. People spoke in a half dozen languages. The wild dogs never ceased their barking. And the singing—everywhere they sang their dark and gloomy songs in a hodgepodge of languages, bemoaning their fate, their *fado.*

At last we came to another set of unmarked doors. These Enéas pushed open without knocking. Inside was the sort of public house common to the poor of the city. The floor was dirt, the tables and chairs fashioned out of old crates and discarded barrels from the dock. Wine was tapped from casks and poured into cups and glasses and bowls, no one like another.

I glanced about the room, and it took but a moment for me to recognize my old friend. He had changed, of course, but the hooked blade of his nose was unmistakable. He wore his head shaved now, and the skin of his cheeks was rugged and raw with the marks of smallpox as well as a single scar that ran on his left side from his cheek to his jaw. His long and elaborate mustaches made no effort to hide the damage, and I sensed he wore his wounds as a badge of honor. Like me, he had grown taller over the years, and more thickly muscled, and he held himself with a tense and dangerous energy I recognized too well. I had fought enough men like the one my old friend had become, and while none of those men had killed me, a few had come closer than I preferred.

Inácio, who had been in conversation with another rough-looking man, stopped talking and turned his head with deliberate malice toward me. Everyone in the *taberna* stared. They would be unused to seeing English gentlemen in this place, and however Inácio wished to respond, it would almost certainly prove interesting.

Inácio rose and strode toward me with the easy, menacing gait I well remembered. He stood only a few inches away, close enough that his mere presence became a threat, and he looked me over with a practiced air of contempt. He folded his arms and flexed them. Veins bulged to the surface of his forearms like rivers on a map. "Stranger, you are lost," he said in English.

"No, I am precisely where I wish to be," I told him.

"I see this before," Inácio said, grinning without any pleasure. "Englishmen come to see how poor men live. Maybe buy something cheap. Hire poor mens to do work. What do you think you will find here? Maybe a dressmaker?"

The men in the room who spoke English laughed at this, more

loudly than the joke deserved. Then the others who did not speak English joined in.

So, that was how it was with him. Even as boys there had been a darkness to Inácio. It was always wiser to be his friend than his enemy.

I bowed to him in an exaggerated gesture. "I had hoped," I said in Portuguese, "you might measure me yourself. You are the seamstress, yes? But be gentle as you measure between my thighs, for I am very tender there."

Inácio did not react other than to set his jaw. All trace of the humorless smile was gone. "You play a dangerous game," he said, continuing to speak in English. "Maybe I make a dress out of your skin."

"If you like," I said. "I suggest you use this." I drew from a sheath upon my belt a dagger, the one I had brought from England—silverhandled, laced with gold, encrusted with rubies.

The crowd let out a collective gasp as the blade emerged. Inácio's eyes went hard, and his muscles twitched as he prepared to grab my wrist. Then he stopped himself. He took a step back and studied my face, moving his head from side to side, trying to take some kind of impossible measure. "No," he whispered. "It cannot be."

"It has been a long time, my old friend."

Inácio paused for a moment and then his face split into a massive grin, this one far less menacing. He opened his arms and took me into a great hug.

Enéas sat in a far corner with other boys his own age, playing at cards, while Inácio and I sat ourselves at a table, both of us with large goblets of wine, both of us drinking only sparingly. I slid the dagger across the table to my old friend.

"You admired it long ago. Now I present it to you." In truth, this was not the dagger Inácio had admired, but a clever imitation I'd brought with me from England. I did wish to gift him the real dagger, but on the other hand I was not so eager to let go of one of the few mementos I had of my father. Perhaps this was a bit dishonest, but no one suffered and all gained. When the misdeeds of my life are inscribed in the Book of Life, I'm not certain there will be ink enough for mention of the false dagger.

"I cannot accept it." Inácio's eyes went wide, but then he shook his head. "It was your father's."

"My father is gone. That life is gone, and you would insult me if you refused a gift."

"A fair point." He pulled the dagger over to his side of the table. "You took quite a risk drawing it before I knew you. You were always eager to take risks, but I think you are more prepared to take care of yourself than you were in the old days. Do you know what else I think? I think you are the mad Englishman whom the Gypsy Dordia e Zilhão claims came upon him like the devils of hell."

"Word of that has traveled quickly."

Inácio shrugged. "Nothing is secret in the Alfama. Nothing is secret in Lisbon. And when Dordia e Zilhão staggers through the street with a smashed nose, people take note. You were not gentle with him."

I frowned. "He irritated me."

"He irritates many people. When we were boys, you could fight well enough, but you liked to solve your problems with words."

"We are boys no longer," I said.

"That is most certainly true," Inácio said, slapping his hand down on the table. "You were so skinny then, and look at you now. You have turned into a bear of a man."

"You are no slight thing either," I said, feeling my way into the rhythm of the conversation. He was taking my measure, which was all well. I was doing the same.

Inácio laughed. "But I was a bear of a boy," he said, raising his wineglass. He sipped only a small amount. "To old friends, Sebastião."

"I call myself Sebastian now."

Inácio leaned back and appeared to consider this fact. He picked up the dagger and passed it from one hand to the other. "So, you are an Englishman in truth?"

"I have lived in England ten years, almost as long as I lived in Lisbon. But more importantly, I can reveal my origins to only a few people I trust. If the Inquisition were to learn who I am, well, I hardly need tell you what they would think of me."

"Sebastian it is, then." He raised his glass again, but still did not drink much. "England has been kind to you, by all appearances."

"Appearances should never be trusted, but I have done well there, yes."

Inácio shook his head. "I still cannot quite believe it. Sebastião Raposa here at my table." He held up his hand. "Yes, I know, *Sebastian*. But you must forgive me. The memories come flooding back."

"That they do," I said. "We had some fine times."

"We did," Inácio agreed. "But they could not last. And now, here you are, an English dandy. Fine clothes, silver in your purse, I suppose. This dagger, once a prize possession, hardly worth keeping."

I did not much care for his tone, but I bit back my anger. Inácio was always impulsive, and he would vent his emotions, even if they were fleeting. A volatile man was perhaps not the most reliable, but that did not mean he was not loyal. Inácio was always poor at keeping his intentions hidden from the world, and that was a form of surety in itself.

"And what have you become?" I asked. "I've heard some stories, my friend."

Inácio snorted. "That I squeeze a few coins out of thieves and whores and gamblers? I own it. And why should I not? This city has taken all it can from me and my family. I would be foolish not to try to do the same. It happens that I do it better than most. God has made me strong and bold, and I must use the gifts given to me. And yet what is good enough for God is not good enough for you, *Sebastian*. I see how you pass judgment on me."

"I do not judge," I assured him.

He leaned forward, scrutinizing me. "Tell me, why have you returned to this place? You were well rid of it."

"I shall tell you everything," I said. "You are one of the few whom I can trust. But first you must tell me if you have any knowledge of what became of Gabriela." I spoke the words calmly, as if they were of no importance. From what Enéas had said, Inácio knew much of what went on in Lisbon, and though his station would be far removed from hers, he might well have kept track of her actions. If he knew nothing, I would not stop my search for her here, but I dared to hope it could be this easy. He would point me in the right direction, and there she would be.

"Gabriela?" Inácio barked. "All these years later, and you still cannot forget that beauty, eh? You were but children then."

Inácio had been a good friend and as loyal as a hound, but his testing the waters of my feelings had, from time to time, angered me. This was such a time. I controlled my breathing. I cleared my mind. This was not a fight I wished to have, nor was this a man with whom to have it. It was Inácio. I had come looking for him, and I had no one to blame but myself if I did not like what I found.

"I am determined to seek out all the old friends if I can," I answered, struggling to sound neutral.

"Hmm," Inácio said. "I hardly think a New Christian lady will be of much use to you."

"I know much may have changed. She might be married, a mother. Regardless, I should like to know."

This time Inácio did drink deeply. He sighed and put down the cup. "I fear I have some sad news for you. After you left—after your father was taken—things became bad for many people. The Inquisition arrested her father as well. And mine. Did you know that?"

I shook my head. "I knew it was possible, but I did not know for certain," I said. "I had no way of learning the details."

"Because you fled."

I did not answer. I had gone and, as far as he could tell, lived a life of ease while he had remained behind to fend for himself. If he felt some resentment, I would not deny him the right.

Inácio shook his head. "So many people were taken after your father. Some said he gave the Inquisitors many names."

I stiffened. "All men tell the Inquisition what they wish to know."

"There's no need for protest. I understand. Men resist, but eventually, once the torture begins . . ." Inácio held out his hands in a gesture of futility.

"Your father was a good friend to mine," I said, trying to return him to the topic. "I am sorry he was caught up in our troubles."

Inácio growled. "But you did not ask about my father. You asked about the girl. She was alone, and she was frightened, and she wed herself to a New Christian merchant—I cannot even recall his name now—only a few months after her father's arrest. She became pregnant very soon after their marriage, but there were difficulties. Perhaps three months before the baby was to be born, she began to bleed and did not stop. That is what I heard. She died less than a year after you left."

I said nothing. I allowed the words to wash over me. All these years I had held on to the hope that I might find Gabriela again someday. All these years she had remained for me the one thing I could reach for to keep me from becoming something entirely hateful to myself. If I were to learn she was married and fat, a contented mother and wife, I could live with the knowledge that she was lost to me. I had become something unworthy of Gabriela, and she deserved a good life and a kind husband. That she was dead, however, that she had been dead nearly the entire time I lived in England, was the cruelest sort of joke. I had passed endless days and months and years yearning for her, made bargains with myself that led me back to her, imagined us married and together—and all the while, she had been cold and rotting.

There was nothing of my old life to salvage. What I had come here to do, I needed to do all the more urgently. I would find the Jesuit and kill him. I would find out who had betrayed my father, and I would make that man pay. I would burn off this part of myself I hated in the fires of vengeance, and then I would see what was left.

"I am sorry," Inácio said. "I see by your expression that you did still care for her. I wish I could tell you otherwise."

"It is better to know," I said, angry with myself for revealing anything. I wanted to reach into my pocket, to take out the scarf and run it through my hands, to smell its false perfume, but it was the last remnant of a foolish dream, and I could not indulge myself. The childish hope that I could have Gabriela back now made me feel weak and simple.

I was determined to show no more vulnerability before my old friend. "This only makes things clearer. All of this destruction was caused by my father's arrest. I have come back to Lisbon to find the man who destroyed my family and destroy him in return."

"Revenge? Against an Inquisitor? That is madness."

"Maybe so, but it is my madness. You would not judge me for wanting this, I hope."

"I understand your desire to set things right, but you must see it is impossible. Were an ordinary man to have hurt you, then you should stop at nothing to punish him. I believe that to my soul. The Inquisition is another matter. It is like taking revenge against the ocean to avenge a drowning."

"I know I cannot destroy all of the Inquisition, but one man is within my powers. That I can do."

"You will end up dead, if you are lucky. In the Palace prisons more likely. All those who know you will suffer."

"I have no intention of dying or allowing them to take me or anyone else. I came here to settle old debts, but I'll admit that may now be a more difficult proposition. I have learned that my father was betrayed by someone for his money. He was robbed. I intend not only to take revenge on the Inquisitor who killed my family, but on whoever arranged for his destruction. I did not come here to gain wealth, but it was my father's money, and if it is in the hands of someone who betrayed him for it—well, I think you understand that I cannot allow this."

Inácio grinned. "You did not come to gain wealth, but you will take it all the same."

"The money means nothing to me," I said. "I only want that it does not enrich my family's enemies. If you aid me in this, much of it can be yours, but I need to learn everything I can about the Jesuit Pedro Azinheiro—where he lives, where he eats, whom he cares for. You cannot order your affairs without knowing much of what goes on in this city. Do you think you can help me with this?"

Inácio was about to speak, but then he paused, noticing the door. A short man with rough clothes and wild black hair entered and eyed the room cautiously. He spotted Inácio and looked to be deciding if he should proceed further or flee. Inácio locked eyes with the man, and he appeared to have his decision made for him.

"Forgive me," Inácio said. He stood and walked over to the man. The man took a step back, and Inácio closed the gap again.

Inácio and the newcomer spoke very quietly, Inácio more so than the stranger. I heard a few of the stranger's words—*very sorry, money, soon*. The man's face twisted with worry, but Inácio said little and showed no expression. Then, without warning, he struck the man in the stomach. It was a hard blow. The man staggered back one step and then fell to his knees. Inácio raised his leg and pushed the man with the flat of his foot facedown into the dirt. The man did not resist. He suffered his humiliation without complaint. Inácio bent down and whispered something in the man's ear. He nodded, and Inácio prodded him with his foot once more—not hard, and it seemed all the crueler for his gentleness.

Inácio returned to the table, his expression neutral, as though he had only gone to relieve himself. "Pardon the interruption. Sometimes business cannot wait."

Inácio was clearly inclined to play games. "That was for my benefit. You wanted me to know you are not a man to be toyed with."

"Perhaps." Inácio smiled. "But the man owes me money, and I have my interests to protect."

"The fishing boats your father left you do not provide you with enough income?"

"My father left me nothing," Inácio said, his voice becoming low and rough. "The Inquisition seized it all, and the loss of it killed him. He sat in those dungeons for over a year, and when they let him out, he was a pauper. He died of shame before another year had passed. The boats I have now, like everything else I have, I earned by my labor."

"Then you have just as much reason to hate the Inquisition as I do."

"Without a doubt," Inácio agreed, "but I also have a great deal to lose. Look at you, Englishman. You will either die attempting to have your revenge, or you will live and return to England—and with money which you do not care for. All I am and have is right here. I cannot afford to make war on the Inquisition. I wish you well, and I hope you succeed in all you attempt, but I cannot spy on an Inquisitor. I would be discovered—make no mistake about that—and I will not land in the Palace dungeon for as same as my father did for your father."

"I understand," I said, and I did. My position here, my disguise within a disguise, protected me. Inácio was right. I did not plan to die, but I did plan to leave. I risked no more than I put upon the table, but a man who remained in Lisbon would risk everything he had. I did not much care for Inácio's resentment, but I comprehended it well enough.

"Perhaps I can help you indirectly. I will not be your partner, for I dare not be, but I am your friend. If you think there is something I can do for you without inviting danger, you must let me know. If I can, I shall."

I took his hand. "It is all I can ask."

Inácio looked away thoughtfully. "And although I cannot ask many questions without attracting notice, if I hear anything unbidden, I shall pass the information along at once."

"Thank you."

"This Jesuit you seek," Inácio now said very quietly. "I know him. We know them all, of course, but this one. He's different. It is said he hates Englishmen. He may well seek you out if you stir the pot."

"I'm counting on it," I said.

Inácio laughed. "Same old Sebastião. I beg your pardon. Sebastian."

"Do you know why he hates the English?"

Inácio shrugged. "He's mad. They're all mad. Maybe hating Jews was too ordinary for him. But you, Senhor *Foxx*—a New Christian turned into an Englishman—if he were to learn the truth of who you are, he would come looking for you sure enough, and he would not come alone."

"He cannot learn that," I said, leaning forward.

Inácio's gaze went dark. "Do not insult me. I may slap a few debtors, but I shall never earn a coin from *them*." He would not even say the word now. Instead he gestured toward the outside with his chin.

"I would not think otherwise," I said. Perhaps Inácio did not think I was the same friend he had lost ten years before. Regardless, he hated the Inquisition, and that would be reason enough for him to keep my secret.

Inácio remained motionless for a moment, as if deciding if honor was satisfied. Then, once more, he slapped the table and raised his wine. "Then we shall drink with joy to your success."

I drank, but I did so without joy.

Chapter 7

I gave Enéas some money and rattled off a list of items
for him to buy. I wished to be alone, and wanted to
offer no excuses. The boy was either oblivious to my
moods or pretended to be. I didn't care which, and I hardly
noticed him disappear into the crowd.

Inácio had become a thief, a pimp, and a fence, and no
doubt indulged in all the terrible crimes such men must,
but I could not mourn my old friend's transformation. Not
now. Gabriela was dead. It had seemed near impossible she
would be alive and unmarried and ready to run away with
a man she had not seen since we were children. Yet part of
me had not only hoped it might be so, but believed it had
to be. I had been able to see our reunion in my mind.

As I made my way back toward Chiado Hill, I passed a
man roasting skewers of fish and vegetables over a waist-
high flame set upon a pile of bricks. I stopped and stared,
feeling the heat against my hands and face. The fire crack-
led and hissed as the juice dripped from the charring and
shriveling meat. I had seen flesh roasted a thousand times,

but only now did I notice the sights and sounds in such detail, taking in their peculiar qualities. This familiar thing was suddenly new and vile. How did no one notice it? How did they not find it repulsive? How was it that people could eat what had been so violated?

The vendor, an old man with tufts of white hair on his thin face, looked up, his eyes alight with hope. "You like, Englishman? I make with you good price?"

Hardly aware I was doing so, I reached into my pocket and pulled out Gabriela's scarf. I dropped it directly on top of a piece of fish. The scarf appeared for a few seconds to resist the fire, and then, all at once, it gave in and burst into flame. The fire consumed the fabric, turning its blue to gold and then black. Then it was ashes.

"You are madman!" the vendor was shouting. His face had gone red, and he waved his hands about wildly.

A crowd gathered to watch the scene. For someone who wished to avoid attention, I was doing a shoddy job. Children and laborers and slaves, a *fidalgo*, a priest, a man in a long leather coat with his face obscured under a wide-brimmed hat—they all stared at me.

"I apologize," I muttered, and handed the man a few coins, enough to pay for all the fish, with a fair amount besides.

The vendor was mollified, and now bowed and thanked me and called after me as I walked away. The Englishman was welcome to burn his rags there any time he wished.

I hated that I made myself the object of gawkers and pointers. I vowed that with the scarf, all my sentiment had been burned away. I would make no more mistakes. I would feel nothing now but resolve and purpose. I had nothing to hope for, and so nothing to lose.

Lest any familiar of the Inquisition had taken an interest in my display, I decided I would not return directly to the inn. Instead I would take a circuitous route, heading upward toward the old castle and then over back toward the Rossio. I lost myself in the crowds.

When I passed the massive Palace of the Inquisition, the very building in which my parents had been murdered, I cleared my mind. I was past idle thoughts and feelings and speculations. I was there to accomplish certain tasks. Nothing else. I was not even a person anymore; I was an embodied goal, and I decided I would stay so until I had finished my work.

As I crossed the Rossio and headed back toward the inn, I saw the man in the leather coat, the one I had noticed when I was burning my scarf. He was turned away from me, so his face was still obscured beneath his hat. He was likely a peasant or laborer, but something about him made me uneasy. Perhaps it was that I had taken such a roundabout route, and yet there he was. There was but one conclusion I could draw. This man was following me.

I walked down a side street quickly, and then turned and turned again. I hurried toward a cluster of boys who played dice in the street, shoving past them and turning again down a tight alley. I did this several more times until I was certain no one had followed. To be absolutely safe, I walked up Chiado Hill to the fine homes of the Bario Alto, and then slowly strolled back down.

When I returned to the inn, I quickly bypassed the common room and climbed the stairs. Outside my closed door, Enéas, who had taken a much more direct route home, waited for me. He had clearly been pacing, and he rubbed his hands together with worry like a comic character in a stage play. His naturally large eyes were like twin saucers.

"My master, I am so sorry. I have failed you."

"In what?" I demanded. I hated how sharp I sounded.

"He insisted he be let into your rooms, and when I told him no, he said that I had not the power to resist his will."

I asked no more questions. I pushed past the boy and entered the room, where Kingsley Franklin sat in the too-small armchair by the window, enjoying the cool breeze from the ocean. Panting heavily within his long coat, he fanned himself with a wide-brimmed straw hat. Franklin gave every indication of enjoying my confusion.

"*Olá, Sebastião,*" he said. "*É hora de falar.*" It is time for us to talk.

I slammed the door and would have accidentally crushed Enéas's head had the boy not dashed out of the way. Franklin was now holding a hand up, perhaps to pacify me, perhaps to give himself a chance to catch his breath.

"Peace," he gasped. "I walked quickly to get back here, and I am not so fit as I once was." He bent forward and breathed hard for a minute, and then looked at me. His face was apple red, but he was grinning, and now he pointed. "But I knew I recognized you. I knew it. I said you looked like a New Christian, but I had no idea it was because you are one."

"What do you think you are doing?" I demanded, more because I needed time to think than because I actually wanted an answer. "Following me upon the street? Have you any notion of how you risked my life as well as yours?"

Franklin continued to jab at the air with his index finger. "I do now, I can tell you. No doubt about it. And no offense meant there. I've always been of a curious nature, so I followed you. That's all. No harm done, Mr. *Sebastian Foxx.* Perhaps a false name that is not a direct translation of your true name would have been a sounder course."

"Sebastian Foxx is my true name now," I said. "And the disguise holds, for no one will look to link me to that forgotten child."

Franklin clapped his hands together. "Well, I did. I linked you indeed."

It was now my turn to jab a finger. It was quite satisfying. "Listen to me. You must forget what you saw and forget what you know. I am Sebastian Foxx, Englishman, and that is all. Nothing more. Do you understand me?"

"I'll not so quickly forget what I know. Nor have I forgotten your father. He was a good man, to be sure, and a good friend. Any son of his, and so forth. If you've come back for some reason, to serve some purpose, you must only tell it to me, and I shall serve you as best I can."

I took a step back and rubbed a hand over my face. I had only just learned of Gabriela's death, and now I must deal with this buffoon.

"My business is my own," I said. "And you truly would be wise to forget you know me. I need not tell you how word of my presence would invite the Inquisition's attention, and you of all men know the harm that could do to you and your business."

"You needn't threaten me," Franklin said. "I'm not your enemy. I only say that if I may be of service, for the friendship I felt for your father, you must tell me, and I will serve."

"I can only say again that my business here is my own," I told him. "If you value your own safety, you will tell no one what you have discovered."

Franklin pushed himself out of the chair. "I can't make a man accept friendship, though the offer stands." Still breathing heavily, he crossed the room to the door. "As does the offer for women." He winked. "I've of late begun frequenting this new establishment, and the Negresses there are—"

"Thank you, sir," I said, holding open the door.

Franklin shrugged and walked out into the hall. I closed the door, went to a chair, and threw myself into it. I leaned back and shut my eyes, and tried hard not to predict what sort of disaster this absurd man was going to bring down upon me. Then I realized the idea of being taken in chain, the idea that Franklin might say the wrong thing to the wrong person, pushed the memories of Gabriela away, and so I indulged in a thousand variations of my arrest and torture and public burning. It was a comfort to me.

Chapter 8

That afternoon I received a note from Settwell saying only that there was an urgent matter we needed to discuss. Eager to distract myself from my brooding and the mistakes I had made that day upon the street, I hurried over to Settwell's house. He attended to me at once, wearing the same faded suit from the previous night, and very likely the same shirt, with the same stains about the cuffs.

Settwell ushered me into his sitting room, and soon the two of us were sipping wine together. It was a congenial but silent meeting, for Settwell said nothing. He smiled hesitantly, looked out his window, and drank more wine. Then he repeated the process. I observed that his eyes were red, as if he had been sleeping badly or crying or drinking far too much—possibly all three.

As he appeared to have difficulty in beginning the conversation, I chose to put him at his ease. "Sir," I said. "I know well that it can be difficult to ask a man for money, even when he has offered it, so if you have invited me here because you have made arrangements to depart, you need only name the ship, and I shall make certain your berth is secured."

"It is not how I should most like to proceed," said Settwell. He set down his glass of wine and rubbed his face vigorously, sending his wig slightly askew. Without troubling himself to correct it, he picked up his glass and drank deeply. "In fact I may not have need of your money. I have asked you here upon a more delicate matter. I hope you will indulge me by hearing what I would say."

"Of course," I said, somewhat surprised. "You need but tell me how I might serve you."

"You know of my predicament," Mr. Settwell began. Now, with one hand, he began to fuss at his wig. "You know I have been ill used and impoverished through treachery. I am at the mercy of vile men. Of course I want to take my daughter to safety, but how much safety will there be in England? I will be free of the Inquisition, but we will face poverty and want, and for a girl, someday a young lady, I think you know what that means."

"You are not friendless," I said. "There will be opportunities."

Having, at last, pushed the wig into something like its previous position, he returned to clutching his drink with both hands. "I do not relish a life of depending upon charity."

"I doubt that you asked me here so that you might bemoan your situation," I said. "If you desire something of me, you need only ask it."

Settwell finished his wine, poured himself another full glass, and then patted my arm. "You are a good man. I hope you will not regret these words."

"I could not," I said. "I owe you my life, and I owe you for giving my parents the knowledge that their son was safe. It must have been their only source of comfort in the last days."

"Very well," Settwell said, his voice now growing hard. "I despise that I must flee this city with my money in the hands of the thieves that took it of me. My daughter will be denied the comfort and freedom that is rightly hers, a state of ease for which I labored all my life. When I lost my wife, I was able to take some solace in the knowledge that Mariana would do well. Now that too is gone, and I cannot endure it."

My pulse quickened and there was a mild throbbing in my temples. I had come to Lisbon to free myself from my own worst self, to exorcise my darkness entirely, but I was yet in Lisbon, and if I could also punish those who had harmed my friend, then I would do so. Gladly. This very moment. I sipped from my neglected glass of wine. "Have you a plan?"

"I do," Settwell answered, "but to succeed, I will need your help."

"You shall have it." I did not hesitate, and I did not lie. The thought of doing something for this man, who had done so much for me, was like a balm. Let him ask me to throw myself into the sea, and I would embrace the opportunity.

Settwell's face lit up. "You are very like your father, Mr. Foxx. Very like him indeed. He, too, was nice in the matter of honor." He took another gulp of wine to steady his nerves, and then began. "There is a pair of merchants, upstarts who have been in Lisbon for but three years and who have prospered beyond all reason. They have used some fair means, but mostly foul. The husband, Mr. Rutherford Carver, is but a straw man, agreeable enough, but not overly clever, I'm afraid. It is his wife who is the mastermind, and she is both cunning and lovely to look upon. Her beauty is such that there is not a man among the Factory who is not enamored of her, which explains, in some small part, why my accusations fall upon deaf ears."

"And how did they cheat you?" I asked, finding myself growing even more eager. A chance to help Settwell *and* scoundrels to be punished. This was a balm indeed.

"The scheme was simple enough. I was in the process of arranging to trade port wines for English woolens. As you know, I'd already been at a disadvantage after my conversion to Catholicism, and much rested upon my success. The Carvers approached me and claimed they could significantly increase my profits if I went into a venture with them. These sorts of joint operations are very usual, and the truth is, Roberta Carver can be quite persuasive. We invested our money, purchased port, and then sold it to an English merchant for woolens, dramatically increasing our profits by taking our payment in gold rather than negotiable notes. We were then to export the gold back to England. The Carvers made sure I understood the shipment was insured, so there was no fear of loss."

"I suspect," I said, "that all was not as it appeared."

"There were no woolens. They bought the port upon my credit and then sold the goods to another merchant for gold. The gold was then warehoused. Using Mrs. Carver's charms, they managed to falsify shipping manifests to make it appear that the gold was on a ship—a very ship that was then seized by Portuguese customs for the crime of exporting gold."

I knew that it was, in theory, illegal to export gold from Portugal. The Portuguese customs agents generally winked at the offense, however, as their economy depended upon foreign, and especially English, trade. Nevertheless, from time to time such shipments were seized to remind the English that Portuguese laws had teeth and that foreigners thrived only by the grace of the Portuguese crown. Such seizures were rarely random, and only those out of favor with the crown ever fell victim.

"So, they claimed the shipment was lost, while they actually retained it in their possession. But surely it was insured. Were you not protected?"

"This is where Mrs. Carver's influence is most pernicious. They have simply refused to pay me what they owe. They are not subject to English law as long as we are here, but to the ruling of the Factory and the consul. The consul dismissed my claim as nonsensical, and, in truth, I was not as careful as I should have been when reviewing that portion of the contract, for insurance in these matters is so standard that I failed to notice its omission."

"Some of this you could not have prevented, and some you might have, but you now have no recourse?"

"That is the sum of things precisely."

"And what do you propose?"

"It is all very simple," said Settwell. He now leaned forward, and for an instant he appeared much like his younger self—energetic and enthusiastic, ready to take on the next great venture. "You have already come here in disguise as a young man of business. We shall take advantage of that. I ask that you present yourself as a man of property, but not liquid wealth, looking to make his way here. The Carvers will seek you out, and because you have no connections, you will have no allies. They will not be able to resist the scent of a naïve and eager young man. You will have to establish lines of credit with a New Christian merchant for this to work, but you are clever, and I do not doubt you can do this. Once you have their trust, they will offer you some kind of bargain, with enough truth to it that they will have to make investments of their own. That means they must accumulate gold. When they have it warehoused, you, sir, will steal it using the skills I know you to have gained in Mr. Weaver's service. The Carvers will lose some portion of what they took of me, and I shall have the means to leave the country. I will not be as rich as I once was, but my daughter will not be a pauper."

I wanted nothing but to kill the priest and be rid of this country, but I could not refuse to help Settwell, and, if I am to be honest, I liked the idea of assisting him with so involved and daring a scheme. More than that, it felt right. He had been harmed, and who was I to deny that he should have revenge? Better than revenge, in fact. Justice.

"How much do you hope to take of them?" I asked.

"Perhaps no more than five thousand pounds. Perhaps as much as twenty. I should prefer twenty, but five will do if it must."

I snorted. "I should think you might hope to live well upon even so meager a sum as five thousand."

"Well enough, I suppose," Settwell answered with a sad smile. "I know it sounds like a great deal of money, but, believe me, they had far more than that of me."

"This is a complicated plan, involving a number of deceptions," I said. "With a fortune such as that in the balance, there will be many dangers."

"Did you expect otherwise here?"

"Certainly not," I agreed. Since learning of Gabriela's death, I had felt nothing but the dull ache of resentment and loss. Now here was something about which I might actually feel enthusiasm.

I stood and took Settwell's hand. "I came here to set matters right," I said. "That is what I shall do. You need only tell me how we are to begin."

Chapter 9

Two days later, Enéas entered my rooms just before noon and set a letter, sealed in wax, on the table. The boy appeared shaken. The color had drained from his face and his hand shook noticeably.

"I was returning from your morning errands, and this was placed in my hand," he explained. "By an *Inquisitor.*" This last word was whispered, the way a Portuguese might speak the name of the devil himself. He then crossed himself and muttered a prayer.

I held the heavy paper and ran my finger along the blotchy red wax. I could not decide how I ought to feel—I was neither afraid nor, despite having orchestrated this contact, gratified. I had set things in motion, and, to whatever extent I could, wished to control how events unfolded. This letter was equal parts promise and threat. I broke the seal and read.

The message was short and imperious. *You are summoned to the Palace of the Inquisition at three of the clock this afternoon.* It bore no signature.

"Is it ill tidings?" Enéas asked, crossing himself again.

"It is growing difficult for me to tell the difference between ill tidings and good."

At the appointed hour, I approached the most dreaded structure in Lisbon. At the north end of the Rossio stood the great Palace, with its four towers and red roof, indistinguishable in many ways from any other large and splendid building in the city. In my mind I had seen myself standing before the Palace, gazing upon it, neck strained. In reality, I chose not to pause. It was, I decided, but another building.

I strode through the great twin doors, surrounded by priests of all orders, though mostly Jesuits, as they hurried about on their thieving and murdering errands. I moved purposefully, as if I belonged—another skill learned from Mr. Weaver—and made my way across the marble floors, past the great oil paintings and gilt statues and altars. So much wealth, bought with New Christian gold, acquired with New Christian blood. I pushed past it all, making note of doors and hallways and means of escape, into the open courtyard of the interior. The note had not said whom I was to meet or where in the Palace to go, but I was an Englishman arriving at the appointed time. I had no doubt the man who invited me would find me without difficulty.

I passed through a quiet garden with a fountain and several statues of saints. Birds sang and fluttered about. I sat on a marble bench, crossed my legs, and placed my hands in my lap. My wig, my velvet coat, my stockings, my silver buckles and buttons, and the lace on my sleeves all seemed so absurd in contrast with the stark Jesuitical black everywhere. No one stared, however. They presumed I had business. Who would enter the Palace if he did not?

So many of my people, my family, had been dragged into this place, put to the question, imprisoned, tortured, murdered. This place was the very heart of Lisbon's evil, the machine that fed upon human flesh and churned out ruined husks. If only, like Samson, I could tear it down. I would gladly suffer torment and blinding and destruction if I could take it all with me. But I had not that choice, and I would have to settle for the next best thing: blood.

I sat for no more than a few torturous minutes before a man in his midforties sat down next to me. He was well preserved, with a youthful face and a disarming smile. His eyes were large and brown and almost feminine. It was Pedro Azinheiro.

The priest had hardly aged since I had seen him last. I remembered Azinheiro walking about the streets of the New Christian neighborhoods, handing out sweets to children while he peered in windows and doorways. We had known many Inquisitors by sight, but this one was particularly notable because of his vanity. Azinheiro greeted the pretty young women with special interest, and he was known to delay or refrain from arrests in exchange for amorous favors. I recalled seeing him, years before, emerging from a neighbor's house. The husband stood outside, his face pale and marked with tears. Azinheiro stepped out, bowed to the husband, his face a parody of seriousness, and then strode off, his posture straight, his head high.

These conquests made him an object of mockery, if only in whispers, but Pedro Azinheiro was not a clown. He was relentless in his pursuit of alleged Judaizers. I wondered what a man like this truly believed. Did he think Portugal remained forever on the brink of a Jewish precipice? Did he fear that New Christian men posed a brewing danger to his church and his nation? Or was he simply a functionary, a man who sought the arrest of New Christians because the Inquisition thrived off their confiscated wealth?

Perhaps if I had not agreed to aid Settwell, I might have struck now. I could have reached out, grabbed the Jesuit's throat, and snapped it within seconds. I had never killed anyone, and yet I knew I could do it. My hands seemed to hold the memory. The Inquisitor would have no chance to respond. The priests all around him would notice nothing until I was already on my feet, running toward the doors. Before the gasps even began, I would be upon the Rossio and vanishing in the crowd.

From there, escape would be easy. I would lose my wig and my English clothes. Buying or stealing plain garb, I would blend into the streets and make my way north to the countryside. It would be foolish to try to leave by ship in Lisbon, but I would be content to walk for days, for weeks if need be, before I could find a place to safely flee.

I had imagined it so many times that my hands itched to carry out the plan, but I had forsworn it. For now. I had sought the Inquisitor, and now I had found him. My task would be to keep the man visible and harmless until I had fulfilled my obligation to Settwell.

"You are Sebastian Foxx?" the priest said in good English.

"I am."

The man bowed his head unctuously. Perhaps he had aged after all. There were more lines about his eyes. His skin appeared drier and veined. He was not, then, a devil. He was flesh and blood, and could die as easily as any other man. I looked forward to seeing it happen.

"I am told," Azinheiro said, "you are prepared to be of some use to us."

I slowed my breathing. I concentrated on the pretense, on the performance. I would need to lose myself, my real self, if I were to make it through this conversation without spilling blood.

"It is not what I have chosen, but it is what I am told I must do," I replied. Easy. Calm. Controlled.

"Having a man who is well situated in the Factory would be of much use to me."

"I am not well situated," I said. The more I played the role, I knew, the easier it would be. Perhaps after a few minutes I would no longer have to will my hands to remain still. "You see, that is the difficulty. I am newly arrived. I hardly know anyone. I don't think I can help you."

Azinheiro pressed his lips together and narrowed his eyes. He appeared bored, like a man who had spoken these words, or similar ones, so many times before that the effort now made him languid. "You will be as much help as I desire. I do not need you to tell me what you know now, Mr. Foxx. I need you to tell me what you know in six months, in a year, in five years—for whatever amount of time we wish you to remain in Lisbon."

This was good news. He wanted an ongoing relationship. That meant he would expect little from me initially. Because it was precisely what I wanted, I thought it best to object. "I am willing to speak a word here or there if it will be helpful, but I do not think I am prepared to continue this arrangement indefinitely. And the notion that you might choose the duration of my stay here, well, I think it preposterous."

The priest sighed. "Your thoughts are of no consequence. You will do as you are told because you are to help me accomplish what has always been off-limits to me. You are to help me uncover the most dangerous men of your nation here in Lisbon."

"My nation? You think the English a threat?" The Inquisition would, in particular cases, arrest and prosecute Englishmen, but usually these victims had been bold and public in their actions. What did this priest have in mind?

"The English are more dangerous than many allow," the priest said. "The fact that the crown depends upon them for their trade has made the prosecution of heresy among them challenging, but I believe there are dangerous men in the Factory—Protestant proselytizers and, yes, even Judaizers."

To this I said nothing.

"You are a man of the Church, and you lived your life in England. You know how these men are."

I nodded, though I had little idea what the priest meant.

Azinheiro appeared somewhat mollified by my agreement, silent and minimal though it was. "Please understand me, Mr. Foxx. I do not hate all Englishmen. Some are good men, like you, no doubt. But there is a particularly vile spirit of greed and wretchedness that is unique to the English character, and it is a threat to the true faith. It is that which must be stamped out like you would stamp out rats, lest their putrid ways and beliefs spread and destroy all they touch."

In a stage play, the priest would have looked wild during this speech. His eyes would have gone wide. He would have torn at his hair and beat upon his breast. Azinheiro delivered no such performance. He might have been speaking of his plans to retile a roof for all the passion in his voice, and yet I understood that he meant these things. There was passion enough, but it was not meant for display.

"I did not know the Inquisition concerned itself with English activities," I said.

The priest waved a hand dismissively. "You need not trouble yourself with our concerns. Only obedience. If you, Mr. Foxx, are useful to the Inquisition, then I cannot see why you may not find the means to prosper, to advance when our enemies stumble. For a man in your position, the path to success may be open and easy."

I made every effort to appear uncomfortable. "I do not love the idea of profiting from the misery of others."

"There is nothing unsavory when a righteous man profits and a corrupt man falls."

I opened my mouth to speak, and then hesitated, only to begin again. I wished to look uncertain, but I feared I looked more like a fish upon a dock. "The crimes you speak of are the English religion. These men come here because they are told they will not be persecuted for their beliefs so long as they follow this nation's laws. I have no interest in deceiving them into breaking those laws. You must remember that I lived as a member of a hated religion in England, and I would not have wanted to be hunted for invented crimes."

The priest shook his head. "You do not understand me, sir. I am not out to invent crimes. That is a lie spread by the English to defame the Inquisition. However, there are men of that nation who do unspeakable things upon our soil. Unspeakable things, sir, I promise you. Those men must be punished. Do you not think so?"

"If they truly commit crimes, then yes, of course."

"And they do. The truth is, Mr. Foxx, the men of some nations are born of baser stuff than those of others. That Jews and Negroes and Gypsies are debased is common knowledge, but I believe the English have the devil's own blood in their veins."

"Sir," I said. "I remind you that I am English."

"Then you must overcome what you are," the priest told me. "I have done so."

"You?" I asked. "You are English?" This was something interesting.

"I am not here to discuss what I am," said Azinheiro. "It is your disposition that concerns us."

"And what is my disposition?"

"You are now my creature," the priest said. "Know this, sir. I have eyes everywhere, and I shall know where you go and what you do. I shall know with whom you speak. Nothing is hidden from me."

"Well," I said with a nervous cough. "Then I imagine we shan't have to speak often."

"Do not mock me, sir. For now, you are to go about your business and make such connections as you can. When you can be of use to me, I shall let you know."

This was, of course, what I had hoped for, but again I pretended resistance. Mr. Weaver always said that in all matters but friendship and love, never to trust anyone who was too agreeable.

"I must be plain with you," I said. "I do not wish to be your creature, no matter the potential rewards."

"And the dangers of refusing do not frighten you?" the priest asked.

"I shall risk them."

Father Pedro barked out a laugh. "The men of your nation, you *freeborn Englishmen*"—he said it with a sneer—"think you must always have a choice. I anticipated as much, and so I shall give it to you." He waved his hand in the air and a trio of soldiers in Inquisition livery appeared before us.

"Are you going to threaten me with arrest?" I asked.

"Of course not. You are of no use to me in prison. I merely wish to show you something."

The priest led me and the soldiers out of the Palace and across the Rossio. The square was crowded with tradesmen and *fidalgos* and foreigners and beggars. The priest gestured toward one corner, where a man worked a small stall selling pastries of some sort. He was a short man, stocky, with thick forearms and a round face that created the appearance—real or illusory—of simplicity. His eyes were narrowed as he handed a customer a pastry and took her coins. Once the exchange was complete, the man bowed as though the woman had been a princess.

"That man," the priest said, "has been of interest to me for some time. He sells *bola de carne,* meat pies. Traditionally they contain pork, but many of his customers are New Christians."

"New Christians eat pork, do they not?" I said. "They are no longer Jews." I had certainly grown up eating pork, knowing it had been forbidden by my ancestors, but that meant little to us. If anything, it encouraged us to eat it all the more.

"If they have nothing to hide, why make a show of eating pork? And why buy their pork from this man in particular?"

"Perhaps he makes tasty pies," I speculated.

"An unusual number of foreigners, particularly Scotsmen, have also been seen to buy from this vendor. The Scots, as is well known, are but a species of Jew. This is more than enough to have him arrested for Judaizing."

"I understand you," I said. "You wish to show me that if I do not cooperate, you will make this man suffer."

"You do not understand at all," the priest said. He turned to the soldiers. "Take him to the Palace," he told them in Portuguese.

I watched in horror as two of the soldiers grabbed the man and began walking him toward the Palace. The third began to collect the food and coins from the stall. Customers and passersby who had been nearby now hurried away, not daring to look back, lest they be tainted by the vendor's crimes.

I had seen men taken away by the Inquisition before. My childhood had been full of such scenes, and that this one unfolded according to the ancient script made it no less dreadful to witness. The man struggled and cried out for help. He twisted his neck to one side and then the other, as if looking for something that would rescue him. No one looked at him, their morbid curiosity crushed by their will to not appear *too* interested.

The man shouted that he was innocent, that he had done nothing, that he was a good Christian, but the soldiers did not react. He might have been a barking dog for all that they seemed to understand him. Then, as he was halfway across the Rossio, the Palace looming before him, the pastry man seemed to accept that it was not a misunderstanding. No one had made a mistake. No doubt he had little enough in his life—his meager business, his creature comforts—and they were all gone. He had seen this happen to other men, and he knew what was in store for him: imprisonment and torture, implication of his friends and relatives, the public humiliation of the auto-da-fé, and, finally, poverty. In a matter of seconds, everything he had had been stripped from him, and there was nothing in his future but torment and isolation and want. He stopped shouting his innocence and instead began to wail, helplessly and hopelessly, as he grieved for all he had known.

I looked at the priest, whose face was apathetic. He appeared to take no pleasure in what he had done, but he demonstrated no sympathy either. He looked like a surgeon inspecting a wound.

It occurred to me that if I had acted upon my first impulse and killed Azinheiro back at the Palace, the pastry vendor would still be plying his trade, worrying about customers and rent, oblivious to the danger that had passed him by. An Inquisitor dead and an innocent saved. Multiply this by days and weeks and perhaps months, however long it would take me to help Settwell. I hated that I had to wait, but I knew now the cost of hesitation. When the time came, and I was free to act, I would not want for resolve.

I turned to the priest. "You wished to show me your power."

"You are not that much of a fool," Azinheiro said casually. "You already know my power."

"Then what has this been about?"

"The pastry vendor has a wife," the priest said. "I am told she is newly pregnant with her first child. Do you think she is also guilty? Certainly hers would not be the first baby born in the Palace dungeons. Shall we punish her for her crimes? Does she deserve the same fate as her husband?"

"I have no idea," I said. "How could I know?"

"Then perhaps we should find out. We cannot be sentimental about sinners simply because they are women or with child. I shall have her arrested if you like."

"I do not like," I said, trying hard to keep the anger out of my voice. Instead I pretended to be another sort of man: I was frightened, I was trapped. I was a fool who had stumbled into something dangerous and powerful.

"Then if you agree to aid me, here and now, without difficulty, I shall overlook her indiscretion in marrying a Judaizer."

"What about the pastry man?" I asked.

"Oh, he is gone," Azinheiro said. "That cannot be changed."

I stood still for a long moment, my eyes cast down. "I see there is nothing to be gained by resisting."

"Now you understand." Azinheiro flashed his patronizing smile. "But you shall find that there is much to be gained by cooperating. Your success is now of particular interest to me, and that means you are in a very advantageous position. I shall make certain you become a very rich man, Mr. Foxx. In return, I hope to see more Englishmen in the Palace dungeons than ever before in history. Does that sound like an agreeable bargain?"

It sounded like madness. "It seems the best bargain I am likely to get."

"That is most certainly true. Good day, Mr. Foxx." The priest now began to walk toward the Palace, and it was clear that he did not intend for me to follow him.

That night a woman cried in the dark of a ramshackle house in the Baixa. Earlier she had wept in the arms of her friends, but they had gone home. Now she sat on a rough chair, arms wrapped around herself and rocked back and forth. She wept for the man she loved. She wept for the life that they would not have together, or the things for which she might no longer dream. She wept in fear for the moment, perhaps tomorrow or the day after, when the Inquisitors would come for her and the baby that grew inside her. She put a hand on her stomach. She had begun to feel a swelling only recently. She might well have made her husband feel it tonight, guiding his hand along the slightest of bulges, and his face would have been as bright as the noon sky.

"Our son," he would have said.

She would have smiled, not troubling herself to point out the obvious. They had both pretended the outcome was assured. Now nothing was assured except disaster. Her husband would be starved and beaten and tormented until he was made to name other sinners. They would make him name her in the end. He would try not to, but no one resisted forever. That was common knowledge. Her husband was gone. Soon she would be gone too. Even if her baby survived birth in the Palace and life in a church orphanage, he would never know who his parents had been, what they had been made to endure.

Her sobs and moans masked the sound of her front door being forced open—it was no difficult thing to force the latch up with the blade of a knife—and the stranger entering her small house. She did not hear him walk upon the warped and uneven floors, and only no-

116 | DAVID LISS

ticed him as he blocked the moonlight streaming in from an open window.

The woman looked up at this man—tall and broad, wearing rough clothes that appeared too big for him. Her face betrayed confusion and fear and then resignation.

"I'm not here to hurt you," he told her.

"Who are you?" she asked, sniffling, wiping her nose upon her sleeve. She hadn't the will to scream or cry out. If a thief wished to cut her throat and take what little she had, perhaps it was for the best.

"I saw your husband arrested today on the Rossio," the stranger said.

She coughed up a laugh. "And you think I need a new man already?"

"No," he said, squatting down so he could look at her eye to eye. She was not pretty, but there was something kind about her face. "I think you need to leave Lisbon before the Inquisition takes you as well. You and your child must be made safe."

"And how can that happen?" she asked, bitterness blasting out the fear and confusion that had been in her voice before.

"You will use this," the man said. He held out a purse and put it on the floor by her feet. "There's enough gold to buy passage to wherever you would like to go. The power of the Inquisition is diminished in the countryside. You'll have enough for food and a place to live for several months, longer if you are careful. You can find work, perhaps another husband. It is the best I can do."

"What do you want from me?" she asked. Her voice was now a throaty whisper, part wonder, part terror. What could he expect in exchange for this chance to survive? To bring her child somewhere safe?

"I want you to live," he said. "I want you to be free of them."

He rose and walked toward the door, opened it, and stepped out to the street.

"Bar the door behind me," the man said. "Lisbon is not safe at night."

Back at the inn, I had Enéas replace the clothes I had taken from Franklin. The innkeeper would never know they'd been missing for an hour. I then poured myself a glass of wine and settled into the armchair by the window.

I did not know the woman. I did not know if she was worthy or wretched, but I did not care. If someone had helped Gabriela all those years ago, perhaps she would still be alive. Helping the woman did not make me feel better, but it was one less thing to regret.

Chapter 10

The Portuguese did not have a culture of public houses, but Englishmen could not live without their wine and coffee and porter, so at the base of Chiado Hill there were more than a few taverns that catered to Factory merchants and the men who served them. Tailors and chandlers and grocers and brewers and a hundred other small tradesmen bought from and sold to the English community. There were also men of other nations—the German architects, Swiss watchmakers, Dutch engravers—all of whom would lend their services to any man, but always chose to drink with the English rather than the Portuguese.

The tavern most frequented by Factory men was the Three Speckled Hens. Up the hill from some of the more unsavory public houses, including the inn where I resided, it was a large room filled with long tables, poorly lit by windows, and always full of tallow and tobacco smoke and the smells of food and drink.

Nearly a week after Settwell and I first discussed our

scheme, we entered the Three Speckled Hens in the late morning. The room was thick with men. Enéas, who trailed behind us, paused to gaze in wonder. He had never seen so many foreigners, so many Protestants, in one place, and he whispered a prayer under his breath and crossed himself, and then prayed again. A portly Englishman observed the boy and laughed, but his fellows whispered in his ear, and the laughter stopped. Even in the heart of English power, a wise man did not mock Catholic faith.

I knew Settwell had not ventured to any establishments frequented by Factory men since he had been cozened by the Carvers and then failed to receive justice, and I wondered how widely knowledge of my friend's circumstances had spread. I found out soon enough. We were not ten feet inside the tavern when all eyes turned to us. Men tilted their heads toward one another and whispered vigorously. Lips parted to show yellow teeth and graying gums as traders laughed and exchanged rumors. I heard a man mutter Settwell's name. It seemed to me an inauspicious way to begin my masquerade as a man with whom to do business.

Enéas ran ahead and found us an empty table. When his calls for beer and chicken, in Portuguese, were met with guffaws, I repeated the order in English. Enéas blushed and looked down. It troubled me how eager the boy was to please and how easily embarrassed he was by his mistakes. He would grow a tougher skin soon enough. There was no other way in my service.

"Wait outside," I told him.

Enéas dropped to his knees and clasped his hands together in supplication. "Because I shamed you by speaking Portuguese? I've tried not to fail you! I've tried to be a good servant, and now you will throw me back to the streets to be tormented and abused. Please, master. I beg of you. I will embarrass you no more!"

I met his gaze. "You have no power to shame me, only yourself. You must wait outside because that is what a servant of your order does."

Enéas sprang to his feet like an acrobat. "Then that is what I shall do!" With a remedy to his blunder presented, his mood brightened considerably, and he hurried to the door.

"That boy dotes on you," Settwell said. "What do you pay him to secure such loyalty?"

"I saved him from his tormentors, and then paid him ten reais."

"Ten reais! You could have five servants for such a sum."

"I don't wish for five servants. I wish for one who will take any risk I ask of him."

I did not miss the resentment that clouded Settwell's face. He would have liked to have ten reais to spare for the loyalty of a servant. He'd been brought so low that such an expenditure seemed the height of extravagance.

Most of the onlookers had, by now, found their way back to their own conversations. The novelty of the strangers had passed, and there was little excitement in watching us eat and drink. After we finished our food, however, we noticed a hovering presence above us, and we turned to see a distinguished-looking man in his fifties, hand-some, with sparkling blue eyes and a smile of unusually white teeth.

"Mr. Settwell," the stranger said.

Settwell rose and, doing a poor job of masking his distaste, intro-duced me to Abraham Castres, who took my hand firmly and looked into my eyes in the way of a merchant trying to take another mer-chant's measure.

"Mr. Castres is the consul, head of the Factory," said Settwell. "The consul's task is to serve as the bulwark between us and the native madness, and he is the final arbiter in all internal disputes." Settwell looked away. "He is meant to adjudicate without bias."

"May I ask what brings you to Lisbon, Mr. Foxx?" the consul in-quired.

I bowed deeply. "Money brings me here," I said with an embar-rassed laugh. It was a mistake to play a role too confidently, for only dangerous men fail to doubt themselves. "I have recently come into property—a good income, mind you, though there are some current obligations. I must take my rents and, shall we say, my future rents, and turn them into ready money. Men I trust have convinced me that the Portuguese trade is the best and most efficacious way to do that."

"It is indeed," said the consul. He thrust his hands in his pockets and turned this way and that, surveying all about him as though he were king and the tavern his kingdom. Perhaps he was right to see himself so. Never had the Factory prospered so much as it had under Castres's leadership, though those profits went mainly to the consul himself and his inner circle of favored merchants. "Many men, through serious application and judicious study, have succeeded precisely as you intend. Others, however, have found themselves in even greater debt." Here he ventured a quick look at Settwell. "Among the most important decisions you can make now is with whom you associate yourself. Make yourself useful to the right men and you will go far. Surround yourself with the wrong sort, and your efforts will be doomed from the beginning."

"Indeed." I was a man pleased to have his own ideas affirmed. "I could not agree more. That is why I am so glad Mr. Settwell has offered to provide introductions."

"Then you two are not previous associates?" asked the consul.

"We have known each other for years," said Settwell.

At the very same instant, I said, "We have only lately become acquainted at my inn."

We had practiced this blunder. Having Settwell appear to lie so brazenly gave me an opportunity to sever ties with him and do so with honor.

I coughed and blushed. "Some men make it so easy to form a friendship that one feels like he has known the gentleman in question for years."

"First impressions are important," said the consul, keeping his gaze upon me. "A merchant must trust his instincts, but those instincts are honed with experience. Come speak to me if you wish, young man. We shall make sure your introduction to Lisbon business is managed by good hands. You do not wish to fall into bad ones."

Castres spoke so that I could not mistake his meaning. I glanced to Settwell and then back to the consul again. "Yes. I shall do that. Thank you very much, sir, for your generosity."

Settwell stepped before me and puffed out his chest. "This gentleman is in good hands, and you're a damned blackguard, Castres, for suggesting otherwise. Have you not yet done enough to me that you must poison my future prospects even as you have already destroyed my fortune? You are like a man who shits upon his neighbor's stoop and then condemns him for keeping a dirty house."

I let out a good-natured laugh that sounded forced and uneasy: I had made the decision to associate with someone, and now I regretted it. I would have to disentangle myself from one man and form ties with another, all without offending anyone. "Come now, Mr. Settwell," I said, my voice rising in pitch, "you can have no objection to me meeting other men of business, particularly one so well placed as the consul himself. That is why, after all, you brought me here."

"I brought you here," said Mr. Settwell, "to show you what a pack of jackals you propose to treat with. Can you not see how they line up to steal your money, as they have stolen mine?"

Castres set a hand on Settwell's arm, but Settwell pushed him away. "Do not lay hands upon me unless you want to resolve our dispute like a man of honor, which I very much doubt."

Once again, all eyes were on Settwell. He pretended—quite convincingly, I thought—not to notice. Locking his gaze on Castres with undisguised malevolence, he reached for his porter and drained the mug. He then allowed it to fall at the consul's feet. From deep in the tavern, someone gasped.

"I know you have suffered some ill turns," the consul said, "but now you blame others for your own mistakes."

"I blame others for their villainy," Settwell responded through clenched teeth.

"You are drunk, sir." Castres's voice began to crack with anger. "I hear you are drunk all too often. Return to your home, and we shall forget this indiscretion."

Settwell had wished to make a commotion, and he had done so. His public humiliation was complete. I could not but admire a man willing to commit himself so fully to a scheme. He had just now proved he was the man the Factory believed him to be: a drunk and a fool, someone men of sense should make every effort to avoid. Settwell had put everything in my hands—his future and his daughter's safety—and that meant I could not fail. I watched Settwell walk from the tavern, his drunkenness mostly an act, and hoped we were not all doomed.

Abraham Castres put his arm around my shoulders. "This is what I love best," the consul said, his voice lively and expansive. The incident with Settwell, now more than a full minute in the past, was long forgotten, as significant as an awkward moment of public flatulence. "A new man, a new face, and new prospects. Lisbon is the very place for a man of business. We have not the possibility of unimagined wealth that a man can earn in the Indies, but not the risks either. You may live in comfort and ease, enjoy the pleasures offered by one of the most beautiful cities in the world, and still quietly and efficiently increase your fortune. How do you like the sound of that?"

"I like it very much." I looked about, straining my neck, making confusion evident. In truth, I was delighted. All my senses tingled. Settwell and I had concocted a scheme, and thus far it had worked perfectly. Such moments were as close as I came to happiness.

"Mr. Sebastian Foxx," announced the consul, as he led me to another table of Englishmen, "allow me to present to you Mr. and Mrs. Rutherford Carver, among the brightest lights in our Factory constellation."

Both of the Carvers rose. Mr. Carver shook my hand, and Mrs.

Carver curtsied. The husband was an unimposing man of some forty years, short and perhaps a bit inclined to be plump, with a slightly jowly face and eyes of a very pale gray that looked, even when he smiled, on the verge of tears. He wore a suit of dark blue velvet and an expertly tailored short periwig. While they were both fine-looking items, I could not help but feel that they were meant for an entirely different sort of man. Mr. Carver was not ugly, nor even unattractive, but he was certainly unimpressive.

Mrs. Carver, however, was a stunning woman of seven or eight and twenty, with a beautiful round face, sapphire-blue eyes, an unblemished pale complexion, and a charming nimbus of bright orange hair that fell in ringlets from under a prim little hat and about her lovely shoulders. And red lips that parted just so as she locked her gaze upon mine. Settwell had told me that Mrs. Carver was a flirt, and I intuited at once that she was a well-practiced one. It was no surprise that many a man had fallen under her spell. I felt some small sympathy for the consul. If he must make a fool of himself over a woman, it should be one such as this.

I joined them at the table, but Castres excused himself. "I fear I have pressing matters of state that call me, but Rutherford and Roberta will make very good hosts, I assure you."

Rutherford Carver called for wine—Burgundy, certainly as an expression of how little he was bound to his host country—and proceeded to pour a large glass for me. While Mrs. Carver watched, apparently hanging upon every word, her husband made inquiries as to what brought me to Portugal, how I knew Settwell, and a variety of other questions meant to measure how much I understood about how business was done in Lisbon. My answers evinced an easy manner, an affect of pretended confidence, and, ultimately, a complete misunderstanding of the situation into which I had thrust myself.

"I hope you will forgive an indiscreet question," said Mr. Carver, refilling my glass, "but to what degree are you prepared to invest in Portuguese trade? Men come here sometimes with a few hundred pounds, and that is all very well for them, but it is not enough to engage with the Factory."

"Are you willing to fully commit yourself?" asked Mrs. Carver, meeting my eyes, and I thought there was hidden meaning in the question.

I blushed and turned away from the lady. "I have very little in ready money," I answered. I was a man made uneasy by the attentions of a beautiful woman, I reminded myself, and would reveal what I did not mean to. "You see, I was forced to settle a great deal of debt when I came into my estate. However, the lands provide me with near a thousand pounds per annum, and though the income of the next few years may already be spoken for, I have been told the surety of my property will be enough to begin my career in this country."

"If you want ready money, you'll need the Jews," Mr. Carver said. "They have the deepest pockets in the city."

"I was told there were no Jews in Portugal," I answered.

Mr. Carver waved his hand about in amusement. "The New Christians. *Convertos,* I believe they are called. It matters not. They love a landed man, and your thousand pounds a year will serve you well. They have a nose for money, those people."

"So I but present myself to one of these New Christian merchants?"

"It is not quite so easy as that," said Mr. Carver with much gravity. "To make these Jews comfortable, I suggest you attach yourself to an English merchant who already has a thriving trade. You will find no shortage of clever men who have a steady business exporting cork and fish and wine and importing woolens. Even the best of us may find an occasional shortfall in funds, and willingness to lend is a fine way to ingratiate yourself."

"I think I understand you," I said, as though I were just able to put the pieces together. "I use my land as surety with the New Christians to borrow money, which I then lend to a dependable merchant for a return for a portion of his profits. But can this be worth the trouble?

Such money as I make from the trade cannot be much more than what I owe for the borrowed funds."

"It is not very profitable," agreed Mr. Carver.

"Then how does pursuing such a course help me?" I asked.

Mrs. Carver leaned forward slightly. "It helps you because in following this course, you make friends. It is an elaborate dance, and we have all learned the steps."

Mr. Carver pulled out his pocket watch. "Gad, look at the deuced time!" he cried out. "I have kept one of my best olive oil factors waiting a quarter hour. What a jackanapes I am! I presume to tell you how to conduct your business, Mr. Foxx, but I make a poor show of it. Will you excuse me, sir? My wife will continue this conversation, and any questions you have, you may address to me at your convenience."

Without waiting for a reply, he shook my hand and left me alone with his wife. She met my eyes with her own, which were wide and slightly moist and almost shockingly blue. She did not turn away, and so, after a brief pause, I did.

"It is a hard thing to come to Lisbon alone, I imagine," said Mrs. Carver. She tossed her head, allowing her ringlets to flow with enchanting effect. "I arrived with my husband, and that was some comfort, but it was nevertheless difficult to adjust to life here."

"It is an odd city," I said, "but not without its own peculiar charm and strange beauty."

"Peculiar charm and strange beauty," she repeated. She pressed her lips together in something between a smile and a scowl. "Yes. I like that. It is a place where many men fail, but it is also a place for new beginnings."

"I hope it may be so for me," I assured her.

"And if you don't mind my inquiring, I noticed you come in with Mr. Charles Settwell. Are you long acquainted with him?"

I blushed and looked away. "Mr. Settwell struck up a conversation with me at my inn, but I don't know him beyond his company and that he appeared very willing to introduce me to the Portuguese trade. Yet after coming here with him, I must wonder if he is the best guide."

"I shall be honest with you, Mr. Foxx," Mrs. Carver said. "Settwell was once a great man, but he has made many mistakes of late. There are some who will say he ought not to have married a Catholic woman and then converted, though his Catholicism is of a very lax variety. His own daughter was baptized into that faith, but he does not take her to church now, and so has irritated both the local authorities and his countrymen. I trust you will be more careful than he."

"I shall make it my business to be so," I said.

Mrs. Carver raised her glass in the air and grinned like a coquette and a predator. "Let us hope you succeed," she said. She tapped her glass against my own, and there was something in that touch that seemed very much like a promise.

Chapter 11

Most Englishmen who came to Lisbon stayed for years. They had time to establish connections, develop a feel for how things worked, and spot their own prey in the herd. I had not the luxury of so leisurely an approach. To advance my connection with the Carvers, I needed a New Christian who would be willing to lend me money sooner rather than later, and that meant someone who would take risks. I needed to find a man with his back against the wall. My connections in Lisbon might be limited, but I believed I knew one man who could help.

Once more, I found myself knocking on the door to Inácio's boathouse in the Alfama. The same young man answered the door this time, but now he grinned. "Englishman!" he cried. "Inácio said if you came I must show you in right away." He opened the door wider.

Almost nothing of the original interior remained. A walkway circled around a great basin of water, which contained two square-sailed fishing boats. In one corner, a pair of men sat on barrels, playing cards and smoking pipes, but otherwise the place was empty.

The young man led me along a walkway toward a door that opened up into an actual house, and I followed the man up a set of stairs to a door on which he knocked. "Inácio," he cried. "*Inglês*."

Inácio appeared in a moment, and waved me inside. He had been sitting at a table, drinking wine and eating salt cod stew and bread. "You want?" he asked.

I held up a hand. "I need your help."

Inácio scowled. "I told you that it would not be easy to aid you. Besides, how hard can it be to find an Inquisitor? In my experience, they find you soon enough."

"That they do," I agreed. "I don't need help on that score. It is another matter."

Inácio leaned forward. "I shall aid you if I can. You know that. But sit. You make me nervous, standing there."

I sat at the table. The onion smell made my eyes water.

"So," he said, swirling a piece of bread through his stew. "This is now what stands in for friendship among adults. You need things, and so you come to me."

I was no fool. Whatever affection Inácio might yet feel for me was tinged with resentment, and it seemed as likely as not he would be looking out for his own interests as well as mine. If he were going to be of use to me, and not a danger, I would need him to understand that my good fortune would be his own.

"It is a matter of business," I said. "Any profit it incurs will, of course, be worth a finder's fee."

He waved the wet bread in a gesture of dismissal, as though this were the last thing upon his mind.

"I need to find a New Christian willing to lend money. Someone who is desperate enough to take a risk on an unknown man."

Inácio barked out a laugh. "You come to me to learn about New Christians. The tables have turned, eh!"

"It is your city now," I said. "I am but an Englishman."

"Englishmen have no difficulty making friends with New Christians. Why do you need my help with this? First you tell me you care only for revenge and justice, and now you are looking to make money?"

"I've agreed to help out an old friend. You recall Charles Settwell, I think."

Inácio nodded. "The English merchant, yes. My father did some business with him as well."

"I owe the man much, and I wish to help him, and time is of the essence. I'd like to know precisely which New Christian is most likely to give me what I want in the shortest period of time."

Inácio pulled on his mustaches and studied me. "Let me think about that. How much money did you say you would give me for this information?"

"I have nothing to give you now," I said. "If it should prove profitable, then, shall we say, fifty pounds English?"

He widened his eyes. "That is a great deal of money for a name. A mere name. And yet you will give me this gift?"

"Should things go as I wish, then it will be no gift, but a payment for services rendered."

He let go of his mustaches, and leaned forward. "Someone, it seems, stands to make a great fortune, and you offer me a good sum, but no more, so another can become rich."

I rose from my chair. "I wished for your help, and I am pleased to compensate you for that help, but I do not care to be put to the question. If you cannot help me, I will find another who can."

"Sit, sit, sit." He patted his hand down. "You have become agitated. I meant no offense."

I sat once more.

"I will show you my friendship by giving you what you ask," he said, "for I have just the name for you. Do you remember Eusebio Nobreza?"

I felt myself scowling. "He was something of a fool, wasn't he? I recall his father was a good man, but the son was a puffed-up popinjay."

"The father is retired," said Inácio. "The son has taken control of the business, and yes, he is a fool. He has made some mistakes, and the debts are mounting. He may take a little coaxing, but I have heard he is eager to make new connections. I think he may be your man. If he resists, you must stick with him, for you will find yourself rewarded."

"Thank you," I said. "And I promise you shall be paid if this goes as I hope."

Inácio grinned. "If my advice is of use, that is all the payment I need. And, of course, the fifty pounds."

A light rain fell, and the air was warm and humid. Buzzing insects swarmed around my face, and though I told myself the effort was futile, I continued to wave them away. I tried to stay dry by hugging the buildings on the uphill side of the Street of the Trinity, not at all far from a house where I lived as a small child, before we moved when I was five or six years old. I recalled these buildings, and recognized the most unexpected details—a missing brick or the floral pattern in a set of tiles. Everything seemed so familiar, but also remote and impossibly distant. Even the people I passed on the street seemed only vague and ghostlike. These were nothing but shadows, illusions, half formed in dreams.

I had things to do, so I shut my eyes to anything familiar and entered the *taberna* to which Inácio had directed me. As I walked into the room, I felt a curious contempt for these New Christians. With each trade and business deal, these men stretched out their necks for the butcher's blade. Each one of them would sigh with relief when his neighbor was dragged off to the Palace dungeons. *It is not me. Not today.* Portugal lived and died by New Christian trade with other nations, and yet the New Christians themselves were grist for the Inquisition's mill.

I approached the barman, hardly more than a boy, with a prominent Adam's apple and a long head with narrow, slitted eyes. He studied me with curiosity, but no alarm. Englishmen were likely not common here, but neither were they unknown.

"Do you speak English?" I asked him.

"All New Christians speak English a little," he answered.

I looked around with the grin of a child looking upon rope dancers. "Portugal's Jews! How marvelous. Tell me, my good New Christian. Have you porter?"

"No porter. Port." The barman smiled at his own humor. "We speak English, but this is not England."

I slapped my hand upon the countertop. "There's port aplenty in England, I assure you. Give me a glass, if you please. I am new to Lisbon."

The man poured the wine into a pewter cup. "I never make this guess."

"You mock me," I said.

"I make joke with you," the barman said, raising an eyebrow. "May I not?"

"I'll be damned for a Frenchman before I resent a man for a good-natured quip," I said. "But let it not cut to the bone, or then we shall have a disagreement." I raised the cup and for a moment had the perverse desire to say the blessing for wine. What would happen? How would these men react? Would they know Hebrew when they heard it? I thought it unlikely. The Inquisitors believed, or pretended to believe, that every New Christian kept secret volumes of the Talmud stashed under floorboards, but I had never seen so much as a Hebrew letter before my arrival in England.

I raised the cup in salute to the barman and took a sip. "By the devil, you keep the best drink for yourselves! This is superior to the finest port I've had in London."

The barman smiled and shrugged his thanks.

I drank again and smacked my lips. "I'm looking for a man called Nobreza. I understand he wishes to do business with an English factor."

"I do indeed," said a voice behind me. "But you are not a factor, are you, sir?" The English was accented, but otherwise flawless. I turned. Eusebio Nobreza was a man with dark hair and eyes, tall, regal in appearance and confident in expression. He wore long mustaches in the style of a *fidalgo,* and a woolen suit of dark brown, drab in color but expensively made.

Because he was a decade or so older than I, Eusebio and I had had little congress in my youth, but I recollected him well enough. He had always been impatient around children and had made a point to shoo me away like a stray dog. As a man in his early twenties, he had been self-impressed and vain of his appearance. Time, however, had etched some lines upon his face that gave him an air of dignity he'd lacked ten years earlier.

"I am new to the city, yet it is but a matter of time before I am admitted to the Factory," I explained. "I am now in the process of establishing contacts among men of significance, and your name has been mentioned more than once, senhor."

"You flatter me," Eusebio said with an affected bow. "Sit at my table and we shall see what we can learn about each other."

I followed him to where an older man sat. He shared Eusebio's narrow eyes and sharp nose, though his hair and mustaches were white, and his hands trembled as he set down his glass of wine.

"My father, Luis Nobreza," the younger man said.

I bowed to him, recollecting that this older Nobreza had done business with my father. He had seemed ever kind and generous in those days, always offering raisins and dates to the children of his business associates.

"I was told to speak to Senhor Nobreza," I said. "How can I be certain you are not the man recommended to me?"

The older man shrugged as if indifferent to the matter. "I am done with trade, I fear. My health is poor and I tire easily. My son now manages our affairs."

"I am certain his considerable skill was learned from you," I said.

"Hmm," the old man said. "An Englishman who flatters like a Spaniard. What wonders shall we witness next?"

"I am indeed lucky to have learned from so great a man as my father," Eusebio said. "And now he sits by my side to make certain I don't forget his lessons."

Was there some bitterness in this? I wondered. Was it something I could use to my advantage? I decided to press the matter. "I too have learned from the experience of my elders. A wise man knows who most deserves his praise."

"Indeed. Sir, can I call for something for you to eat? The ham is excellent." The younger Nobreza gestured toward the smoked hams and dried pork legs hanging from the ceiling like talismans against evil.

I studied him. "Ham, you say."

Eusebio scowled, but his irritation was almost comic. "It is always thus with you Englishmen. I know not what you've heard, but we are Christians. We eat like Christians."

I laughed. "I confess, I have never quite understood your circumstances though I have heard of them. Are you Christian by choice, or are you coerced?"

Eusebio cocked his head. "I will reply, but what of your religion? Did you join it by force or by choice?"

"In England, no man is coerced into his faith," I assured him.

"But *when* did you choose?" Eusebio asked. "We worship as our fathers did, and they as their fathers. Is that choice?"

I nodded slowly, as if considering these matters for the first time. "You raise a fine point. I shall have to think on it. And I thank you for your offer of food, but I shall decline. At this moment, I am only hungry for gold!"

"The single-mindedness of the English," said the younger man.

"It is what makes them so useful," said the older. "What sort of business do you wish to do, Mr. Foxx?"

I leaned back and did my best to appear thoughtful. "I have property, sir. Very sound property."

"But no ready cash," Eusebio speculated. "You wish for me to advance you money that you might trade with it."

"Yes. You have come right to the heart of the matter."

Eusebio smiled. "I have dealt with newly arrived Englishmen before, and your circumstances are not unusual. I am always eager to lend money to a solid man who will return the investment, but I am less eager to engage in business with a man for whom no one will vouch. The lands that will act as surety are very far away."

"I can offer documents—" I began.

"Documents are made out of paper, and they are of little value when the lands in question are so distant," Eusebio interrupted.

I was not willing to argue the point too vigorously, since it was, in fact, my intention to forge any documents I might require. "The difficulty," I said, "is that everyone feels much the same. How am I to establish myself if I cannot find someone who will take a risk?"

"I am afraid that is your concern, not mine," the younger man said without a hint of satisfaction. "If you seek men who love risk, you must visit Amsterdam. Here in Lisbon, caution is the guiding principle."

"I am sure you understand," Luis said, in a more conciliatory tone, "that the wheels of commerce must turn with all deliberation if they are to keep turning at all. My son can little afford to give you credit until your worth is established."

"My father's way of business served him well for many years,"

Eusebio said. In other words, it was a way of doing business that kept him solvent and out of debt. Dismissed, I rose, thanked both the Nobrezas, and went back over to the barman. I drained my glass of port and ordered another as I considered my options. There were none and unless I could find a man more desperate to lend money, I would have to grow used to the idea that I would not be leaving Lisbon any time soon.

Chapter 12

I now found myself in the awkward position of courting projects but with no money to invest and courting
investors while commanding no projects, but I had no
choice other than to hope the timing of each effort would
resolve favorably. I returned to Inácio, hoping for the name
of another New Christian, since Eusebio was unwilling to
do business. Inácio merely shook his head.

"They are all fearful," he said. "You know how it is with
them. Take my advice. Go back to that *taberna*. Spend
some time. Spend some money. Get Nobreza to trust you.
You won't find a better prospect."

I consulted with Settwell, who agreed that Eusebio was
a good prospect, though perhaps not the man he would
have chosen first. Nevertheless, Settwell thought it better
to stick with Eusebio now that I had approached him, lest
I appear fickle. I tested the waters with Kingsley Franklin
as well as he sat eating his dinner in the common room of
his inn. Franklin leaned back and placed his hand on his
great stomach.

"I envy you, young sir," he said. "Striking up new business, making conquests. The money. The whores."

"There are no whores involved in my question," I said. "I wish only to know if you are familiar with Nobreza."

"I did business with the father," Franklin said. "He was always dependable. The son was a bit weak, but that could serve your interests. If you are looking for someone to bend to your will, he might be your man."

I returned to the New Christian *taberna,* and though Eusebio still showed no interest in doing business, after a week or two he did regard me with a friendly smile and a nod. It was little enough progress, and I wanted more, so I was encouraged when, two weeks after our initial meeting, I received an invitation from Rutherford Carver to meet him at the Three Speckled Hens to discuss possible uses for my ready money—should I secure a loan and find myself in possession of any.

Making my way through the crowded coffeehouse, I found the Carvers sitting alone at a table, drinking wine and discussing a story in a London newspaper—one fairly well used and evidently rather old. With one hand Mr. Carver wiped his perspiring brow with a handkerchief while waving the other through the air as he articulated some point. His wife nodded, giving him her full attention.

Mrs. Carver looked, if anything, more striking than I recalled. She wore an ivory gown, cut low in the front to expose a generous swath of her creamy bosom. Atop her head sat an undersized hat, like something one would find upon a child's doll, and under that, her orange hair spilled out upon the shoulders of the gown like wine upon a tablecloth.

I bowed to them, and they invited me to sit. Mr. Carver poured me a glass of wine. "So very grand to see you again, Mr. Foxx. How are you liking Lisbon?"

"I like it very much," I said, "though I am ready to begin making some money."

"Spoken like a true man of business," Carver said, laughing heartily as though he had said something extraordinarily clever. His pale face reddened with the effort, and his eyes moistened. "I do advise patience. These things can't be rushed. You must establish yourself first, though a man such as you, with property, need not be in any hurry."

"I should describe myself as eager, not hurried," I said.

"The game of it!" He laughed again and slapped his hand upon the table. "The thrill of the hunt, eh? I know your mind, sir. I know it like I know my own. But you must wait until you are established. That is the thing here, sir. Reputation. Name. These are the sum of the Factory man."

I laughed politely along with Rutherford, even as I observed, from the corner of my eye, how Mrs. Carver turned her pretty face away, her pale skin flushing. Did her husband embarrass her, or did she merely wish to create the illusion that he did?

"Tell me, sir," I said, once all the laughter about nothing had died down, "how can I establish myself when everyone waits until I am established? It is a bit of a paradox, is it not?"

Mr. Carver spread his hands, as though the great mystery had just unfolded itself before us. *"A vida em Lisboa,"* he intoned in utterly unaccented Portuguese. "That is life in Lisbon."

Mrs. Carver turned to me, her movements languid and unconcerned. "It is the difficulty all new men find. You will have to be bold. That is what separates the successful merchants from the ones who grow weary of the effort and slink back to England. Are you bold, Mr. Foxx?"

"I hope I am bold enough," I answered.

"Have you found yourself a Jew yet?" Mr. Carver asked. "That is the way, as I've told you."

"I have begun to build some contacts there," I said, leaning back like a man pleased with himself.

"Contacts are easy," Mr. Carver said. "Any man might strike up a conversation. It is the *substance,* sir." Here he drove his index finger toward the ceiling. "The substance is what matters. With whom have you been speaking?"

I told him about Eusebio, and Carver nodded, his ebullience somewhat diminished in the face of real business. "A solid enough man. I know of him. He does not have the fattest purse in the city, and he tends toward caution. Trying to get out of his father's shadow, but he's afraid to strike out alone. You know, his father was the most useful Jew in the city once. There wasn't a soul in Lisbon better able to convert gold to notes and back again."

Mr. Carver now had my full attention. According to Settwell, my father had been deceived by a scheme involving the conversion of gold to notes. Of course, many men engaged in such practices, and there would always be those among the New Christians who would need conversion to export their wealth. Even so, this was a fact worth noting.

"Do you think the younger Nobreza is of no value?" I asked.

"If he lends you money," said Mr. Carver, "that is value enough."

"Since our own arrival in Lisbon," Mrs. Carver said, "we have made something of a business in dealing with new men. We well recall the difficulty of our first few months, and we have found it profitable to seek out those whom others are yet to trust and get their money first."

"Are you proposing a venture?" I asked.

"We are," Mr. Carver said. He finished his glass of wine and stood. "Dependent upon your having funds, of course. I should love to tell you more, but the consul has requested a meeting with me, and I do not wish to make him wait." Here he giggled, though at what I could not have said, and observing that nothing amusing had transpired would have been rude. "I leave you now in my wife's capable hands."

I rose and shook his hand, doing my best to hide my annoyance. The man had invited me, and now he hastily departed. In fact, their scheming was so overt that even I, someone who earned my bread through trickery and pretense, found it hard to play the part of the innocent. It was likely this scheme had worked before. How could a new man, such as I pretended to be, resist the twin allures of established trade and a beautiful woman?

When Mr. Carver was gone, I sat down once again with his wife.

"We are very fortunate to have the consul's attention," she told me, turning her face away prettily, showing me the appealing lines of her profile.

"I do not share in your fortune. It seems every time I try to sit down with your husband, he has somewhere else to be."

Mrs. Carver shook her head. "He and I are partners, and as long as you have one of us, you have us both. You should be pleased, for it is of great advantage to you to do business so early with people who have the consul's ear."

"I am grateful for your attention," I said, "and I am doubly grateful that you speak to me so plainly. I hope you will always do so."

Her eyes narrowed slightly. "I am not one for prevarication, sir. Perhaps that is not wise for a woman of business, but I was not built to deceive."

"Only to delight," I ventured, for flirting seemed to be the order of the day.

Mrs. Carver watched me as she raised her glass to her lips and drank. When she set her cup down, she said, "We seek a relationship of mutual advantage in *business*. Nothing more. I hope you make no improper suggestion."

"I would not dream of it," I answered.

"I know what is said of me," Mrs. Carver said. "A woman who would do business must be a virago, unless she is pretty, and then she must be a whore. I am what some men call pretty—"

"I should think all men," I said, for I did not think an abrupt end to the flirtation would be credible. She played an interesting game, and I was not entirely sure I understood it.

She held up a hand. "Please. No flatteries. They are not welcome."

"I beg your pardon," I said, turning away, affecting embarrassment.

"I merely wish to inform you that I know of these stories and I despise them. I am a married woman, and you must make no mistake about what that means. You and I may do business together and we may be friends, perhaps, in time, but do not insult me by pursuing more."

I could not but admire her strategy. It was the bold seductress who began by pushing away her intended victim. It would, of course, make the seduction all the more believable when it came.

"I accept your terms," I said after a moment of what I hoped appeared to be chastened contemplation.

She tossed her curls. "Perhaps you think ill of me for saying I know myself to be pretty. I acknowledge that nature has favored me, and to some degree, I make use of those advantages, just as a clever man makes use of his wits and a strong man of his brawn. Some gentlemen are inclined to offer advantageous terms because they admire my appearance. It is no secret the consul treats us well for it. I also know that some say I am degraded, and that my husband and I prey upon those bewitched by me."

"I have heard all these things," I admitted.

"I know you have, and I thank you for not pretending otherwise. But in spite of what is said, I do not lift my skirts for business prospects, and I never deceive men into believing so. My husband and I should like to do business with you because you have property to support your investments, and we would like to profit from your risk. That Mr. Carver absents himself indicates not some absurd opportunity such as to be found in a stage comedy. It indicates that he is a man of means and his presence is required elsewhere. So you must make do with the wife, though I flatter myself that it will be enough."

It took me a moment to think of a reply. "Do you speak to all your potential partners thus?"

Mrs. Carver laughed and a genuine smile illuminated her face. It was a sudden flash, a glimpse of something divine and secret. I did not doubt that men would endure many hardships to see that smile. "I am more direct with some than with others, but I am honest with all. I think you and I have a great deal of money to make together, and I do not wish that to be spoiled by misunderstandings. You strike me as a man of sense. As such you must have some inkling of the challenges a woman in my position faces. I would hope you would not add to them."

"Madam, I have never heard a woman speak so bluntly, but I would be a fool to do anything but honor your direct address. It is true that I admire your beauty, but I can be no more blamed for my appreciation of your face than you can for wearing it. But, if I may be honest, you are by no means the only beautiful woman in the world, and a man cannot have every woman he desires—nor will he desire every woman he finds pleasing to gaze upon. I certainly hope I may be able to admire something without wishing to possess it. Rest assured I am content to take pleasure in your conversation and the gold that is born of our association."

She held out her hand and I shook it, and the silk of her glove felt cool and somehow alive. "Then let us begin making money," she said.

What she proposed was this: I would secure, by what means I could, two thousand pounds to invest into a shipment of cork and port wine. The Carvers would sell the shipment to their London brokers, and they would divide the profits, with two-thirds going to the Carvers, one-third going to me. "Despite appearances, it is an excellent opportunity for you. We have built a reputation with the New Christians and the customs men, and we can obtain prices impossible for you. Our ships are never searched and never molested, whereas you, as a new man, would be subject to unfair scrutiny. You profit less than if you struck the bargain yourself, but you take virtually no risk."

"Can you truly guarantee your ships won't be seized?" I asked.

"Of course not. All ships may sometime be seized or lost in storms or taken by pirates. I cannot promise you nothing will go amiss, but I can promise you that you shan't find a safer exchange. You take the least risk possible, build your reputation, and learn more about the trade."

I felt it was time to move another piece on the board. My fingers had touched only pawns thus far, but now it was time for something bolder but subtler—a bishop or knight. "You have done me the honor of speaking directly, and so I must return the favor. Mr. Settwell has implored me not to trust you. I do not know him well, but I also have no reason to doubt his motives. He tells me that you exploit your relationship with the consul to abuse men on the margins such as he— and such as I."

I searched the lovely pallor of her face for signs of embarrassment but saw none. If anything, the twitching at the corners of her mouth suggested irritation.

"You know me and my husband no better," she said, "but you can see Settwell is a drunkard. He has lost money through his own poor investments, and he is embittered by our success. You may allow him to dissuade you if you like, but I cannot see how that will serve your cause. I suggest you ask about and see whose reputation is stronger."

I had raised the objection and accepted the explanation. She would surely be satisfied and have no cause to question my sincerity. Now it was time to move the pieces a bit further.

"Tell me," I said, "if we were to conduct business in your preferred method, how would we proceed?"

"When you have your money, we shall convert it to gold, which is then given to our agent, who provides the goods. We ship those goods to England. We are paid in gold, which we then transfer back to credit."

"Is there not a risk in holding so much gold? Isn't the money vulnerable during that phase?"

"Our warehouses are extremely secure," she told me, and it was what I most wanted to hear.

I widened my eyes. "Lisbon is a beautiful city, but a lawless one. How secure can these warehouses be?"

Mrs. Carver held my gaze for a beat longer than good manners required. "Shall I show you?"

I shrugged. In truth, this was the very offer I had hoped would be proffered.

Prior to leaving the Three Speckled Hens, I summoned Enéas and spoke to him briefly, explaining what I needed him to do. Enéas did not like it. I saw tears form in his eyes, even as he nodded his understanding.

"Perhaps it is too much," I said. "If you cannot do it, I shall not hold it against you. I know what I ask."

Enéas took a deep breath. "No, I shall do it. For you, because I owe you everything, but also for me, for how can I live with myself if I refuse you?"

I put a hand on the boy's shoulder. "I admire your bravery, however bombastic."

Enéas grinned shyly. "We shall see if I can do this without pissing my trousers. Then you may admire my bravery."

Few paths ran straight up Lisbon's hills from the river, but rising from almost the direct center of the Palace was an unusually wide street that had become the center of activity for the city's goldsmiths. The industrial warehouses lined the river, but the best-guarded commercial buildings in the city were on or near this main thoroughfare.

Foreigners, especially Englishmen, were in abundance, as were *fidalgos* and functionaries employed in the East India office and other royal trading services. The occasional carriage rattled up and down the cobbles, and there was no shortage of sedan chairs. The poor and the clergy, however, were far fewer than upon nearly any other street in the city.

It was the population that marked the street as different, then, for the buildings themselves appeared no stronger or better fortified than any other. Some of the houses were marked with ornate cornerstones announcing the name of the resident goldsmith, but most were subtler. When a man kept thousands of pounds' worth of gold in his basement, and he lived in a city thick with cutthroats and thieves, it was perhaps the wisest course not to advertise.

Mrs. Carver led me up the Street of Goldsmiths more than halfway to the Rossio, and then cut off to the east, toward the Bario Alto. She walked with her gloved hands on my arm, smiling softly to herself, but saying nothing. She kept her eyes directly before her, not turning to look at a beggar with no arms who called to her; when a leper kneeled before her, she stepped deftly aside. She made no comment and none was necessary. I knew it was impossible to live in Lisbon and allow oneself to be affected by the ubiquity of suffering. There was simply too much of it.

If Mrs. Carver could not aid everyone, however, she did, from time to time, toss a few coins—once to a Moorish woman with one eye and a shockingly thin baby strapped to her back, another time to a little girl who bled from two welts on her face. Sometimes a look of sadness passed over her face, and I marveled at the complexity of the human soul. That this woman was a villainess was beyond dispute, but I never suspected this concern for her fellow human beings was a show for my benefit.

Mrs. Carver stopped at a building on the side street, near a little clearing by a steep staircase. It was an unremarkable house, though clearly an affluent one, of solid white stone crowned by two stories of elaborate tiling. She removed from her coats a key to open the door. Its lock was sturdy enough, but nothing impressive. Once we passed within, however, we found ourselves in a vestibule, poorly lit by a small skylight, with another door—this one of heavy oak, and protected with three complicated-looking locks.

"It appears but an ordinary house," Mrs. Carver said, something of a theatrical air in her voice, "and it is not upon the Street of Goldsmiths itself, so there is nothing to draw attention to it. No one should be tempted to break it open. If a thief should try, he will find himself faced with three locks no man alive could pick."

"Very good," I said. I did not believe a lock had been made that a man could not pick, and I was as skilled in the art as any. "Are there guards to protect the building at night?"

Mrs. Carver was leaning toward a lock, but she turned to me and smiled. Her lips appeared so red, and her teeth so white, in the dim light of the vestibule, that there was something simultaneously demonic and angelic in her appearance. "Not outside," she said, "for that would only draw attention. Inside is another matter. You shall see soon enough."

She opened the three locks one by one and we then found ourselves in a long and narrow corridor with a low ceiling. At the end of this we came to another locked door. We next descended a gloomy staircase, Mrs. Carver clinging once more to my arm. The air was now cool and damp and smelled of mold and rotting wood. At the bottom we came to another long chamber, this one made of stone and undecorated, which felt more like a crypt than a vault.

At the end of this chamber stood two young men, both bearded and extremely thin, with pistols and swords, and with wineskins hidden, hastily and poorly, on the floor behind a small table. They recognized Mrs. Carver and spoke to her deferentially. Even so, they permitted her to pass only after questioning her, at length, about me. Once we proceeded past these sentries, we gained entrance to a large room with an even lower ceiling than the hallway. I was made to stoop lest I strike my head. Small windows permitted shafts of light to pierce the gloom, revealing a series of cages, like prison cells. These contained not men but bars of gold, sacks of coins, and collections of gems. Here at last was what I had come for, the goldsmith's vault, where the Carvers, among others, kept their gold. This was the place from which I would have to steal it.

Such stores were not uncommon in Lisbon. Portugal was among the wealthiest of European nations, not because of its own industry or resources, but because for the past half century, Brazilian gold and diamond mines had provided a steady stream of treasure to the homeland, most of it dedicated to funding new palaces and churches. Such wealth as actually fell into civilian hands often remained locked away in warehouses like this one.

I looked around, affecting approbation. "I believe this warehouse is very secure."

It did indeed appear to be so, which meant it was going to be difficult to steal the Carvers' money. Difficult but not impossible. Not by any means, and I was already beginning to put together a plan.

"May I see your vault in particular?" I asked.

With the guards watching us, we walked down the aisle of cages. We came to one in the middle of the row, to which Mrs. Carver gestured. "Ours."

I peered inside and saw that it was entirely empty, which presented certain problems to the thief who wished to rob it.

Mrs. Carver laughed upon seeing my expression. "Our money cannot grow in the vault. It is out upon ventures. When our ships return, our money is replaced."

"So for our arrangement to work," I said, "I will have to secure funds when your money is between investments."

"Yes, that is how it must be."

I nodded, as much to myself as to Mrs. Carver. More than anything, I wanted to give Settwell the money he needed to flee the country, but I was not prepared to rob just any merchant to do it. This was about justice, not wealth, and it would have to be the Carvers' gold I stole. And that meant I would have to, once more, prepare myself to wait.

Chapter 13

M rs. Carver took my arm as we strolled back along the Street of Goldsmiths. The most direct path to the Three Speckled Hens was along a steep incline, and we had to choose between walking down a series of winding streets or taking a narrow stairway hacked out of the steep hillside. As it would soon be dark, I suggested the quicker route, though the dangerously angled stairs provided a perfect place for thieves to attack. A woman of Mrs. Carver's station would never take it alone. Nevertheless, she showed every sign of feeling safe with me.

The moment we stepped upon the first of the stairs, two men approached from below. They were Gypsies, rough ones by the look of them, but even such men as these rarely risked molesting English men or women in the light of day. The street behind us was now empty, however, the few laboring men and aging housewives who had been loitering about scurrying away like startled cats.

"Hold, lovely lady," one of the Gypsies said in Portuguese. "I would gaze upon you a bit longer, for you look less like a mortal creature than an angel of heaven."

"Your skin is like marble and your hair like fire," said the other. "Will you suffer me to touch it?"

"Get out of my way," Mrs. Carver returned in their language. "You dare insult an Englishwoman in broad daylight? Have you urgent business with the hangman?"

"No urge to die, but a score to settle." A third man now approached from behind us, and I recognized him at once. It was Dordia e Zilhão. He walked with the easy and confident gait of a cat approaching a wounded and helpless bird. His face was no longer bruised from the beating he had taken, but his nose sat swollen and crooked upon his face, curiously at odds with his fanciful mustaches. Even so, he held himself like a man triumphant. With one hand he tapped a long dagger lazily against his pantaloons. "Are you surprised to see me, senhor?"

Because I had tasked Enéas with finding Dordia e Zilhão and selling to the Gypsy information about where he might find the Englishman who had bested him, I was not surprised to see him in the least. Nevertheless, I glanced nervously from one man to the other. "I suggest you consider carefully before you venture into dangerous waters."

"You know this man?" Mrs. Carver asked. She tried to sound indignant, but her voice cracked. This, I suspected, was the sort of lady who appeared indomitable, but only because she was so good at controlling all around her. She spoke with authority and liked to say shocking things, but doing so put her in command. She did not like it, I now saw, when events were not of her ordering. Perhaps that was why she chose a dishonest path—secretly pulling the strings certainly made outcomes more certain.

"He attempted to rob me upon the street," I explained to her. "It went poorly for him."

One of the men grabbed me and spun me toward Dordia e Zilhão while pinning my arms firmly behind my back. I now balanced dangerously upon the edge of the stairway. A single push would send me tumbling. The end result might not be death, but at the very least bones would be broken.

The other man similarly handled Mrs. Carver. She gasped as the Gypsy's hands gripped her shoulders, and her already pale skin went nearly translucent and then blossomed with pink. There was no misunderstanding the look upon her face. It was pure terror. Anything could happen, she knew. These would not be restrained, and she had lost all control of the situation, of her life, of the world.

Best to end this quickly, I decided. I had known Dordia e Zilhão would seek me out eventually, and so I had thought that rather than wait to be surprised, it would be better to meet him on my own terms—and in a way that would best serve my interests. When I had devised the idea of manipulating the Gypsy so that he would attack when I was with Mrs. Carver, I thought only then that these were two people who deserved such punishment as they deserved. My opinion about Dordia e Zilhão had not changed, but whatever Mrs. Carver had done to Settwell, I found I did not have the stomach to see her suffer.

"The lady has no part in this," I said, trying to draw attention back to me. I had no illusions that a reasoned plea would persuade my attackers, but I thought it might distract them from Mrs. Carver, if only for a moment. "Let her be on her way, and you and I will resolve our differences in any manner you choose."

"You make no decide," Dordia e Zilhão said in English. He grinned at Mrs. Carver. "I now take your clothes, as I ask before, but I shall also have her clothes, and more. I shall make you watch while I enjoy this woman, and then I slit your throat. What say you now, Englishman?"

Mrs. Carver said nothing. Fear had left her nearly paralyzed, and seeing how these men tormented her, I felt the anger in me begin to swell. My own culpability was now forgotten. It hardly mattered to me. I desired only to lash out, to feel flesh and bone yield to me. I could not lose control, however. I told myself that. It became like a prayer. I could not lose control. I could not let the will to hurt envelope me.

I am afraid, I told myself. I am a frightened merchant.

"Someone has surely observed this assault and alerted the soldiers," I said, letting my voice squeak. It had been hard to speak, but once I began, playing the role came easy. My training and experience and memory took command. "They will be here shortly. Now, as I am a man of honor, I shall meet you when and where you choose, and we may settle our differences. That is better than you deserve, and you had better take advantage of what I offer."

"He squeaks like mouse!" Dordia e Zilhão cried. "I tell you, mouse, I first have spoken to the people who live near, and they know what happens to them and their families if they cross Dordia e Zilhão, whom they fear—and wisely so. You should have done the same. As for soldiers, I have given promise of meat and drink if they do not trouble me. I regret to say, there is no one to help you. Honor is for up your arse."

I met his gaze. My heart beat steadily. My muscles were relaxed. In moments like these, when anger was about to meet action, I was most at peace. The urges calmed and the voices quieted. I was outnumbered, but I had faith in what my mentor had taught me. I need only wait until I found the best moment to press my advantage and make sure Mrs. Carver would not fall. The anticipation was torture, but the knowledge of what would come after was as soothing as wine.

"I say you must let us pass," I said in a loud voice, hoping to sound arrogant.

"Your talk means nothing." Dordia e Zilhão raised his long dagger and pointed it at my face, letting it dangle but inches from my left eye.

The Gypsy's elbow was locked and his arm firm—a threat, not a prelude to a strike. Even so, a sudden movement might cause me to lose an eye, and I willed myself not to flinch. Mrs. Carver was still too close to the stairs. If I moved now, the Gypsies could easily push her out of spite.

Dordia e Zilhão lowered the blade slightly, letting it rest on my cheek. I felt warmth and then wetness as the sharp edge cut my skin. Mrs. Carver gasped and then something like a whimper, a wounded-animal sort of noise, escaped from deep in her throat. For my part, I did not react. The cut was shallow. It would not scar or even bleed much. What mattered to me was that Dordia e Zilhão had committed himself, and I could now act with impunity.

From the corner of my eye I saw the man behind Mrs. Carver begin to grind his hips against her. "I want this one when you are done with her," he said to his leader. Mrs. Carver squeezed her eyes shut and tears began to trickle down her cheeks.

I could tolerate no more. I thrust my heel into the shin of the man behind me, and at the same time I crouched down and to the left, sensing Dordia e Zilhão would thrust up and right with his weapon. He did, and the dagger flashed forward, striking hard into his own man's cheek. The blade penetrated the flesh, and I heard the crack of teeth breaking and a more disturbing sucking sound as the blade ripped other teeth out by their roots. The man cried piteously as his face blossomed with blood. He staggered back, flailing his arms, horrified by his wound but unwilling to pull the dagger out himself. It flopped out of the side of his face, pulling down and widening the wound until it at last dropped upon the ground. At that moment, the man lost his balance and began to tumble down the steep staircase.

Now free, I rolled off to the side and away from Mrs. Carver. Dordia e Zilhão was now holding the bloody dagger, which he had snatched from the ground.

Taking the stance of an experienced duelist, Dordia e Zilhão thrust forward at me, but I danced backwards, close to where the hill plummeted downward. I stood facing my enemy while, to my right, the other Gypsy still held Mrs. Carver from behind on the top of the stairway. I moved toward Dordia e Zilhão and then sprang in the opposite direction, landing hard, forcing my elbow down on the base of the neck of the other man. He went down at once, and Mrs. Carver was knocked backwards by the impact. I grabbed her by the wrist and jerked her forward to keep her from falling.

She staggered but regained her footing. Dordia e Zilhão, now the last man standing, brandished his blade. His face was red with anger and twisted into a mask of fury, but there was fear there too, and that made him dangerous. He would be willing to do anything to preserve his honor, including sacrifice himself if it meant hurting Mrs. Carver.

"Get behind me," I snapped at her.

She began to move, but Dordia e Zilhão struck, lashing out quickly and suddenly. He meant to cut a wide gash across her face, destroying her beauty. I saw it in time. I struck his wrist hard with my forearm, and the blade flew free. The Gypsy was now disarmed, and the danger was essentially over.

When I set this encounter in motion, I had hoped a heroic rescue might alter favorably the balance of power with Mrs. Carver. Because I had orchestrated the attack, I also believed I would have no difficulty keeping the lady safe. I had clearly miscalculated, and the callous assault upon Mrs. Carver's dignity infuriated me.

I lunged toward Dordia e Zilhão's right, and as the Gypsy turned to face me, I shifted and struck the thief from the left, driving my fist into the soft spot on the side of his head. It was like a hammer blow. I felt something yield and Dordia e Zilhão's eyes rolled upward. He fell to his knees.

It was enough, and the fight was won, but I did not want that it should be over. Here was a man who would have mutilated a woman out of spite. He would have raped her and allowed his friends to do the same. Perhaps I'd been wrong to provoke him, but Dordia e Zilhão had turned from an equal to prey on an innocent—like all men of power in Lisbon.

With my left hand I grabbed the thief by his long locks, and with my right I struck him in the jaw. I did it again, and then again and then again. I felt nothing, not the pain in my hand or the pounding in my head. I was only dimly aware of Mrs. Carver calling my name. Only the touch of gloved fingers on my forearm—so cool and gentle and tentative—broke through in the way no shouting or pain could have.

"Please," she said. "You need do no more."

I looked at Dordia e Zilhão, whose head I still held up by his hair. His nose was smashed once more, now flattened and utterly destroyed, and blood bubbled from his nostrils and mouth. Several teeth were missing and he struggled to breathe.

I let go and the Gypsy dropped to the cobblestones. Mrs. Carver, her hands still on my arm, straightened me up.

"I am sorry." I panted heavily, and sweat rolled down my back and off my face. My stink was pungent in my nose. I lowered my eyes because I could not stand to look at her. Beauty was the last thing I wanted to see. I forced myself to speak, though the words came out with great difficulty. "He tried to hurt you, and I was angry."

"Do not say you are sorry," she answered, raising my chin so I had to look into her brilliantly blue eyes. Already she had regained composure. The order in her world was restored. I had restored it, and I could not help but wonder if, because she had brought me into her world, she told herself that she had played a part in her own rescue.

"You saved me," she said, the relief in her voice unmistakable, "and I shall not forget it."

Around us, people began to peer out windows and step into the thresholds of their doorways. An Englishman and Englishwoman stood among the bloodied forms of defeated thieves. One was badly hurt. Perhaps he would die. Perhaps not. In London I would have run before constables arrived to restore order and apprehend anyone who looked troublesome and unimportant. Here, there was no need to hurry. Mrs. Carver must have been thinking much the same thing, because she looked at me and managed a sad smile. *"A vida em Lisboa,"* she said in a raspy whisper.

"A vida em Lisboa," I agreed.

She took my arm, and as though departing a country dance, we walked from the men I had bested. Already the memory of the blind rage began to fade, pushed away by certainty. Mrs. Carver was a manipulative woman and extremely dangerous, but the gratitude she felt now was real. Things were different between us. The power was mine.

Back at the Duke's Arms, I sat in my armchair, my head buzzing with a thousand incoherent thoughts. I tried to ignore the throbbing in my knuckles as I used my uninjured left hand to lift a cup of wine to my lips. I was content to sit there, to be still, to do nothing and think of less, for hours.

I had nearly lost control of events, but I had not the energy to condemn myself. Nor did I wish to think of Roberta Carver, how I had seen vulnerability in her today, and how it made me think differently of her. It was much easier, I realized, to see her as nothing but a cruel villainess, but it seemed she was, like all people, more complex than surfaces suggested. Perhaps even more complex than most I've known.

This was, I knew, a dangerous turn of thought, and I chastised myself at once. I could ill afford to think kindly of her. She had behaved with ill intent, and now she must pay for her actions. It was what I knew to be true, and yet I did not quite believe it.

After some time, I drifted off into an uneasy slumber, but I do not believe it was long after that I was awakened by a soft knock at the door, and I groaned, thinking it must be the intolerable Kingsley

Franklin. Perhaps he had seen me slip up the stairs, noticed my swollen hands, and now wished to make endless conversation about it. I waved at Enéas to get the door, and closed my eyes.

Then they snapped open. I smelled a now-familiar perfume. Roberta Carver entered the room, closing the door behind her, leaving Enéas on the other side. Her hand trembled as it left the doorknob.

"What do you do here?" I asked her. It was a genuine question. I could not fathom her purpose. She toyed with me, did she not? So why take this step? Did she believe I was not yet sufficiently ensnared?

"You do not wish to see me?" Her voice was low and hoarse. Her blue eyes were rimmed with red, as if she had been crying. Her hair was disordered, with curls coming free. For all that, she was still striking beyond words.

"You deliberately mistake my meaning. Why do you risk coming here, observed by all? People will talk."

She took a step close. "People already talk. What will they say—that you and I are behaving scandalously? They say that about me and every man with whom we do business. And although I do not like it, my husband encourages these rumors. He will not know the truth when he hears it."

She had taken the time to follow her actions through all possible outcomes. This, I realized, was what she did. She took not a step whose consequences she had not calculated.

I took her hands. This woman was beautiful, yes, and her boldness was alluring. She was also a predator, one whose cunning and care made her especially dangerous. She was, I reminded myself, a woman who had chosen to wound Settwell, a guiltless man with a vulnerable child. I did not want to care for her or become closer to her than I already was. I did not wish to be the sort of man who saw goodness and worth where there was only beauty. And in truth I still mourned Gabriela.

But then again Gabriela—who had been good, who had been worthy—was gone, and this woman stood before me. Perhaps it did not matter if she was cruel and greedy. She was beautiful and she wanted to be with me, and perhaps that ought to be enough.

"Roberta," I said, using her Christian name for the first time, "I cannot allow you to place yourself in danger."

"I was in danger today," she said, "and you did not hesitate. I care for Rutherford. I truly do, but he is not like you. He does what I tell him. You are . . ." She swallowed hard. "You are unafraid."

I turned away from her, for this was, perhaps, the thing about myself I liked least. I wanted to be afraid, but she wanted me fearless. I knew it was true, and I knew that she had now moved beyond manipulating me. What I had done for her today had altered her sense of me, and I supposed it altered my sense of her as well. I did not want it to, but I could not deny it.

She put a hand on my shoulder and turned me to face her. "How little you understand people," she said. "You think I insult you?"

"I know you do not," I said.

"Then what is wrong?"

I drew her toward me. I believed, to the core of my being, that doing so was a mistake, but I did it all the same. A man could only fight his nature on so many fronts before something gave way. I kissed her and she returned the kiss, hot and hungry and greedy. Her breath was sweet, and her hands clutched me tightly. I could feel how much she wanted me, and if there was anything false in it, I could not detect it.

Then I pushed her away—I realized suddenly and horribly that I had no choice. It was something that could never be. Not here. Not in Lisbon. Not while I pretended to be something I was not.

I had undergone the ritual of circumcision after converting to Judaism, under the rites and regulations of Judaic law. This was perhaps a year after my arrival in London, and as this is an ordeal normally experienced by newborn infants, the less said of my recollections of this observance, the better. Setting aside the awkward and painful nature of the experience, it had left its unmistakable mark, and if Roberta were to see me unclothed or to touch me, she would know me for a Jew.

My mind raced. Was there some lie I could tell? Some deception to explain everything away? Of course there wasn't. Roberta, like me, was a schemer. She might pretend to be satisfied by some explanation of sickness that required surgery, but she would eventually see through the lies. A whisper to an Inquisitor would be enough to destroy me at any moment. I could not let that happen, for it was not only my life in the balance. I could not endanger myself if it meant imperiling Settwell's cause.

I cursed under my breath. "I will not commit adultery," I said. I hated how weak it sounded. How foolish.

Roberta grinned at me, and I believed it was because she already had an answer prepared for this objection. "*You* would not be committing adultery. That sin would be mine alone, and I think I can endure the guilt." Her eyes were moist and her cheeks flushed.

I almost forgot my resolve as I looked at her. But my desire for her was only a feeling, an urge, and I could tame it. "No, I won't do this to you."

"It is for me to decide what I will do," Roberta said, but I could see that already irritation and anger were replacing longing. She felt rejected, and that could be very dangerous.

I was now upon the thinnest of ice. I could not let her believe I had sent her away or that she had embarrassed herself. I took her hands once more and kissed them. I dropped to my knees and looked up at her. "Were you unmarried, or even estranged from your husband, no power in the world could keep me from you."

"What do you care for my marriage?" she asked, yanking her hands free. "Forgive me for saying so, but I don't think there is an Englishman in Lisbon who hasn't attempted to bed me, yet you refuse when I offer myself." Suddenly her eyes went wide. "There is someone else, isn't there? No man of spirit refuses to cuckold a rival, and I have seen that you are no coward. Who is she? Who is the woman you love?"

There was only one thing I could say. "*You* are the woman I love. I loved you from the moment I first saw you, from the moment we first met. I have not been able to stop thinking about you. I have lain awake nights in agony for the want of you. And today, when those Gypsies attacked us, I would have died gladly to save you. There is no danger I would not face for you, Roberta, but I will not share you with another man."

"That is foolish," she said, but she sounded unsure of herself.

"Do not tell me it is foolish to love you. If you leave your husband, I will be yours, but not before."

She was struck silent as she stared at me in disbelief. I had refused her and flattered her vanity all at once. I had to hope it would be enough.

She took a step back. "I cannot leave Rutherford. There are matters of business . . ."

"Business?" I demanded. "I talk to you of love, and you speak of business?"

"You don't understand," she said. "My life back in England was . . . not easy. My father was cruel to me, and Rutherford took me away from that."

"All English fathers are cruel," I said. I didn't believe this, but I wanted her to tell me more about herself. I wanted to better know her—that I might more easily outwit her, I told myself, but even as I made these claims, I knew I was lying to myself.

"Not like mine," she told me. She met my eye. She would not look away as she spoke of this, and I knew it to be a matter of pride for her. "He was not merely cold or neglectful or stern, but he delighted in causing pain to others, and to me in particular. There were four of us, two boys and another girl, and I was singled out as the one on whom anger and frustration and the desire to hurt might be safely vented. My father not only tolerated this, he encouraged it."

"Your mother?" I asked.

"My mother would have cut off her own arm to please my father. It was what he wished, and that was the end of the matter."

"Roberta, I'm sorry—"

"I don't want sorry," she told me. "Sorry is nothing to me. I care nothing for words. Words are false, by their very nature. I care only for actions, and I know who you are, for I have seen your mettle when it most counted. I cannot believe you will turn me away now."

"But your husband—" I began feebly.

"My husband is my concern," she said, more softly now. "I value him in ways you cannot imagine. He was kind to me when I needed someone to be kind."

"You need only have waited half an hour to find someone else who would be kind to one such as you," I said.

"But it was him!" she snapped. "You are a man. You can't know what it is to have no power of your own. You might look at Rutherford and see someone weak and unimposing, but he was my rescuer."

That, it seemed, was what she valued most.

"To leave him now would be to ruin him," she said more quietly. "There are too many matters of business unresolved."

"And there always will be," I said, sounding bitter. "There will always be a reason not to leave him. You may be grateful to him for rescuing you from an unkind parent, but you were a prize beyond anything he might have hoped for."

"I am a person, not a prize," she said.

"Can you not see that I am saying the same thing?" I said. "I want the person, not a fleeting association. Until I can be with you, we may be business associates and we may be friends, but I will not be your amusing little lover."

Roberta nodded stiffly, her manner supremely controlled. "I see."

"I hope you do," I answered.

She wiped a tear from her eye with her index finger, sniffed in a breath, and left the room.

I was breathing hard. I walked over to my cup of wine, and when I picked it up I realized my hand was trembling. Had I salvaged things with Roberta? I could not be sure, but if she had left wishing to sever ties with me, so much of what I had done in Lisbon had been for nothing. I drank until the cup was empty and then poured myself another glass, and when it in turn was done, there would be more.

Chapter 14

I had hoped to be done with Lisbon before the end of summer, but August turned to September and though things progressed, there was no end in sight. I observed the festival of Rosh Hashanah, the new year, in isolation. I remained in my room and read from my prayer book and dedicated my thoughts to the holy day.

As I considered my weeks here in Lisbon, I could not but take satisfaction in what I had accomplished, even if it were not yet enough. I engaged in small deals, made some profits. It was nothing remarkable, but it was credible, and I began to make a name for myself. I met with Rutherford and Roberta Carver with some regularity, planning out our business together. There was always a tension now with Roberta, and I could not tell if she looked at me with anger or with longing. I avoided being alone with her, or even sitting next to her. I hoped she believed in my anguish, and, much to my surprise, I found myself hoping she did not mock me behind my back.

Inácio, Franklin, and Settwell had all given me the same

advice, so I went to no Portuguese *tabernas* but the one Eusebio frequented. I established my base of operation, and I did not stray from it, for there was no advantage in spreading myself too thin. I became a familiar fixture there, the Englishman who hoped to cajole this New Christian or that into offering me credit.

Every now and again, I recognized a man who walked into the tavern. I saw Senhor Meldola, who specialized in importing English and Dutch foodstuffs, and Senhor Cardozo, a dealer in whale oil and ambergris. My father had done business with them long ago. Each time I prepared myself for denials, even an altercation and flight. But who would recognize a grown Englishman of business as being the skinny thirteen-year-old son of a New Christian merchant last seen almost ten years earlier? All took me for what I appeared to be and sought nothing beneath the surface.

Eusebio remained guardedly social with me, but his father gave every sign of enjoying my company. Eusebio would make polite conversation and ask after my health, but no more than that. I understood that when he was ready to do business, he would let me know. And so it went until that afternoon in September when everything changed, the day the Inquisitor walked into the *taberna*.

There was no truce, and there was no understanding. Inquisitors did not make a point of avoiding New Christian *tabernas,* but there was simply no advantage in entering them. Inquisitors wanted that men should eat and drink and speak freely so their agents would overhear anything blasphemous or otherwise significant. Everyone knew that there would be Inquisition familiars in the tavern—in every tavern—but Inquisitors hoped that now and again someone with something interesting to say would drink too much and feel a little too safe.

All of which explained the sudden silence when the Inquisitor entered the room. Someone was going to be arrested. Why else taint this tavern forever, make it the place where an Inquisitor might walk in at any moment? The newcomer, with his black robes and his gold cross, pulled back his hood to reveal the face of Pedro Azinheiro.

Azinheiro smiled at the room as though he had not stunned them into silence. Every man present had lost a friend or a relative to this priest—I was sure of it. Azinheiro had been an Inquisitor for more than twenty years, longer than any other in Lisbon. It was hard to imagine anyone more reviled and feared by the city's New Christians, and yet he did not look to be a Daniel in his den of lions. He gave every appearance of a man who had entered a pleasant-looking eatery, where he expected to make friends shortly.

He walked to the barman with an easy saunter. There he cleared his throat and, in a cheerful voice, ordered a cup of wine. He watched while it was set before him, and as he picked it up, smiled to himself as if remembering a funny joke.

No one spoke. No one dared. I knew it was not out of fear of the priest, but because the first man who reentered his conversation would be suspected of being too comfortable around the Inquisitor, and thus very possibly an agent of the Inquisition. And so we all sat in silence, none eating or drinking, while Azinheiro sipped his wine and continued to smile. Occasionally he hummed.

At last he finished his wine. He wiped his mouth with his clerical sleeve and slapped the pewter cup down. Every man in the tavern held his breath. Maybe the Inquisitor would leave. Maybe his presence there did not mark the end of anyone in particular. Maybe he wanted to send a message that no one understood or could heed. They could worry about its meaning later, in the comfort of their own homes, away from Azinheiro. It would make sense then, surely. But now, it would be enough for him simply to depart.

He did not. Instead, he leaned toward the barman as though readying himself to share a great confidence, and with all the good humor in the world, ordered another cup of wine.

The barman hesitated a second, his long face twisted with confusion. Perhaps he toyed with the idea of asking the Inquisitor—as politely as he could, of course—if he would not mind considering taking his wine somewhere else. Perhaps he was merely too terrified to move. Then, like a man on a carriage startled out of an unexpected slumber, the barman roused himself, shook his head slightly, and poured the wine.

That was when I rose to my feet.

All eyes were upon me as I strolled over to the counter. Had anyone asked me, I could not have said what it was I was doing, what I intended. I had moved beyond thought. I saw only the counter and the back of the Inquisitor, with his head bent, and just enough of his grinning old mouth. I felt a relentless thrumming in my temple, a staccato drumbeat, neither urging me on nor dissuading me from my course.

I leaned against the bar, my forearms flat, my fingers intertwined. "Another cup of wine," I said to the barman. When it arrived, I drank it down, almost all at once. I then turned to the humming Inquisitor.

I had expected that I would need to call upon all the skills I had learned from Mr. Weaver to contain my anger, but much to my surprise I found myself already quite in control. It was not that, seeing him again, away from the Palace of the Inquisition, I did not wish to kill Azinheiro. I did. I wished to remove my hidden dagger and slice Azinheiro's throat and watch while he writhed upon the floor like a fresh-caught fish. I could see it clearly—the priest's body below while I stood with blood splattered upon my hands, my clothes, my face. I could taste the coppery residue in my mouth. It could not happen now, but it was, I believed, inevitable, and perhaps that was why I was so calm. I was where I should be, moving closer to my goal.

"Good afternoon," I said to the priest.

The Inquisitor nodded at me. "And to you."

So, we did not know one another. That was how the priest wanted it. Then why had he come to the *taberna*? Did he want to remind me of his power and his presence, or had he something else in mind?

"What do you here?" I asked. I kept my voice low, though the barman had stepped away, not wishing to hear anything. For all that, it was the sort of question I might have asked if I had not known the priest.

"I drink wine," said the Jesuit. "I am thirsty."

I tapped the side of my cup, and the barman refilled it. I took another long sip. "You've had your drink, and your thirst is quenched. Now you must consider that you are making these men uncomfortable."

The priest turned to me. This was evidently a man who believed deeply in his own cleverness. "Why should they be uncomfortable if they have nothing to hide?"

"Do you jest?" I asked, meeting his eye.

The Inquisitor picked up his cup and began to swirl the contents. He studied them like an augur for a minute. "You are very forward, sir."

"The English are a direct people," I assured him. "Perhaps you know a thing or two about the English character."

The priest narrowed his eyes. "You are also bold."

"Simply observant."

"Then I shall return your English bluntness and tell you I expected you to be even bolder," the priest said, barely above a whisper. "You falter, sir, and that makes you of no use. I am here to offer some support."

Of course the priest was monitoring my actions. I knew he would, and there could be no place I would be more observed than a New Christian *taberna*. So what kind of support did Azinheiro intend to offer?

"I shall tell you the truth," the priest said, now more loudly. He wished this part of the conversation to be overheard. "I was thirsty and wanted a drink. I was thinking of something private and amusing, and I hardly even noticed where it was I walked into. I did not mean to make anyone uneasy."

"You've had two glasses of wine," I said, moving away from him, as though my business were concluded. "Surely your thirst is quenched."

The priest picked up his cup and drained it. "Indeed it is. You have convinced me. Good day, Englishman."

He turned from the bar, walked the length of the tavern, and stepped out into the street.

I continued to drink the port, but I did not turn around. I wondered if, in sending the priest away, I had poisoned my own well. I had rid them of the Inquisitor, and that could be regarded as no small favor, but had I also marked myself as someone too comfortable with Azinheiro? Then I heard the men whispering. They had overheard Azinheiro's last comment, and they were repeating it. *You have convinced me to leave.* The New Christians were gazing at me with wonder and respect.

I stared into my wine and waited for something to happen. A few minutes later, I felt a hand upon my shoulder. I turned around and saw old Nobreza staring at me, his eyes wide and sparkling. "Mr. Foxx, would you join me at my son's house for dinner tomorrow afternoon?"

At last some progress with the Nobrezas. The pleasure of it was admittedly lessened by the knowledge that the Inquisitor had made it possible. More than that, it was what the Inquisitor himself desired. I had come to Lisbon to set the pieces on the board, but I now had the uneasy feeling that it was the priest's hand moving them from square to square.

Chapter 15

Unlike in London, where the fashionable eat their evening meals as late as six or even eight in the evening, in Lisbon dinner was still commonly served, in accordance with older customs, between noon and three in the afternoon. If a man wished to dine later, he would invite his guests to stay the night.

I had no particular wish to visit Eusebio's home, which was only a few streets over from the house in which I spent my childhood. I would not walk down my old street, and I would not look at that house. There were certain things that could not be endured. It was easier to sit down with the Inquisitor who had arrested my father.

Only shortly before I left the inn did I realize that my meal would be ending as Yom Kippur began. The evening services for the holiday were called Kol Nidre, named for the central prayer—a plea for forgiveness for vows broken against one's will. For foreign Jews whose families had previously converted under the Inquisition, Kol Nidre held special significance. In London, many Jews believed that their distant relatives in Portugal secretly practiced Judaism while pretending to observe Catholicism in public. I had never had the heart to tell those I met that while I could not be certain, I did not believe there were any such clandestine Jews remaining. Generations ago, such families existed. My patron, Mr. Weaver, told me his had been such a family. I, however, had never met a secret Jew, never seen a furtive sign of hidden observance. Such people no longer existed. The Inquisition and time had done their work.

I shut out all sights, all smells, all sensations, and walked until I found myself outside Eusebio's house. It was much as I remembered it, an unremarkable three-story building in the middle of its block. I was admitted at once and led into a sitting room by a mulatto woman who gave me a glass of port without troubling to inquire if I wanted it. Perhaps she spoke no English and thought it would be easier that way. As soon as she set the glass before me and curtsied, she hurried out of the room as if escaping my noxious Protestant vapors.

The room overlooked the downward slope of Chiado Hill, and from a chair I gazed out at the houses below, and at the river beyond them, before glancing at the room. The furnishings were new and fine, with detailed woodwork and velvet cushions. Beneath the line of the window, the walls were decorated in elaborate tiling depicting the labors of Hercules. I studied the pictures for a moment and again looked out the window to the distant water, watching the light play off the waves and the flutter of lax sails upon the ships. There was, I supposed, a bakery nearby, and the air smelled of fresh bread and scorched rosemary. The sunlight was bright and somehow revealing. I remembered something—not an event, but a feeling, of being a child and smelling this air and basking in this light and being happy. The memory disturbed me, and I shook it off.

I looked up as a woman walked into the room. Eusebio's wife. She was tall and quite lovely in the Portuguese way—poised and formal, but also graceful. There was something in her manner that struck me as regal, and I found myself staring at the sea-green gown that hugged her arms tight and flowed down to her ankles. She had dark hair and green eyes and a long, thin nose, slightly flattened at the bridge, giving her a touch of imperfection that served to render her utterly perfect. It was that flatness that struck me, that made me understand instantly who she was, that robbed me of all uncertainty.

It was Gabriela.

I felt something tighten within me—my stomach, my heart, my capacity to breathe. Gabriela. Alive. Before me. Standing. Inclining her head.

I felt as though I were looking at her through a long tunnel. I felt as though the ground under my feet buckled, and it took the greatest exertion of will not to hold on to the walls for support. She was here, alive, well. This moment, this encounter, was real.

Time seemed to fall away. Here was Gabriela, and I was a thirteen-year-old boy again, contriving one excuse after another to spend time with her. I was fifteen, upon the London streets, howling with rage at the years and miles between us. I was eighteen, in a darkened bagnio, so drunk my head pounded, hardly even aware of the woman who lay beneath me as I told myself, again and again, that I had forgotten Gabriela, that I never thought of her any longer.

I saw a look of confusion cross Gabriela's beautiful face—no doubt a strange expression had passed over my own. I blinked, turned away, and when I looked back I knew my face betrayed nothing to suggest I was anything but an obsequious English merchant, eager to make his fortune. Whatever I felt, I would hide—for now—as Mr. Weaver had taught me.

I also knew that what had happened was no coincidence. I had not by chance found myself allied to a merchant married to Gabriela. Inácio had done this. Inácio had lied about Gabriela being dead and then sent me to Eusebio. Why? Did Inácio hate me because I had escaped the Inquisition, had escaped Portugal, had gone to England?

Did he think me wealthy now, and this visit to Lisbon an indulgence? Was this a joke to him? Inácio had been crushed by the same forces that had cast me to better shores. Perhaps he wished to make me pay for it.

That I could make no sense of his motivation hardly signified. I could not depend upon my ability to read people, not those close to me. I could spot a thief at fifty feet, and tell within a moment's conversation if a husband and wife were well contented, but I could not see into the hearts of those whose actions affected my own existence. It hardly mattered why he had deceived me, only that he had.

Behind Gabriela stood the same mulatto who had answered the door, because—of course—the lady of the house would not enter the room alone to meet a strange man, particularly an English merchant. The serving woman stood with eyes unfocused, there if anyone should need her, but otherwise no more than furnishing.

A rich floral scent, perfume or natural, struck me suddenly and made me light-headed. My heart raced. I thought my ears buzzed until I noticed a fly hurling itself uselessly at the window. The *tap tap tap* of it was thunderous in my ear. I recalled that, ten years before, I had not said goodbye to Gabriela, and I did not have to. I was alive and she was alive. We were in the same room. We were always supposed to be together, and now, it had come to pass.

Was she truly more beautiful than other women, or did I merely see her that way? It did not matter, because she transcended beauty. She was goodness. My mind moved forward—all my plans for Lisbon took a different shape. Whatever Gabriela was now, I could not be worthy of her in any context until I had purged myself of darkness. I must help Settwell, discover who betrayed my father, and kill the priest. Then, perhaps, we could—could what? I did not know, but now possibilities existed where there were none before.

Gabriela curtsied and smiled. Her lips, far redder than recalled, parted to reveal white teeth. Perhaps my gaze was too intense, for she lowered her eyes. "Mr. Foxx, you are most welcome in our home. My husband and his father will be here shortly, but I did not wish for you to think yourself neglected. I am Senhora Nobreza." Her English was good, better than I recalled, though her accent was thick.

I rose too and met her eyes before I bowed. I wanted to give her this chance to recognize me. Perhaps she would say, *My God, it is Sebastião!* and throw her arms around me, and I would forget my vows to right wrongs in Lisbon. Perhaps I would not need them any longer because Gabriela would make me whole. If only she recognized me, everything could change, at this moment.

She did not, and I layered falseness over mask over disguise. It was the only way I could survive the evening.

"Senhora Nobreza. It is an honor. I thank you for making me so welcome." My voice was as even as it was glib.

"You are very kind," she said. "May I sit with you?"

"I should be delighted," I said, attempting to appear good-humored, but feeling myself spiraling into despair. She did not know me. She had forgotten me. All this time—nearly ten years—almost half the time I had been alive, I had believed myself in love with her. When I thought she was dead, I had felt all that was good vanish from the world.

I remembered every detail of her face, though it had changed somewhat in its maturation to perfection. I would have known her anywhere. I could have picked her from a crowd of thousands, but she did not see me standing right before her. She had forgotten my face, perhaps even my name. I saw a vase on the mantel above the fireplace, and I could imagine it in my hands. I could feel the weight of it. I knew precisely how it would feel to throw it against the wall, to see it shatter into fragments, to smell the dust of old pottery. I would not hurt her. Never. But I yearned to see destruction all around her and for her to know what she had done—that she had shattered me just as surely.

I took a breath. I sat in a stiff armchair, and Gabriela sat across from me on a settee, with her back to one of the windows. The light reflected off her hair, and she appeared to glow like a Madonna in a painting.

"Senhor Nobreza does not often invite Englishmen to our home, and in the main I am not sorry, but when he told me of what transpired with you and the Inquisitor, I was delighted that he made an exception."

"I shall make every effort to conduct myself so as to be a credit to the English nation," I said, settling into my role, taking comfort from the falsehood I projected.

"I have no grievance against the English," Gabriela said. "You must not think so. It is only that having foreign guests in one's home brings attention, and we do not like attention."

"I imagine not."

"You do understand that as an Englishman you are not exempt from arrest by the Inquisition?"

"Yes, I have been told that."

"And the Inquisitor you spoke to—he is known to dislike the English."

"His conversation has led me to understand that to be true," I agreed.

She leaned forward. Her high-necked gown revealed nothing, but her breasts strained against the fabric. If she noticed my eyes upon her, she gave no sign. "Then why did you take such a risk?"

I wanted to ask her why she cared. Of what concern could it be to her why I did anything? The words threatened to erupt from the very core of me, but I pushed them down. I became what I pretended. "I did not think I took a risk by stating what was obviously true. I neither threatened nor insulted nor belittled the Inquisitor. I observed that he made the men in the tavern uncomfortable. I spoke what he already knew."

"And you think it is not dangerous to speak a truth known to all?"

I remembered once, as a boy, I had said to her in a fit of anger, *I wish I did not lack the power, or perhaps the courage, to change things for our families.* She had turned to me. *I know it is not a want of courage.* I thought now that I could repeat my childhood words to her. Would she remember?

Instead I smiled with patronizing indulgence. "I did not worry about propriety, senhora. My concern was that I witnessed an injustice, and I did not much like it."

"Perhaps that stands in England, but here things are different. Would your fine principles save you if an Inquisitor came for you?"

"If an Inquisitor comes for me, he shall get more than he bargained for. I shan't go quietly."

Damn my tongue. I cursed myself, but I kept my face impassive, and I pursed my lips like a fool who cannot distinguish between bravado and truth. I would never again speak to her without pausing to consider my words, but I feared the damage was already done.

Gabriela sucked in a breath. "You are very direct."

I considered how I might retrench. "I am alone here, with no one to protect and with, as yet, no fortune rooted in this country. I have nothing to lose, and I flatter myself I would be able to escape to the protection of my countrymen if I had to."

I had been staring out the window as I spoke, but now I turned to Gabriela. She was flushed. My efforts to soften the force of my declaration clearly had not worked. Gabriela did not recognize me, but I had certainly grabbed her attention.

The Nobrezas, father and son, arrived and we all retired to a fine dining room with a large, ornately carved table in the center. A massive chandelier hung overhead, and there were perhaps three dozen candles lit, though ample light yet streamed through the windows. By the fireplace was yet another elaborate scene done in tiles—this time images from the Trojan War. I glanced at an image of Achilles, his face twisted in his mighty rage, and I looked away.

We ate chicken roasted with potatoes, and a fish stew with greens and crusty Portuguese bread, and there was a hearty Douro wine. Upon the table were bowls of olives and figs and dates. The conversation was light and informal, and after a few minutes, I gave myself over to the insignificant chatter of people who little know one another. I hardly allowed myself to glance in Gabriela's direction. I became what I pretended to be: an Englishman after New Christian gold.

I learned that Gabriela and Eusebio had been married only ten months, which surprised me. A New Christian woman her age ought to have been married for years, with several children by now. There was something to this, a story not spoken, but neither of them hinted at it in any detail. Once, when I involuntarily looked at Gabriela, I observed a slight darkening of her cheeks as she turned away.

After dinner, the serving woman brought in another bottle of Douro and Gabriela excused herself. I allowed myself to watch her as she left the room, and nearly sighed with relief when she was gone. How, I wondered, did Eusebio pass his days abroad knowing that she awaited him at home? How did he compel himself to leave this house?

Eusebio said, "She is beautiful, do you not think so?"

I forced myself to simulate polite admiration. "You are a most fortunate man."

"I am," said Eusebio with a smile of genuine pleasure. Perhaps he truly loved her, and so perhaps his heart would be broken when I fled with her.

"I hope," I said, "that you take no risks inviting me here. I would hate to see any ill effects of my talk with the Inquisitor befall you or your family."

"You have marked yourself to be both honest and courteous, and

I believe the Inquisitor will not target you for that. Indeed, if I read his face right, he looked at you with something like respect, and a man who earns respect is a man worth doing business with."

"That Inquisitor in particular—I gather he does not like Englishmen. Do you know why?"

Eusebio stared at me. "I will not gossip about an Inquisitor."

"Of course not. Forgive my ignorance," I said. Eusebio could still not be certain that I was not an agent of the Inquisition or that I would not, perhaps, someday become one. A man in Eusebio's position would never intentionally say something that could be used against him. The wrong word here or there might return to haunt him years from now.

"I know it is difficult for you," Eusebio said. "The English are used to speaking without reservation. But you, Mr. Foxx, are more sensitive to the particularities of life in Portugal than many of your countrymen. A New Christian merchant looks for such qualities."

There it was. Forward movement at last. I was not foolish enough to believe I had truly earned Eusebio's respect. More likely, Eusebio recognized that there was some status to be gained by being the one to do business with this Englishman. "Does this mean you are prepared to extend me credit?"

"If you can present me with a reason to do so, a specific investment, then we may discuss it further," Eusebio said, spreading forth his hands. "If I cannot help you, you are free to go elsewhere. Otherwise, I wish to do business with you exclusively."

I nodded. I did not want to tell Eusebio I had a venture lined up with the Carvers and was but awaiting a New Christian to lend me money. That would have sounded desperate and calculating. I needed to make Eusebio believe that he, and not the Carvers, was the engine that drove this English merchant. I would eventually get what I wanted from Eusebio, and that was enough for now.

We stood and shook hands, and raised our glasses to each other, and made many promises of friendship. It was all well. I was on my way to helping Settwell. I thought I could affect the arrangements I needed with only minimal contact with Gabriela, and that would be best for now. Next I would learn who had betrayed my father, and then I would be able to complete my business in Lisbon and, once more, escape.

Chapter 16

This time I did not trouble to announce myself. When the boathouse door opened, I forced myself inside. I didn't know if it was the same young man who had admitted me before. I didn't look.

I walked at a steady clip along the slick wood, entered the adjoining house, and climbed the stairs. At the top, I pushed open the door. I was prepared for anything, my senses alive and tingling, and yet I was hardly aware of any of it. The part of myself I most recognized was gone, hidden deep within my rage.

Inácio was sitting on a chair, a very young girl, no more than thirteen, on his lap. Her dress was unlaced and falling about the shoulder, and on seeing me she pulled it up and fled the room.

Inácio's expression was cold and hard. He remained seated. "I know we are old friends, but you test my patience."

I took a deep breath, struggling to pull myself free of the tendrils of anger. I would at least hear what Inácio had to say before I acted. "You lied to me," I said, speaking through clenched teeth.

"Did I?" Inácio asked. "I don't recall doing so."

"Gabriela. You told me she was dead."

Inácio's eyes widened, a pantomime of surprise. He leaned forward. "And she is not?"

"She's married to Nobreza, the man to whom you sent me. Am I to believe that is just a coincidence?"

Inácio now rose from his seat. "You may believe what you like. I heard she was dead. I also heard Nobreza was a desperate man. I am pleased to learn she is alive, however. She was always very pretty. And have you done well with Nobreza?"

I unclenched my teeth. "Yes."

Inácio shrugged. "Then I have done well for you. I put you in the way of business, and I accidentally, but happily, found your lost love. I think you should be thanking me, not barging in here, offering me insult."

I took a step closer.

Inácio held out his hand. "I have told my men to treat you kindly, but if they suspect you mean to do me harm, it will not go well for you. I am sorry I gave you wrong information. I never meant to. You can believe that or not."

Had I made a mistake? It had felt so much like a contrivance, but now I began to wonder. My anger so unbalanced me that I found it impossible to tell what was reasonable and what outrageous. For what possible reason would Inácio have lied? The man was a scoundrel and, apparently, an abuser of children, but our friendship surely appealed to the best part of him. Even if resentment had led him to lie to me about Gabriela, even if he had been motivated by pure spite, why would he have sent me to her husband?

"How can I know you are telling the truth?" I asked. I felt more in control, yet the idea that Inácio toyed with me buzzed within my ears like a mosquito.

"I cannot prove that I am," Inácio agreed. "There are many false stories that circulate in Lisbon. You need to decide if I deliberately chose to lie to you or merely passed along something I believed to be true. If you see only what you expect to see, you will miss what is before your eyes."

How had I let myself fall prey to my anger? It was the very reason I had come to Lisbon, and now here it was again, poisoning everything I touched as it had back in London.

"I'm terribly sorry," I mumbled, and turned to leave the room.

"Wait," Inácio said.

I paused and looked back.

Inácio stood with his hands by his sides, palms out. "I am not so blind that I can't see why you are angry. You loved her, and then you thought her dead, and then you find her married. Of course this is a terrible blow. I do not want you walking away from here thinking you have broken our friendship." Inácio grinned, and the scar on his face seemed to glow in the candlelight. "I have also, from time to time, let my passions rule."

I sighed. "Thank you, Inácio."

"This incident never happened, so it requires no forgiveness. But if you avoid me hereafter, that shall be another matter."

He held out his hand, and I shook it. I did not entirely trust him now, but I did not entirely mistrust him either. I did not know what to think. Both Inácio and Roberta had said I was a poor judge of people, and perhaps it was so. Perhaps it was even good. Maybe this uncertainty was the very state of equilibrium which I sought. I could not say I liked it entirely.

When I stepped inside my rooms at the Duke's Arms, I found the curtains drawn and several lamps burning, a pointless waste of oil, for it was not yet fully dark. I was about to call out to Enéas to scold him, but then I saw a man sitting in the dim light of the room, apparently waiting for me. I straightened my back. My muscles tensed, and my breath came slow and deep. Weapons, exits, advantages. I took it all in. And yes, the opportunity to strike at someone felt like a balm. Inácio was—perhaps—guilty of nothing, but the rage was still there, seeking an outlet.

The man sat at my writing desk, with his feet propped up, and a glass of my wine in his hand. One of the lamps rested but a few feet away, illuminating half his face, making his features twist and contort with the flames.

It was Azinheiro.

No doubt he expected groveling and obeisance. I should now genuflect, make certain his wine was sufficiently full. Perhaps he would like some bread and cheese. Might I call for some cold meat?

Let him menace another man if he wanted that. The only courtesy I would show him was forbearance from breaking his neck. "What are you doing here?"

Through the curtains, the last of the day's light began to dim. Yom Kippur, the Day of Atonement, would soon begin, and I stood talking to a priest of the Inquisition.

"I am told you took dinner this afternoon with the merchant Nobreza," said Azinheiro.

I said nothing, waiting to see if he knew about my detour to visit Inácio.

"Your meal was, I hope, productive for your business," the Inquisitor pressed.

"It was," I said. "And now I am eager to return to my work, which is why I rushed home."

I grabbed the bottle of wine off the writing desk and poured myself a glass. The sun had not set, so the Yom Kippur fast had not yet begun. I swallowed my drink and counted off all the reasons why I could not kill this man right now. Chief among these, of course, was that murdering an Inquisitor would interfere with my ability to help Charles Settwell. There were others too. I would become a wanted man, and fleeing the country would be difficult. It had all seemed so simple when I first conceived the notion: Get Azinheiro alone and kill him. Well, here we were, alone. A thrust of a blade or a twist of the neck. It hardly mattered. But then, what of poor Mariana? What of Gabriela? What of the man who had betrayed my father? That simple plan had built itself layers and complexities.

There was no helping it. There was nothing to do but drink more wine with a murdering Jesuit. I poured another glass for Azinheiro and handed it to him, wishing it were poisoned.

"I do not like you coming here uninvited," I told the priest. I did not know if it was dangerous to be so blunt or if it helped preserve my disguise, but I wasn't worrying about a little breach of decorum.

"I am sorry to displease, but there are matters that require my attention. You have me to thank for the invitation to Nobreza's home after all."

"It is true that your appearance at the *taberna* set these events in motion," I said, "but I cannot engage in trade if you wish to oversee my every movement."

"I have no interest in doing so," the priest said. "For now I am interested in making certain that you are dependable."

"What can I do to prove it?" I asked.

"Something rather simple," Azinheiro assured me. "You are going to help me discover evidence against Eusebio Nobreza."

I was so startled I took a step back. Perhaps striking now was not so terrible an idea after all. I needed to keep Azinheiro occupied and happy for the time being, but I would not betray another man, another New Christian, not to preserve my disguise or further my revenge. And I especially would not betray Eusebio, whose wife might well be caught in the ensuing vortex.

"Evidence of what?" I demanded. "I see no sign that Nobreza is guilty of anything."

Azinheiro appeared unaware of my tone. "You are to find evidence of Judaizing."

Rather than be tempted to hurl my glass at the priest, I set it down. "Nobreza is no Judaizer, I assure you."

"Because if he were, you would have noticed? Do not be naïve. These people are clever and secretive. They have had generations to learn to hide their rituals and satanic observances."

I shook my head. "I'll offer no assistance in this." And remembering to find a credible context for this position, I added, "I have spent *weeks* trying to find a New Christian who will extend me credit. I do not see why I should work to see ruined the very contact I have labored to cultivate."

"You will see the value if the arrest comes *after* he has lent you money but *before* you have repaid it," Azinheiro said with the mischievous grin of a man who has just outwitted his interlocutor. "You see, I will order things to your best advantage. That is one reason to do as I say. Another is because you have no choice if you wish to remain in Portugal. What should the Factory men think if they were to learn that you were secretly of the true church? You would have no future here. No present, perhaps."

This was what the Inquisition did. It knew how to corner men like beasts, to deprive them of options. Azinheiro had no idea who I was or what I intended, and yet he managed to outmaneuver me all the time. I could not betray Eusebio to protect my scheme, could I? For a moment I considered how convenient it would be for him to vanish into the Palace prisons, and for Gabriela to find herself without her unworthy husband. Maybe it would not be too difficult to arrange for her safety in my agreement with the priest. She was a beautiful woman, and Azinheiro would not question my motives.

And then I could set about murdering infants and pregnant women! Why not? Sink part of the way, then there's no point in resisting the urge to become a complete and irredeemable wretch. No, it was unworthy even to consider such things. I hated that the Inquisition's poison had even tempted me. Yet I could not help anyone by refusing to cooperate. For all my will to defy the Inquisition, I knew

Azinheiro could easily find someone else perfectly happy to advance his own career by destroying a New Christian. If he wanted Eusebio, then he would have him. Perhaps Gabriela would only face ruin and shame, but more likely she too would be charged and imprisoned. If she did not then betray enough of her friends, she would be subject to torture. I had no choice but to appear to cooperate with the Inquisitor until I could devise a more permanent solution to this problem.

"I don't care for it," I said.

The priest shrugged. "It is life in Lisbon."

Time, then. It was what I needed. I had to secure my deal with Eusebio, lure in the Carvers, steal their money, and get Settwell and his daughter free. I had to do all that before Pedro grew impatient. As of this moment, time was running out.

"I see I have no choice but to obey."

"Then you see clearly enough," the priest said. "Now, let us catch a Jew."

Chapter 17

It took a frustrating week of intermittent meetings with Rutherford Carver, who always had some other place he needed to be, but at last I was able to secure the details for the exchange. Roberta and I now went to great lengths to avoid each other, and when we were in the same room, we stood apart, trading furtive glances, but risking no more.

I would use my false claims of lands in England to provide a surety from Eusebio for two thousand pounds, an amount equal to what the Carvers themselves would provide. For this plan I did not actually need the money, simply the guarantee that it was to come so I could convince the Carvers to keep gold in their vault at the goldsmith's. I hoped that once their next shipment came in they would have more than just the two thousand, but the lesser sum would suffice. A man might live very easily upon that amount.

With a sense of grim satisfaction, I realized that after so many weeks I was prepared to bring my dealings with the Carvers, the Nobrezas, and Settwell to a close. Then all would be easy. I saw myself on a ship's deck, sailing from the Tagus to the open sea, my arm around Gabriela's waist. Where in this picture was her husband? Overboard, perhaps. Where, for that matter, were the agents of the Inquisition, who might find themselves perturbed when they discovered the death of one of their own? These were, I supposed, important details—but the thought of the sea air, the idea of Gabriela so close, tempted me to indulge in the fantasy. Reality would impose itself soon enough.

I turned these thoughts over and over, circling them endlessly until I grew angry with myself and then, as a consequence, everyone and everything else. I forced myself to do arithmetic problems and Latin declinations, but the moment my concentration wandered, I returned to Gabriela on the deck of that ship, and the wind and the sun and the fluttering fabric of her gown, and it would all begin again.

This had gone on for several days before Enéas began to notice. "The senhor is not himself," he observed, "and when a man is this distracted and sleeps this poorly, there can be but one explanation. The senhor is in love!"

We were walking to a meeting with the Carvers, and I answered only with a glower.

"It is the Senhora Carver, is it not?" Enéas said. "The fiery red hair, the creamy white skin. I have seen many men desire her, but *she* desires only you, senhor."

"Thank you for your opinion, Enéas," I said. "I am lucky to have an advisor such as you in these matters."

"And how could she not love you?" he cried. "A handsome man, and a courageous one! A man of action and one of principle! A man who rescued poor Enéas from a life of misery and want. That she loves you proves the worth of her mind, and yet you push her away. It is most curious. Perhaps it is not Senhora Carver, then. Perhaps it is—"

I set my hand down hard on the boy's shoulder. "It is not your concern. I would prefer not to speak of it."

Enéas nodded, and the grave look upon his dark features suggested he understood he had escaped something terrible. "I will be more careful to mind my tongue. I never wish to offend the senhor. I am grateful for all the senhor does."

"That is good," I said. "But I don't need expressions of gratitude. I need only loyalty—and, perhaps, some privacy."

"And you deserve such things. I will respect your wishes. Even so, I will say only that though I am young, I know much of love. A great deal of love. I am very much, in my own way, an oracle of love, and the senhor need only ask for advice, and I shall give it."

"You still appear to be talking."

Enéas studied me. "What is strange to me is not that you resist her beauty, for there are many beautiful women in the world. What is strange to me is that you resist her nature, for you and Senhora Carver are very much alike. Very well suited, I think. That is strange to me."

"What is strange to me is that you are still speaking of this," I said.

"And to me too!" Enéas agreed. "I cannot imagine why I don't stop. My loyalty prompts me to speak the truth even if the senhor does not wish to hear."

"I should very much like it if your intelligence would prompt you to be quiet before the senhor administers a beating."

"The senhor has not beat me in all these weeks. I think it unlikely he would begin now," Enéas said. He glanced at my face. "Though certainly not impossible."

Three hours later, I sat at my desk in my rooms, going through my correspondence. There was a damned lot of it for a man only pretending to engage in trade. I could not imagine how much there would be if I sought to make money in earnest.

I had shoved my papers aside in disgust when I heard the knock at the door. I knew it was the boy before I called for him to enter. Turning and sighing, I was about to warn him against offering any more advice, but then I saw Enéas's pale complexion, his trembling lips.

"What is it?"

"It is Senhor Franklin," Enéas said.

"Is he hurt?"

Enéas shook his head. "I saw him upon the street, senhor, speaking with the Jesuit, Father Pedro." On saying the Inquisitor's name, Enéas crossed himself.

"Go on."

"I could not hear what they said," the boy explained, "but the priest gave Senhor Franklin gold."

"You're certain?" I asked.

Enéas nodded.

I thanked the boy and sent him away. I returned to my desk and closed my eyes. So Franklin was an informant. I had liked him years before and now, though the man had become somewhat ridiculous, I liked him still. I knew that men did what they must to survive in Lisbon, but it was one thing to give the Inquisition information under duress, quite another to receive money for it.

Franklin knew who I was, but I'd not yet been arrested. That could only mean he'd taken money for promising to keep an eye upon me. Perhaps he might grow desperate later and pretend to have then discovered my true nature, but it seemed to me more likely he would continue to sell innocuous details of my comings and goings.

This changes nothing, I decided, though I was now determined to keep a careful eye on the innkeeper.

When I left my rooms that afternoon, I found Franklin waiting for me at the foot of the stairs. "Mr. Foxx, how go your ventures?"

"Very well, thank you," I said, making a point to meet the man's eyes and smile.

"I should very much like to discuss them with you," Franklin said, hurrying after me as I made my way to the door. "I know I don't appear to be much these days, but once I knew the Factory as well as any man."

"I should like that myself," I assured him, hardly slowing my pace.

"Just name the time, sir," Franklin said.

"I shall do so," I replied.

I headed out to the street, Enéas trailing behind me. I did not look back, but I felt certain the innkeeper watched after me until I was well out of sight.

I left Enéas outside the Three Speckled Hens and went in to meet with the Carvers. They were both there, and I was relieved not to be alone with Roberta. It unnerved me how she watched me, searching for signs that my eyes lingered on her. It troubled me not because I disliked it, but because I liked it rather too much. I sat with Rutherford between us, keeping my gaze on the plump man, wondering what she had told him to make certain he always acted as a buffer. Was I too bold in my advances? Was I untrustworthy? Was Rutherford willing to overlook my designs on his wife because he had designs on my money?

Roberta sat slightly apart from us, placing one hand over the other, and looking off into the distance. Meanwhile, Rutherford and I discussed matters of business for the better part of an hour. His chief area of interest seemed to be how I might secure my connections with Eusebio, though he continually distracted himself with tales of his own conquests among the New Christians. These stories were relevant, he assured me; if I paid attention I might hope to emulate his success. Rutherford appeared to believe, to the depths of his soul, in his own greatness, although he surely also recognized his wife's contributions.

After some time, Rutherford saw a pair of Factory men he wished to speak with and excused himself, promising he would return momentarily. It was the first time since the incident in the inn that Roberta and I found ourselves alone together.

Roberta looked at me, then lowered her face and turned away. When she looked back, she was blushing only a little, and smiling awkwardly. "I thought I was too old—and too married—for this kind of foolishness."

"I don't know that this is the best place to discuss this," I said quietly.

"Then where?" Her voice was quiet but harsh. "All those private conversations we have together? Where else can I speak of what I feel when you will not ever be alone with me?"

"Roberta—" I began, but she raised a hand for me to stop.

"You need not say it," she said, flicking her fingers upward in dismissal. "I don't blame you. I wish I had not made a fool of myself in your rooms. I understand that your interests are too closely bound up with ours for you to feel like you can reject me. You do not have to deceive me to do business with us. I wish only to know the truth. I want—I want to stop wondering. I want to stop lying awake at night, dwelling upon the same absurd things over and over again in an endless circle until I think I should go mad."

I admired her frankness—and felt a tug of pity—but it was too late to veer from my chosen course. "I have told you how I feel, and you have no cause to doubt me. Until you are ready to leave your husband, speak not of love. I cannot bear it."

"I love Rutherford. He is kind to me, and I do not wish to betray him. Not utterly. But he is not enough. Can you not understand that?"

"I can," I said. And I did. I, who had traveled across Europe and embroiled myself in a thousand mad schemes because I despised who I had become, understood this kind of existential dissatisfaction all too well. But what did she truly want from me? Passion? Redemp-

192 | DAVID LISS

tion? She claimed to love me, to want me to bring her something she was missing, but all the while she planned to steal my gold. I could hardly tell her lies from her truths.

"You will give me nothing?" she asked.

"I have told you how I feel," I said, keeping my voice steady.

"I cannot forgive you." She brushed some dirt off her glove. "I can forgive you for spurning me, but you should never have kissed me. I cannot forgive you that."

It was then that her husband returned. I remained for another quarter hour lest I seem conspicuous. Then I departed, making every effort to look like a man hurrying off, all the while wishing I could steal Roberta's money so I could stop pretending to be too in love with her to take her to my bed.

It was time to secure the loan. I wrote at once to Eusebio Nobreza, telling him that I had a business prospect. Eusebio wrote back and invited me to his home two days hence. It was not as soon as I would have liked, but there was no helping it. Furthermore, I told myself, if there had been a polite way to suggest another location, I would have done so. I did not want to go to that house and see Gabriela—and, simultaneously, I wanted to go most desperately.

I met Eusebio at his home at midday. There was no sign of Gabriela, and I felt many things, but chief among these were relief and despair. Nevertheless, the elder Nobreza was there, and I had come to take genuine pleasure in Luis's company. He accompanied me and Eusebio into the study, where we drank excellent Madeira and spoke of nothing significant until I forced the issue.

"Sir," I said, "I believe I may have found a prospect with a pair of English merchants called Carver."

"I know them," Eusebio said. "They are on firm ground. What do you require?"

I did not hesitate. "Two thousand, English."

Eusebio was silent for a long time. Would it hurry him along to let him know that I needed his money so I could kill the man who wanted to cast him in chains? Somehow, I thought it would not.

Then Eusebio appeared to end an internal debate. "Send me the details in writing," he said. "I shall look it over and, based on the reputation of the Carvers and your merits as a person of character, I shall secure your credit should the venture appear well conceived."

I smiled. All was in play. Now I wanted only for the Carvers to receive their funds from abroad and place their money in their vault.

"I am very pleased that we shall do business with this Englishman," said Luis, raising his goblet. "You are the most curious of men, Senhor Foxx. You are as polished as a courtesan and as blunt as a German. I have told my son that, in my opinion, you are a man whose honor we may depend upon."

I rose and bowed to both men. "You flatter me."

"I speak the truth," Luis said with an amiable smile.

"Do not think Mr. Foxx is not driven by greed, just like all the rest." Eusebio's mood appeared to have shifted quite suddenly. He cast me a sour expression. "You Englishmen exploit our wealth, the same as the Inquisition."

"We do not seek to exploit you," I said. "We work with you, sir. Is it not the English who aid New Christians in secreting wealth out of the country? Were it not for us, nothing of what you earn could be safe."

"In the main, that is true," Eusebio said, though the look upon his face suggested the admission was distasteful. "Forgive my dark mood, Mr. Foxx. This system is not of your devising. I know that. But I am trapped within it, waiting only for the hammer to fall and for everything I have, everyone I care about, to be taken from me."

"I cannot claim to understand what it is to live as you do," I said. "But know this: if I can serve you in any way, you need but ask."

Eusebio nodded. "You are kind to say it. Many Englishmen have sweet words, but few will put themselves at risk for one of my kind."

"Let us pray, sir, that you never have cause to put my words to the test."

I followed one of the servants to the door, but when I turned to leave, I realized Luis was behind me. "Forgive my son, Mr. Foxx. He is very bitter sometimes, and who can blame him? But I am glad the two of you have come to an understanding."

"The younger Senhor Nobreza honors me with his confidence," I said.

"He would be a fool if he didn't. You will join us for dinner tonight to celebrate?"

"I do not wish to impose upon your son or make work for his wife," I answered, perhaps too hastily. I could not sit down to a civil meal with Gabriela and pretend she was nothing to me. I had done it once, but I thought to do so again would break me.

"Then have dinner with me now. We shall go to a *taberna* together. You do business with the son, but does that mean you cannot be friends with the father?"

"Absolutely not," I said.

"Then you shall eat and drink upon my bill."

I followed the older man to the street and a nearby *taberna*, where we took a quiet table by the fire. Luis ordered a plate of roast pork. I called for chicken.

I winked at the older man. "Come, sir. You may be candid with me. Is the pork for show?"

"I cannot be candid with anyone, for anyone could be an agent of the Inquisition, even you, sir. My son or his wife could be in their service and I would not know. But I shall tell you truthfully, for there is no secret in it. We are not Jews. We have not been Jews for generations. There would be no New Christians if we were permitted to marry Old Christians. My parents and grandparents made a point of showing they were not Jews by eating pork, but for me and my children it is but one of the foods we eat, one we ate when we were children and which, perhaps, reminds us of better days. It is ironic, do you not think, that pork should be the meat most likely to produce nostalgia in one of my kind?"

"So you do think of yourself as a distinct people."

"We must do so. The laws of this nation keep us a people apart."

"And if you were to escape Lisbon with your wealth and live wherever you chose—how would you live then?"

"It is something I do not dare to dream of, and so I do not think on it."

"Has no one ever escaped?"

"Once we were permitted to move to the colonies, but no longer. As for other means of leaving the country, they are difficult. You mentioned Englishmen who take risks to help my kind. Do you know the merchant Charles Settwell?"

"I have met him," I said, measuring his response. "I know he is not well thought of by the Factory men."

"I should say nothing," Luis told me, "but I will tell you this much. He was a great merchant at one time, and he did not shy away from helping his New Christian friends."

"That is very admirable. But why should a man hesitate to do what is right? The Inquisition takes those whom it pleases. Evidence is but trumpery, after all."

"I suppose the trick is to keep them from wanting you. My son exports nearly all his money because the less he has here in Lisbon, the less attractive he is to the Inquisition."

"But why earn it if you send it away?" I asked. "Can it be retrieved?"

Luis shrugged.

"So there is a way," I said.

"Reimporting money is risky, but not so risky as leaving it here. You can ask Mr. Settwell about that." Luis examined his cup of wine, as though curious at its strange ability to loosen his lips.

"Has Mr. Settwell done such a thing?"

"No, not himself. But he saw its consequences on others."

I understood we were now talking about my father. "Tell me."

Luis shook his head. "Some things are better not spoken of by a New Christian."

Was this what had happened to my father? Had he brought money back into the country? Had some enemy discovered what he had done and betrayed him?

"Let us talk of other things, then. I do not wish to ask you to wade through the thicket of the forbidden." I finished my cup of wine and poured another for both myself and Luis. I then called for a second bottle. I had not been drunk since arriving in Lisbon, but I now began to feel the wine coursing through me. It would be good to drink too much. I was in no danger tonight, and surely if anyone deserved a little taste of oblivion, it was me. I also thought it would be good for Luis to drink too much—far too much, for then he would require assistance in getting home. The thought of seeing Gabriela was too alluring to deny. It would be enough to catch a glimpse of her. Just to look at her face and, perhaps, have her smile at me for showing a kindness to her husband's father.

I raised my cup to Luis. "To new friends."

We were well into our third bottle when I began to direct the conversation back toward subjects of particular interest to me. I spoke of my potential business opportunities with the Carvers and how certain the investment appeared. I gossiped briefly about Roberta's reputation, because doing so would amuse and disarm, and then I returned to the vexing problem of credit. "I am glad we are moving forward with our partnership," I said. "I only wish he had proved amenable even sooner."

"So do I. I had hoped as much from the beginning, but I do not attempt to alter his mind in matters of business," Luis said, stroking his long mustaches. "Not because I would not choose to offer assistance but because doing so would be counterproductive. If I told my son to lend, he would withhold, and if I told him to withhold, he would lend. He must do things his own way, and even if his own way is not best, I say nothing. Better he should learn those lessons now than later."

"I understand entirely. In truth, I hardly know what I will do if this venture succeeds. Profits come in gold, and while I know there are secrets to converting gold to negotiable notes without the customs agents or the Factory learning of it, I would have no idea where to begin."

"The Englishman has not been born who did not wish to conceal his business from the customs agents, but why should you wish to conceal your doings from the Factory?"

I shrugged. "Let us say that I don't wish to draw attention to myself too soon. A man can make enemies if he rises too quickly."

"Interesting," Luis said. "Most men are eager to draw as much attention to themselves as they can. But you are right that doing so can be a double-edged sword."

"I am as eager as any Englishman to make my name," I said, finishing the bottle and signaling for a fourth. I used the pause to concoct a plausible story. "I have a sister at home and she is in want of a dowry. I confess one of my hopes in coming here was to earn enough that I might send her the profits. I do not want it said of me, however, that I am weak and womanish because I put my family before trade."

"You are a good brother," Luis said.

"It is a love match. But the young man she favors is well born, and to inherit land and title. His parents will not consent without a sufficient dowry. He cannot defy them in this matter. I could attempt to smuggle the gold out of the country, but you know well there are risks."

Luis smiled as he poured a cup from the new bottle. "You must have this gold before you worry about the risks of possessing it."

"You are right in that, senhor. I am building castles in the air."

Luis drank and said nothing. I let the silence linger. Silence was often better than words.

Luis said, "We have methods." His voice was hardly above a whisper.

"I beg your pardon?"

"Methods of converting gold to paper. You know we dare not keep our money in the country, and exporting gold is, as you say, dangerous. There are mechanisms for making the exchange. There are bankers and goldsmiths here, a network of them, and they have served our people for many years. These are foreigners and noblemen and criminals. The less you know, the better, and I know little enough myself except how to work the network. I used to deal with their representatives directly. Indeed, when I was a young man, a good portion of my income came from acting as a gold discounter."

"Do you still have these contacts?"

Luis laughed. "None of us go anywhere except the prison or the grave."

"Then, if I were to find myself with gold, perhaps more gold than you might expect . . ." I let my voice trail off.

"We do not often aid outsiders," Luis said. "It would be frowned upon, but in this one instance, for the sake of your sister and your loyalty to her, I shall do what I can for you."

"It might be a large sum."

"The sum does not matter," Luis said with a dismissive wave. "Gold is gold."

I raised my cup. "You are a good man, senhor. I drink to you."

Luis saluted me in return.

"This ability to convert gold to notes," I said. "Can it be reversed? Can you convert notes to gold?"

"Why should you wish to do such a thing?"

"Not I," I assured him. "That would be of no use to an Englishman. I simply wondered about the story you mentioned before—the man who brought money back into Portugal. Surely it came in as paper, but once in the country, the foreign notes would have to be turned back to gold."

"That is it exactly," Luis said, having forgotten his earlier reluctance.

I was on the cusp of information I desperately desired, but I did not know if I should risk asking for more. I might frighten the older Nobreza. On the other hand, I might never be in a better position to learn the facts.

Fortunately, Luis required no further pushing. "It was a New Christian trader—one with excellent ties to the Factory. He dreamed of amassing enough wealth to bribe his way out of the country. He wanted to take his wife and his son along with his son's friend and her father." He paused as if to elaborate, but shook his head. "Wheels needed greasing, however, and the Factory is ever cautious."

The friend and her family. Gabriela. If my father's scheme had succeeded, we would all have escaped, as I'd known then.

"What happened to this man?" I asked.

Luis shook his head. "Too many people learned he had the money, and he was betrayed. One of his enemies turned him in to the Inquisition so he could seize the notes for himself."

"Who was it?" I asked. "Do you know?"

Luis snorted. "An Englishman, of course. Who else would do such a thing? But if you like ironies, I have one for you. This New Christian's ruin unleashed a wave of destruction. Many others fell, including the man who betrayed him. He was once quite rich, and now he runs a second-rate inn for Englishmen. Indeed, it is the very inn in which you stay."

I stared at Luis. "The betrayer was Kingsley Franklin?"

"It was indeed."

Two hours later, I stood on the stoop of Eusebio's house, pounding upon the door with my left fist while my right arm looped Luis's torso in an effort to keep my friend standing. He opened his eyes, looked at me, and burst out laughing. Then he closed his eyes again.

I was a little drunk, but my senses had been sharpened by Luis's revelation. Franklin had betrayed my father. This news had filled me first with confusion and then with rage. Franklin's taking money from the Inquisition now meant little. Turning against my father years before—that was unforgivable.

I had no idea what I should do with this information. Kill Franklin? I had come here to take justice upon an Inquisitor, not to go on a bloody rampage, slitting the throat of any man who had wronged my family. Yet I could not walk away from this either.

One of the Nobreza servants, an elderly woman with a displeasing, crumpled face, opened the door and ushered us inside. I led Luis to the parlor and set him in a chair. As I turned around, Eusebio and Gabriela entered the room.

I had to struggle to keep myself from staring at her. Her white gown clung enticingly to her body, exposing much of her shoulders, and her skin glistened in the dim light. I had tried to prepare for her beauty by reminding myself what she looked like and what effect she had upon me, but all that work was for nothing. Looking upon her face was like a blow, forceful and unexpected. Here was the woman I should have married. In another life, I might have escaped with her when we were young. We might have fled to some tolerant land. We would now have children together, perhaps many, and we would be living in contentment. In that life, I was a different person, a man untroubled by remorse or rage. I was gentle and kind and could love without reservation.

"What is this?" Eusebio demanded, interrupting my reverie. "He is an old man, and you took him out and got him drunk."

"He got himself drunk," I said. "I merely encouraged it."

"I thought better of you, Foxx."

I attempted to hold myself like a dignified man, though I suspected

I was making a poor show of it. My balance was not at its best. Given the right sort of incentive, inebriation could be shrugged off; I knew from experience that if an assailant were to attack, I could recover well enough. Conversation, however, was a bit more challenging.

"Good senhor," I attempted, "let us not make much of nothing. Your father is not a child. He and I enjoyed good food, drink, and conversation."

Eusebio shook his head. "I know that in your nation, consuming great quantities of drink is a sign of manhood, so I shall not hold this against you. Not this time. However, if you should abuse my hospitality again, I shall have to rethink our business arrangement."

I bowed low and long. I did not fall over. Triumph! "I have offended where I did not intend to, and the blunder was one of ignorance, not malice. I have much to learn of your country."

Eusebio appeared to be considering the merits of this apology. I, meanwhile, was considering slamming Eusebio's face into the wall.

"Get me a glass of wine," Luis cried from his near-sleep. "I am thirsty."

"Bring him water," Eusebio snapped at his wife. He took one last look at me and Luis, and then left the room.

I now found myself alone with Luis, who had slipped back into a stupor. I kneeled before him and began to remove the older man's boots. They came off fairly easily, which was something of a relief. I did not know if I was prepared for a complicated operation.

I knew I should leave. Now. Before Gabriela returned. Being alone with her was madness, and I was not in full control.

I stood cautiously, but before I could make my way out of the room, Gabriela entered with a crystal pitcher of water and a goblet upon a pewter platter.

"You are very kind to him," she said, setting the platter down near her sleeping father-in-law. "I know he enjoys your company."

"And I his," I said. I took a step back. The room, which had seemed well lit a moment ago, now appeared too dark for a man and a woman accompanied only by an unconscious old man. "I am sorry to have offended you tonight. I truly meant no harm."

Gabriela had poured water into the cup and was now bent over Luis, gently tipping it to his lips. I admired her shape under her gown, but I would not let my eyes linger.

"To my mind, it is good that Luis has a companion," she said. "Like many men his age, he longs to have someone to talk and listen to. But until you have concluded your business with my husband, you should not be *too* good a friend." She stood and looked at me. "Eusebio can be guarded about his position."

She shared confidences with me! More than that, what she told me was at the expense of her husband. This was almost as good as a kiss. "It is hard to live in the shadow of a successful father," I said. "Your husband wants to be his own man. I understand that."

"Was your father a great man?" she asked, still serving the water to Luis.

"Oh, yes," I answered.

Gabriela set down the goblet and studied me, as if trying to puzzle out some mystery, but then seemed to shake away the notion. "I am trusting in your honor, Mr. Foxx. I hope you will be good to my husband. Our luck has not been the best. There have been some missteps, and some debts, and we cannot withstand any more ill turns."

"I understand," I said, though I did not. Was she warning me off? She did not recognize me, but could it be she felt some ember of what had been between us?

"I want," I told her, "only that everyone should benefit."

Gabriela looked at her father-in-law, slumped in his chair, and now snoring quite loudly. Then she gazed about the room and seemed to notice, for the first time, that she was, for all practical purposes, alone with me in the gloom.

"I must go," I said.

"Good night, Mr. Foxx."

"Good night, senhora."

"Mr. Foxx."

Grateful for the excuse to look upon her once more, I turned around.

"This is much to ask and I know it is not your religion, but it would look good for us—make a good impression upon those who watch—if you would join us for church this Sunday. To entice an Englishman to come to mass with us would help my husband's standing. It would also protect us, at least a little. The Inquisition may be less likely to persecute New Christians who stand some chance of bringing Englishmen to the faith."

There were few things I desired less than to attend a Catholic mass, and I knew that my attendance would not impress Inquisition spies the way Gabriela believed it would. Nevertheless, she thought it would make her safer, so I could not refuse her. I did not want to disappoint her, and I did not want to miss an opportunity to see her again.

I bowed. "I would be honored."

She smiled. "I do not believe it will put you in additional danger or I would not have suggested it. If you wish, you may meet us there, outside the Igreja de São Domingos. It is upon the Rossio. Do you know it?"

It was the official church of the Inquisition itself, hard by the Palace. It was there that Jews, my ancestors and hers, had been made to kneel and submit to the Catholic faith. "I can find it."

"We shall see you there. Good night, then."

I turned away from her again.

The outing had been something of an experiment. It had been my intention to extract information and a promise from Luis, and I had encouraged the old man to drink to that purpose. Unfortunately, our excess had been so great there was a chance he would not remember his promise. But I had seen Gabriela. That had been one achievement.

I made no vows to myself. I resolved to do nothing and to refrain from nothing. I would do my duty and for the rest—well, I would see what my duty allowed.

Chapter 18

Word of newly arrived ships always circulated quickly among the English taverns, so the next morning I was hardly out of bed before learning the vessel upon which the Carvers' previous investment depended had safely returned. This, I knew, was the moment it would all come together. My line of credit was secure, which meant the Carvers would not only put gold in their vault but would keep it there pending the next major transaction—one in which they hoped to steal everything I had borrowed, ruining both me and Eusebio.

The time for waiting had come to an end. Settwell would have justice and liberty. Those who had stood against me and my family would face their punishment. As for Gabriela—my thoughts on that could wait. I had indulged in too much drink the night before. I was now master of myself, but my head felt slightly heavy and my thoughts sluggish. It was not the time for considering new courses of action.

I made every effort to hurry out of the inn, having

206 | DAVID LISS

Enéas dress me quickly and gather together my things, but when I reached the bottom of the stairs I found the massive form of Kingsley Franklin blocking my path.

"Mr. Foxx, I'd have a word with you."

I looked at the man who had betrayed my father. For years I had assumed that if anyone had given my father's name to the Inquisition it had been out of necessity. I would not blame a man for attempting to survive. Those were the rules of the game. But here was the person whose actions had led to my father's death, and he had done it out of greed, not pain or fear or desperation.

"I am very busy, sir," I told Franklin.

"You are not too busy for this conversation."

"You will find that I am," I answered, pushing past the large man.

Franklin grabbed my arm. I spun toward him, and the innkeeper took a step back, alarmed like a man who has just stepped upon a snake. He raised his hands to show he meant no harm. "Mr. Foxx, if I have given some offense, then I beg your forgiveness."

Putting Franklin on his guard would do me no good, and so I forced myself to smile. "Of course not, sir. I'm merely in a hurry. But we shall resolve things soon enough, I promise you."

I breakfasted with Settwell, who expressed pleasure at the news that all the pieces were in place. After we ate, Settwell brought Mariana down to say hello, and I spent the better part of an hour with the girl, reading poetry to her and then discussing the verse.

"Father does not often have guests," she told me. "You must be special."

"I am not special," I said. "I am, however, an old friend. I have known your father for many years."

She nodded. "You are both very old."

"Your father is much older," I said, laughing. "I am still quite young."

She studied me for a moment. "Will you be too old to marry me when I am grown up?"

"By no means. I shall happily wait."

"Then I accept your proposal," the girl told me with delight. "You shall marry me, and we shall escape Lisbon."

"Mariana!" Settwell cried out. He had been across the room, reviewing a newspaper, but now he stormed toward the girl, his hand raised.

It was an awkward business to interfere with a parent's discipline, but I blocked Settwell's approach with my body. "Did the girl say something wrong?" I knew well what her mistake had been, but I wanted Settwell's temper to cool.

"I am sorry, Father," Mariana said. She walked around me and presented herself meekly. "I forgot myself while speaking to Mr. Foxx. I know better."

Settwell had recovered himself. He knelt before the child and embraced her. "You *do* know better," he told her. "I am sorry to have frightened you, but you *should* be frightened. If the wrong person were to hear you say such a thing, he would take you away from me forever. Do you understand? You and I would never see each other again."

She clung to him more tightly now. "I forgot myself because Mr. Foxx is so kind, and because you had him in our home."

Settwell rose, taking the child with him. He set her down in a chair. "I do trust him, but that does not matter. You must be on your guard at all times. You must never say naughty things, even with people who will cause no trouble."

She nodded and hugged her father again.

Settwell walked over to me. "I am a freeborn Englishman. You cannot know how I hate telling my own child she may not express her thoughts."

"I understand you," I said.

"I know you do. For the love of God, Mr. Foxx, you must get me the money I need to escape this wretched country before I lose my daughter."

To that end, I met with the Carvers that afternoon at the Three Speckled Hens. I shook Rutherford's hand and bowed to Roberta, and then took a seat after calling for coffee.

"I have great news," I said, pretending to be ignorant of their own.

"You must be quick to beat the winds of rumor in this city," said Rutherford with jollity. "It is said that the Jew Nobreza has finally extended you a line of credit."

I grinned like a boy given a prize. "He has indeed. I find I am ready to commence my career as a Factory man."

"You'll not become a Factory man so easily as that," Rutherford said. "It will take years of dedication and canny choices before you are admitted."

"But it is a start," Roberta said, looking about the room—not looking at me. "We must encourage the young man."

Rutherford slapped the table. "We must indeed. And I do. I do encourage him. Are you encouraged, Mr. Foxx?"

"I believe I am, sir."

"And Eusebio Nobreza, no less. That man could teach a whole tribe of Hebrews to pinch their pennies. Teach them by example, I tell you. However did you win over the miser?"

I allowed myself to color slightly as I shrugged. "I was not aware that he was any less agreeable than any other man. I merely presented my case to him. He knows I can support his advance with funds at home, and even these Portuguese understand the value of English rents. I admit, I did strike up a friendship with his father, whom I find to be very agreeable."

"Old Nobreza!" Rutherford cried out. "That scoundrel. Ha-ha! In his youth, they say, he rutted half the Jew bitches in Lisbon. Get at the son through his reprobate father. Clever, sir. Clever."

"I admit I was not attempting to be clever. Merely to be agreeable."

"You may confess your secrets to me, sir," Rutherford said with another slap on the table, "but tell no one else. If anyone inquires, you cleverly sought out a weakness and you exploited it. That, sir, is how you become a Factory man. Is that not right, Roberta?"

"It is never ill advised to be clever," she said, twirling a strand of her red hair and gazing at nothing in particular.

"No, it is not. I trust you will listen to my wife, sir. She knows what's what."

"I believe you," I said.

"Then shall we do business?" Rutherford asked.

"By all means. I shall apply the line of credit to your transaction when you give the word."

"I have good news. Our ship from Brazil has returned, and once our goods clear customs and we can convert our holdings, there will be fifteen thousand in gold in our vault. Of course much of that will go into other ventures. Nobreza will wish to hold on to his money until the last minute, so when we are ready, I will let you know. Then we may proceed."

So there it was. And fifteen thousand, too. Settwell could not complain about so great a sum. It tripled what he had originally asked for. A man might never want with so much.

I looked at Roberta. Her eyes, cold and blue, lingered on mine for a moment and then flicked away. She but awaited the opportunity to steal my money, and I the opportunity to steal hers.

It was a strange thing. She had deceived my friend, a man to whom I owed an immense debt. The Carvers' crime against Settwell had been unforgivable. It was not a slightly unscrupulous take on usual trade—it was theft, pure and simple. What I intended was, of course, much the same, but my scheme had the virtue of being retaliatory.

For all that, I felt remorse at what I would have to do. I had known many thieves upon the London streets. Some stole out of desperation, and some because it was all they knew. Some stole for the pure joy of taking what belonged to another. Was Roberta one such as that? I had seen her at her most unguarded moments, and I did not think that she was. Roberta Carver was alive and vital and daring and certainly dangerous, but she did not seem cruel. Still, people grow accustomed to their own actions. Thieves never dwell upon the harm done to those they steal from. Even murderers grow numb to their crimes. Was that what had happened to Roberta?

I could not know, but I was determined that no amount of speculation would interfere with what I had to do for my friend's sake.

She was waiting for me in my rooms when I returned to the Duke's Arms. She had given Enéas a few coins to vanish, and had amused herself in my absence by drinking my wine and—I was certain—going through my things. I had been raised in Lisbon, and so I expected as a matter of course for my possessions to be searched. I left nothing I wished hidden where it could be found.

"I've so wanted to see you," Roberta said when I entered the room. "You will not send me away?"

She stood by the window, the yellow sunlight illuminating her blazing hair and nearly penetrating the very pale blue of her gown. Her blue eyes sparkled as she watched me, and I knew she had been crying.

I led her to sit across from me in one of the rigid and unforgiving chairs. "Roberta, please don't do this. It is unendurable."

She looked away. "I cannot leave him, Sebastian. I cannot do that to him. He would be lost without me, and he has done me no harm. It would be cruel."

"But to betray him with another man would not be cruel?"

"Not if he never learned of it," she said with the slightest of smiles.

I kissed her. How did it happen? I hadn't intended it, and her words about my cruelty had stung, but there we were, kissing. Then she stood, and her arms were around me, running down my back, and I pressed against her. I put a hand on her breast and felt her hard nipple. She gasped and her warm breath was on my face, and I nearly lost myself in the sound of her breathing, deep and urgent.

Somehow I pulled away. "Roberta," I began, but could say no more.

"What kind of a man are you that you would refuse the advances of a woman you desire?" Her voice was throaty.

"A miserable man," I answered, and for once I told her the absolute truth.

"There was nothing false in your kiss," she said. "You do want me."

I did not trust myself to speak.

"I do not know what I shall do." She looked away.

I took her hands. "My lovely Roberta, do nothing. I wish I had not made you unhappy by asking of you what I must have but you cannot give. I cannot change my own nature, and even less yours, but I can give us a respite. Let us speak of this no more until our business is complete. I shall think on my resolutions and you on yours. When we have completed our affairs, we will see if either of us has a new way out of this impasse."

"A truce in love?" she asked, smiling again.

I nodded. "Yes. A truce."

She put a hand to my face. "My dear God, I do love you, Sebastian Foxx. I wish I did not, but I do. I will not torture you, but tell me you love me. If I am to be kept apart from you, I must hear it. Tell me you love me."

"I love you, Roberta, with all my heart." The lie came out more easily than I would have anticipated.

* * *

Three days later I received a note from her husband. Their goods had cleared customs. Their gold would be in the vault in two days at the most. It was time for me to let my Jew know I needed the money.

I sat down as I read. Now I would take Roberta's wealth, and I hoped that I would not destroy her.

Chapter 19

The next day was Sunday, and I met the Nobrezas outside the Igreja de São Domingos as agreed. It was an old church, its construction having begun in the thirteenth century, but it had only been completed after I had left Lisbon, and its style reflected more of the previous century than the Gothic style. The façade was white and unadorned, but its lines were baroque and pleasing to the eye. Its loveliness belied the fact that it had witnessed the deaths and forced conversion of thousands of Jews.

I felt a wave of uneasiness wash over me. I did not wish to be inside a church, let alone the church of the Inquisition. Yet it was not the crimes of the building that troubled me—it was how familiar it all felt. I had never before been in this church, but I had worshipped in others much like it. I knew the liturgy, all the things I was supposed to do and say, though, of course, I could not reveal as much. I had spent the first half of my life participating in a religion that was not mine, one that would not accept me. I had done it for thirteen years, and my father and my grandfathers and their fathers had done it for their lifetimes. Going inside felt like a capitulation, but I would do it because the web of lies I had created demanded it of me—and because Gabriela had asked me to.

Both Luis and Eusebio shook hands with me outside the church. They were eager to show off their English friend, and I was determined to give them a good show. I would act befuddled and fascinated. I would ask questions and make polite remarks. I knew the role I was to play and I would play it. Behind the two men, Gabriela nodded at me, but she said not a word. I removed my hat and bowed.

As we walked in, Eusebio stood next to me with Gabriela and Luis behind us. "I understand," Eusebio said, "that it was my wife who asked you to come with us."

"She did," I agreed. "And I saw no reason to refuse. It is a small thing for me. I sense it is a greater thing for you."

"The English are proud," Eusebio said. "They do not like to be seen showing any more respect for the true faith than they must. For a man like you to come to a foreign church when you do not even speak our language—I know it cannot be easy."

"I am not overly nice in matters of religion. And as I have come to Lisbon to make money, I do not see why I must stand upon ceremony in matters of so little import."

"The Factory men may not like that you come," Eusebio said. "This may cost you in their esteem. Efforts to conform to our ways are not condoned."

I hardly cared, as I had no intention of dealing with Factory men for long. "I am here to be my own man, not to bow to the Factory," I blustered.

Once inside, Eusebio led me to their pew, and I took my seat. I felt a kind of numbness wash over me. The candles, stained glass windows, statues, singing of the choir, cool of the stone—they all brought me back to my boyhood. The air was thick with incense and the odor of unwashed bodies. I could imagine standing in a church not unlike this one, holding my father's or my mother's hand, feeling protected and loved, if unaware of the danger all round us.

I settled into the service. Gabriela sat on the opposite side of Eusebio, and so was difficult to see, which was for the best. Occasionally Luis would whisper a word of explanation or clarification, but otherwise all proceeded much as I expected. Of course I did not take the communion wafer, but as I was dressed as an Englishman, that surprised no one. I began to think my time in the church would pass without event.

Then, as the priest rose to deliver his sermon, he nodded toward another priest in the audience. I recognized him instantly. The dark robes. The handsome face and slightly graying hair. It was Pedro Azinheiro, gazing out at the worshippers with his mouth puckered into something like a smile. I had the distinct impression I was precisely where the Jesuit wanted me.

I tapped Luis and gestured with nothing more than a tilt of my head. "It is the Inquisitor from the *taberna*. Strange he should be here."

"Not so very strange," Luis said. "This is his church. Indeed, he is the one who suggested that it would be a useful thing for us to invite an Englishman to join us."

I nodded as though this answer satisfied me, but I felt the bristling of the hair on the back of my neck. Something very dark was coming together. It was the way I felt when violence brewed on the streets in London. A man would fall in behind me and another would look across the street and I would know it was about to begin. Every shaft of light and flickering candle caught my attention. I noticed every cough and rustle of clothes. There was nothing to do but wait for Azinheiro to make his move.

It did not take long. I soon understood the nod between the two priests. The sermon was upon a subject clearly chosen by Azinheiro.

"For centuries now, this country has fought a tireless war against the nefarious influence of Jews," the priest began. "Though we have offered these interlopers every opportunity to embrace the true church, still they plot against us, against our faith, and against our souls. They remain in our midst, willfully resistant to the blessings of our Savior."

All around us, parishioners leaned forward to look at the New Christians in their midst. The presence of an Englishman made the Nobrezas a particular target. Some people were subtle, but others began to stare in open hostility. As the priest droned on about the Jews killing Christ, poisoning wells, spreading plague, and murdering Christian children, the mood in the church became increasingly restless. A woman sitting directly behind me hissed. When I turned to look at her, her gaunt, pockmarked face blanched in horror and she crossed herself.

"The Jew made the evil eye at me!" she whispered to her husband.

"I think it is time to leave," I said quietly to Eusebio.

He shook his head. "If we leave, we will look guilty."

"Of what?"

"Of being Jews," he snapped back.

"If you don't leave, these people will be whipped into a mob against you."

He looked straight ahead and set his jaw. "That is a chance we must take."

"The devil take your chance," I said, now growing angry at Eusebio's stubbornness. "Your first duty is to protect your wife."

The same woman who had hissed at me now cried out, "The Jews are uttering curses! Spells. I heard them speak in English, calling upon the devil."

There was general murmuring in the crowd. So many people were whispering and rustling upon their benches that it was difficult to hear the priest, who was speaking with great energy on the subject of circumcision.

The woman behind me jumped up. "Something bit me! The Jews called upon the devil to send a creature to bite me."

I stood up and faced her. "That would be rather indirect, would it not?" I asked her in Portuguese. "If I wanted you bit, I would do it myself and circumvent the intermediaries. Though now that I look upon you, I think it would indeed be preferable to conjure a devil for the task."

I knew well that the best way to defuse the anger of a crowd was to replace their rage with amusement. I would willingly play the clown if it would soothe the mob.

"My friends," I cried out. "Do not think I wielded the power of the devil to transform this woman's face into the likeness of a rat. It is how I found her!"

Our accuser was now crimson with rage. Her husband, also red-faced, stood and jabbed a finger at me. "You owe my wife an apology!"

"If you married her," I rejoined, "you owe an apology to yourself."

The congregation was howling with laughter. I knew I was far from securing a victory, however. I had to find a way to transition from chaos to order. I waved to attract the crowd's attention. When they at last settled down, I said, "Let us be calm. I believe the good priest was trying to tell us something. I beg you continue, Father. I have quieted the disruptions."

I held out a hand as though inviting the priest to resume speaking. His face was almost as red as that of the woman I had insulted. I had manipulated the crowd so that resuming the sermon would incite laughter. The priest would have no choice but to move quickly toward ending his sermon with, perhaps, an unremarkable passage of the Bible.

The priest cleared his throat and began to flip through his Bible, setting aside his prepared remarks. Then I noticed Azinheiro toward the front of the church, whispering to a young man who sat next to him.

The priest was just readying himself to speak when the young man leapt to his feet and pointed upward. "Look! Our Savior weeps! He weeps at the sight of Jews in his presence!"

I glanced where he pointed and saw a stained glass window depicting Jesus on the cross. A dark tear of liquid trailed down the figure's cheek. I looked up and saw an accumulation of water on one of the rafters above the window. A slow but steady trickle of water had been falling from the rafter, making its way down the wall, and pooling in the vicinity of the crown of thorns.

The Portuguese were a superstitious people, and a weeping Jesus could prove a very dangerous thing. Had Azinheiro arranged for the dripping water or merely noticed it previously and kept the fact in reserve? It hardly mattered. Quickly, over the bubbling excitement of the congregation, I said, "It is but dripping water."

I knew at once that I had made a mistake.

"The foreigner denies the miracle!" one man cried out.

"He will not believe in the tears of our Lord!" another called.

Throughout the church, people glared at the Nobrezas, shouted at them, pushed against one another to get closer. I could feel the violence brewing in the air, like the moments before a rain fell. It was coming, and nothing could stop it now. The only option was to run for shelter.

"We dare not stay!" I cried to Eusebio.

This time, to my relief, Eusebio agreed. He took Gabriela by the hand and kept behind Luis, himself directly behind me. I pushed as gently as I could through the angry congregants who were now in the aisles, hurling insults. For now it was nothing worse than words, but I knew it would be a near thing to escape even once we were outside the church. If the rumor spread quickly enough, a crowd could materialize almost out of nowhere, and we might be overwhelmed by numbers. No amount of physical strength could protect us if fifty assailants came for us at once.

At last we reached the doors. A few men tried to block our passage, but I shouldered through. From the corner of my eye, I saw one of the men I had just shoved aside place a hand upon Gabriela's breast. He turned to his friend to say something, a leering expression upon his face. I lashed out. I grabbed the man by the wrist and, using my other hand, bent it back quickly and brutally. The bone gave a satisfying snap, and the man cried out in pain.

Gabriela looked on in amazement, but Eusebio had already moved ahead. I did not wait to see if the man's friends wished to challenge me. I herded the Nobreza clan out.

No one on the square was yet aware of the mayhem in the church. I believed I might be able to usher the Nobrezas quietly back to their home. In the absence of scapegoats, the anger of the crowd would soon abate.

Then the crowd began to emerge. They were led by the upset husband. He pointed a finger at me and, so everyone upon the street might hear him, yelled, "They are Jews, and they deny a miracle."

Gabriela turned suddenly. "What do you want from us?" she cried. "Have we ever hurt you? No, but the minute someone whispers poison in your ear, you lust for our blood. *You* are the devils."

I looked at her, regal and proud and angry. What she said was as true as it was foolish. I admired her courage, but as my goal was to get her away from these people alive, I wished she would keep her bravery to herself.

The man's wife put her hands to her ears. "She curses me!" she screamed. "She has sent devils into my mind!"

I turned to Luis, whom I trusted more than Eusebio. "I am going to create a distraction. Use the opportunity to get your family home."

Luis nodded. He did not question or offer protest. He was a New Christian of Lisbon, and he knew that it would be madness to refuse an opportunity when one was offered.

I strode toward the man who made the accusation and said, "I am an Englishman, and I do business with the Factory. Who dares accuse me of being a Jew?"

"Then you admit you are an unbeliever!" the man crowed in triumph.

"Yes, but a Protestant one." I risked a peek quickly behind me and saw the Nobreza clan making a safe escape.

"And you keep company with Jews," the man began, beginning to raise his hand to point again.

I had heard enough. I lunged forward and delivered a blow to the man's stomach. He was gaunt, and there was almost nothing between his belly and his spine. I felt my fist connect with something hard. The man yelped and doubled over. His wife shrieked. The crowd began to surround me now, and I suspected further fighting would go hard for me. There were dozens of them, moving closer, angry and wide-eyed with religious frenzy. In all likelihood, none of them would be particularly skillful fighters, but numbers would more than compensate. I could see how it would be. They would drag me down, and I would be immobilized, possibly killed, as they trampled and kicked me.

I was ready. I had saved Gabriela. Maybe this was for the best. Maybe it was the best thing that could happen to me. I had forgotten about Settwell and his daughter; I only felt tired, weary of my quest for revenge and the endless tasks that sprouted from it like hydra heads. I was tired of lying to everyone, to Roberta Carver most of all. I wanted it to be finished.

Then I saw a familiar face emerge from the crowd. Pedro Azinheiro approached, smiling smugly. He pointed at me. "Back away, my friends," he said. "That man is to be taken to the Palace of the Inquisition. He is under arrest."

Chapter 20

I did not resist. My moment of surrender had passed, and I realized that being arrested was likely the best thing that might happen to me under these circumstances. The fact that it was Azinheiro who arrested me almost certainly meant I was safe. If the priest wanted to harm me, he surely could have done so without going to all this trouble. The question, then, was what the Inquisitor intended.

I was flanked by a soldier on either side, and Azinheiro walked before us. These were not unreasonable odds by any means. I considered killing all three of them and making my escape, but, as always, that would mean failure elsewhere.

I wondered what would happen when we reached the Palace. I had vowed I would not be brought inside, that I would kill and be killed first. Could I enter willingly now, hoping that I might eventually be released?

The breaking point would be chains, I decided. If they attempted to constrain me, I would fight. My greatest advantage would be surprise. I offered no resistance now, and perhaps if I caught enough of them unprepared, I could make my way out.

I remained silent as Azinheiro led me the brief distance along the Rossio to the Palace. We passed through the doorway of the great building, and through an open courtyard. Azinheiro brought me down a set of narrow stairs, and then down another. Finally I found myself in a large basement room, at the center of which was a rectangular table, scratched and covered in wax and ink stains, with chairs alongside. Sconces lined the wall, but only a few were lit, and the room was full of flickering shadows. It smelled of old smoke and sweat and rat droppings.

With a sweep of his arm, Azinheiro invited me to sit, which was very polite. Good manners are important before torture.

"You created quite a stir in that church," Azinheiro said. His eyes were wide and bright, and his face seemed to glow. This was pure pleasure for him. He lived for moments such as these and, I vowed, he would die because of them.

"Certainly one of us did," I answered.

I was in the Palace. I was even possibly in the very room to which my father had been brought, where he spent too many moments of his last weeks on earth. None of it mattered. The building did not matter, and the man did not matter. This was only a place, the Inquisitor only an enemy; I had been in worse places and defeated worthier opponents.

Azinheiro made a clucking noise. "You are forgetting your place, Mr. Foxx."

"What is this about?" I demanded, pretending to the arrogance of a freeborn Englishman. I imagined the liberties that were my birthright formed a sort of armor, strong enough to protect me from whips and pincers and red-hot irons! "You ask me to gather information on the Nobrezas, and then you nearly have them murdered in a riot of your own creation. Had I not been there—" I stopped talking.

Azinheiro smiled. "You are not so clever as you think, but not so dull as I feared."

"You wanted me to intervene on their behalf. You wanted me to save them so they would better trust me."

Azinheiro shrugged and said, "You've proven your willingness to assert yourself before. I was very impressed at the *taberna*."

"What if I had not done so?" I demanded. "What if I had been too frightened and ran away? What if I had been hurt or killed?"

"Those things did not happen," Azinheiro said.

So it had been a calculated risk. Perhaps I would have failed and the Nobrezas been killed, dragged down and torn apart by an angry mob. Perhaps I would have been killed as well. That would have proved a loss, but not a catastrophic one. The game goes on and on. There is nothing to be won—the goal is to continue playing.

"Now," Azinheiro said, "Eusebio will be in your debt. I have driven him into your arms. He will confide his secrets to you, and he will lend you money. With your aid—and with his confessions—he will soon enough be in a position that he cannot ask you to repay it. His property shall become the Inquisition's, and I give you my word you will not be asked to return the sum. You shall advance, and your creditor shall vanish. This arrangement will work very well, over and over, I should think, until your place in the Factory is secure. And then we shall discuss the menace of Protestant heresy."

The priest was cunning. His plan would almost certainly have worked had I been what I pretended. But I wasn't, and none of those clever machinations would do much good when I stuck a blade in his throat.

Azinheiro growled irritably at my silence. "You have no answer?"

"It is not just to deceive a man," I said. "It is not Christlike."

"I shall worry about what is Christlike," Azinheiro said. "You worry about your choices, for they are stark. You may either grow rich and powerful, or you may become an enemy of this Church. I suggest you bring me something useful soon, Mr. Foxx. I would hate to suspect you of having come under their Judaizing spell."

"That is why you've brought me here," I said. "You want to threaten me."

"I want to show you what will be your fate should you succumb to the enemy," Azinheiro clarified. "Let us visit the dungeons."

"I do not wish to go," I told him. I find it is good, every now and again, to say something honest, even in the most dissembling of relationships.

"I am not inviting you. I am telling you," Azinheiro answered.

"No." I placed my hands upon the table. "This little game of yours has gone on long enough. I am an Englishman, sir, and I shall not be treated this way."

Azinheiro stood. "You may either go into the dungeons upon your own volition or carried by soldiers, but go you shall. Other Englishmen have doubted the resolve of the Inquisition, and they spent more time within these walls than they would have believed possible."

I doubted that he would imprison me simply for defying him. Azinheiro orchestrated torment and death and useless confessions, but he was not, I believed, cruel for the pure pleasure of it. No, here was a man who liked to watch the wheels turn and the gears grind. And I was the Jesuit's bait, not his fish. He would not squander what I had to offer simply to prove he could.

"I refuse," I said. "Throw me in irons if you like."

The priest smiled. "You are very clever, sir. You know I value you too much for that. You are only of use to me if you are free. Mariana Settwell, however, is another matter. She could quite easily be taken away from her father. Yes, I know about your friendship with that drunk. I know everything that happens in this city. Everything, sir. So now I give you another choice—a real choice. You may follow me or you may walk out of this Palace right now, but if you do the latter, your friend will never see his daughter again."

I cursed myself and I cursed Azinheiro and I cursed myself again. The Inquisition had been eyeing Mariana since before I had returned to Lisbon—Settwell had told me as much—yet my actions had placed the child in greater danger. My plans were slipping away from me. Innocent people were being caught in the swirling vortex of vengeance. The things I touched were withering. If only I had just killed the priest and fled when I first arrived, none of this would have happened. I had become too bold, too ambitious, and I now had to extricate myself from all of these tangles without further hurting Settwell or his daughter or the Nobrezas.

My body shook with rage as I rose from my seat.

Wordlessly, I followed Azinheiro down a series of corridors and another dark stairway. This one was guarded by a single soldier, who recognized Azinheiro and immediately proceeded to unlock a heavy wooden door. I yearned to reach out now, to snap the priest's neck, but I controlled myself. Soon, I promised myself. I needed only to pass his test and get free. It would be but a matter of days.

The door opened, and the stink of excrement and rotting food assaulted me. Azinheiro did not seem to notice and, with a thin-lipped smile, gestured for me to step inside.

The floor here was dirt, and the gloom was broken only by the occasional low-burning torch upon a sconce. A space perhaps the length of three men separated two walls of cages, most of which were unoccupied. Three of them, however, held men who sat alone upon wooden benches that served as beds, staring at us with the wide-eyed expression of broken animals. I forced myself to look, to understand that this was what my father had endured. In one cage sat a familiar-looking man, head down, eyes red-rimmed and hollow. It was the pastry-seller. He'd lost a great deal of weight, and his head wobbled on his neck.

In one of the cells, a man rose and limped forward. He was dark-skinned, clearly a Moor, and his beard hung long and tangled. Even in the dim light, I could see his hands were covered with cuts and clots of dried blood.

"What is that man guilty of?" I asked.

Azinheiro shrugged. "Heresy. He failed to condemn his neighbor for possessing a copy of the Mohammedan holy book, though he knew the book to be there."

Unwelcome as this all was, I would not waste a glimpse into the fortress of my enemy. I noted the apparent strength of the cells, the kinds of locks used, the number of guards stationed within. If he would make me look, then I would let nothing be lost.

"I have seen enough," I told Azinheiro.

"But we have only yet begun our tour," Azinheiro answered. He led me along to the far end of the chamber. There another guard stood before a door, and this led to a similar room but smaller and with half as many cells. All of these were empty save one, which held a frail old woman curled upon on the earthen floor. She breathed loudly and in pained rasps.

"What is her crime?" I demanded.

"Heresy, I suppose," Azinheiro said. "She is not one of mine and I forget the details."

"It is obvious she is ill," I said. "This is no place for an ailing old woman. Have you no doctors to see to her?"

"It is her soul that is in danger," Azinheiro answered. "Her body is of no consequence."

From there Azinheiro led me out the far door and up another set of stairs. This brought us to a hallway, at the end of which was a large chamber that smelled strongly of urine. Here were three tables with leather straps affixed to them. Chains hung from the wall, and in the corner stood a hellish contraption with a long pole arm, from which dangled straps of leather.

"If the Portuguese applied the same ingenuity to engines of commerce as they do to those of torture, perhaps you would not be dependent upon foreigners to keep food upon your tables."

Azinheiro shook his head. "I don't think you sufficiently understand the point of this tour."

"I understand everything," I said. "You wish me to see what will happen to me should I fail to cooperate."

"Perhaps you do understand. Your secret protects you, but only so much. Your Englishness protects you not at all. I would have every Englishman in Lisbon in these dungeons if I had the power."

I turned away. "I see I have no choice but to act as you tell me."

"None. You have two weeks to bring me actionable information about Eusebio Nobreza. Otherwise, you will understand the reach of the Inquisition far better than you would like."

From the Rossio, I walked directly up toward the Bario Alto. At the Nobreza house, I was shown in at once, and Luis met me in the hall. He took both of my hands in his own and breathed a sigh of relief. Then he embraced me. His tears pressed against my cheek.

"I'd heard you were arrested," Luis said, once he let go. "We feared the worst."

"I was taken to the Palace, but nothing more passed. It is perhaps more desirable to frighten an Englishman than it is to take action against him."

Eusebio and Gabriela now appeared, and together we all walked into the parlor. Gabriela began at once to pour glasses of Madeira, but all the while she kept her eyes upon me. I tried not to meet her gaze.

"You saved us today," Luis said. "That crowd would have torn us apart had you not come to our aid."

"He nearly set that crowd upon us," Eusebio groused, "with that foolish comment denying the miracle."

228 | DAVID LISS

I could not deny the truth of the accusation. "That was a mistake. I sensed a crisis and spoke before thinking. I apologize for it."

Eusebio sighed. "No, you must forgive me. Whatever mistakes you made, you had a clear head and a strong determination. I am in your debt."

I bowed. "I did what I thought best. It is easy for me, as a foreigner, to take risks you never could. I depended upon my nationality to protect me."

"Your Englishness may not be the shield you imagine," Luis said. "I beg you to be careful for your own sake. You may not be so fortunate next time."

"I would be curious to know how you were so fortunate this time," Eusebio said. "Why did they not detain you further?"

"I believe they determined there was nothing for them in holding me," I answered. "It is true they will arrest Englishmen, but only when there is good reason. I am new to this country, with few connections and little wealth available for confiscation. To keep me in the Palace would be to anger the Factory and gain nothing in exchange."

Eusebio studied me for a moment, but said nothing. He was clever enough to recognize that even if the Inquisition saw no profit in imprisoning me, it would certainly never neglect an opportunity to exploit a vulnerable Englishman.

I lowered my gaze. "They asked me to report questionable activities on all New Christians," I admitted. "Naturally, I agreed, but I shall tell them nothing. I shall always say—truthfully—that I see nothing of the sort."

"Hmm," Luis said. "This could work to our advantage. If they have a friendly agent watching us, one who will never speak ill of us, then are we not safer than if we did not know the identity of the person who might report us?"

"I don't know," Eusebio said. "If we do business with him, the Inquisition will inevitably turn its gaze upon us."

"And if we back out now," said Luis, "the Inquisitors will grow suspicious."

Eusebio nodded. "True enough. It's a damned precarious position."

"For my part, I shall protect you any way I can," I said. "They cannot threaten me with anything to make me falter."

"You are in Lisbon, and must protect yourself as we do," Eusebio said. "If you are arrested in earnest, you shall name anyone you know. You think you won't, but everyone does."

"I do not wish to impose myself on you," I said. "I can only tell you that I would lay down my own life rather than condemn another man to the Inquisition. They may torment me, but I shall never speak a word against anyone in this house." I bowed once more and left the room.

I had just reached the front door when Luis called to me. "Hold, sir. A moment."

I paused and turned to face him. "I wish I had not come here. I only wanted to make certain you were unharmed."

"Eusebio is angry because you acted the hero before his wife," Luis said. "His manhood is injured, but he will see the logic and his desire to do business will win out. I promise you. I shall certainly do everything I can to convince him you are precisely the man you say."

"I thank you."

"In other words," Luis said in a whisper, "I shall lie to my own son on your behalf."

What had Luis learned? "Have I not given you every reason to trust me?"

Luis smiled. "That you have, but that is not the same thing as being honest. I shall be blunt and tell you I've long suspected you were not what you seemed. Your look and your coloring made me suspicious, but I was not entirely certain until you revealed yourself in the church. Your Portuguese is near flawless, hardly the halting speech of a man in the country a few weeks."

I said nothing. No one else had noticed, but I had been caught out. The question now was what this meant for my relations with the Nobrezas.

Luis nodded to himself and looked wistful, as if remembering something. "I will ask nothing more. I do not wish to know. Secrets are never safe in Lisbon, no matter what we may vow to ourselves. I believe you are not here to harm us."

"On my honor, that is true," I said quietly.

"Then it shall suffice. Perhaps the day may come when there will be no more secrets."

"I hope that day will be soon," I said. I replaced my hat and departed.

Chapter 21

When I at last returned to my inn, Franklin heaved himself from behind the bar and waved.

"Mr. Foxx, sir. You are wanted."

I planned to ignore him, but instead I stopped in my tracks. Inácio sat near the innkeeper, drinking Franklin's beer.

I looked past Franklin. "Inácio, what do you do here?"

Inácio rose and walked toward me. "A word in private, if you please."

I muttered an incoherent excuse at Franklin and led Inácio up the stairs. Enéas waited there, and looked stunned to see Inácio enter with me, but was wise enough to say nothing. I waved him away and gestured for Inácio to sit.

I poured him a glass of wine and sat across from him. "I am surprised to see you here. I did not think you were the sort of man who frequented English taverns."

"I'm not," Inácio admitted. "But I heard that you were arrested by the Inquisition, and I wished to make certain you were not detained."

This was curious. Was he truly worried for my well-being, or did he merely fear that he might somehow be caught in the web if the Inquisition came after me? "How did you hear it?"

Inácio snorted. "I hear everything. A man in my position must."

"And what would you have done if they had not released me?"

"What could I have done? Nothing. But if you were released, I wished to know of it at once."

"Why?" I asked. "How is that information useful to you?"

"It is useful to me," Inácio said, his voice slow with anger, "because you are my friend. Or have you forgotten that? Are you so convinced I played some little game with you about Gabriela that you think I would rejoice to see you taken by the Inquisition?"

I shook my head. "Forgive me. That you are here is proof enough."

"This city makes us all fear our own shadows, but the time to doubt yourself is when it seems a man plots against you when he has nothing to gain." He grinned. "Now, if toying with your heart had gold at the end of it, then you should mistrust me."

I managed a smile. "That is the old Inácio! And I thank you for your concern. It is a complicated business. The Inquisitor I seek is trying to get me to turn against Nobreza."

"I thought you were here to kill him, not give him New Christians."

"It is complicated," I said, "and the less you know, the better."

Inácio nodded. "Agreed. Tell me nothing else. I shall tell *you* something, however. I hear things, and it has come to my attention that your barman below is in the Inquisitor's pay."

"I know," I said. "I have been avoiding him since I found out. No doubt he wants to learn about my plans so he can pass the information along."

"Very likely. That priest is the devil himself."

"Do you know anything about him?" I asked. "Why does he hate Englishmen so much?"

"I shall tell you what I've heard," Inácio said, "though I don't know if it is truth or rumor. They say his father is English, and that he raped his mother."

I leaned forward. The explanation might have been pure fancy, but it was certainly interesting. "Who was this man?"

Inácio shook his head. "A merchant, the stories say. A young man who had too much to drink, and found a *fidalgo*'s daughter out on the street later than she should have been. Perhaps she was meeting her lover. I don't know. But he not only took her, he hurt her. Apparently the mother is addled now. Some say she is cloistered in a convent here in the city, though I know not if it is as a nun or in the care of nuns."

"Hmm," I said. "It sounds like a revenge play, but it would explain a great deal."

"Your life is a revenge play," Inácio said. "Who are you to judge?"

I laughed. "It is good to talk to you again, Inácio." And it was. I had no intention of giving myself over to trust entirely, but it seemed as though, in his clumsy way, Inácio wanted to look after my interests.

Inácio picked up his wine. "Tell me. You cannot toy with this Inquisitor forever. Next time he will not let you out of the Palace. You will have to act soon."

"I intend to. It may be you can help me with something."

Inácio coughed. "I told you that my help must be limited."

"No one need know it is for me, or to what it is connected. Can you get me a mule cart and have it left for me at a location I tell you at the time I tell you?" It was, after all, a simple thing, and having Inácio tend to this meant I'd expose myself to fewer people in the city.

Inácio narrowed his eyes. "You will give me the money in advance?"

"Of course."

"And a small fee to compensate me for my time and knowledge?"

I inclined my head. "A small fee."

"Then it shall be my pleasure."

* * *

When Inácio left the room, Enéas came back in and threw his arms around me. I allowed the boy to embrace me for a moment. "What is it?"

"I heard that the Inquisition took you," he said. "I am relieved you are well."

I shook my head at the wonder of it. I had come to Lisbon to kill a man, to take one life in the hopes of remaking myself into something less violent. How had all these other things happened instead? How had I come to be a father to this orphaned child?

"I would not let them keep me," I said. "Who else would make certain you did not return to your criminal ways?"

"You're the one planning to rob a vault," Enéas said. He grinned as he spoke, but then studied my face to make certain he had not insulted me.

I smiled just enough to let him know he was not in trouble.

"After you have taken the gold and done what you need to do, you'll leave Lisbon?"

I nodded. "I can't stay. I've taken too many risks."

Enéas cast his eyes down.

"You will have to learn much better English if you are to do well in London."

The boy's eyes lit up. "Of course. I will work very hard. I will learn the language and I will be the best English servant in London. And when I am older, we will go deer hunting together. It is what Englishmen like to do, is it not? We will ride through London, shooting deer, and it will be a very good time."

I nodded again. "It will be a very good time," I agreed.

Chapter 22

All was prepared, and I needed only darkness. I sat in my room without troubling myself to light a lamp until I felt it was time to go. Then I slipped noiselessly through the Lisbon streets.

It was after midnight. Most *renegados* had long since fallen into drunkenness or violence. But I did not take unnecessary risks. On every street, I clung to the shadows. I turned corners with silent caution. The sky was domed with heavy, gray clouds, but it was nearly a full moon, and occasionally its light pierced through.

Down the street from the nondescript building that held the vaults, I reviewed my plan and scouted the area for any unexpected travelers. On the far end, Enéas would meet the mule cart that Inácio had secured. Once the cart was in place and loaded, we would have to drive it through the streets quickly; the trick then would be getting it to Luis Nobreza without attracting the notice of any soldiers. There were few patrols at night, but it would only take one. Any Portuguese soldier we might encounter would be inclined to inspect the cart. If he discovered several thousand pounds' worth of gold, he might choose to keep it.

There was nothing for it. I could not steal gold and transport it across the city without taking risks. I approached the building's door. No sign of movement, no sound of footsteps. I was alone. I had just heard the bells chime midnight not five minutes before. It was time to begin.

The door was heavy and the lock solid, but it was no more complicated than other locks I had dealt with before. I took from my pocket a leather roll that contained my picks and went to work. The tapping of the picks echoed through the streets, though only a trained ear would know the sounds for what they were. A passerby would think it nothing more than the tap of rat claws on a tin roof. More importantly, almost anyone out at night would have his own secrets to attend.

At last the tumblers turned and the lock's bolt retracted. I pushed the door, wincing at its long and mournful groan, and stepped into the foyer, where I faced the second door and its locks. These were trickier, but at least now I could work without fear of discovery. I set to it, not troubling myself with the noise or how much time I took, and within ten minutes the door was open and I looked into the long hallway. I moved forward, my soft leather boots making only the occasional hissing scrape.

At the end of the hallway, I came to the door of the vaults. This was the most dangerous part of the operation. If there were guards who would be in a position to surprise me, they would be on the other side. This door had three more locks, each as complex as those on the front doors. I could not hope to gain access in less than five minutes, and picking these locks, I would generate far more noise than I would like. Unfortunately, it was my only option.

Beginning at the top, I began to prod and poke the first lock's interior, and it clicked open in less than a minute and with little noise. This, I hoped, was an omen of good things to come—but it was not.

The second lock was sluggish and awkward. Once I dropped a pick, and the metallic clink might as well have been a cannon roar. Shortly after that, I momentarily lost my footing as I leaned forward, and my elbow thudded against the door. I cursed myself and proceeded. Finally it gave, and the third lock offered far less resistance. It had taken closer to ten minutes than five, but I now slowly opened the door.

No one awaited me at the head of the dark stairwell, but I had no way to be sure what lay below. The blackness might contain any number of men waiting for me. I had seen no dogs during my visit with Roberta, but that did not mean they were not there after hours; silence meant nothing, as dogs could be trained not to bark. There was no dog smell, however. Only the cool and damp of stone, and a tang like old piss.

I began to descend the stone staircase, taking each step with deliberate slowness. The stairs were steep and narrow by English standards, and there was no railing but the rough wall. I tried to control my breathing and commanded my eyes to adapt to the gloom. To adapt there had to be light, however. Here there was none.

When I reached the foot of the stairs, I turned in the direction I was reasonably certain was north and began to move toward the last door. There was still no sign of any guardians, which did not comfort me. Far better to deal with the protectors now than to wait for them to emerge. Although if I was lucky, it might well be that Roberta and the others who stored gold here were deceived, and the space was far less well protected than they imagined.

At last I had groped my way to the final door, to the room with the vaults. Here would be the most difficult lock of all, and I knew I was already behind schedule. I had to act quickly if I was to get the gold. Once more I cleared my head, thinking of nothing, letting my hands do the work.

At last the bolt turned and the door swung open with the sonorous groan of old iron. I was in. I waited a moment, listening for any signs of movement. Nothing. I was alone. I wished I had known it earlier, since I could have struck a light. Now I took from my leather bag a torch and kindling box. After several false tries, I managed to spark a flame.

There it all lay before me. Ten cages on the left and ten on the right. Now that I had light, I fished into my coat to look at my watch. I had under half an hour before Enéas was due to arrive with the mule cart. Seeking out the Carvers' vault, I stepped forward, raising the torch. The cage contained six crates, each with fifty pounds of gold bouillon. All told, three hundred pounds to carry, but worth just over fifteen thousand pounds sterling. I could, without too much difficulty, carry one box at a time up the stairs and toward the door. Then Enéas and I could get the crates on the cart. The first box, and maybe the second, would not be overly taxing, but I knew my legs would begin to weaken from the climb. I needed to give myself sufficient time to take quick rests before each load.

As I calculated the difficulty, I saw a shadow rise above me from behind. I dropped the torch and began to turn, but then felt a tremendous amount of pain.

The room now stank of wine and rotten breath. And my head hurt. How long had I been insensible? I didn't think very much time had passed, but there was no way to be certain.

I opened my eyes just enough to make out the scene. I was still near the vault, on the floor where I had fallen. Two men stood over me, one drinking from a wineskin. He took a long gulp while his fellow looked on anxiously.

"Not so much, you greedy son of a whore. That's our last one."

The man with the wineskin swallowed and wiped his mouth with the back of his hand, and then spoke with a Spaniard's accent. "I know it is the last one, which is why I mean to savor it. Good Rioja wine. Not your Portuguese piss." He took another drink.

"Save some for me, Jorge." The second man, whom I could see

better, was a little slip of a thing, hardly taller than a boy, and very skinny. He hopped about as he spoke, and he had a small, sharp nose and protruding lips—a birdlike man indeed.

The Spaniard, however, was big enough, with huge hands and a massive nose. It had been broken in the past, likely more than once, and now it sat round and wide atop his face, like a great turnip. "Quiet. If you could take the wine from me, you would, but you can't and so you won't. If you ruin these last few sips, I'll kill you like I did the thief."

I felt contentment overtake the throbbing pain in my head. If a man is to be waylaid while going about his business, he can only hope to be waylaid by drunkards such as these. They thought me dead, when I had only taken a lump and a headache for my pains. With my eyes still slits, I continued to watch and wait, but I could see I would need little art. As drunk and foolish as these two men were, I might as well have been sitting up and watching them openly.

The Spaniard took one more long gulp and handed the skin to the smaller man. "Not too much, now. A little girl like you don't need so much as a man."

The Portuguese lifted the skin, and I saw his hands were shaking. He swallowed and then began to drink more. The Spaniard snatched the skin away.

"That's enough for you, missy."

"I never seen a man murdered before," the Portuguese said.

"You haven't seen no one murdered yet," the Spaniard snapped back. "He was a thief, and killing a thief is no crime. It's what we get paid for. But we're going to have to move him, otherwise we'll need to explain how he got so far inside without us noticing. We'll dump the body on the street and be done with it."

"I don't want to touch him. It will anger his ghost."

"His ghost won't care, but yours will if I kill you for refusing to help. Grab hold of one arm, I'll grab the other. He's a big fellow."

The Spaniard moved toward me and staggered. He grabbed onto

the little Portuguese to regain his balance, but overcorrected, and the two of them nearly fell to the floor together. While they tottered comically about like a pair of clowns at a country fair, I launched myself to my feet and struck out at the Spaniard. I knew I had to dispatch him, or nearly so, with the first strike. It was always dangerous to attack so large a man, even if he was drunk and unskilled. I put my shoulder into the blow, driving my fist forward as Mr. Weaver had taught me, connecting with the man's jaw and never slowing, never relenting, until I had completed the arc.

Time seemed to stop, so perfect was the punch. Blood shot out of the Spaniard's mouth, splattering the face of the Portuguese behind him. That tiny man stood frozen with terror as I stepped forward. The Portuguese raised his arms to protect his face and cried out, "Jesus, save me from the ghost!" I hated to be cruel to so harmless a man, but I had not time for kindness. I struck the little man in his stomach. The Portuguese's arms came down, and I saw his eyes were wide, his mouth open, his teeth already flecked with blood. The poor fellow had only been doing his business, and it was a hard trick of fate that such business should put him at odds with my own. Still, it had, and there was no doing things by halves. I struck again, this time to the side of his head, knocking him so hard that he bounced, like a child's plaything, into the wall and then collapsed upon the floor, motionless and broken.

A fraction of a second later and I would have been dead, but I saw the shadows shift in the flickering lantern light, and I dodged as the Spaniard wildly swung a shovel at me. He had not been dispatched. He had apparently not even gone down. He was bloodied, but also now crazed and determined. He waved the shovel like it was a magic sword. "You think I can't take a punch or two? Haven't you seen my face, thief?"

I grunted in dismay and jumped back as the Spaniard swung again. The shovel struck the dirt floor so hard that it was momentarily stuck. I rushed forward and, using my momentum, brought both my hands down, clamped together, upon the soft part of the Span-iard's temple. The big man looked up just in time to see the blow, but not in time to move. I hit hard and true, and the Spaniard stag-gered, his eyes rolling toward the ceiling. He fell, face forward, to the floor.

I paused only long enough to regret doing harm to men merely fulfilling their duty, and then I took the lantern and went to work at once upon the vault door. I had it open in less than five minutes and grabbed the first crate. I had not accounted for the weight of the wood, which added a good ten pounds to my load. I was already tired from the exertions of fighting the guards, and my head throbbed painfully, but none of that mattered. It couldn't. Struggling for bal-ance, I began the painful climb up the narrow stairs.

As predicted, I began to struggle by the third crate. Stars swirled be-fore my eyes. I wondered if I had been more seriously hurt than I had first allowed. My arms grew leaden and the muscles in my thighs spasmed with each step. But though my chest heaved and sweat poured down my face, stinging my eyes, I pressed on. I would slow but I would not stop. Fifteen thousand pounds' worth of gold was enough money to right a wrong, to save a family, to soothe the sting of a debt too great to ever be paid.

I was halfway up the stairs with the final box when I felt my foot slip in something wet—my sweat, possibly my blood. The box fell and I stumbled. I could see it all: I would crash to the floor below, striking my head, the gold box landing atop me. Perhaps I would die in the accident, or perhaps be hurt and live to be discovered in the morning. I would then find myself under arrest, facing the royal au-thorities and the Inquisition.

Somehow I steadied myself. As though operating under its own volition, one of my arms shot sideways, striking the wall and revers-ing my momentum. I caught the box that had eluded my grip. The incident had lasted only a few seconds from beginning to end—my life seemed to be over, and then all was as it had been.

I finished the climb, taking each step just a little more slowly.

I had stacked the crates in two rows of three near the front door. I now peered outside and there, as I had planned, and as I had hoped, was the mule cart. Enéas sat slumped over with the reins.

"All is well?" I murmured.

"Well," came the response in a nervous whisper, hardly recognizable as a human voice.

It might have gone faster with two men loading, but Enéas was small, and I did not want to risk one of the crates dropping and breaking. The cart was only ten feet from the front door. After hauling the crates up from the subterranean vault, this last stretch would be easy, almost a rest.

It took only a few minutes for me to load the crates. And there it was. Settwell's money. Settwell's revenge. Justice served and a debt paid—if not in full, then at least in part. With this task completed, there was nothing to stay my hand. Azinheiro would die, and I could extricate myself from this cursed city before anyone else came to harm.

I jumped on the cart and said, "Let's go."

The cart did not move.

"Go," I hissed.

Enéas sat still.

I leaned forward and tapped the boy's shoulder. Before I saw Enéas's head fall heavily to the side, I felt the hot liquid on my hand. Even in the dim light, I saw the black blood everywhere. Enéas's throat had been sliced open.

He had not been the one to whisper.

The moment I realized what had happened, I also knew someone came toward me from behind. I could not move to either side, for I was pinned in place by the crates, so I dove down and forward, grabbing a pair of legs, and feeling a body tumble before me. The man was only on the ground for an instant before he leapt like an acrobat to his feet.

Dim moonlight pierced the clouds and I saw a bald head, mustaches, and a scar. I saw the flash of teeth and a dagger in the man's hand, silver-handled, laced with gold and glittering with rubies.

Inácio.

My vision clouded. Blood pounded in my ears.

"You owe me," Inácio said, reading the question on my face. "You thought we could be friends again after your father destroyed mine? You were gone too long, Sebastião. You made the mistake of thinking I was precisely what I appeared to be."

I was surprised, and not surprised. All along I had known I could not trust Inácio. I had suspected him of playing his own game and seeking his own angle, but I had not anticipated this cold hatred. I had not imagined, for a moment, that I could be for him what the priest was to me.

"My father didn't destroy yours," I said, my voice low. "They were both destroyed by the Inquisition. How can you not understand that?"

"Your father seduced him with his Jew charm. He said, 'Come work for me. It will be easy money. We will both benefit.' And my father believed it. He believed it, and he died for it."

I held myself in readiness, but still I could not credit what I had witnessed. Inácio had been toying with me since our first meeting. He had told me Gabriela was dead for the pleasure of seeing my distress and then sent me to Eusebio—why? To further confound me? For the simple pleasure of twisting my feelings? Now he had killed Enéas and planned to rob me. I had never trusted him entirely, but I cursed myself for having been blind enough to trust him at all.

"It is a fool who blames another victim rather than his enemy," I said.

"What? I should be like you and try to take revenge on the Inquisition? That is absurd. Instead, by putting you and Nobreza together, I've given them reason to take notice of your precious Gabriela. Now, *that* is revenge. You can think on that when I kill you with your father's dagger and take this gold, which has been a nice surprise. It will be no more than a week before Gabriela is in chains in the Palace."

Inácio raised his knife, expecting me to charge him, but I did not move.

"They're going to rape her, you know," Inácio said. "All the pretty ones are raped. Maybe not in the first few weeks, but after a while the guards can't resist the temptation."

Inácio stood, the mule cart to his back. He could not escape with the gold unless I was dead, and I knew it. Inácio needed to force a fight, to put me at a disadvantage. But I would not take the bait. He would either have to flee without the gold or face me directly.

"So be it," he said, as if I had explained all of this out loud. He ran at me.

Inácio was big, and he charged like a bull, but I also knew he was cunning. I watched his eyes, not his body—even in the moonlight I could see them shift—and knew his plan was to go low, to cut my legs. I leapt out of the way and spun around the instant he dove.

He was on the ground now, and I remained standing, with the full advantage. I kicked Inácio hard in the side. He grunted, but with the momentum of the kick leapt to his feet, hardly worse for wear. He yet held the dagger.

He charged again. I sidestepped, but this time not quickly enough. Inácio was on me, his weight pinning me to the ground. He stretched his forearm across my chest, immobilizing my arms, and with his free hand raised the dagger.

I drove my forehead into Inácio's face. I made poor contact, bloodying his nose at worst, but it was enough to make him loosen his grip. I drove a punch into the side of his head, and Inácio fell off me. He scrambled quickly to his feet. He looked at me for a moment, seeming to take a measure of me and the situation, and further off into the blackness of the Lisbon streets. I could see his face shift as he made a decision.

"Revenge or gold!" I cried, as he ran down the street. "You can't have both."

I would not follow him. I would deal with Inácio later. Settwell came first, before justice or mourning for Enéas. I hated that it was so, but I gritted my teeth and stepped onto the cart, grabbing the reins.

It was half past two in the morning when I reached Eusebio's house and brought the gold inside. I was soaked with sweat and my head ached beyond anything I had known. My back throbbed and my arms stung. I was hardly aware of any of it. Enéas was dead. Inácio had betrayed me. But still there was a touch of relief. I was close. I nearly had what I needed to help Settwell, and once that was done, I would be free to settle scores, to deal with Azinheiro—and now Inácio.

I had planned to have Enéas free the mule as soon as I took the gold off the cart, but now it was one more matter to tend to alone. I drove nearly a mile down the street, untethered the animal, and ran the distance back to Nobreza's house. Both beast and cart would be claimed before dawn, vanishing into the endless churning sea of Lisbon's poverty.

When I returned to the house, there was only a single lamp lit in the sitting room—no one would wish to lead a neighbor to ask questions or make reports—but the entire house was awake. Luis Nobreza was involved in a heated argument with his son, and Gabriela watched them, her expression unreadable. She wore a wrinkled gown she had hastily thrown over her nightclothes, and her hair was loose and wild.

When I walked into the room, Eusebio spun on me. "You walk into my house as though it were your own?"

"Your father instructed me to do so," I said, making every effort to keep my voice civil. "I have no wish to cause trouble."

"Enough," Eusebio snapped. "Where did this gold come from?" When I did not answer, Eusebio pointed at his father. "Did you even think to ask? There is something criminal or heretical here. Do you want this Englishman to stain us with his taint?"

"There is no taint," Luis said. "It is business. It is what we do, what we've always done. Senhor Foxx asked if I could convert the gold, and I said yes. I've done as much for your and our friends for decades."

"Well, you shan't do it this time. Get rid of the gold."

"I can't do that," I said. "I no longer have the means of conveyance."

Eusebio walked over to me and jabbed a finger into my chest. "Then I suggest you flee. You run as fast and as far as you can, because I want no part of this money, and I shall report you and your scheme to the Inquisition this very morning."

"No, you won't," I said. I was angry and tired and hurt. I had seen Enéas's body lying dead in the cart. And so patience for Eusebio eluded me. He complained and threw up obstacles. And he had Gabriela. That was the most unforgivable thing of all. Keeping her for himself, when he was weak and cowardly. I was the only thing that stood between her and ruin, and her whining little dog of a husband didn't even know it.

I pointed at him. "You won't invite the Inquisition to ask questions. You don't think they'll ask questions you don't want to answer? You don't think they'll take this gold and link it to your father?"

"Maybe they should," Eusebio said. "Better he should be in the Palace prison than remain a powder keg in our house, waiting to explode."

Eusebio's face had reddened with rage, but the moment he spoke, regret washed over it. He was already turning to apologize to Luis, but it was too late. I was already across the room, grabbing Eusebio by his shirt and lifting him off the ground. I thrust him into the wall hard enough to knock down paintings and dislodge candles from their sconces. Plaster under the wallpaper cracked. Little clouds of dust puffed out.

"My father was dragged off to the Palace dungeons, and he died there, so do not speak of incriminating your own. I will rip your tongue from your mouth before I let that happen. Do you doubt me? Do you?"

"No," Eusebio gasped. He pushed back against me, though he lacked the strength to make me move. "Now let go of me. They were but empty words."

I relaxed my hand, and Eusebio stumbled but remained on his feet. "This is Lisbon," I said. "Words are sharper than blades."

All was now silent. Eusebio stared at me, eyes wide and limbs shaking. Gabriela stood nearby, a hand over her mouth. She knew. I could see it on her face, but she said nothing.

"Who are you?" Luis asked. "I see no reason not to tell us now."

"I'm a dead man," I said. "I pray you do not become like me."

I began to walk off. Luis followed me and grabbed my arm before I walked through the front door. "What is this money about? Truly?"

"A debt," I explained. "Long ago, a man fulfilled a promise to my father and saved my life. That money is his. He needs to flee the country, and the money will allow him to save his daughter. That is as much as I will tell you."

"It is as much as I need to know," Luis said. "I will have your notes by this afternoon. I shall bring them to you or send them by someone I trust. It is probably better that you do not come back here."

I nodded. "You are a good man, senhor. I am sorry to have brought trouble to your house, and I am sorry to have behaved so poorly toward your son."

Luis smiled. "You have a hard time containing your anger."

I snorted. "That is what it looks like when I succeed in containing my anger."

Chapter 23

The message from Luis came at almost noon. He did not think it safe to be seen at an English inn himself, and instead he told me to go to the Rossio and wait near the cluster of tailor shops. I hurried out and made my way to the crowded square, conducting some business at stalls and then leaning against a wall and smoking a pipe as though engaged in nothing more important than watching the crowds. From time to time, I was able to keep myself from thinking of Enéas and his cruel and pointless death.

I saw no sign of Luis and began to despair of his coming at all. What if something had gone wrong? What if Eusebio had followed through with his threat, or the family had been taken by the Inquisition for some other reason? I had not told Azinheiro anything of note, but if he had grown impatient, then all might have ended in disaster.

That was precisely what I feared when I saw one of Eusebio's servants, an elderly man whose name I did not know, approach. The fellow was dour-faced, so it was hard to read anything in his expression.

"Is something amiss?" I asked at once.

"No," the servant said. "Come with me."

I followed him out of the square and down a series of winding streets. Then, at an intersection, he said, "The third house on your right. The door is opened."

"Whose house is it?" I asked.

The servant shrugged. "If I do not know, then I cannot say."

I understood about such places. They were often owned jointly by New Christian merchants, purchased by a *fidalgo* on their behalf, and used for secret meetings. Often there were multiple entrances so men could attend without being seen to enter together. I could not understand why Luis would need to meet in secret. I wondered if I might be stepping into a trap, though traps did not frighten me overmuch. Traps were set by men. Men could always be made to talk.

I walked into the hall. There was an entrance on the left—a well-lit parlor that caught the midday sun in an almost blinding luminescence. There Gabriela waited, already rising to meet me.

She held out a leather envelope toward me. Her expression was unreadable. "Your bank notes," she said.

I stared at her. With the light of the window behind her, illuminating her sky-blue gown, she looked like something more than human. Her dark hair, tightly bound, glinted in the sunlight. Her face was red and puffy from weeping, but still her beauty was almost painful. And we appeared to be alone. The two of us, with no witnesses. Did she know what she meant to me? Did she mean to inflict this torment?

"Thank you," I said, my voice a rough croak. I entered the room and turned so she would have to move away from the window, her dress regaining its intended opacity.

"It is for Mr. Settwell, isn't it?" she said, swallowing hard. "It was always rumored that it was he who helped you escape, and we know he is in trouble."

I nodded. Words did not come easily.

"Is that why you've come back?"

"It is why I stayed so long," I said.

We stood five feet from each other, taking in each other's faces, neither daring to move or look away. Her green eyes were fixed on me, and the bow of her mouth was pressed hard together.

"I cannot see how I failed to notice," she said at last. "But after what you said—and then my husband's father told me that you wanted the money to save the English merchant who liberated you." She shook her head. "It all became clear."

"People see what they expect. And I have changed."

"That is beyond doubt," she said.

"Do you judge me?" I asked her, hardly believing what I heard. "I have loved you, Gabriela. All this time, across these years and these miles. You want to know why I came back? I told myself it was for revenge, and then to help a friend, but it was for you. It was always for you."

"We were children then," she said. Her eyes were downcast and her voice was very quiet. "And I am married now."

Was she shy? Was she afraid? Did she need me to be bolder? "What does your marriage mean to me?" I asked. "Eusebio Nobreza is nothing. He cannot stand between us."

"Is that what you expect? That the past ten years can simply be erased?" Her voice was louder now. Harder.

"I don't know what I expect," I told her. "But I had to tell you the truth."

She looked at me, her eyes cold and without tenderness. "The truth is that we grew up together and we liked each other and you were sweet and kind to me. What is that compared to Eusebio, to whom I owe everything?"

"He is not worthy of you," I said. "He is a weak—"

"I owe him *everything*," she repeated, this time more sharply. "After my father died, I was made to live in a nunnery. I tried to make myself useful, to belong there. I sought to take orders, if you can believe such a thing, because I knew that it would be a better life than anything that awaited me outside. The abbess—she was kind to me and sympathetic to my plight, but she died, and the woman who replaced her had always hated me. And . . . I was not treated well."

I reached out for her, but she snatched her arm away.

"No. I don't want sympathy. I wrote to a friend, telling her what I endured, and she told Eusebio. He came and paid the outrageous fee the abbess asked, and took me away. He brought me back to his house and told me I owed him nothing, that he would forget what he had paid the convent. But I did not want him to send me away. I loved him, truly loved him, for saving me. I have been happy with him. I don't need a man who throws others against walls or steals gold or plays games with the Inquisition. I need a man who will take care of me and protect me and be a coward if that is what it takes to survive. I need *him*. So stop pretending we're children. All of that is gone."

"I thought—" I began, but I hardly knew how to continue.

"I cannot imagine what you thought," Gabriela said. Her tone was soft, but the words cut all the same. "You look at me and do not see what is there, but what you wish to be there."

Could that be true? Roberta had said as much of me, and the little faith I had placed in Inácio had proved to be too much.

I stood in silence, feeling the sting of her words, and feeling foolish for having believed there would be something still between us. Those long years I had held on to the hope of her, the memory of what we had felt for each other. But did I have any notion of how much of it was real and how much invented? What I knew now was that the love I felt was for someone as unreal as any creature of myth. She bore no connection to the angry woman standing in front of me.

Yet, for all the humiliation I felt, I still had to try to save some part of that past. "I will get you out of this country," I told her.

She shook her head. "Have you heard nothing I said? Your love for me is the love of a child. I will not run off with you."

"Both of you," I said, trying to save face, yes, but also seeing things more clearly now. Of course it was madness to think she would leave her husband, but I could still serve her. I had an obligation to do so.

"All of you," I told her. "I know Eusebio has smuggled money out of the country. I will get you out—you and Eusebio and Luis. You will go where you like."

She blinked at me. "You would do that for us? Why?"

I looked at the woman who had consumed more of my thoughts than any other person, any other idea, and I understood that this was not the Gabriela I had dreamed of. She was gone, as much a memory as the boy who had loved her. Time and circumstance had remolded her as surely as they had remolded him.

"Why?" she asked again.

"Because for sins of one man against another, the Day of Atonement does not atone until they have made peace with each other."

"What does that mean?" Gabriela snapped.

"I hope someday you will know. For now it is enough to explain that I need to undo the past. You have a husband, and you love him. I have no desire to hurt anyone. Not ever again."

"How will you do it?" she asked.

"I don't know," I said. "Not yet. But I will figure out a way." I thought of Inácio's threat the night before. Time was running out for the Nobrezas. "Soon. Within the week."

Here she was, the woman I had loved all my life, and I had just let go of her. While I felt a deep and terrible sadness welling up inside me, I also found, to my surprise, something like comfort. She was gone, but not beyond my helping. I could do something real and undeniable for her. Maybe that would be enough.

"I am sorry I was cruel to you," she said at last. "I misjudged you."

"Don't be sorry," I said, turning to leave. "And you did not misjudge me. You understand me all too well. If I had the same understanding of myself, perhaps things might have gone better."

Chapter 24

Wanting to waste no more time, I made haste as I pushed my way through the streets, my leather envelope of incredible wealth tucked into my breeches so that no pickpocket could help himself to what I had acquired through blood and sacrifice. I had to make my way around a procession carrying the bones of some saint or another, but otherwise the streets were empty. Tonight was All Hallows' Eve, and the superstitious people of Lisbon would already be preparing for an evening of prayer, clutching crucifixes and rosaries, hoping to keep the spirits of the dead away during the most haunted night of the year. Then tomorrow would be All Saints' Day. The streets would be mobbed. Every church in Lisbon would be alight with candle and full of song. I would, by then, be in pursuit of my own vengeance instead of Settwell's. I would tend to Franklin. I would make Inácio pay for his crimes. I would kill Azinheiro, and then I would flee the country with Eusebio and his family. And then? Well, then, of course, I would become a happy man, ready to lead a productive life.

I laughed at the absurdity of my plan. How could I be transformed? I had come to Lisbon to exorcise the darkness, but everywhere I went was the gloomier for it. I no longer pursued these things because I believed they would improve my life. I did them because they needed doing. Where a broken man like me might make his home thereafter, I could not guess.

At Settwell's house, the old mulatto woman let me in at once, and Settwell rushed to see me. "Well?" he asked.

I held the envelope in my hand already, lest his joy be somewhat diminished by seeing me pull his wealth from my breeches. Settwell snatched it away. He peered inside and his eyes widened. He took a few steps backward and forward. He opened his mouth to speak, but laughter erupted, and he put a hand up to silence himself as though he were a little girl.

"You have done it," Settwell said. "The money, right here. In my hands." He reached out and clapped my shoulder. "By God, sir, whatever I did for you, you have repaid me. You have more than repaid me. You have served justice and given new life to me and my daughter."

Mariana, sensing the excitement, came running down the stairs and threw her arms around me. "Mr. Foxx!" she cried. "What did you bring me?"

"Mariana!" snapped her father. "Do not be rude. Mr. Foxx has other things to worry himself about than geegaws for little girls."

"For ordinary little girls, to be sure," I said. "For special little girls, I have no more pressing business." From my pocket I pulled forth a cleverly carved little wooden duck, trailed by a train of ducklings. I had bought it in the Rossio before meeting Gabriela.

Mariana squealed. "I love it. This is the best present I have ever received!"

"Now run along," Settwell said. "Mr. Foxx and I have tedious business to discuss."

The girl pouted, but she did as she was told. Once she was gone,

Settwell poured two glasses of port and handed one to me, though I had the very distinct impression he would rather have kept both for himself. We tapped glasses and drank.

"From nothing to fifteen thousand. I would never have believed it. I can never sufficiently thank you for what you have done."

"No more thanks. Wrongs have been righted, and that is all that matters. But now we must discuss how you will leave the country. Were you on your own, it would be no difficulty, but I cannot think the Inquisition will simply allow you to leave with a Catholic child."

"She is my daughter," Settwell said, his voice very hard.

"That little matters, and you know it. She is the seven-year-old Catholic child of an Englishman. The Inquisition will regard her as a prize."

"The Factory will protect us. The consul will never allow my child to be taken."

"The Inquisition has taken English children before. You yourself have said so. And I need not remind you that you cannot expect help from the consul and the Factory."

Settwell laughed. "Well, then I was a penniless merchant, down on his luck. Now I possess a fortune of fifteen thousand pounds. They will forget any past disagreements."

"You cannot reveal that you have the money, not so soon after it is stolen from the goldsmith's vault. I propose circumventing the Factory entirely. We shall hire a coach and a few soldiers as protection from bandits. I will come with you to make certain the soldiers do not turn coat. We will then go to Oporto, and hire a berth there to France or Italy. You will not be known, and so you will be seen as simply another Englishman. Mariana will be invisible. Once you come ashore, you will easily find transport to England."

"Yes, yes, that sounds fine," Settwell said as he paced about the room with a kind of frantic energy, "but I'm not entirely certain I'm ready to leave Lisbon—not now. Maybe I shall remain a little longer, see what bargains I can strike. It never hurts to add a few pounds to one's holdings. I should think in less than a year, I could double this money."

I could not credit what I heard. "Are you mad? The goal was to get you free of this country. I did not steal that money so you could wager it upon trade."

"It's no wager, and I shan't squander the money. In any event, it isn't your money, is it? It's mine, and what I choose to do with it is my own business."

"I risked my life to buy you your freedom. Enéas gave his life to do so. He was murdered during the robbery."

"What? The little Gypsy boy? You can get another, surely."

I set down the wine with great care. "I valued him for who he was, not how quickly he could deliver a message. I did not put him in harm's way so that you might have one more opportunity to rise in the Factory."

Settwell stared at me, and his gaze was now stony and cold. "It doesn't particularly matter what your intentions were. You did what I asked because it was your obligation, and what I do next is none of your concern. Now, if you are going to snap at me thus, I shall not like it, so I bid you a good day."

I felt blood pounding in my throat, in my temples. Could it be I had misjudged yet another person in my life? His indifference and foolishness struck me with near physical force. I closed my eyes for a moment and look a long, deep breath. "If anything happens to that child because of you, you will answer to me."

"It is very good of you to care for her, but I am Mariana's protector, and she shall be well." Without further commentary, Settwell strode out of the room, leaving me to find my way out. I waited until I believed I could step out upon the street without knocking down the first person whose looks I misliked.

* * *

When I returned to the Duke's Arms, Roberta was waiting for me once again. She had hired a private room, and left a message for me to find her there. I prepared myself, making certain I felt nothing when I walked through the door. She sat with her fingers wrapped around a cup of wine. Her eyes were red and her face haggard. Her green dress was rumpled, and I saw mud strewn along the hem.

"Roberta, what has happened?" I asked, doing a tolerably good imitation of someone who did not know.

"I am ruined," she answered. She rose to her feet and threw her arms around me, pressing me tight, her hands clutching my back desperately. She smelled of sweat. After a moment, she pushed herself away, and began to pace. "Our vault at the goldsmith's was robbed. Fifteen thousand pounds' worth of gold taken. We have nothing, now. We have worse than nothing. Much of that money was debt that we owed others."

"But surely the goldsmith will compensate you," I said, forcing my face into an expression of concern. "He must have purchased insurance for his holdings."

She shook her head. "He swore he did when we agreed to use his services, but it was a lie. His insurance was long unpaid, and there will be no consequences to him for his lie. I can no longer help you make your fortune. I am so sorry, Sebastian. Forgive me. Pity me, too. It will be all we can do to get ourselves back to England."

I led her to sit down. "You must have other options. You are well established in this city. You have friends. The consul worships you. Surely someone will lend you money. You need only have a loan for a few months to make enough to reestablish yourself, I should think."

She shook her head, almost violently. "No one will lend money to people who lose what they have. We are tainted. Even the consul will scorn me now."

I expected her to ask me for a loan, but soon realized I was mistaken. Roberta was broken, and I had broken her. I wished I had not done this to her—if only she had left Charles Settwell alone, none of this would have come to pass.

"What can I do for you?" I asked, and not only because I wished to play my role. I did want to help her. I wanted to erase her anguish—and to ease my own. I had done what needed doing, but here was yet one more woman I had brought low.

She looked down at the scratched and beer-logged wood of the table. "You can do nothing. I only wanted to tell you before you heard from someone else. Perhaps the money was the only thing you cared for, and I wished to see for myself if that was true."

"It is not true," I said, taking her hand. "I don't give a damn about the money." It was among the few honest things I had ever said to her.

"I think you have truly loved me," she said.

I said, "I have. I have loved you, and I love you yet." Did I really care for this predator and thief, who destroyed without remorse? At that moment, I believed I did. Perhaps it was merely her vulnerability that made me think so; perhaps it was my own.

"If there had been money," she said, "if there had been wealth enough for us to rise above gossip and rumor, then who can say what might have eventually happened? Now I have no choice. My lot is to be a good wife to a ruined man."

I did not wish to speak the words, but I could not quite prevent myself. "Is there no way to find this thief and reclaim what was lost?"

"The money is gone—either converted or driven out of town or sailing upon the waters. No one would dare leave stolen gold lying about for long. Even though I believe I know who took it, there is nothing I can do without proof."

"Who do you think took it?" I asked. I attempted to keep my voice even, but after I spoke I realized that it had been a mistake. Surely I should have been emotional upon hearing such news. The layers of dishonesty were becoming a bit too complex even for me.

She laughed bitterly. "I did not think he had the wile to do it, but

I am sure it was that villain, Charles Settwell. You recall I told you to keep your distance from him."

"I do," I said, trying to sound no more than concerned and curious. "Why would he steal your money?"

"He tells the world that Rutherford and I tricked him into losing his fortune. I have no doubt he told you that as well. I recall how cautious you were when you first met us, though we hoped honest dealing would erase your doubts. He has repeated this lie so many times, I think he may even half believe it, though he is far too canny to lose himself entirely in a fabrication."

"If he did not lose his money through trickery, then how did he become what he is now?" I managed to ask.

"Bad business. Isn't that what always happens? He lost the last of his fortune when he brought in a wool shipment two weeks after we had flooded the market. We hadn't done it out of malice, you must understand—we managed to buy a great deal of surplus, and we delivered what we bought. Had Settwell but asked us to stock our goods in the warehouse for two weeks that he might bring his goods to market at the same time, we would have accommodated him. English merchants do such things for one another. But he did not, and he was forced to sell at a loss. We never set out to compete with him. We simply were better at commerce than he was. That is why he does not forgive us."

Forgetting myself, I asked, "Is there proof of this?"

"All Factory transactions are recorded," Roberta answered, looking at me askew. "That is why no one believes him when he speaks ill of us. The Factory has been convinced of his dishonesty. The records show why he was ruined and how little we had to do with it."

I would have to review the records myself to be truly satisfied, but the story could be true. Assuming it was, then I had ruined an innocent couple, in order to steal money for a man who had lied to me. Had I done wrong? Was the debt I owed Settwell—for my father's sake as well as my own—so great that it rendered this kind of deception meaningless? If Settwell had approached me and said that he wished to rob an innocent couple of their hard-earned wealth, would I have done it? Was the debt vast enough that I would have set aside my own objections? Perhaps. But Settwell had not given me the choice. That was a violation of trust and an abuse of the bond that existed between us.

And what of Roberta? This story undid everything I believed about her. If knowing her to be cruel and selfish had been a barrier before, what now? What was this woman sitting before me other than strong, and clever, and utterly betrayed by me?

I had come to Lisbon looking for atonement, and had found only more transgression. No matter what it took, I would fix what I had done. I would make peace with Roberta Carver, and to do so, I would find a way to replace the fortune I had stolen. I would break open the treasury of the Palace of the Inquisition if need be to set this right. "I will help you. I will find you the money you need."

"It is too late for that," she said. "You cannot simply hand me fifteen thousand pounds. Our reputation in Lisbon is destroyed, and no amount you might reasonably lend us would have any effect on that."

I stood up so rapidly that Roberta gasped. My chair nearly toppled. The table rattled. "Go nowhere and do nothing," I told her. "I will find your money. I will do whatever it takes. I will not let this stand."

She permitted herself a sad smile. "The way you say it, I can almost believe it is so. I have seen you when you are determined. I know you think nothing can stop you, but I don't believe even you can save me from this."

"You must believe it," I said. This woman had seen me at my worst. She had seen the monster that lived in my heart as I beat the Gypsy almost to death, and it had frightened her, but she had not turned away. Almost everything I had ever said to Roberta Carver was a lie. Even now, I could not tell her who and what I was, and yet in some ways she knew me better than anyone and loved me still.

"You do not know what I am, but I swear I will make things right."

I could not deceive her about what I had done—not forever. For now, I would begin to earn her forgiveness by recovering the money she had lost.

After Roberta left, I sat alone in the private room for a quarter hour and then walked into the common room, where Franklin was waiting for me. The usual easy grin was gone from his face. His eyebrows were knit together and his mouth set in a tight frown.

"Mr. Foxx, sir. A moment of your time."

I pushed past him. "I am busy now."

"You are always busy, and I think I know why, but I cannot be put off any longer. A moment." He gestured with his head back toward the private room.

The last thing I wanted was a meeting with a man whom I might, perhaps, be killing in just a few days. I had been avoiding Franklin precisely because I did not want to listen to his light banter and foolish jokes. There was no point knowing him better. I wanted to keep him an abstraction, but Franklin was clearly determined to make doing so difficult. I sighed and followed the large man back inside.

"Whatever you have to say, I do not wish to hear it," I told him. "Particularly not now."

Franklin closed the door behind him and looked at me. "You don't wish to hear it. That much is true. But you need to. For some time now, I've been taking gold from an Inquisitor named Pedro Azinheiro, who asked that I report on your comings and goings."

That Franklin would admit this surprised me.

"I suspect you have found out," Franklin said, "which is why you've been so disinclined to speak to me."

I did not answer. I wasn't prepared to tell him the truth, that I knew he had betrayed my father, so what else was there to say?

Franklin sighed. "You know how few choices I have. You know better than most. If an Inquisitor asks, you say yes. Someone else will do it, so it is better to take the gold and stay out of their dungeons. But I want you to know I've told him nothing—not about who you are or why you are here. I've reported to him about your comings and goings, such as anyone might see, and nothing more than that."

"Why are you telling me this?" I asked. "What do you expect from me?"

"I tell you so that you'll be careful. I expect nothing, except, perhaps, your understanding. I've wanted to warn you sooner, but you would not listen. In the meantime, I've said nothing about anything you might not wish to speak of—the Englishwoman, the Portuguese tough. But sooner or later, nothing I have to say will matter. If he wants you, he'll have you."

I stared at Franklin, his wide eyes and red cheeks. Perhaps he had betrayed my father years before, but now he was trying to find some way to do the right thing. He was trying to make peace with the son of the man he had wronged.

Could I make peace in return? If I had truly come to this city to remake myself, was I not obligated to accept Franklin's efforts to atone?

It was ultimately a matter for another time. Now I had other and more pressing matters to tend to. "Thank you," I managed. "I appreciate your candor."

"It is no more than my duty to the son of a man I admired," Franklin said. "I have done what I could, and I will do all I can. If I can serve you, Mr. Foxx, you need only ask."

Before I acted, it was important that I confirm Roberta's story. I owed that much, and more, to Settwell. But there was nothing to be gained from asking permission to review the Factory records. I was not a member and, as a new merchant, it would be assumed I was looking to gain some kind of advantage over the established men in the city. Therefore, rather than request something that would be denied, I took the initiative to find out the facts on my own, in the most logical and expedient fashion. That is to say, I broke into the consul's house.

Men not actively on guard against deception have little defense against it, but even so, obtaining the information I desired proved easier than I would have expected. The mansion in the upper reaches of the Bario Alto was the consul's private residence, but also a semi-public building and the center of activity for the Factory. Meetings among merchants and with Portuguese officials were held there, and Anglican Sunday church services were conducted in the spacious ballroom. So I entered the building through the back, walking through the kitchens with the scowl of a busy man who resented the lesser beings around him. None of these would dare to question a prosperous-looking Englishman. I climbed the massive stairway, and, under the scrutiny of portraits of past consuls and Factory men, barked orders at a succession of servants until I found the room that held the records. It was a large, sunlit space full of overwrought furnishings and overstuffed bookshelves. The room was empty but for a pair of clerks. I stabbed a finger at one and told him what I wished to look at. He never thought to question the order, and I was soon sitting before a thick folio of handwritten accounts.

There, in the ledgers, was precisely the transaction Roberta Carver had described. I could find no evidence of anything like what Settwell had told me. Settwell had lost his money through impetuous mismanagement. I had, without doubt, been deceived.

I departed the house back through the kitchens. I did not wish to see anyone who might recognize me.

What would I do? What *could* I do? I could not pauperize the man once more. Even if I wished to, Mariana remained in danger, and I could not endure that the child's future be sacrificed because of the foolishness of the father. I did consider all obligation to Settwell to be discharged, however. Indeed, Settwell was now in my debt.

I would demand ten thousand pounds' worth of the notes. Five thousand pounds was fortune enough, and considering how ill-gotten it was, Settwell could not complain. I would insist upon—indeed, oversee—Settwell's return to England, where he would live very comfortably upon his stolen money, if not quite so comfortably as he had hoped.

I would then return the ten thousand pounds to Roberta. She would initially refuse them, of course, but I would make certain she took them all the same. The money had been stolen, and their names had been tainted, but the notes would enable the Carvers to discharge their debts and return to England in good standing. Their dreams of mercantile conquest would be, at least temporarily, at an end, but they would be independent and have a sizable fortune. As for the five thousand pounds I would still owe them, I had some ideas about how I might make that up, and perhaps a surplus as well, though I could not guarantee I would survive the effort.

Once back in England, assuming I yet lived, I would confess everything to Roberta. Perhaps she would forgive me. Perhaps she would not. Perhaps it did not matter. She was another man's wife, after all, and while I had thought we had been deceiving each other, I now understood that I, alone, had been deceiving her. She would, in all likelihood, spurn me. Why should she do anything else when she had no notion of who I truly was? Still I would do what I could to make amends.

There was nothing to do now but see Settwell and reveal to him how things would proceed. He would not like it. Based on his behavior this morning, he would behave badly. I very much hoped things would not end violently.

Chapter 25

Whatever I intended to say to Settwell, I forgot it the moment I approached the house. Neighbors gathered outside, whispering to one another. The old mulatto woman was weeping and pulling at her hair, and an elderly priest stood arguing with Settwell. I had no idea what any of it meant, but I knew it would be a terrible idea to investigate while the priest was still there. I remained in the shadows, watching and silent, for the better part of an hour until the priest left, the neighbors retreated, and Settwell and the wailing mulatto returned to the house.

I waited another half hour and then approached the door. Trying the handle, I found it open and entered without being announced. Settwell stood in the parlor, drinking wine. His face was a mask of grief.

"The worst has happened," he said without looking up. "The Inquisition has taken Mariana."

I stood motionless. "Tell me what happened."

"An Inquisitor arrived here," Settwell said, "with an

army of priests and nuns. They said that I had proved myself an unfit guardian for my daughter, who had expressed a wish to be raised in a proper Catholic home. Mariana, of course, denied it, but the priests merely said that children were reluctant to admit such things in front of their parents."

"Where will they take her?" I asked.

"Eventually, she shall go to a family that will raise her. For now, I think she is at a nunnery, though they would not tell me which one."

I considered my options.

Then Settwell said, "They know about you."

I felt everything inside me grow tight and coiled. "What do you mean?"

Though I had asked, I already knew what he meant. I was exposed. The Inquisition knew I was an escaped New Christian. They knew I had deceived them from the moment of my arrival in Lisbon. All of my disguises were done. I felt my body course with a curious admixture of panic and joy. The most dangerous men in the city would come for me now, but my fetters were broken. I could meet them without pretense.

Settwell sighed. "One of the reasons the priest said they could not leave her with me was because I consort with unrepentant Jews. They spoke the name Raposa. They know about you, and they mean to capture you."

"You must speak to the consul. He will help you," I suggested. There were things to do; that was all. There had been things to do before, and there were different things to do now. Only the details had changed.

"I can expect no help from the Factory!" Settwell shouted. He stomped upon the floor and raised his balled fist at me. "The consul can do nothing in these cases. I'm not the first Englishman whose child has been lost this way. Once the Inquisition takes them, they are gone. They are gone forever, and you know it. Indeed you told me as much earlier."

I stared at Settwell. There was more to this story. I had not been looking for signs of deception from him before, but I sought them now, and I was sure he held something back. "You say that, and yet you do not seem to believe that it is so."

"There was but one thing I could offer them to make them relent," Settwell said.

I drew a long dagger from the secret sheath along my leg. Settwell had surely traded me for his daughter. "You fool," I said, my voice low and raspy. "You know the Inquisition does not bargain. They mean to have both me and Mariana."

"I know that, but I had to take the chance. I had no other choice."

"Your choice was to depend upon me to get her back. It is what I do."

"It was too great a risk," Settwell said. "I am sorry." He looked at the floor, and he would not raise his eyes.

I examined the room, as if for a sign of what would come next. "What is their plan?"

"They will take you as you leave the house. Then they will release Mariana."

Everything around me became clear. I saw every blemish in each piece of furniture. I saw every line upon Settwell's face. Each tick of the clock was distinct. A fight was coming. I was determined to make it a good one.

"You are lucky they bargained for a child," I said. "If you had betrayed me for any other reason, I would be obliged to kill you."

"Once I saved a child for your father. Now you save one for me."

"My debt was already canceled," I hissed, "when you deceived me into ruining an innocent family to feed your greed."

Settwell paled further. He looked down and muttered something I could not understand.

"Yes, I found out about the Carvers. Now give me the banknotes. You've earned none of that money, but for your daughter's sake, I will let you keep some small portion."

Settwell shook his head. "The priests knew about the money too. That was the other part of the bargain for getting Mariana back."

My identity was exposed, Mariana was taken, and the money vanished. I could not imagine how things might be worse, but I was certain I would find out, and very quickly. I checked the daggers in my sleeves and the one at my ankle. I gripped the knife in my hand more tightly. I had come to this city to do violence, and I had found reasons—good reasons—to postpone my confrontation with the Inquisitor. It could wait no longer. The choice was no longer mine, and what happened in the next few minutes would affect the lives of the Nobrezas, the Settwells, and the Carvers. All of the people I had touched were doomed if I could not unmake my mistakes.

"What are you doing with that knife?" Settwell asked. "They are going to arrest you. They have soldiers."

"They don't have enough," I said as I approached the door.

Settwell moved before me. Not too close, for he was afraid, and he kept his eyes cast downward. "I know I deceived you, and perhaps you are right to be angry, but that was merely business. Do not go out there looking to fight. You will be killed."

"There is no avoiding danger. They have come for me, and I cannot go with them."

"Then what of Mariana? They will think I've warned you. They will punish me by refusing to return her."

"They were never going to return her, and you know it. The Inquisition takes. It does not give and it does not bargain."

"They will give her back!" Settwell cried. "Consider what you do. It has been years since they have burned anyone. They will arrest you, question you, hold you, but you are an Englishman now. In due course, they will let you go if you but give them names and publicly speak the words they want to hear. It is a little humiliation, but you will survive. You must depend upon that."

"No," I said. "I will not surrender to the Inquisition."

"There is no choice," Settwell nearly shouted. "Have you ever heard of a New Christian resisting the Inquisition when they come to arrest him?"

"I am not a New Christian," I told him. "I am a Jew." I walked out of the house.

They were, as Settwell had said, waiting for me. Six soldiers in livery, carrying muskets so ancient it was reasonable to hope they might kill their wielders for me. And there, among the soldiers, was Azinheiro, his wide-brimmed black hat perched atop his head, his long black coat fluttering in the breeze. He stood staring at me, his handsome face bright with anticipation. He had spent his entire life hunting Jews. At long last he was about to catch one.

I stood on Settwell's stoop and looked at the soldiers. I looked at the priest. I noted the contours of the street. I felt the wind and the moisture in the air and examined the light.

"An old friend of yours, a rather low fellow called Inácio, came to visit me," the priest said. "He tried to sell me some information. Though of course, we paid nothing for it. It seems you are not a man of the Church after all."

"I was once," I said.

"This Inácio said you have come here to kill me."

"I have," I said.

"I am told I arrested your father," Azinheiro said. "I do not recall it, and I have not checked the records. I'm sure they would refresh my memory. But they say you fled, and now you are back. Now you too will be made to answer for your sins."

"No," I said. "I won't."

"Do you mean to resist so that we must kill you?" Azinheiro asked.

"I have no intention of being killed," I said.

"Come now," the priest said, and there was something in his voice. Perhaps he sensed the coming violence, like static in the air before a storm. "You cannot fight six armed men and hope to live. Your bravado will not protect you if one of these soldiers fires a musket at you."

"Your men can't fire their muskets if they are dead," I said.

One of the soldiers began to cock back the hammer of his weapon. I threw my knife at him, striking below his helmet, directly in his eye. An instant after I threw the blade, I leapt forward, taking hold of the primed musket and pointing it at another soldier, who was lowering his own weapon. I squeezed the trigger, allowing the musket to explode directly at the soldier, whose chest burst into a red mist.

Twisting out of the way, anticipating and sowing confusion in the tight quarters, I closed the distance with another soldier, grabbing his musket by its snout and pointing it up. I then yanked it free and used it as a club to strike its owner. The blow landed with crushing force, caving in the helmet, and the soldier was down. I turned quickly to another enemy and swung the musket hard and fast into the man's throat. Something snapped. The soldier gurgled and turned purple in the face as he fell with blood bubbling on his lips.

I pulled the blade free from the face of the first man I had killed, and it came out of the eye with a sickening slurping nose. I pivoted and released the missile directly at one of the two remaining soldiers. This one stood some fifteen feet away, and was readying his musket. My knife blade penetrated the man's neck. The weapon discharged at the sky.

There was but one soldier left, and he was more than twenty feet away. I grabbed one of the still-loaded guns from the ground and held steady for an instant, then dodged for cover just before the other man fired. The shot missed me, and I sprang forward, knowing I had time. When there was but five feet between us, I pulled back the hammer and discharged the ball into the man's torso.

The violence had been brutal and merciless. It had also been swift. It had taken less than half a minute to dispatch the six soldiers. In the midst of the fallen men stood Azinheiro, looking stunned. In his long career he had seen men tortured and mutilated. He had overseen brandings and piercings, eyes gouged and fingers broken and severed. He had seen men and women burned alive. Never before had he seen soldiers of the Inquisition struck down while performing their duties. No one had ever dared. Now here were six of them, lying twisted upon the ground in pools of blood. Most were dead, the rest were dying.

I stood, breathing quickly and steadily, my pounding pulse a distant rhythm. I knew the Inquisitor's expression. It was the look of a man who discovered, too late, that he had taken on the wrong enemy.

I had by now retrieved the long knife that I had used to kill the two soldiers. It glistened with blood. Grabbing the priest by one arm, I pressed the blade to Azinheiro's throat. "You will tell me how to get the girl back to her father, or I will kill you now. And then I will find out from someone else."

"You cannot get her back," Azinheiro said. "She is in my mother's care, for I could trust no one else. She will be treated well for a few days, until a family can be found. I could get her out for you, but you would have to trust me, and I fear you will not do that."

"No," I agreed. "I cannot trust you."

"You can't win, you know. There is a reason no one has ever dared to harm soldiers of the Inquisition."

"The reason is that men have families they will not endanger. I have none. You killed them all, priest. That is why I dare to do what I do."

"You do have friends," the Inquisitor said, his words rushed and stumbling, not risking the passage of an unnecessary second. "The girl, for one. We have determined, thus far, that she is a good Catholic, but what if we are mistaken? What if she is a heretic? What if you have corrupted her with your Jewishness?"

"She is a *child,*" I hissed.

Evidently, the priest saw no point in responding to this. "And then there is the family Nobreza. Even as we speak, soldiers of the Inquisition are at their house—"

I let go of the priest and ran. I did not know if I could reach Gabriela in time, but I had to try. The priest was going nowhere. I would find him later. He would tell me what I needed to know. And then he would die.

When I reached the house, I knew it was too late. There was no sign of habitation, and wooden planks had been nailed across the door, a sign I knew too well. I did not have to get close to read the parchment attached to the boards. I knew what it would say. The house now belonged to the Inquisition. Neighbors were out in the streets, talking in excited whispers, horrified at what had happened, delighted it had not been to them, and fearful they would be implicated when the Inquisitors went to work.

I retreated into a dark alley. The staggering losses of the past twenty-four hours were almost beyond my ability to tally. Enéas was dead. Roberta was ruined, and the money I had stolen from her was in the hands of the Inquisition. Mariana had been taken, and so had Gabriela, her husband, and Luis, a man who was perhaps my only true friend in Lisbon. I had been exposed, and I could not return to my inn lest I be arrested myself. They would not make the mistake of trying to apprehend me with anything less than a small army this time, and I could not be certain of my ability to defeat the next force they sent against me.

This, then, was the end of the road. I was out of options and out of hope.

At least that was what the Inquisition would think. Mr. Weaver had always said that my greatest strength was that I did not give a fig for what happened to me. I was willing to take risks other men would shy from because I did not fear the consequences. I knew that this was what separated me from other people. It was, I believed, the darkness that lived inside me. The time to embrace it was now. I would be the monster the Inquisition had created.

I had never killed anyone before today, but now six men lay dead at my hand. I could not say I felt much in the way of regret. They had stood against me, and they intended to harm my friends. Friends who were now imprisoned in stone and steel, guarded by blade and musket. They resided in a prison from which there had never been any rescue because there had never been any attempt—until now.

I had a few days. I knew that much. They had to seek a family for Mariana, and she would not be harmed in the meantime. As for the family Nobreza, each of them, like all New Christians, had been taught since childhood how to manipulate the Inquisitorial system— what to say and how to say it to avoid torture and receive the lightest penalty. Only a fool claimed true innocence, for that only made the Inquisitors angry. Instead, they would confess to small crimes— lighting candles on Friday or refraining from work on Saturday. Yes, I refused to eat pork. Yes, I muttered a prayer in Hebrew whose words I did not understand. The Inquisitors devoured these lies like they were sweets.

Gabriela and Luis and even Eusebio would be well for two or three days. By that point I would know what to do. I needed only time and resolve.

I sat down in the dark alley and lowered my head onto my arms, folded across my knees. Anyone watching me, knowing what I had endured that day, would think me giving in to despair, but it was not so. I did not weep. Instead, I began to think and to plan. I did not know precisely what I would do, but I knew a large number of men were going to die, and if all went well, I would not be one of them.

Chapter 26

I had little hope that my plan would work. The boy I
paid to deliver the note was a stranger, and might well
simply pocket the money. Even if the note was received, I
could not depend upon its recipient coming to my aid.

If only I had Enéas here to help me, I thought. That
faithful boy who had trusted me, who was now dead because I had, in turn, trusted the wrong people. Again and
again, I destroyed those I touched—the kind, the well
meaning, the innocent. I wanted Enéas's help, of course,
but what I needed more was to believe that I was somehow worthy of his loyalty.

I was in a bagnio in the Alfama. It was a terrible place of
crooked floors and warped walls. The building smelled of
boiled onions and unemptied chamber pots. The woman I
had paid for sat in the corner of the room, her arms hugging her knees. She was the prettiest in the house, and the
proprietress said she was the prettiest in the Alfama. It
might have been so. She was tall, olive-skinned, and green-
eyed, with curling coal-black hair. She'd smiled at me and

showed me her white, even teeth. I had taken her upstairs without further comment. When I entered the room, I told her to leave me alone. She had done so, but the look of terror on her face made it clear she thought I was a madman.

After the fight with the Inquisition soldiers, I had bought new clothes—plain woolen trousers and a shirt and a vest. A wide-brimmed hat, I hoped, concealed much of my face. I wanted to look like an ordinary Portuguese, and I suppose I did, but when I caught a glimpse of myself in the room's mirror, my crazed expression frightened even myself.

I had to do something. I had to do many things, but how could I? How could I wrest Gabriela and her family from the Inquisition? How could I find and free Mariana? And how could I save Roberta when the money I had taken from her was gone?

At last came a knock on the door. I gestured for the woman to answer it. If it was anyone other than the man I had sent for, I would need to act quickly.

When she pulled open the door, I let out my breath. It was Kingsley Franklin.

I pulled the large man inside and closed the door. Franklin looked around, and watched the woman seat herself once more in the corner. Franklin smiled at her.

"I suppose you've paid her so you could hide out here for a few hours. But maybe someone ought to sample the goods." He grinned at me, but seeing my expression, lost his own sense of humor.

"Have you heard anything of this afternoon?"

"Begging your pardon, sir, but I believe they've heard of those events in Rome by now. You struck down fifteen soldiers of the Inquisition."

"It was somewhat less than that," I said.

"They came to the inn and seized your things. They found a book of Jewish prayers among them. They nearly arrested me, but a parcel of Factory men descended upon them like locusts."

"Factory men?"

"They may care nothing for me," Franklin said, "but I am an Englishman, and that is sometimes enough. The Factory will do all it can to protect its own. I'm safe for now."

"By the time I am done with them, there won't be anyone left to arrest you."

Franklin shook his head. "I understand your anger, but you can't fight your way out of this. Fighting is why you are a fugitive."

"I had no choice. I was discovered. They were coming for me. It was resist or be arrested."

Franklin nodded. "You'll be wanting a way out of the city now, I suppose. I'll do what I can for you. Money. Documents. You must tell me what you need."

"No," I said. "I can't leave." I quickly told Franklin about the Nobrezas and Settwell's daughter. I did not tell him about Roberta Carver. The truth was too bitter for words.

Franklin shook his head. "Your friends are gone, Mr. Foxx. They're beyond your help. As for the little girl, you might be able to get the priest to tell you where she is if you are still determined to harm him."

"Yes, but I need to find him. Soon."

"Then you're in luck," Franklin said with a grim smile. "Tomorrow is All Saints' Day. The streets will be crowded. You'll never have a better opportunity to approach him unseen."

It was obvious. I should have thought of it myself. "I know the priest's church, so it will not be difficult to intercept him on his way. I then find out where he is keeping Mariana, and I kill him. Before word spreads, before mass is even over, I must find and liberate the girl. If I get Settwell and his daughter to you, will you see them out of the city? Can I depend upon you for this?"

Franklin nodded. "You can, sir."

"Then I will deal with my friends in the Palace dungeons."

"I understood you until that last part. How exactly will you attend to that?"

"I don't know," I admitted. "But I shall manage something. If I have to kill every priest in the Palace, I will get them out."

Franklin shook his head. "By the very devil, sir, I know you mean it, and I half think you can do it."

I studied the innkeeper. His face was red, his beard patchy, his eyes heavily bagged—and yet for all that, there was a spark about him, as though he were enjoying the adventure.

"Why are you so eager to help me, Mr. Franklin?" Perhaps I wanted to hear him confess. Perhaps I merely wanted to make certain his motives were good.

Franklin laughed. "Because I must, Mr. Foxx. I hate this city, and I hate what it's done to me. You're not the only one who wants revenge."

It was a clear morning, bright and cloudless, and the streets were full. The bakers fired up their ovens early, and the stalls on the Rossio were filled with breads and pastries and fruits. An hour after dawn, despite the brilliant sunlight, there were candles in every window. An hour after that, the streets were lined with processions as the penitent brought flowers and offerings to their dead before church. There were beggars and soldiers and *fidalgos,* priests and nuns and monks. Rarely had I seen the city so full of people.

There was only one procession I cared about, making its way to the Igreja de São Domingos. I found an alley and waited. I pressed my back against the wall and allowed the chants and the songs to wash over me. This was the moment so long delayed. This was the reason I had come to Lisbon, but any sense of satisfaction had vanished. No matter what happened next, it would not change the fundamental facts that Mariana was in the hands of the Inquisition and

Gabriela was in the Palace dungeon. None of these things would have happened if I had not been here, and yet I wanted to believe I was not to blame.

When the Inquisitor passed, it was like picking fruit. He walked in a group of penitents, candles thrust forward, eyes down, mouths mumbling song. Ordinary people surrounded the priest, not other clergy, not other Inquisitors. I simply reached out, grabbed Azinheiro's shoulder, and pulled him into the alley between the São Domingos church and the Hospital Real de Todos os Santos. I released the priest and let momentum do its work. Azinheiro skidded along the ground, sliding through beggars' excrement and dirty rags.

The buildings on either side of the alley were both tall, and it was twilight dark toward the center. I squinted as I looked at the priest upon the ground, enjoying his confusion for only a fleeting second. This was not about pleasure. It was about necessity. Before Azinheiro could cry out, I pulled him to his feet and hurled him forward into the wall. The priest's head struck, and he was dazed, which had been my intent. Grabbing his arm, I pulled him deeper into the alley's darkness. The priest complied, unable to resist. Quiet groans escaped his lips, but nothing more. His mind would be racing, trying to find a way out of this, trying to find the words that would save him.

I shoved him forward again. Azinheiro stumbled, but did not fall. He struggled to right himself, to stand like a man and be master of his own fate. For decades he had watched as men were helpless against his power. He would not like knowing what it felt like on the other side.

I moved farther in. The buildings to either side of us leaned closer as the alley progressed, and there was just enough space for me to walk without angling my body. The light of the bright November morning hardly penetrated. All was gray and shadow. I thrust the man up against the wall once more, and the back of his head again made contact. The priest cried out and this time slumped to the ground. He sat still, looking up. His full lips moved soundlessly. He showed no sign of trying to rise.

"You know why you are here?" I asked.

"I do not care," the priest said. He swallowed hard, closed his eyes, and then gazed at me with an expression of outrage, as if I were violating the fundamental laws of the universe itself. "You are an unrepentant Jew, and your every word and deed proves why this Inquisition's work is vital."

I knew there was no point in debating a man such as this. The world bent and contorted itself to fit his understanding, not the other way around. I could not make him see reason, could not make him regret his actions. It would be a mistake to try. My business wasn't persuasion—that was the Inquisition's concern. I merely resolved injustice long neglected.

"You have destroyed countless lives," I said. "Your actions have caused people to die, including my mother and father. You have robbed the innocent to fill the Inquisition treasury. You have stolen my friend's daughter and you have dragged others, for whom I care, to your dungeons."

The priest looked up. "I have done no wrong, and I fear no judgment, certainly not from a Jew, and least of all from an English Jew."

I took out my long knife. "We shall see," I said. "Where is the girl, Mariana Settwell?"

The priest's dark eyes were wide with disbelief and fear. Had he ever felt powerless before? Had he ever worried for his own safety? In all his years of stoking the fires of terror and inflicting pain and extracting confessions, had he ever wondered what it would be like to feel those things himself?

I put the knife to the Inquisitor's face, just under his eye, and slid it along, making a shallow cut. The wound bled freely but not copiously. It was meant only to suggest the seriousness of the situation.

The priest began to weep. "What are you," he asked, "that would do this to another man?"

The question was like a blow to my belly. "How can you ask me that? You who have done such things for longer than I've been alive?"

"But I served the Holy Inquisition. You serve nothing."

"I serve the ideas and the people I honor," I said. "I'll ask you once more, and then I'll take out your eye, so consider your next words carefully. Where is the Settwell child?"

The priest nodded. "She's with my mother, in the Conceição dos Cardais."

I knew it: a small Carmelite convent dedicated to the care of the infirm, in the Bario Alto. I could get Mariana and bring her back to her father. Then I could—I could do what? I still had no clear notion of how I would get the Nobrezas out of the Palace, but I knew one thing for certain: if the Inquisitor left this alley, Mariana would not remain at that convent for long.

Yesterday I had killed in self-defense. Could I truly kill a man in cold blood? I had always believed that when the moment came, I would be equal to the task. Now here it was, and it was no longer simply a matter of rebalancing the scales of justice. A child's life, a parent's love, hung in the balance, and yet I found that murdering a man, even the most hated of men, was a harder thing than killing in the heat of conflict.

The priest managed a weak smile. His eyes grew bright. He knows, I thought. He sees my hesitation, and he means to exploit it.

"You turned me into something vile," I said. "I will not let what little is merciful in me spare you."

The priest shook his head. "Can you not see the hand of God in this? You *think* yourself a demon, but like all men, the struggle between heaven and hell rages within you. You have come all this way, done all these things, only to discover what you could have known all along: that you are not so bad as you believe. Perhaps you are no worse than other men."

"Your talk won't save you," I said, but I wasn't sure if it was true. Where was my rage now? I thought about my parents: my mother's hasty farewell on the Factory quays; my father, whose face was hard to recall. I remembered my love for Gabriela and how she was gone forever, married to Eusebio.

"Do what you must, my son. I have never acted in any way not in accordance with the teachings of my faith. I am at peace."

The priest did, indeed, appear to be at peace. "Your delusions of rectitude mean nothing to me," I said as I probed myself for the will to strike. "All that matters is that I will know I have done what I have to do."

The priest's smile grew. "Kill me if you think it will help. I will answer to my God in heaven, and I have no fear of what is to come."

I did not recall seeing him rise, but the priest was now on his feet. He wiped at his bloody face with his sleeve and took a few slow steps away from me, never taking his eyes off me. He looked like a man easing himself away from a vicious dog. That was how he saw me— as an animal, dangerous and deranged, but one that might yet be soothed. Even now, at this moment, he did not understand what he had done to me.

I took a step forward, but only one, before I heard something—a great beast hidden in the earth, groaning in pain. I felt it in my feet, vibrating up my legs. Then the noise came from everywhere. It was like the voices of the damned, breaking free of hell, a deep and awful rumbling. The walls all around began to shudder until the stones sprouted veins. I was stilled by the realization that something immense and dreadful was happening.

A brick fell from high above, grazing the priest along his skull. Azinheiro cried out, and blood gushed from his forehead. Another brick fell, exploding into dust, and then the ground was no longer vibrating, but heaving and rolling like the waves of the sea. Cracks erupted in the soil, and the earth began to spit forth dust and pebbles. The rumbling grew louder and from everywhere there were screams and the sounds of stone grinding, grinding, grinding against stone. Bricks and tiles were now raining down, creating a wall of debris in the space between me and the priest. It had been mere seconds since I first noticed the growling, and now I could not reach Azinheiro. The alley had become a death trap. It would, in seconds, become a tomb. I knew I had to do the thing that came least naturally to me.

I fled.

It was like an invisible hand had pulled free the thread binding together the alley and it had unwound into a pile of rubble. The air was full of dust. I escaped from the narrow confines, though my face and arms had sustained a hundred small wounds. A trickle of blood ran into my eye from a cut just above my hairline.

It was more than the alley. More than this street. All round me, buildings shook upon their foundations, folding in upon themselves and crumbling as though made of sand. I had run uphill, away from the Rossio, so I could not see how the great church and the hospital and the Palace fared, but I watched as house after house fell forward or inward, Lisbon's structures unmaking themselves. Statues toppled like toy soldiers. Crosses spun from church roofs, becoming deadly, spiraling missiles. The worshippers packing the streets dropped their effigies and candles and ran, but where could they go? The entire city was ripping itself apart. I looked up at a distant hillside and watched as houses—dozens of them—buckled and slid into the sea. How many died in that one instant? Already the injured and the dead lay in the street, struck by debris and trampled by the crowd. There was blood everywhere. Shrieks of terror and cries of pain echoed through the broken city, which had only minutes—seconds!—before been a glittering jewel, the pride of Portugal and the envy of Europe. Now it was a landscape of hell.

Then, all at once, it was over. The ground ceased to shake and the buildings no longer trembled. From every direction came snapping as stone and brick settled. Distant crashes sounded as structures weakened by the quake gave out, but these were sporadic, like the popping of wood in fire. The massive church I stood near remained standing, though fissures marked the walls.

An eerie quiet began to spread across the city. Everyone held themselves still, stopping where they were. That a city could collapse had, minutes ago, surely seemed impossible. Now the fact that it could stop seemed equally unlikely, and the survivors gaped in wonder and respite.

Then came a new chorus of cries of pain and loss, and the screams of the injured and the dying. Horses and donkeys brayed. Dogs barked and howled. Broken bells clanged. Women called for their children, those from whom they were separated and those who lay dead on the ground or in their arms.

From across the expanse of these many hills rose a collective wailing. It swept across the city like a wave as tens of thousands of people fell to their knees and cried toward the heavens.

"You have been punished!" called out a priest. "You have tasted God's wrath, and he has punished you. Repent! Repent lest you anger God further."

I took quick stock. What mattered? What was important? There were wounded who needed tending and the trapped who needed rescuing, but anyone could do such things. What needed doing that only I could do? The priest? I looked back toward the Rossio, but that course was futile. The priest was buried under rubble or had fled to safety. There was nothing to be done there.

Gabriela? She was in the Palace, and even a casual glance around the city told me that the largest buildings had survived the quake. Smaller structures lay in rubble, but the palaces and great churches, the mansions and fine houses, though scarred and cracked and beaten, yet stood. Gabriela would be as safe as anyone, ironically enough, inside the Inquisition dungeon.

But what of Roberta, in her house upon the Bario Alto? She might be alive but buried under rubble. She might need my help. I had destroyed her life, but perhaps I could now save it.

I ran uphill and to the west. As I rose higher, I could see that the Palace of the Inquisition indeed still stood. Everywhere else lay the injured and the dead, stood the weeping and praying. Houses were but stews of stone and tile and wood, as though crushed by giants. In places it was hard to find the streets, so covered was the ground with the splayed remains of homes. The air smelled heavy with dust from the broken brick and ceramics, and smoke from the fires that were burning everywhere. They were small fires now, but they would grow. With all the candles lit for the holiday, there could have been no more dangerous time for a disaster of this sort.

A man lay upon the rubble, his left arm crushed to pulp, his eyes wide and unreasoning. I sped past him. A woman tried to recruit me in the search for a missing priest. I ran past her. It was not that I did not care. I wanted to help them all, but I could not. Until I had seen to the people I cared for, the strangers would have to fend for themselves.

The Carvers had rented a fine detached house on a street of sturdy buildings, and here the city seemed strangely untouched. Roberta's house was comparatively sound. Part of the roof had fallen into the street, the windows were all broken, and the door was open and askew, but the house remained. I ran inside and stopped in my tracks. There was a body on the floor, a woman of middle years, a Portuguese servant by her dress. Her throat had been cut. There were footprints and streaks in the pool of congealed blood. There had been a struggle.

I rushed ahead, calling Roberta's name. I could smell no fire burning, but the air was full of shit and piss and vomit. Other people had died here. Paintings had fallen from the walls, which were cracked and smashed, but still stood. The ceilings had fallen in places, coating the furnishings with dust and knocking chairs and statues onto their sides.

Then I heard the weeping. I ran to the stairs, but they too had collapsed. Then I realized that the weeping did not come from above, but from the parlor. There, amid the debris and chunks of plaster and brick, sat Roberta upon the floor. Her face was bruised, black where she had been struck, and her lip and nose were bloody. She wore a nightgown that had been torn down the middle, and clutched the ragged sides to hold them together. A blanket rested over her shoulders.

I knelt beside her. "Roberta, what happened? Where is your husband?"

"Dead," she said. She did not look up. Her body heaved with crying, but no tears fell down her cheeks. She had none left.

"What happened to you was before the tremors. What was it?"

"Tremors?" she asked vacantly.

"What happened to Rutherford?"

"He was murdered," she said. "He was killed."

I felt my pulse quickening. I scanned the room as though whoever had hurt Rutherford might still be present. "Who killed him?"

For the first time, she met my eyes. Her gaze was dark and terrible. "You did," she said.

That was when I noticed what was in her hand. It was a dagger with a familiar silver handle, laced with gold, encrusted with jewels.

She told me about it, her voice flat and empty. She awoke the night before to find her husband in her bedroom. Another man stood behind him, pressing a blade to Rutherford's throat. The stranger was large, with a scarred face. He had a shaved head and long mustaches. He grinned with unrestrained pleasure.

Rutherford's eyes were wide with horror and disbelief. He wore no wig, and his close-cut hair was damp with sweat.

286 | DAVID LISS

"My name is Inácio Arouca," the man with the jeweled blade said. "I do not care if you know it, because you will not survive to see the morning."

Rutherford whimpered when he heard this. Frightened though she was, Roberta did not allow herself to make a sound. She sat up. A single candle burned in a wall sconce—lit by this beast of a man, perhaps—and from her bed she searched for something she could use against him.

It did not have to be a deadly weapon. She did not have to kill him. She just had to stagger him long enough that she could escape—she could elude him. She was sure of it. She was swift and he was large. She knew this house and he did not. She only needed a moment, a weapon, an opportunity, and if she could make it to her neighbor's house, she would be safe.

"What do you want?" Roberta asked, trying to keep the terror out of her voice. It was foolish, she knew. A man like this would expect her, want her, to be frightened, and defiance and pride would only make him angry. But defiance and pride were all the power she had right now.

"I want to discuss your friend, Mr. Foxx," the man said.

"Foxx," snapped Rutherford. "What of him? He's no one to us."

The man laughed. "Is that what you think? He is not no one to your wife, I promise you."

Roberta blinked away her tears. She was shaking her head without realizing it. Rutherford could die, they could both die, and the last thing her husband would hear was that she had nearly betrayed him with another man.

Inácio shook Rutherford a little, as if to wake him. "You are not seeing things as they are, Englishman. Your wife was bedding Foxx. But that is not the worst of it. It is not the worst of it that he is a liar and a scoundrel, a Jew who escaped the justice of the Inquisition and has now returned to stir up trouble. No, for you the worst of it is that he stole your money. Yes, it was he who broke open your vault and took your gold. He schemed with another Englishman called Settwell, and then carried away all your wealth. You have nothing now because of him. I am doing you a favor by killing you."

Could it be true, Roberta wondered, but even as she thought the words, she knew the answer. Of course. Everything made sense now. They had thought they were cultivating Foxx, but he had been cultivating them. She had shown him their vault, and he had noted every lock and door. She had thrown herself at him, and he had pushed her away because he did not care for her . . . and because he was a Jew, as she would have quickly discovered. Too late, she understood.

"I never betrayed my husband with him," Roberta said, looking away from Rutherford, not wanting to see his eyes. "You are mistaken."

He grinned. "Maybe yes, maybe no. Perhaps you did not care that he was a Jew. Perhaps he could not have you, for his secret nature would have been revealed. But you wanted to, I'll wager. Perhaps you threw yourself at him, and he scorned you. Ah, I can see by your face it is true. What lies, I wonder, did he tell you to make you believe a man would choose not to take such a beauty? They must have been convincing."

She hated herself for being so transparent. She made her face a mask. She would reveal nothing else. She would give up not an inch of ground. No matter what happened, he would have no more easy victories.

She had to think. They had been ruined and betrayed and now they were going to be murdered, and it was all Sebastian Foxx's fault. But there must be a way out.

"He is clearly your enemy," Roberta said. "He is our enemy as well, so why have you come here?"

"Because I want to hurt him," the man said, "and if he knows he caused your deaths, that will bring him much pain. This is what must happen, because he needs to see that everything he touches will come to ruin. I am the hand of God in all this. I am here for justice. Do you understand me?"

Roberta nodded, wanting only to placate him.

"Good," he said. "Now, remove your gown and fuck me. If you make certain I enjoy it, I will let you and your husband live. If you resist, I will kill him and continue, giving you one more chance to convince me."

"Please," she said. "I don't want this."

The man pressed the blade to Rutherford's neck.

"Just do what he says," Rutherford said. "It doesn't matter."

"Your husband is a sensible man," Inácio told her. "I suggest you be sensible too."

This could not be happening, she thought. She would not let it happen. She needed some way to change this, to undo it, to remake it.

"Please," she said. "If you let us be, I will pay you. We have money—gold our creditors don't know about. It is yours if you simply go."

"What gold?" His eyes widened. "How much?"

"One hundred and twenty reaís," she said. "In a bag. You can take it and run."

She could see that Inácio was interested. Likely he would want both the money and to hurt Foxx, but she was distracting him, changing things.

"Very well," he said, not even trying to keep the deception from his voice. "I accept your bargain. Get me this money, and I'll enjoy a Portuguese whore instead of an English one."

She nodded quickly, but she wasn't ready. Not yet. The Portuguese were religious and superstitious. Even the depraved ones, perhaps especially the depraved ones, took their oaths seriously. He wanted the money, so Roberta was determined to make him earn it. "Swear upon Christ and all the saints that you will let us go if I give you the money."

Inácio appeared to struggle with this demand for a moment, and then, at last, he nodded.

Roberta slowly drew back her covers and crossed the room, feeling Inácio's eyes upon her as he hunted for her shape in her formless gown. She trembled from cold and fear. She came to a dresser, and with a shaking hand began to pull open a drawer. This was her moment.

With a comb in hand she lunged. There was a flash of silver in the dim light and Inácio's eyes went wide as she plunged the sharp teeth into his forearm, the one holding the dagger. Inácio dropped the blade and staggered backward. The comb had gone deep into his flesh, maybe two inches, and he was howling with pain.

Rutherford dropped to the floor, and was probing his skin for signs that his throat had been cut—as if he would have any doubt about it.

"Get up!" she screamed. She should have fled, she knew, but Rutherford wasn't moving, and she was still waiting for him, even as Inácio pulled the comb out of his arm and strode forward, his face a skeletal icon of fury.

"Are you mad?" Rutherford barked at her. "You have to do as he says!"

She saw now that he wasn't going to escape. He had put his faith in this man rather than her, rather than himself. He didn't rise even as Inácio picked up his fallen dagger. He didn't resist even as Inácio pulled back Rutherford's neck and raised the blade.

That was when Roberta ran to the stairs and hurled herself down. The house was dark. That was her advantage. That was what would save her. She would not think about what would happen if she failed. She would not think about the wet sound she'd heard, the noise of metal on flesh, the horrible, horrible gurgling. Rutherford was dead, but all she would think about was the door, getting there first. Finding it first. She would increase the gap between herself and Inácio because the house was dark and he could not see her, and she knew where she was going.

But it was the darkness that undid her. Inácio had already killed Isabela, their one remaining servant. Roberta knew it was her when one foot caught something heavy and soft just as the other slipped in a hot, sticky liquid. Even as she began to fall, Roberta knew she could not recover. She would go down, and he would be on top of her, and she would not get up.

She hit the floor hard. Pain shot through her elbow. And then a rough hand grabbed her hair, pulling her back so forcefully she blacked out for an instant. She felt nothing but sickening confusion and nausea. She was on her back now, her hair wet with Isabela's blood. Or was it her own? Or was it her vomit? Had she voided her stomach without noticing?

Inácio had her down, pinning her arms to the floor and breathing his fishy breath on her. He smelled of sweat and tobacco. Blood from his arm, the wound she had made, dripped in her eye and stung.

Inácio grabbed the collar of her gown and ripped. Her breasts were exposed, and she felt his hands on her, wet with sweat and her husband's blood.

He didn't have his dagger.

She lay very still, willing herself not to feel his rough pawing, while her hands gently searched the floor, feeling through the stickiness, probing around Isabela's body. And then something hard and cool. Metal. The handle of the dagger.

She sliced through the air. She should have gone for his neck or his face, but she was too afraid. Instead she went for what was closest, the arm she'd already stabbed.

Inácio screamed and fell away from her. Somehow she rose. Her hair was wet with blood. Her breasts were still exposed. Her mouth opened as she screamed and lunged at him again, and she knew she looked like a demon of hell. Even as her mind closed, as reality fell away, she knew she had to win, and she cried out to him that she *was* a demon of hell, that he had betrayed his oath to Christ, and that Satan was coming for him.

She stabbed at the air, hoping to cut him again, but he jumped back. And then he ran. He found the door, and flung it open, and disappeared into the night.

Roberta slammed the door shut, but she did not move from the front hall. She held the knife, ready for him to come back. She would wait, for he would return, she knew it, and she would kill him, and that would be so much better than going upstairs and finding her husband's body and facing everything that was to come.

I listened to the story, my emotions ranging from maddening anger to admiration. She had fought off a man who possessed twice her strength. In the direst of situations, she had remained cunning and resourceful. She was a marvel, and I had destroyed everything she held dear.

She was very still after she'd told me what had happened. We remained in that house full of corpses, in a city full of even greater death, and neither of us said a word for I know not how long. Then she spoke again.

"You cheated us." Her voice was frighteningly controlled. "You stole our money, and you ruined us. I offered myself to you. I gave you my heart, and you trampled upon it."

"I did. I was deceived into thinking you a villain."

She pushed herself back, scrambling like a crab in her haste to move away from me. She ignored the pieces of broken glass and brick that cut into her palms. "You make excuses for being a monster?"

"It is what happened. I wish to God it had not, but it did. I can't change that, but I can help you now."

"Help me with what?" she demanded. "Burying my husband?"

"I shall help you survive in this ruined city," I said.

"What do you mean? What ruined city?"

She didn't know. She had been sitting here for hours, and she hadn't noticed the quake.

"Roberta, open your eyes. Inácio didn't make the windows break and the plaster fall from the walls. Look outside. The city has been destroyed by an earthquake."

She looked around, seeing her surroundings for the first time. Tears rolled down her cheeks. The world had become what she most feared, I realized. It was a place of chaos and disorder, where even the most meticulous care and carefully crafted plans would never provide a safe harbor. Above all else, Roberta wanted stability and safety, and now every last shred of those things had been taken from her. She was lost.

Except that I would not let her be lost. I would save her. She had nothing, and both of us—indeed every person in Lisbon—were now vulnerable in a city that would, over the coming hours, descend into bestial madness. What did Inácio matter when soon this city would be ruled by the desperate and violent, men who would make Inácio seem tame by comparison? I would let him go. I would let Azinheiro go. I would save the people who mattered.

"There are things more important than revenge," I said aloud.

I rose and walked through the ruins of the house until I found the maid's room. Two or three plain dresses hung upon her wall. One of them smelled fairly clean, and I brought it to Roberta. "Put this on."

"Why? What does it matter what I wear?"

I took her by the shoulders and tried to make her look at me. "It matters that you live."

She laughed bitterly. "You ruin me, then try to save me. You are mad."

"I have wronged you, and you have come to harm. I cannot undo that, but I can do everything in my power to protect you now."

She tried to push herself away, but I dug my fingers into her shoulders. She leveled her gaze at me. "What do you care what happens to me now?"

I nearly told her I loved her, for I was now certain I did. What had stood in my way before? I had loved what was best about her, but I could not love the wily and deceptive Roberta Carver. That woman was a scoundrel, as broken as I was, caring for nothing but money. Now I knew that the Roberta Carver I had pushed away was a fiction. She had broken faith with her husband, certainly, but she had not been a trickster or a thief. I had been drawn to the woman as she was. The things that had repelled me were lies fabricated by Charles Settwell.

Someday, when she was safe, I would tell her this. I did not think she could forgive me, but maybe she would understand. "I was deceived. I hurt you," I repeated. "Now I pledge my life to see you safe. That will have to be enough."

I did not intend to go anywhere. I needed Roberta dressed so we could react quickly should we need to, but the streets were the last place I wanted to be. People would be frightened and their actions would be difficult to predict. While she put on the gown, I went to the kitchens, where I found food, water, wine, and ale. These supplies would keep us alive. Unfortunately, we were wealthy in the only way that now mattered in Lisbon. There would be people who would do anything to obtain what we possessed.

I went back to Roberta, who had returned to the floor, her arms wrapped about her knees. I sat beside her. She said, "You are all I have now, aren't you?"

"Yes."

"Then I must accept your help, though I hate you, mustn't I?"

"You must."

"What will happen to us?"

"We will survive," I told her.

She looked out the window, though still seeming not to see any details. "There are so many dead already."

"Yes," I agreed.

"Did they not believe they would survive?"

"They behaved foolishly," I said. "They made poor choices. They stood when they should have run or ran when they should have stood. We will do none of those things."

"I suppose I must be grateful, but how can I not hate you?" she asked.

"You may hate me if you like," I told her. "You may swear to take revenge upon me, and I'll not resent it nor resist it. I will help you plunge a dagger into my heart if you like, but you must promise not to harm me until you are safe. Once this disaster is past us, then you may do what you like. But not before. Do you promise?"

She nodded.

"Then we shall be well for now."

The moment I spoke the words, I regretted them, for once more the earth began to shake. The groans of people and buildings and the earth itself echoed throughout the city. Roberta reached for me, but I broke away. I grabbed her wrist and yanked her up, tugging her out of the house and toward the street, which was wide and so the safest place.

Roberta was like a woman asleep. I had to pull her every step of the way. Her glassy eyes turned this way and that and saw nothing. We had hardly crossed the threshold and stumbled out into the street when her house swayed slowly to the left, then violently to the right. It shuddered and then folded in on itself, collapsing in an orderly pile, like a closed book. Only a cough of dust and debris betrayed any sense of violence.

All around us, houses were falling. They vomited stones and tiles and timber. Those buildings that had survived the first quake had been weakened, and now the second quake ripped them apart at their cracks and fissures. I wanted to flee, but there was nowhere to go, and so I stood in the middle of the street, surrounded by the terrified, the wailing, the desperate and the dead-eyed, holding Roberta, who pressed her face to my chest, while everywhere the buildings of Lisbon came undone like soap bubbles popping in a basin.

The sound was incredible, all of it reverberating across the newly empty spaces. The church at the end of the block buckled. In the distance, another church began to heave back and forth like a pendulum, and then it was gone, as though the earth underneath it had vanished. And far off, the Palace of the Inquisition swayed and began to crack. Under the pressure of its movement, it ejected bricks like a fighter spitting out teeth. The massive structure rocked as though picking up momentum, and the walls began to bend in an almost beautiful rolling motion. Then the Palace, the seat and symbol of the Inquisition's power in Lisbon, began to fall in upon itself. And Gabriela was within.

The world had turned to chaos, and I knew I needed to impose order and structure. I needed the destruction of the city to conform to my rules. I would not let the end of the world keep me from rescuing Roberta and Gabriela and Mariana. There was confusion and violence and death everywhere, and none of it would stop me. I understood that this was the place and the time I was built for. All my loss and anger meant I belonged here. My broken soul was made for this. I was a devil, and this was the pit. Everything in my life had led me here, to this moment, when the world around me at long last was a fit place in which I might dwell. I had come home.

I took Roberta's hand and led her down the center of the street, farthest away from falling bricks, and together, with careful and wandering steps, we began to walk.

Chapter 27

I guided Roberta through the streets, which were full of the crying, the wounded, and the praying. Twisted bodies lay everywhere. We saw severed limbs and heads, and corpses cut in half. Buildings burned all around us. Fissures had opened in the earth, five and ten and fifteen feet wide, winding their jagged way across streets and under the ruins of houses.

We reached a little garden where strolling *fidalgos* and English merchants had often liked to look upon the rolling hills of the city. Now we stopped to gaze at the wreckage. From our elevated position, Lisbon looked as though it had been blasted by an invading army. Hardly a church or mansion remained whole. Where there once were buildings now was smoldering rubble. Other sections were engulfed in violent flame, and great clouds of smoke and soot lingered in the air. Ironically, to the east the Alfama had taken some damage, but this poorest part of the city was also the best preserved.

A great swell of people moved toward the river. "They're

trying to escape on ships," Roberta said. "We should hurry before there is no more room."

"No," I said. All of Europe had read of the earthquake in Lima the year before, in which waves had followed the tremors. I would not risk such a fate—not with Roberta. "There are too many of them. There will be chaos and violence, and perhaps even great waves."

Roberta looked down. "Then all those people will die," she said.

I followed her gaze to the English quays and the collection of inns and taverns that had been built up around it.

"Oh, hell," I said. "I believe I have to go down there after all."

Still holding Roberta's hand, I made my way down the hill toward the Duke's Arms. The crowd of people grew thick as I approached the tavern. I pushed and punched by those eager to get on board ships, on barges, on anything that floated.

"You said it was dangerous down here," Roberta said.

"That's why we need to be quick. I have to find someone and get him safe."

"Who?"

"Kingsley Franklin, the man who betrayed my father."

Roberta studied me. "Why?"

"Because I think he's sorry for what he did," I said.

"I don't understand you at all," Roberta told me, but offered no more objections.

Pulling Roberta behind me, I entered the Duke's Arms, which had been shaken in the quakes but was not seriously damaged. Every surface was covered with dust, and a few rafters had fallen from the ceiling. Pots and mugs and food lay on the floor. It looked like a great wind had blown through the common room.

No one was inside but Franklin, who sat at one of the tables, his mug full, his feet up. A grim smile was spread over his ruddy face.

"God took his deuced time, but He got the job done," Franklin said. "This city needed a good leveling." He took a swig from his mug. "You and the lovely lady have earned a drink, I believe."

I shook my head. "We need to get to higher ground. We should do it soon."

Franklin shrugged. "Lima. I read about that. But what does it matter? Maybe a great wave will come. Maybe not. I had nothing, and now I've even less. What can you tempt me with that can compete with the privacy of my own tavern and all the ale I can drink?"

"I have friends in the Palace dungeon," I said. "I mean to rescue them."

"That again." Franklin raised his mug. "Good luck to you, sir. I shall see you in hell, and toast you once more."

"Mr. Franklin, the Palace lies broken, and within there is a fortune. Gold, jewels, bank notes, coins. All of it stolen. I suspect, with the entire city in chaos, that fortune is largely unguarded."

Franklin set down his mug. "Go on."

"I want your help. I want you to come with me to save my friends, steal from the Inquisition, and then rescue Charles Settwell's daughter. You can sit here and wait for death, or you can have your revenge on the Inquisition by taking its money and defying its cruelty."

Franklin took a long drink and rose. "Let's go."

If Franklin felt any sadness at the thought of leaving his tavern, possibly never to return, he showed none of it. He stepped out into the street, squinted at the press of people pushing toward the river, and began trudging uphill. He breathed heavily and steadily. He was a big man, and easily winded, but he was not weak, and he seemed no stranger to exertion. We made swift progress.

After a few minutes Franklin stopped. He cocked his head, and turned to me. "You hear that?"

"What?" Roberta's eyes were wide with alarm. "What is it?"

I heard nothing but the distant wailing and calling of names and endless barking of dogs. Then there was something more, a low hissing. It sounded like wind and sand blown hard against a wall. Next came the panicked screams, thousands of them.

I turned around. The crowds in the streets, already far below, were pressing back, away from the water. Indeed, the water had pulled away from the shore, and the great Sea of Straw seemed to be shrinking. Packed masses were shouting and pointing. Those closest to the water were visibly shoving those nearer to land, but they were packed in too tight. No one could move.

I looked to the expanse of the Tagus, beyond the ships, and saw a wall of water, perhaps sixty feet high, closing in at impossible speeds. Nothing I had ever seen had filled me with such awe. This was the hand of God, the mighty fury of nature, a power so incredible and unstoppable it made me want to laugh at the futility of my life and my struggles.

Franklin stood next to me, staring at the wave. His face was blank.

"Run!" I cried. I gave Franklin a shove, grabbed Roberta's hand, and began to move.

The large man roused himself from his stupor and began to move farther up the hill. I set myself to the task of gaining altitude and doing it quickly. Roberta climbed too, scrambling mightily, summoning all her strength. I took pleasure at her effort. After all she'd witnessed, after all she'd endured, she still wanted to live.

The angle was steep, and the loose white sand gave way under our feet, but death was behind us, and we dug in with our fingers. Twigs and burrs and shards of rock drove into the flesh under my fingernails. I did not turn around until I heard Franklin cry out.

"Help me!" he called.

Twenty feet behind me, Franklin had stumbled. Clouds had passed before the sun, darkening the sky, and the wind pushed toward the river. A panicked mass, ready to overtake and trample us both, approached. Beneath us the wave foamed and roared, and prepared to crash against Lisbon. A deafening sound blasted forth, dwarfing the noise of the quake that morning. Water sprayed over us.

Then, like a great rug being tossed across the shoreline, the wave struck. Countless people were thrown backwards, their bodies broken by the force of impact. Blood streaked through the air like comet tails. So many terrified people, trampled and drowned. The wave hit hardest to the west, tearing through warehouses and homes like they were made of mud. The Duke's Arms was washed away, as were the houses above it. The very ground under my feet might be pulled toward the sea, and I scrambled backwards lest I be sucked into the destruction. To the east, water tore stone and tile from the great Palace, but even farther east the Alfama, once again, was spared.

Already the lucky ones who had escaped were streaming past me, and Franklin was disappearing under their feet. I began to push against the crowd, shoving blindly, unable to believe what I saw. It seemed as though half the city was now underwater, and for the blink of an eye there was stillness. Then the water began to pull back in a violent rush. After it did, the thousands who had been standing upon the quays were gone. So were the ships that had been in the Tagus—some dashed against the city, others simply swallowed by the river.

What hadn't been destroyed by the impact of the wave was being taken by the water's retreat. Buildings and stairs and trees were all being ripped away, and from halfway down Chiado Hill, it was but mud and wreckage. I tore my eyes away and looked down at the dirt where Franklin lay, arms over his head as people trod on him.

Roberta waited ahead. "Go!" I cried to her, and then shoved into the crowd, knocking a half dozen men down, and clearing a space around Franklin. I reached down and grabbed the Englishman by his massive upper arms and pulled him to his feet. His nose bled, and he would have a nasty black eye, but he appeared to be otherwise unharmed.

"You came back for me," Franklin shouted above the noise. "You are your father's son."

"That is a conversation for another day," I said, and prodded the man forward, looking to get away from the hillside before it crumbled into the river.

I moved Franklin along, making the big man run as quickly as he could. I would not now lose Roberta. Saving Franklin at the cost of being separated from her would be too much to bear, but I found her in the crowd ahead, gazing with the hundreds of other survivors at the destruction below.

In the distance, the crying had calmed. We heard no more screams, but some low moans echoing off the river, now swollen with drowned bodies. Along the shore I saw only a few sluggish forms wandering amid the tattered remains of inns and warehouses. They staggered like the dead brought to life, and all around them, the true dead lay at horrible angles. There were too many to count, and they were only a fraction of the souls who had, minutes ago, crowded the harbor. Thousands were dead, but the people I cared about might yet be saved.

Chapter 28

I could not have said what I had imagined, but when I reached the Rossio, my mind went blank. The Palácio da Independéncia was broken but not destroyed. The great hospital was partially in ruins, but it stood proud compared to the surrounding buildings, many of which were unrecognizable. The Palace of the Inquisition had taken a great deal of damage, but parts of it stood yet, and I remained hopeful.

The dead lay in the square. How many were there in the city, buried and burned, crushed and drowned? A quarter of the population? A third? Half? More? Everywhere, the living were on their knees, praying that God not punish them further.

The great front door of the Palace of the Inquisition was splintered and broken, and Franklin and I walked through, side by side, with Roberta trailing behind.

"You can't truly intend to go in there," she said. "What you said before. You didn't mean it. You couldn't have."

"I have friends in the prison," I said. "I mean to get them out."

"And you, Mr. Franklin. Do you mean to do this?"

"I do," he told her. "I mean to make myself useful to Mr. Foxx, and if I can get rich in the bargain, I shan't complain."

Dust and blood covered the tiled walkways. Priests rushed about, carrying their own wounded, fetching water, bandages, whatever else was needed. A small fire burned in the cloister, but no one tended to it.

One of the priests scowled at us. "There's no help for you here," he said. "Seek it elsewhere."

"Is this your Romish charity?" Franklin asked, putting his meaty fists to his bulging sides. "I ain't impressed."

"What choice have we?" snapped the priest. "There is nothing but survival. I cannot help you."

"I'm not here to ask for help," I said, "but to offer it."

"Oh," the priest said, eyeing Roberta skeptically. "Well, I suppose we could use more hands. The wounded priests are to be found down that hall. Ask Brother José what you can do to—"

"What of the prisoners?" I interrupted.

"The prisoners?" the priest repeated, incredulously. "I haven't the time to concern myself with them. Men of God have been injured."

I stepped forward, grabbed the man by his robes, and threw him against the wall. He struck with his feet well off the ground and crumpled to the floor. "You will find the time," I said. "How many are there, how do I get to them, and where are the keys?"

The priest held out a key ring. "I have them here. Please, don't hurt me. There are seven men and three women in the prisons. The entrance is down that hall and to the left. I do not know if it is accessible. No one has checked on them."

They'd been left to die of thirst or starvation, buried alive. I took the keys and stepped away.

"Go down there if you like," the priest continued, smirking. "I'll find some way to seal you in. You may die with the heretics, for you are clearly one of them."

I swiftly stepped toward the priest, grabbed him by his hair, and smashed his head into the wall. Something cracked, but I did not know if it was tile or the priest's skull.

Roberta screamed and put a hand to her mouth. "You killed him."

"I might have," I said. "Likely not."

"But he's a priest."

"That signifies nothing," I said. "Beggars who bow to the communion wafer when it passes in the street are holier than these men. They are Inquisitors. I will not show mercy to them, not for an instant."

We walked down the hall and found the heavy wooden door that led to the prisons. I fumbled with the keys on the ring until I found the right one. When I opened the door, I was struck by the stench of the prison below—the stink of sweat and piss and shit and rotten food. I cursed and descended the stone stairs into near-total darkness.

At the bottom of the stairs, I found embers in a fireplace. Everything in the small chamber was coated with dust from the ceiling, but it seemed as though the building had not crumbled belowground. I lit a torch and handed it to Roberta.

Her hair was wild, but her eyes appeared focused and her face was set with determination. She was returning to herself. She had sat weeping in her house before, but now tears were a luxury she could not afford, and instead she wore the hardened shell of suffering and endurance. I knew it well.

"Stay close," I said.

We unlocked the next door, and this led us down a long corridor that forked. To the left, I knew, was the women's prison, to the right the men's. I had walked this path before. We went left first. I stormed through the door and, seeing there were no guards, grabbed the torch from Roberta's hand. Franklin hung back, eyeing the halls for signs of trouble.

There were eight cells here, but only one was occupied. Gabriela and an old woman I did not know sat together, holding hands and saying the Hail Mary. Gabriela was in prison for Judaizing, but she recited the prayers of her tormentors. She had not even the comfort of the religion for which she was punished.

I stepped forward and began to insert keys into the lock.

Gabriela looked up, her eyes wide with disbelief. "Sebastião. Why are you here?"

"I'm here to rescue you," I said.

Gabriela began to weep. "We shall be executed for this."

"There has been an earthquake. Surely you felt it."

"We did," Gabriela said. "How bad is the damage?"

"Lisbon is gone," I told her. "Destroyed beyond repair, I think." The true key went home with a satisfying click. "I am taking you back to England with me. All of you."

The old woman in the cell with her stood up and spat. "I'm not going anywhere," she said. "Not with Jews. It's your fault I'm here, and it's your fault that God is angry enough to punish the city. When the priests come for me, then I'll leave, but not before."

"That's your choice," I said. I helped Gabriela to her feet. She looked over and saw Roberta holding the torch, and next to her, Franklin.

"Who are they?" she asked.

"These are my friends," I said. I gestured toward the innkeeper. "That is Kingsley Franklin."

"And I am Roberta Carver, once a merchant, now a widow. Mr. Foxx has saved and ruined my life."

"That may be his particular skill," Gabriela answered.

"Let's get the men," Franklin said, breaking up the conclave of aggrieved women.

In the men's prison there were three times as many cells. Men were no more inclined to heresy than women—women were just less likely to own property for the Inquisition to steal.

I moved through the prison, opening cells and explaining to the men what had happened. The prisoners who were strangers to me fled. When only Luis and Eusebio remained, I gathered my people around me.

"There are fires and destruction everywhere," I said. "I've seen no soldiers to keep the peace. Lisbon is lost. We must head out of the city on foot, and then find passage by cart or horse, perhaps toward Cascais. There we will buy passage on a ship—or steal a vessel if we have to."

"Do you think God sent a bolt of lightning to Lisbon?" Eusebio snapped. "That we alone are struck? There will be damage at Cascais, and any viable ships will be gone."

"Then we will continue by land," I said.

"How far do you mean for us to go?" Eusebio demanded.

"We will walk to Spain, if necessary. To France. I care not. We are leaving this cursed country. This is your chance to be free. I do not claim that God has destroyed the city so that we could have this opportunity, but the opportunity has come, and it would be a crime against God not to seize it."

"And what shall we live upon during our sojourn through Europe?" Eusebio demanded.

"Our riches," I answered.

"What riches?" demanded Eusebio. "You think we are a bottomless source of wealth? The Inquisition took everything. We have no more riches."

"The Inquisition took everything from me too," I assured him. "It took everything from Mr. Franklin. Before we leave this building, we are going to take it back."

"You are mad," Eusebio said as we climbed the stairs. It was the fifth time he'd said it.

"Maybe," Franklin said, "but I think it is closer to daring than madness."

Eusebio's doubts did not anger me, but they were beginning to irritate me. I turned to him. "What would you have us do?"

Eusebio said nothing.

Luis spoke up, perhaps not liking to see his son humiliated. "Robbing the Inquisition is dangerous."

"Being alive has become dangerous," I said. "Lisbon is in ruins, and there are no laws, and we will have to be bolder than our enemies if we are to survive."

"You speak of enemies, but we have none," Eusebio said. "If we leave this building, we are free. We don't need to antagonize the Inquisition. This is but greed dressed up as something noble."

"You all know who I am and you know my story. The Inquisition took everything from my family, including the right to leave. My father spent his life laboring in the hope of someday having enough to free his family, and the Inquisition killed him so they could take his wealth. I am taking back what is mine. I intend to stop anyone who gets in my way. If you want my protection, you have it, but you must do what I say. And believe me when I tell you that you will need me. The moment the sun goes down, every *renegado* in the city will be out to slit throats and take what he can find. Every building left standing will be looted. If we don't take this money, someone else will, and the difference will be that it does not belong to their blood."

"That hardly justifies theft," Eusebio said.

"I will not argue this with you." I turned to face him. "Either go or join me and be silent." I continued up the stairs, and Eusebio followed behind. I let out a little breath of relief. I could not say for sure that I would have left Eusebio.

At the top of the stairs were five priests standing in a close huddle and speaking rapidly. When I emerged fully, I saw that there was a sixth person standing behind the priests—the old woman from Gabriela's cell. She thrust a crooked finger in our direction. "That's him. He's the one behind it all."

One of the Inquisitors, a man of about thirty with hooded eyes and massive eyebrows, stepped forward. "Back to your cells," he snapped. "Return at once, or you will face greater punishment."

I understood him to be the sort of man who threw in with the Inquisition because he enjoyed power and the freedom to harm others with impunity. In this crisis, he would naturally become the leader, and would prove ruthless in the execution of his duties. Such men were truly dangerous and so were best dealt with swiftly.

I held up my hand, indicating that no one should move.

The priest's face began to redden. "Return to your cells, I say, and beg Jesus Christ to forgive you."

I struck him hard in the jaw, clipping the priest strongly enough to crack his teeth, but carefully enough not to seriously hurt my own knuckles. A perfect punch, just as Mr. Weaver had taught me. The man's eyes rolled back, and he fell to the floor.

Franklin lashed out at another priest. Franklin was neither swift nor skillful, but he was large, and his big hands carried a great deal of force. The man dropped.

"It's the mad Jew!" one of the other priests cried, pointing at Franklin.

"He's the mad Jew," Franklin said, shaking the pain out of his hand. "I'm a mad Protestant."

I lunged at the priest who had spoken. I grabbed his head and pushed him hard into the wall. I turned to dispose of another priest, but saw the man already had the point of a blade emerging from his chest. Behind him stood Luis, yanking free the sword. I had hoped to avoid unnecessary killing, but clearly the elder Nobreza had his own plans. The man had lived in Lisbon all his life. He had his own debts to collect from the Inquisition, and I would not tell him to stay his hand. I nodded at Luis and grabbed the last priest, throwing him to the floor. "Where is the treasury?"

"If I tell you, you will kill me," the priest said.

I turned to Franklin. "I wonder if it is possible to force information from a man, even if he knows he will be killed after he speaks. Some kind of torture perhaps?"

"Do you know who can answer this?" Franklin said. "An Inquisitor. Let's put one to the question."

The priest swallowed hard, and then pointed down a long corridor. "The door is at the end. I know not who has the key."

Franklin and I began to walk in the direction the priest had pointed.

"He's helpless," Gabriela said behind us. "You cannot kill him in cold blood."

I turned and saw that Luis had taken out his blade once more and was raising it over the fallen priest.

"If we don't, he will get help and they will try to stop us," Luis said. There was no eagerness in his expression. He showed no signs of relishing the violence. This was grim necessity.

"There is a hallway full of butchered priests," she answered. "Do you think it won't occur to them to check the treasury?"

I eyed the prostrate priest thoughtfully, and then stomped upon his knee and heard something break. The man cried out.

"That will slow him down," I said, and began to walk toward the treasury. Luis sheathed his blade.

Gabriela hurried to walk beside me. "Are you going to allow the freedom offered by the quake to turn you into a fiend? What have you become?"

"The Inquisition turned me into a fiend," I said. "I will be what they made me if that helps me protect my friends."

"You do not have to be cruel," she said. "You used to be kind."

"When we have what we've come for, and we escape, I shall not do these things any longer. But we are in the heart of the palace of the enemy, and I cannot afford to show mercy to those who least deserve it."

"No," she said. "I suppose not. But I wish you were someone who could find a way."

Not surprisingly, none of the keys on the chain opened the entrance to the treasury. The heavy wooden door, however, was cracked from the building's shifting weight. Franklin and I found large stones, loosened from the wall, and began to take turns smashing them against the door. I feared the stone would crumble, but it was solid. The door was not. Three blows, and it cracked further. The door soon turned to splinters. I used my boot to clear the path, and then we entered.

There was a brief stone hallway before the room opened up. There were no windows, but with Roberta's torch we could see inside the chamber, and it made us gasp. It was not a huge room, but it was large enough, with rows of shelves lined with sacks of coins and boxes of gold bars. There were cases of jewels and stacks of fine clothes and silks and bags of spices. There were silver dishes and candlesticks and picture frames. There were gold necklaces and earrings and rings. There were riches beyond imagining. Kingdoms could rise or fall upon such wealth.

Then I caught a glimpse of something in the flickering light. It was a leather envelope I recognized. I grabbed it, looked inside, and then handed it to Roberta. "This is yours."

Roberta looked at the notes and then met my gaze. "This doesn't give me back what I've lost," she said. "Do not think this undoes your crimes."

"Nothing can undo my crimes, but this gives you money."

There were other stacks of notes, and I chose to concentrate on these, examining papers to make certain they were negotiable. There were thousands of pounds there—I could not guess how many, and I did not wish to take the time to count. Whatever the amount, it would have to suffice as my revenge.

"Take as much as you can in large notes," I said, "but we need coins and gold and jewels to pay for what we need upon the road. Do not overburden yourselves, and pick small coins if you can find them so we won't draw attention to ourselves. Be quick. We mustn't stay longer than we have to."

When we had finished collecting as much as we could reasonably take—a literal fortune, I supposed—we began to head for the exit.

"Where shall we go now?" Gabriela asked.

"We will find a place for you to take shelter for the time being. I am not done in this city. I must find Mariana Settwell."

"And then?" Roberta asked.

"Then we flee."

Chapter 29

Anyone who has ever dared to imagine hell has probably summoned a picture very like Lisbon on that day. Buildings lay in ruins. People wandered the streets, bloody and wounded. Both men and women wailed and huddled upon the sidewalk. All around us fires gave off heat and belched smoke, and the sky was already dark with ash, falling back upon the earth like rain. Roads that had been open for centuries were now blocked off.

Roberta and Franklin and I had seen it earlier, but the Nobrezas stared in open horror. The world was broken, and no words would suffice.

"We must go now," Eusebio said, his voice shrill. "Why must we wait?"

"I will not leave yet," I said. "My responsibilities are not fulfilled."

"I have no further responsibilities here." Eusebio turned to Gabriela. "You will come with me. We have money and we will have our freedom."

Gabriela shook her head. "We dare not go without

him," she said, keeping her voice low. She stroked his sleeve. "There will be thieves and murderers. How can I be safe among so many desperate people? We need Sebastião."

I turned away, but her moment of intimacy with her husband did not sting. The pain was not there. Stepping forward, I put a hand upon Eusebio's shoulder and drew him away from the others. I did not care for Eusebio's hurt pride, but I wished to keep the man from quarreling with me at every turn. "You have skills, and I have skills," I said quietly. "It happens that mine are better suited to surviving in a ruined city. Let me protect you and your wife and father and see you safe from this nightmare. You will then take the money you carry, and your own skills will serve you well in London or Amsterdam or Paris. There you will thrive."

Eusebio took a step back. "I will trust you for now, but I do not like it."

We continued walking east, toward the Alfama. The streets were still full of the wounded and the lamenting, but here there were more houses standing.

"I know this street," Roberta said. "Is it not where your friend Settwell lives?"

I nodded. "That is where we are going."

Roberta stopped. "I shall not enter his house."

"There is no time for that," I told her. "There can be no grudges now. All of you will go where I say and do what I say. In return, I will get you out of here alive if that can be done."

"I can't," she said. "Everything that has happened is because of him. I lost everything, and it was his doing. Rutherford would be alive if Settwell had not deceived you."

"I know," I said. "I don't ask you to forgive him, only to tolerate him. Once, long ago, he did something for my father. He saved me. Nothing can erase his crimes, but for the debt my family owes him, I must try to help him."

Roberta brushed a loose strand of hair from her soiled face. In that instant, she looked, if only fleetingly, as she had before her life had come undone. "I don't understand you, Mr. Foxx. Your loyalties will destroy us all."

"They have kept me alive all my life. I won't abandon them now."

We found Settwell huddled in his parlor, sitting on the floor, his back against the wall, his arms around his knees. The house seemed strangely undamaged. The same could not be said for Settwell, whose complexion was pale, and whose thin hands trembled like those of a man with a palsy.

Roberta stared at him but said nothing. He appeared not even to notice her, nor the others in our little band. He looked only at me.

"The city is destroyed," Settwell said. "It is gone, like a sand castle, washed away by the waves."

"I know," I said.

"Mariana is out there somewhere," Settwell said. "She may be dead. I was such a fool."

"You can lament your mistakes and resolve to do better when you and your daughter are safe. In the meantime, I believe I know where to find her."

"I don't deserve your help," Settwell said.

"No," I agreed. "But Mariana does."

I checked the house to make certain there was food and drink, and then took what I needed to replenish myself. I rested for a little while, not wanting to go out until I felt prepared. Then I rose. I told the others to bar the door and light no lamps. "Kill anyone who tries to force his way inside," I said.

Settwell came and stood beside me. "Take me with you. I can help you."

I shook my head. "No, I don't think you are made for such things."

"Is this because you don't trust me?" Settwell asked.

"In part," I told him. I waved Franklin over. "Do you have any interest in giving the Inquisition even more reason to hate you?"

He grinned. "This is better than robbing the treasury all over again."

Chapter 30

It was growing dark, and night would be a far more dangerous time. We could not be the only ones who had realized Lisbon was full of wealth for the taking. Some of the fires that had raged before had burned out. Others had spread. There was no knowing which perils would grow and which would abate. The time to act was now.

We made our way upward once more, ignoring the suffering that we could not alleviate. We did not speak. We kept our heads down and skirted the fires and the rubble. We found the way around closed streets and avoided alleys. As we walked, the city began to shake again. The grinding and the screams struck up in what was now a familiar chorus, but the rumble was less terrible. Everything that could fall already had.

Franklin and I stood in the middle of a street, sticking our arms out for balance until the quake passed, and then continued on our way.

It is disorienting to travel in a city whose landmarks have been obliterated, so the gates of the Conceição dos

Cardais appeared unexpectedly as we trudged up the hill. It was a small and unexceptional Carmelite convent, but because it remained standing, it appeared a palace. Bricks and tiles had come dislodged, and statuary had collapsed, but for the most part the building and the grounds were unharmed, and the gardens looked calm and beautiful. Birds fluttered in the standing trees. Outside, Lisbon was hell, but this looked like paradise, safe and tranquil.

Inside, the nuns must be thanking God for sparing them. They must be wondering what they had done to deserve mercy when so many others had received none. I myself asked the same question.

I was tempted to speculate that it was the presence of Mariana, an innocent. But then were all who had been crushed and burned and trampled and drowned and torn apart by the sea evil? Was this earth-quake the work of an avenging God, or was its joy and misery distrib-uted merely by random chance? I had to believe the latter. The idea of a God that would wipe out an entire city—a city of vile Inquisitors and *fidalgos,* yes, but also one of beggars and children—was too dark to contemplate. I wanted no part of such indiscriminate violence. I much preferred the idea of justice narrowly delivered.

The door of the main building was unlocked. It was dim and cool inside, and even if it was not the finest convent in the city, I marveled at the beautiful wood carvings, the detailed paintings with their frames of gold. While most of Lisbon starved, here were grand stair-cases and elaborate tilings. Here were rich furnishings and tapestries. Everywhere I looked, I saw gold and silver and velvet and silk.

"Lovely place these nuns have," Franklin observed.

"In two days it will all be worth less than a loaf of bread."

Franklin nodded with some satisfaction. "The earthquake is level-ing in more ways than one."

A nun in her drab Carmelite habit came toward us slowly, arms folded in her sleeves, head slightly lowered. She was an older woman, perhaps fifty, with olive skin and a face that would have been consid-ered ugly in her youth, but now gave her a distinguished appearance.

Her habit was filthy and streaked with blood, and her face was covered with soot. "What is it, my sons? Are you hurt? Do you want shelter?"

I took a step back in surprise. Given all I had seen and done in the past twenty-four hours, nothing could have shocked me more than a nun offering kindness unbidden and with no motive but the desire to do right. I had forgotten such people existed within the Church.

"Your convent is open to all?" I asked.

"We have been spared this terrible destruction," the nun said. "God has preserved us for a reason. I pray you do not abuse our charity, for we wish to serve as many as we can."

"You believe God preserved your convent? Do you then think God destroyed Lisbon for its crimes?"

"I cannot know the answer to that," she said, now studying me with skepticism. "It serves me nothing to ponder God's plan. I can only ponder His plan for me. Senhor, there are men who will choose to take advantage of the chaos in the city. If you are one of them, I beg you leave. There is gold enough to be dug up from the ruins. Let us be to tend the sick and feed the hungry as long as we can."

"I would never keep you from that task," I said. "We do not need help, however. I seek someone within, the mother of the Jesuit Pedro Azinheiro."

The nun looked startled. "Sister Juana Maria? What do you want with her?"

"She has something that does not belong to her."

"What is that?"

"A child," I said.

The nun, to my surprise, took a step forward. "You sound English. Are you her father?"

"No," I said. "I am his friend. I've come to fetch the girl for him."

"Why does he not come himself?"

"Searching the streets of a ruined city is a task for which I am better suited than he," I answered. In the hopes alleviating her concerns, I added, "The girl knows me. She will tell you so, and that I am her father's friend."

"I am made to understand he is not a good Catholic," the nun said, again quietly.

"He is not even a good man," I replied. "I cannot say he is a good father, though I do not believe he is a terrible one. But I do know he loves this girl, and what is more important, she loves him. The Inquisition took her from her father as a pawn in a larger game, not because it had any concerns about her soul. Sister, my father was taken from me by the Inquisition. I do not want this girl to become what I have."

"You do not fear the Inquisition's wrath?" she asked.

Franklin snorted. "I've never met a man who feared it less."

"The Inquisition is broken," I said. "If not forever, then at least for now. Its priests will be too busy protecting their gold to worry about a little girl, and if you wish to protect yourself, you need only say she vanished in the chaos. I have seen people crushed and buried alive. I have witnessed I do not know how many thousands swept away by the sea. No one will disbelieve you."

Still the nun remained motionless.

"You say you believe you were spared to do God's work," I pressed. "Do you believe keeping a child from her father is God's work?"

She sighed. "You speak the truth, senhor. We live or die by the Inquisition's pleasure, or at least we used to. Perhaps, as you say, things may be different. For now, at least, all this suffering and destruction will allow me to tell a plausible lie. Do you swear by the blood of Christ that you will return this girl to her father, and that you will keep her safe?"

"This could complicate things," Franklin muttered.

"Sister," I said, "I am a Jew, and I will not take that oath."

She blanched, turning white beneath the grime on her face. "You are the priest killer."

"I am someone who did not wish to be killed by priests," I offered.

"And if I do not do what you say, will you kill me too?"

"If you attack me with a knife, I may be forced to handle you more roughly than I should like, but if you only try to block my path, I believe walking around you will prove sufficient."

The nun continued to stare. "For a murderer, you speak with a great deal of reason."

"Then perhaps what I did was not murder," I proposed. "Perhaps it was justice. Perhaps it was even God's justice. You, too, give every sign of being a woman of reason. I shall let you decide if it must always be murder to kill an agent of the Inquisition."

"This man has been wronged by the Inquisition priests," Franklin said. "He has seen his family and friends imprisoned and killed. The Inquisition came to drag him to the same fate. That's why he killed those men. It can't be a crime to destroy those who would destroy you."

"Killing is always a sin, but not all of us believe the Inquisition does God's work," the nun said very quietly. "I will help you if you swear by whatever you value that you will do what you have promised."

"I do swear," I said, "upon the memory of my father, and of his parents, and of all those who have died in the Inquisition prisons. I swear by the God who led my ancestors out of Egypt and who set me free from Lisbon long ago."

She stared at him. "Set you free? Then you have come back? By choice?"

"Yes, Sister. I returned here to atone for the crime of leaving others behind."

"It seems to me you have done much to atone for since your return," she said.

"That," I said, "is one point on which we shall not disagree."

* * *

The nun led us up a long staircase whose gloom had not been broken by the lighting of its lamps. "Do you also promise not to hurt Sister Juana Maria?"

I began to grow weary of these promises, but I said, "I have no desire to hurt anyone. I want to bring the child to her father. I would like to believe I will not have to harm an aging nun in my efforts to do that."

We approached a door, and the nun knocked. There was no answer from within.

"It is odd," she said. "I thought she was in there with the girl."

I heard the muffled sound of a child crying, and I recognized it as Mariana. "Have you a key?" I asked the nun.

She shook her head.

I examined the door. It was too heavy to break down, and it was clearly barred from the inside, which meant picking the lock would do no good. "Fetch me an axe," I said.

"No," she answered. "I cannot let you destroy holy property."

"Do you mean to say that your desire to return this girl to her father vanishes if doing so means harming a door? It is too late for such niceties. I am here, and the girl I have come for is in there. That means the door is opening or coming down."

Unwilling to leave the room unattended, I sent Franklin to go with the nun to find the axe. While they were gone, I pressed my ear to the door. I thought I could hear Mariana crying again, but maybe it was just my pulse pounding in my ear.

At last, Franklin and the nun returned. I went to take the axe from Franklin, but the big man shook his head.

"Let me be of some use," he said. "I'm stronger than you. And you will need to rush in once the door is down. If I am good at anything, it is mindless work. If there is thinking to be done, better it should be done by you."

322 | DAVID LISS

I managed a thin smile. "That may be the most eloquent confession of stupidity ever uttered."

Franklin began to swing the axe. With each strike, the nun winced, as though something she loved were being hurt. It took five blows and then the lock was off and the inner bar broken. I pushed through the door. Inside I saw an elderly nun sitting with Mariana on her lap. In front of them, with a sword brandished in his hand, was Pedro Azinheiro.

Chapter 31

It was a spare room with a wooden floor and a single bed. By the large window was a bench with a red velvet cushion, and upon the wall was a massive painting of the Virgin holding the infant Jesus.

"Mr. Foxx!" Mariana cried. "Have you come to take me back to Papa?"

I didn't take my eyes off Azinheiro, but I managed a smile. "That is exactly what I've come to do."

"I don't like it here," she said.

"Hush, child," the older nun said. "We have treated you well."

"You can't have her," Azinheiro said, though he took a step back as he spoke. His skin was all bruises and bandages, but none of his wounds struck me as serious. He thrust the sword in my direction, but the action did little except inform me that he had likely never before handled a blade.

How many times would this man attempt to take what mattered to me? It was enough. I would endure it no longer. I did not want to savor his death or make him suffer or beg. I did not need him to understand his crimes or repent them. I wanted him dead.

"Why can I not have her?" I said, speaking slowly, planning how I would approach. In just a few seconds, it would be over. I would do what I had come here to do. At long last, Azinheiro would be gone.

"Because you want her. You've done enough damage. Killing my soldiers and the men at the Palace. And robbing the Inquisition! Did you think I would not hear of that? You think yourself some sort of avenger, but you are nothing but a thief, taking our money."

"And where did the Inquisition get that money?" I demanded, moving slightly to the right and in, crowding his sword, making it more difficult to gain any momentum with it. I was nearly in position to strike. "Does the Inquisition have any purpose but to hoard more gold? I'll not quibble with you, priest, about which of us is evil. I only wish to know if I was mistaken in my belief that priests were not allowed to use swords."

"I shall have to confess the sin," Azinheiro said.

"I doubt you shall live long enough to do so."

Azinheiro laughed, and he appeared to believe in truth the advantage was his. "How can you stop me? If I see you reach for a weapon, I will run you through."

It was time. I could move now, reach in, grab his wrist hard and twist it. The sword would drop. I already heard in my ears the clang of metal on stone. I would twist his arm, and he would cry out and fall to his knees. I would take his head, and twist, and it would be over.

Why, then, did I not take the opportunity? Why did I still talk? "You may be willing to commit the sin of wielding a blade, but I have observed in a dozen ways that you have made no habit of studying its use. I've spent the past ten years of my life training in the arts of fighting. Are you so certain you can have the better of me?"

Azinheiro blinked several times. I suspected he was still trying to think of a way out of this situation that did not involve a direct confrontation with me. Likely he knew he had made a mistake, he had challenged in arms a man who outclassed him in every conceivable way. He wanted only an honorable means to escape.

"Look around you," I said. "The city is in ruins, and the Inquisition is scattered. Your world has come to an end, but this child's has not. Let her go, and I will let you go."

The words were out of my mouth before I understood them. Did I mean it? I did. I did not want to kill him, though I knew he did not deserve to live. Perhaps I did not want to be remade. Perhaps I did not want to let go of the anger and be transformed. Perhaps I did not want to discover that killing him made no difference, that I would always remain who I now was. All of those things were true—but they were not, I realized, the main reason.

I simply did not want to kill a man, no matter how terrible, in cold blood. The desire was nothing but memory.

"Let her go," I said, "and you can live. Never cross me again, and I shall not come after you."

"If I let her go, you will have no reason not to kill me," he said.

"You deserve death," I told him. "You deserve it a thousand times over, but more than that, the girl deserves to be free. Release her, and I will leave you. I will leave Lisbon. I will be done with all of it."

"I don't believe you." With his free hand, Azinheiro reached out and grabbed Mariana from the nun and pulled her close to him. He pressed her to his body and laid the blade across her chest, just under her throat. Her eyes went wide, but she held still.

"Now you dare not attack me," the priest said. "You are going to let us both walk out of here, otherwise the girl dies. All the fighting skills in the world won't be able to prevent it. Whatever else you have done, you will not do this. I will not let you return this child to her English father."

Rage pulsed in my head. I felt my fist tighten into a hard ball. I had offered to let him live. I had agreed to walk away from my reasons for being here. After all I had endured to get to this moment, I was prepared to show mercy, and now he pressed a blade to this girl's throat.

Azinheiro said, "You think me cruel, but I am trying to save this girl. Better she should come of age in the true church than with a drunk and a thief for a father."

"That is not your decision to make," I told him.

Azinheiro grinned. "It looks to me like it is. She will stay in my care or she will leave this world entirely. She can enter the kingdom of heaven as an innocent. Which shall it be?"

I hesitated a moment. I liked to consider myself a man of principle, and there were things to which I did not like to stoop. That said, I decided that no one in that room—including myself—mattered except Mariana. Getting her back to Settwell was my purpose, and everything and everyone that stood in the way of that was expendable. I had tried the path of clemency and forgiveness and it had yielded nothing. It was time for another way. And so I lunged forward and around Azinheiro, yanking the priest's mother to her feet.

I did not trouble myself with threats. I simply caught the old nun in a headlock and began to squeeze. Her thin body, bony and delicate, writhed against me. Her skin was dry as paper, and what little air she could suck in rattled in her chest.

The nun who had helped us screamed, but Franklin grabbed her arm to hold her back. His expression was neutral, like a man at an execution who knows nothing of the condemned's crimes.

The old nun began to thrash. I moved to tighten my grip on her, but relaxed it slightly instead. I did not want to be hurting old women no matter whom I was trying to save. I could not go through with it. Even threatening her was more than I could endure.

Azinheiro, meanwhile, pretended toward bravado. "Ha, you think I care what happens to some old nun? Kill her for all I care. It will get you nothing."

"The old nun is your mother," I said, stalling while I figured out how I could extract myself from this nightmare. "You don't want her to come to harm." And then I knew what I would do. "But it's too late!" I shouted.

I pushed her head to one side and tossed her toward the other nun to break her fall. Pretending to kill her was a risk. Azinheiro might have struck at Mariana out of retaliation, but I knew human nature well enough to expect that he would, if only for an instant, look over to see what had become of his mother.

When he did, I reached out to his wrist and twisted. The sword fell, and I released my grip, catching the blade smoothly. Meanwhile, with my other arm, I pulled Mariana toward me.

I now had the weapon and the girl. Mariana hugged me. I felt the moisture of her tears dampen my shirt, but she made not a sound.

I looked up. Franklin had the priest in a headlock, much as I had held his mother. He struggled, but Franklin, as he had said, was strong, and Azinheiro could not escape.

"Put him there," I said to Franklin, pointing with the sword to a chair in the corner. Franklin gave the priest a rough push, and he went crashing into the chair.

I then gently removed Mariana's arms and handed her over to Franklin. "Go with my friend downstairs. I shall be there in a moment, and then we'll go to your father."

"I don't know him," she said, looking at Franklin. "I want to stay with you."

"You can trust him, Mariana. I promise."

"I'll take good care of you," Franklin said. "A man would be a fool not to do as Mr. Foxx wishes."

Mariana nodded and they left.

I stood in the room with Azinheiro and the nun who had admitted us, who was now bent over Sister Juana Maria. The old woman sat on the floor, looking somewhat dazed. Later, I would feel remorse for how I had treated her, but I pushed those thoughts away for now. She had been treated roughly, but no one had been hurt. Not yet.

"She will be well," the nun said to Azinheiro. "She only needs some air and rest."

She turned and glared at me, but her gaze conveyed nothing I hadn't already said to myself.

"Take her away," I said to the nun. "I have business with the priest."

"There will be no violence in a house of God," the nun said.

I laughed. "Is this a new rule? I spent my childhood in Portugal, and I have never heard of such an injunction before. I suggest you visit the torture room of the Inquisition Palace."

The nun helped Sister Juana Maria. She turned back only once, looking at her son mournfully.

The priest sat in the chair in the corner, looking small and defeated.

"I shall let you walk out of here," I said. "No priest of the Inquisition has ever done so much for a Jew, but I will grant you this gift today. I suggest you take it."

"Why?" the priest asked.

"My reasons are my own," I told him. I had not fully sorted them out for myself, and I was in no mood to explain them to him.

"I don't believe you," he said.

I shrugged. "I can't change that, but all the same, I am letting you live, and I am letting you leave. Perhaps when I am gone, you will believe me."

I turned to walk away, and the priest hurled himself out of his chair. Apparently, the sword was not the only blade with which he had armed himself. He had produced a small knife, which he thrust at me. He was slow and clumsy, however, and I easily sidestepped, grabbed his arm, and pushed him roughly against the wall. He landed hard, and his head smacked against stone. The knife fell from his hand and his eyes rolled momentarily, but he did not collapse.

With my left forearm, I pinned the priest to the wall by his throat, while with my free hand I took a blade from my belt. I was having difficulty coming up with reasons not simply to kill him and be done with it.

"Perhaps I made a mistake," Azinheiro gasped. "You are not a murderer. What you did to my mother was vile, but I understand you did it for the girl. You don't wish to harm me, so let me go."

"So you can try to kill me again?" I asked. "So you can abduct children and destroy families?"

"I must do those tasks appointed to me," he said, "but you need not hurt anyone. You are not so cruel."

"I am what you have made me."

"I did not make the Inquisition," Azinheiro said. "I was but a poor child. I would have starved, ended up a soldier or worse, had I not found a home there. And if I had not been the one to arrest your father, it would have been another. You may hate the institution if you like, but its agents are only fallible men."

"It is a poor excuse. I shall not have it."

"Revenge gets you nothing, my son. Seek forgiveness instead. If you kill me, how will you feel later?"

"It is difficult to say," I mused. "But I know if I don't, you will hurt others, and their pain, their blood, shall be on my hands."

"Do not your Jewish practices have a day of atonement?" the priest asked. Seeing my startled reaction, his eyes sparkled with hope. "Yes, I have studied your beliefs, and I know such things. Men may atone for their sins. Is it not wrong to rob me of my chance to atone?"

I let go of the priest and then pushed him to the stone floor. "How will *you* make amends, priest? How will you atone for killing my parents? How will you atone for destroying people simply because their ancestors were once Jewish? How will you atone for the pastry man, whom you destroyed because you did not like his customers? What can you say to me that will unstain your hands or give me back my family, my friends, the wife I will never have? Let me hear what you have to offer."

The priest said nothing.

I kneeled over Azinheiro and put my hand against the priest's throat once more. His pulse thrummed under my grip. "If your Inquisition survives this earthquake, will you go back to them? Will you work all the harder to make up for the money they have lost by arresting more New Christians? Or will you tell your masters that you now know what you did was evil? Will you tell them you must wash your bloody hands and repent? Which is it?"

The priest closed his eyes. "I am what I am," he said. "I cannot be anything else. But you, my son, have a choice now to be one thing or another. When you killed before—that was violence meeting violence. You fought to survive. You must now decide if you want to be guilty of murder."

If I let this priest live, he would continue to do evil. He would use his authority to take and ruin lives. I could prevent that. I could make it so this madman never hurt anyone again. Perhaps there was no pleasure or even satisfaction to be had from killing Azinheiro, but killing the priest was the right thing to do. Letting him live was weak.

I chose to be weak.

"I can't make you be someone other than who you are," I said. "It is not my place to do so. That is what the Inquisition does. It is not what I do."

I turned toward the door. Azinheiro rose, coming shakily to his feet and steadying himself against the wall. He was silent. It would have been beneath him to thank me for my mercy. I was not even sure it was mercy; I was even less certain it was the right thing. I only knew that it was what I had to do.

As I began to descend the stairs I saw a shadow pass behind me. I turned in time to see Kingsley Franklin, having once more picked up the axe, bringing the weapon down toward Azinheiro. The priest managed a startled cry and raised his hand, but it was too late. The axe struck the top of his head and drove in, almost perfectly centered, to the bridge of his nose.

Franklin, surprisingly agile, jumped back to avoid the spray of blood and brains as the priest toppled over onto the floor. I remained motionless, looking at the body of the priest as a halo of blood formed around his prone body. Franklin now stepped toward me, hands raised.

"I thought you might suffer a bout of morality," he said, "so I figured it best to be on hand to do the business."

"Why?" I asked, my single word catching in my dry throat.

He shrugged. "I told you. Your father was a friend. Figured it was the least I could do. You get to enjoy knowing you made the hard, righteous choice, *and* you get to see the priest get what's coming to him. It's a thing of beauty, when you consider it." He wiped with the back of his hand at a few drops of blood that had collected on his forehead.

My eyes shifted back to the dead priest. "That may be putting it strongly."

Franklin shrugged again. "You're not angry, I hope."

"In truth I hardly know what to feel," I said, "but it is not anger toward you."

"Good enough for me," he said, and headed down the stairs.

Chapter 32

Outside the convent, Mariana's hand felt warm in mine. The air was cool around us, and it smelled of smoke. Night had fallen while we were inside, and a sheet of gray clouds covered the sky, like a lid coming down on a pot. Scattered fires lit the city, but otherwise all was dark.

"We should stay here tonight," Franklin said, "and find the others in the morning."

"I doubt the convent will welcome us now."

"You might be surprised. They're meant to offer forgiveness."

"Mr. Franklin," I observed, "we left a priest with an axe in his skull in one of their chambers. I'm fairly certain we have worn out our welcome."

"Maybe so, but they won't do much about it, will they? And the cold glares of a bunch of dried-up old women may be better than crossing the city in the dark."

"Safer for us, perhaps. I cannot say what dangers the others might face without us there to protect them. We must go to them."

"Do you really wish to cross this hellish landscape with a child?" Franklin asked.

"Honestly, I cannot know any course that is safer than another. It's all madness, so it may as well be madness upon our own terms."

Franklin shook his head in wonder. "Mr. Foxx, if I had not known your father, I would be surprised to meet a man as honorable as you."

And yet, you betrayed him, I thought. The anger, however, did not rise to the surface. Franklin had been given a chance to redeem himself, and he had taken it. It was true that, in part, that redemption had included cleaving the skull of a priest, but he had done it for the most moral of reasons. He had helped me. I would not forget that.

We moved out into the broken, burning streets, populated by the dead and the half dead and the murderous. I wanted only to pass unseen. Though frightened, Mariana understood that she had to remain quiet. She gripped my hand hard and walked with her lips pressed together. Franklin, however, knew nothing about stealth, and each step he took announced our presence to anyone who cared to notice. I had to hope his size would deter any attention he attracted.

The destruction appeared worse in the flickering dark than it had in the light of day. There were gangs of men upon the street, armed with knives and swords and hammers and makeshift clubs and pikes—whatever they could get. Some were small groups, only three or four, and others twenty or more. I tried to keep clear of them, but once or twice we were looked over by gaunt men. They were beasts who had been kept upon leashes all their lives by the Inquisition and by ancient custom. Now they were set free. They had no laws to follow. There was no one to tell them they could not carry blades or force themselves upon any woman who caught their fancy.

Over the course of the day, my rough clothing had been stained with blood and shredded. Both Franklin and I were bedraggled and harmless enough in appearance. As long as we did not encounter that species of man so depraved that he wished to sate his lust upon a child, I hoped we would be safe.

In that walk back to Settwell's house, we saw wicked things. I wished I could have shielded Mariana's gaze, but she was young and perhaps would not remember what she did not fully understand. A quartet of men, standing facing one another, pleasuring themselves in unison; a pair of gaunt and shirtless boys searching the dead for useful trinkets; a group of laborers beating a Dutchman for sport. The man was upon the ground, his arms raised in futile defense, as they struck him with sticks and stones. There were more than a dozen of them, and though I ached to save the man, to lash out against his tormentors, I did not dare try. I could not risk Mariana's safety, not against so many foes. The Dutchman caught my eye and cried out for help, and I made myself turn away. I knew that of everything I had seen and done that day, this moment would be the one that came to me as I lay awake at night, but I kept walking all the same.

As we rounded a corner we came upon a half dozen soldiers, and I feared the worst. These underpaid and armed men would be more dangerous than any gang of thieves. One drew his sword before I could react. "State your business!" he demanded.

"Please, senhor," I said, hoping humility would win the day. "My business is mercy. I bring this child to her father. I promised to find her and return her to him, and that is what I do and where I go."

I expected the man to scoff, but he only nodded. "Have you stolen? If so, confess now. It will go easier on you."

"No, senhor," I said. "I have stated our business true."

"Submit to a search."

Something in the man's tone told me that it was the right course, and I agreed. The soldier gestured to one of his men, who came forward and ran his hands along and inside our coats and pockets. The soldier then backed away and told his commander that we had nothing of import upon us.

In all my time in Lisbon, I had never seen soldiers behave so efficiently and honorably. "Senhor, you and your men do brave work, keeping the peace," I said.

The soldier snorted. "All it took was for God to stamp his boot upon us that we might do so. It was His Grace the Count of Oeiras who has ordered things properly. While the king flees the city and hides in the countryside, the count has paid us what we're owed and organized patrols. We comb the streets looking for able-bodied men to help with the rescue. We should recruit you were it not for the child. We also look for thieves, and all we find shall hang in public at dawn as a sign that the law still reigns in this city."

"You do well, senhor," I said. "Strange to consider Lisbon might be better for all this destruction."

"I've thought the same," the soldier said. "This lot will be disinclined to agree, however." He gestured behind him and I saw, for the first time, that the soldiers pulled five men along upon a train. Their hands were bound behind their backs and the rope twisted around their waists. "Thieves all, and they shall swing at first light."

I looked over at the men, hangdog and defeated. They were no doubt hungry and thirsty and tired of walking behind the men who would kill them. I turned away, but then looked back again.

The third man in the train looked familiar, and so I stepped closer and saw that it was the Gypsy Dordia e Zilhão. His face was battered and bruised, most likely from what he had endured in the earthquake and its aftermath, though the contours of his face might have changed after the beating I had delivered. His lips were cracked, and it was plain to see he was parched. He lifted his bloodshot eyes, both so blackened that he looked to be wearing a mask. He'd broken the bones around them. He began to say something to me, but clearly the pain and effort of speaking was more than he was willing to endure, and he slowly dropped his head, wincing slightly at the movement.

I turned to the soldier. Dordia e Zilhão was no friend of mine. He was a thief of the worst kind, who preyed upon the weak and the lost. He had abused Enéas beyond imagining and he would have raped Roberta. Yet for all that, I had harmed him, tricked him into injury and ruin, not once but twice. Did I not owe him something? Perhaps if I spoke a kind word or two, I could convince the soldier to move the Gypsy from the ranks of the condemned to the rank of soldier. With so many lives blasted out of existence today, was there not here an opportunity for some good, the chance to turn a man from something vile to something useful?

There was, however, a limit to the number of favors I dared ask the soldiers, and so, instead, I said, "Senhor, if you have no preset course you must patrol, might I impose upon you to offer us escort that we might see this child home?"

Whatever doubts the soldier had entertained about me now vanished. A man who wished soldiers to accompany him was certainly honest. "Senhor," the soldier said, "I have seen horrors and suffering today that I should not forget if I live a thousand years. I would be forever in your debt if you gave me the opportunity to look upon something good."

And so it was we made our way back to our friends under armed escort. When we reached Settwell's house, I saw the curtains part and then Settwell came running out of the house and grabbed Mariana and hugged her. The two of them wept. Whatever else might be said of Settwell—that he was a liar and a thief and a fool—there was no doubt that he loved his daughter, and that he had suffered for his mistakes.

When Settwell finally let go of Mariana, he stood and embraced me. "I have wronged you," he said, "and yet you braved what I dare not imagine to save my daughter. I know you did it for her and not for me. That does not matter. I am at your command for as long as I live."

"We shall see," I said.

I turned to thank the soldiers and was surprised to find all six of them sobbing like children. I had been so full of rage toward the Portuguese, had seen so much of their worst nature, that I had forgotten what a sentimental people they could be.

"Senhor," I told the soldier, "I thank you for what you have done for us and what you mean to do for the city." I cast a glance at Dordia e Zilhão. Perhaps it was not too late to ask for more. "That man there—the one with the blackened eyes. What is his crime?"

The soldier wiped his tears upon the back of his hand. "We caught him and a fellow beast attempting to rape a novice nun. Her arm was crushed under a fallen building. When we rounded the corner, the friend was lifting her skirts while that one was pulling down his breeches. Why, have you something to say on his behalf?"

Whatever impulse toward mercy I had felt abruptly withered. "No. I thought I knew him, but I see I am mistaken. I hope he hangs slow."

"As slow as can be arranged," the soldier agreed. "This destruction shall turn every man into either his best self or his worst self, and the worst ones must be made to suffer."

I did not disagree. I thanked the soldier once more and turned back to Settwell and his house. It was time to make ready to leave Lisbon forever.

Chapter 33

I set out provisions, and we ate and drank in silence. I had not explained my plan in detail to the others, because I was not entirely certain it would work, and I did not wish for them to see me fail. It was not for the sake of my pride, but rather for their sense of security. They needed to believe I was competent, and given what these people had experienced, the slightest falter on my part could fill them with uncertainty. To survive what lay ahead, they would need to believe survival a possibility.

I believed we had a chance, the next morning, to escape the city quickly and safely, but I could not be certain the vehicles I sought were still where I hoped. This location, too, had dangers of its own. Best to say nothing of this, but to keep my group moving and believing we might yet safely flee.

We dared to make no fire that night, but it did not get very cold. I propped myself against the wall near the front door. My plan was to sleep lightly. I wished to see none of the others, nor to speak with them—not about anything unrelated to our survival. I wanted to consider nothing else until we escaped Portugal.

I think the others could tell I was in no mood for conversation. I made it until near midnight without any of them bothering me. Then I was disturbed by the one member of the group I was not sorry to see: Luis. The old man came in and sat down next to me, lowering himself with stiff difficulty to the stone floor.

In the day's excitement, I hadn't noticed if Luis had recognized Franklin. How could I explain my willingness to forgive the man who had sold my father to the Inquisition?

"My creaky bones," Luis said as he finally settled. "I can recall when the simple act of sitting did not feel like a victory, but I suppose you were not yet come into your beard then."

I said nothing. I wasn't being deliberately unfriendly, but I could think of no reply to the idle chatter.

"You have managed to collect quite a varied group of survivors," Luis tried again. "Lovers and would-be lovers, enemies and friends. I cannot blame you for not wanting to be among them."

"And an English merchant turned innkeeper."

Luis nodded, watching me carefully. "Yes. A strange choice."

"I believe he's changed," I said.

"Can a man truly change so much as that? Can he redeem himself for such crimes?" Luis asked.

"I pray to God he can."

Luis's face darkened. "Do you know what I think? I think redemption does not matter. I don't care how much he regrets what he did to your family. I don't care how much he wishes to atone. It will not bring back your father. It will not rewrite the pain and destruction he caused for a few gold coins—coins the Inquisition took from him as soon as they were stolen."

"No," I agreed. "It won't. The past cannot be remade, but the future can be."

Luis laughed cruelly. "I did not think you so philosophical."

"It is something I have been trying to learn, senhor—trying to believe. For sins of one man against another, the Day of Atonement does not atone until they have made peace with each other."

Luis narrowed his gaze. "What does that mean?"

Of course he did not know the liturgy any better than Gabriela had. He would not recognize a prayer from the holiest day of the Jewish calendar. His forefathers had been Jewish, but he was not.

"It is the reason I came here," I said. "And it is how I am trying to live."

"Well, if it is so, there is a difficulty, because I will not make peace with him. I will not forgive him. Leave the traitor behind."

"No," I said. "He helped me rescue Mariana. He tried to warn me about the Inquisitor."

Luis shook his head. "And if he betrays us all again?"

"He won't. He, too, wants to survive. He would only betray us if he were a creature of pure malice, and I am sure that is not so."

Luis began to say something, but apparently thought better of it. "I suppose I am not the only one of your refugees who must endure the presence of an enemy."

"There is no helping it," I said. "Mrs. Carver must pass the night in the house of the man who orchestrated her ruin."

"Ruin was coming for everyone," Luis said. "Settwell's scheme is now beside the point."

"That is true," I agreed, "but her ruin would have had a different shape. Her fortune is gone, her reputation in tatters, and her husband dead. All of those things began with me. If I'd never come here, her life would not have taken such a turn."

"But perhaps her life would already be finished," Luis said. "It is a fool's game to predict what would have happened."

I was silent.

"Did you seek for those terrible things to happen to her?" Luis asked.

"I sought her poverty," I said.

"But you believed you were pursuing justice."

"I was wrong."

"Men make mistakes," Luis said. "You made yours with a good heart and just intentions. I know of no instance in these affairs where you deliberately did evil or sought to harm those you believed blameless. No one can know the results of his actions. You may pull a drowning man from a lake, and that man might be a heartless killer. Does that mean that when you see a man struggling in the lake you must pass him by?"

"Of course not. The man could just as well be a saint as a demon. Most likely he is neither."

"But if he is a demon," Luis said, "and you saved him, do you blame yourself for your actions? Perhaps it is human nature to do so, but the impulse is wrong. At any given point in our lives, Mr. Foxx, we can only make the best choice given to us. Choices are in our power, but consequences are not. You must continue to make the best choices you can, and face the consequences bravely."

I managed a weak smile, certainly invisible in the darkness. "You are a wise man, senhor."

"Just an old one," Luis said. "A man learns a few things as he travels the decades, even if he does not mean to."

"Then tell me this," I said. "I came to Lisbon to pursue justice. I came to kill a man I believed I needed to kill. I found him at the time of my choosing, and as I was about to take his life, that was when the city came apart. What does it mean? Was this the intervention of God, telling me not to kill the priest?"

Now it was Luis's turn to laugh. "You suffer from the arrogance that afflicts all who look for omens. The wind blows east, and you ascribe it some meaning in your life, but the wind blows east for all men, not just you."

"But not all men were about to confront such a person when the quake began."

"Is it the only time you encountered the priest?"

"No, I had spoken with him many times before that—and, of course, after."

"And none of those times the earth shook?"

"You know it did not."

"Then that is your answer," Luis said. "Tens of thousands live in Lisbon. When the earthquake struck, women were giving birth and men dying. Offers of marriage were being proffered and those offers were accepted or rejected. Secrets were revealed and concealed. Men committed crimes or advanced schemes. They wrote poems and struck bargains. Lovers came together for the first time and broke apart forever. Oh, I suppose more than a few men merely sat about picking nits or pissing in pots, but how many besides you were engaged in business that felt monumental? What makes you believe God was speaking to you and not one of them?"

I was curiously comforted by Luis's explanation of my insignificance. "Thank you, my friend. I am glad you are with me."

Luis grunted as he pushed himself to his feet. "Don't think me anything but selfish. I depend upon you to help me survive what comes next."

"As I depend upon you," I answered.

I drifted off from time to time, but I was awake when Roberta came into the room and sat next to me, almost precisely where Luis had. I listened to her breathe for a few minutes, but said nothing until she spoke.

"I know you're awake."

"Yes," I said.

She fell back into silence, and I began to wonder if she had fallen asleep. Then I heard her breathing change, and I understood she was crying.

"I know nothing about you," she said.

"That is probably for the best," I told her.

"You are a Jew," she said. "An escaped New Christian. And you came back here seeking revenge against the Inquisition. I pieced that much together."

"Yes," I said.

"And Senhora Nobreza. You knew her when you were younger."

"Yes."

"You loved her?"

"Yes."

"You came back for her too, didn't you?"

"I did."

"Then you love her still?"

Why did she want to know? Did her question suggest there had been some thawing in her heart? "I thought I did when I came here, but she and I have changed. We were children then, and so much time has passed, but more importantly, life has made us different than what we were. She is happy with her husband."

Roberta was silent for a long time. I imagined she must be thinking about her own husband, killed by Inácio, killed because of me. Then I saw something glimmer in the moonlight. I realized Roberta was holding something out to me.

"Senhora Nobreza said she thought this was yours. This is the blade that man used when he attacked me."

I looked at the dagger and shook my head. It was nothing to me, a replica. It was meaningless when I had given it to Inácio, but it had become so much more. Now it would belong to Roberta.

"You should keep it," I told her. "You've earned it with your courage."

"I was not brave," she said. "I was terrified."

"Anyone can take risks when he is not frightened. To act, despite fear, is the soul of courage."

"Were you frightened," she asked, "when you did all those terrible things? When you fought those men?"

"No," I said. "I was too angry to be frightened."

Roberta was silent for a long time. At first I thought it was because she did not believe me. Then I thought it was because she did.

"What is your secret?" she asked. "How do you summon anger of such strength that it drives away the fear?"

At this I laughed. "You don't understand. The only reason I am here, in this city, is to purge myself of that anger. I want, more than anything else, to be afraid, but I'm not, because for so long I haven't cared if I lived or died."

After a long while she said, "Why did you refuse me? I want to know the truth."

"Because you did not know I was a Jew."

Now it was her turn to laugh. "Do you truly think that would have mattered to me?"

"I did not fear bigotry," I said, "but discovery. I couldn't let you know I had been lying to you. And I refused you *because* I had been lying to you. I didn't trust you."

"But you trust me now? Why would you? I have told you I blame you for everything that has happened."

I took in a deep breath. "I can't begin to explain everything, and I don't wish to—not while we are here. When we're safe, when we are free of this city, then you may ask what you like."

"Why? What will be different then?"

"*I* will be different then," I said.

"How will you be different?"

I turned away from her. "I hope I shall be afraid. It is what I wish to believe."

I was awake before first light. Despite Settwell's financial reversals, his larder remained well stocked, so I filled sacks with cheeses and dried meats and fruits. I found some bread, two days old, but soon enough no one would complain. I filled old wine bottles with water. They would be heavy to carry but there was no helping it, and with any luck, we would not be traveling on foot for long. I divided the goods among as many bags as possible, keeping in mind the strength of each in the party.

I then ate a breakfast of stale bread and cheese rind. Franklin joined me, and we discussed the route. Then Luis arrived. He glared at Franklin for a long time, and the Englishman left. Even after he was gone, Luis remained silent for several minutes, then turned away and looked out the window.

"How certain are you that we shall be able to escape the way you claim?" he asked.

"Fairly certain," I said. "But there can be no way to know what we might face."

"I am not a young man," Luis said, "and the journey will be hard."

"You shall be well tended to."

"Even so," Luis said. He turned to look at me. "I cannot be sure I will survive what is to come. After yesterday, none of us can be certain. I want you to have this." He held out a letter, folded several times and sealed with wax. "Do not open it unless I am dead. It contains things I would have you know about your family. I will tell you them myself when we are safe, but now is not the time. Yet I could not risk that I might die without your knowing."

"It will be a hard thing not to open it," I said.

"You seem like a disciplined man to me," Luis said with a sad smile. "I can't stop you, of course. I can only tell you that my preference is that you wait either for a time of quiet or for my death. If you honor me, you will honor my wishes."

I put the letter in the pocket of my coat. "Then it shall be as you ask."

Half an hour later, we were upon the street. There were more soldiers about than during the previous night, and it was hard to walk fifty paces without observing groups of three or more, muskets at the ready. They appeared tired, but something made them seem like a new version of their old selves. In the wake of the disaster, they had found purpose and, from what I had been told, leadership. I had no idea who this Count of Oeiras was, but the soldiers had spoken of him with such reverence, and he evidently had taken charge of the kingdom.

Had we been searched, as we had the previous day, we would have been marked as thieves and so condemned to death. I had not troubled to count the wealth we had taken. I was fairly certain none of the others had either. The money was abstract now, and it would remain so until we were free of danger. I supposed it was in the many tens of thousands of pounds, perhaps even more than a hundred thousand—enough for all of us to live well for the rest of our lives, should our lives last beyond the next few hours and days. The soldiers were now one more threat to our safety, but I hoped a group such as this, with women and a child and an old man, would attract no notice. My hopes bore out. The soldiers we passed nodded to us or offered quick exchanges of news and advice, but no more than that.

I led the way. Behind me walked Luis, Gabriela and Eusebio, Settwell and Mariana, and Roberta. I had placed Franklin in the rear. We could not head directly to our destination, for the streets were collapsed and burning. We moved east, uphill, before finding a clear path to the Alfama. As we crossed the Rossio, we saw a newly constructed scaffolding with more than a dozen bodies dangling from ropes. Perhaps one of them was Dordia e Zilhão. I looked away.

In the Alfama, everything was surprisingly calm. Many of the fires from the previous day had gone out. Refugees, such as we saw, were docile—in mourning or confusion, but the panic of the previous day had dissipated. Soldiers crossed our path every few minutes, keeping the peace and troubling no one who showed no signs of ill intent. Once I saw an old man stumble, and a stranger set down his pack and his own concerns to help him to his feet. The hour of Lisbon's destruction was also its finest. Stripped of its wealth and corruption, its priests and its *fidalgos,* it was but a collection of human beings, with all their flaws and all their virtues.

As we walked, I sensed Luis moving beside me. "You are sure there will be a boat where you are going?"

"Nothing is certain, senhor. Certainly not any longer, but I believe so. I hope so."

"And we shall be safe on the ocean, you think?"

"Safer than here."

I had no plan to brave the open sea. We would hug the coastline north until we reached Spain and were free of the Inquisition's grasp. From there we would buy passage on a ship, or barring that, procure a carriage and proceed on land until we reached France. Then, by land or sea, to Calais, and from there across the Channel to the first English port available.

At last we came to the heart of the Alfama and the house I sought. I looked up and down the street to be certain there were no soldiers, and then kicked in the door. Inácio's stronghold smelled strongly of fish and the Tagus. I led the group down the hallway to another door, which opened to the cavernous boathouse. It was dark, for there were only a few small windows toward the ceiling, but even in the gloom, I saw a single large boat, intact. It had but one mast and a square sail. It was not meant to travel far, and would offer no protection from the elements. Traversing the waters on such a vessel would prove rough going, but it was our way out of Lisbon, and I meant for us to take it.

I remained motionless for a long moment. I knew little enough of sailing, and I had no idea if any of the others had more experience, but there were oars, and the prospect of hard labor heartened me. That was something I could do. So long as we kept within sight of the shore, and the weather did not turn foul, we would endure.

Settwell moved forward to the boat. I watched him examining it, running his hand along the inside, checking the rigging. He was a merchant, and I supposed that required him to know a thing or two about sailing vessels. He certainly acted like a man who knew what he was about.

Settwell had set in motion the events that had hurt so many people and had betrayed my friendship and loyalty. But I could not summon any real anger. He had used his lies and his guile, for that was his nature, just as I used fists and blades. Perhaps he had learned something. Perhaps he only knew he had become rich. I chose not to make it my concern.

He came back over to us and took hold of his daughter's hand. "I should not choose to take her to India, but I think a run along the coastline should prove manageable," he said.

Mariana looked at the boat, and then her father. She leaned against him hard, and he crouched down to whisper encouraging words into her ear.

"Even a lion may love its young, but that makes it no less dangerous."

It was Roberta. She stood next to me, as unkempt and filthy as the rest, though no less lovely for it. She was raw now, wild and unbound by society's restraints on her femininity. There was a pure and raging beauty to her.

"There must be a truce between you," I said. "We must work together."

"Yes, I know. Still, quite a band of followers you've assembled."

"I am attempting to do what's right. You must promise me there will be no trouble."

"I shall make none," she assured me. "I want to live. And the truth is, I cannot say how much harm your friend has really done me. I would have been ruined in the quake, and Rutherford—that was not his doing. No one could have predicted or prevented it. I am too tired, too frightened, to hate anyone."

I looked at her. "Not even me?"

"You least of all," she said with a sad smile. "Perhaps when this is all over, I will hate you, or perhaps my feelings will be of an altogether different nature. I cannot know, but I look forward to the leisure of discovering what I feel when I'm not fatigued and terrified."

"It was not long since that England was the last place you wished to go."

"And now I cannot see it too soon," she said. She leaned toward me, her face tilted up toward mine, and whispered, "Get me there quickly. Please."

Her voice, her breath, were like cold water on a sleeping man. I roused myself from my reflection and began to direct my survivors to make ready. I had some load the boat, others check the rigging. Franklin I sent to seek out the latch that released the secret door. He found it along the river side of the house, not well hidden. It was a circular crank with a handle, which the big man rotated in a few massive heaves, lifting up the false stone barrier.

Light now streamed in. The Tagus was still choppy and rough, but the sky beyond was blue and nearly free of clouds. A beautiful day for sailing.

"Everyone but Franklin, climb in," I said. "It's time to go."

Eusebio was first, and offered a hand to Gabriela. Settwell and Mariana followed. And then Roberta and finally Luis. They sat there on the splintering wooden benches, all of them, not just Mariana, looking like children, hands in laps, waiting for the adult to tell them what to do. How had I become that person? I was now the responsible one. Heaven help us.

"We are joining them, yes?" Franklin asked me.

"Not quite yet," I said. "You have to help me untie the ropes."

He snorted. "I thought you were worried I was too fat to take with you."

I smiled at this. "I suspect you will be thin before we get to the end. Now, let's get to it."

The ropes were bound tightly, and untying them was hard work. I was bent over, negotiating a particularly stubborn knot, when I heard the unmistakable sound of footsteps approaching from the hallway. I ignored it for a moment, continuing the work, and I did not look up until I was ready.

When I turned, I saw Inácio, who stood five feet behind Franklin, pistol out. A broad grin spread across his imposing features. The arm that held the pistol was steady, but the other was wrapped in bloody bandages, still wet. I took no small amount of pleasure in the knowledge that Roberta had hurt him, perhaps badly.

"This is the end for you," Inácio said. "Did you not think trouble would come?"

"I expect it every moment," I said. "Now is as fine a time as any."

"Brave talk, but talk accomplishes little. You came to me with your talk. *Oh, let us be friends. Let us forget how you suffered while I prospered.* That talk meant nothing to me."

"Yes, I worked that out," I said.

"It's sad, do you not think? Everything you've done and endured, and it comes down to this."

I turned to Franklin. "Get on the boat, and take her out. Leave without me. Get them safely to Spain and then France. I'll find another way out of the country."

Franklin stood frozen. "If I attempt to take the boat out, he'll shoot us."

"If he turns his gun on you long enough to shoot you, he'll be dead. He won't take the chance. It's me he wants." I presumed that was the case. This was his boathouse. If he had wanted to leave, he would be gone already. Had he been lingering here, hoping I would show? Had he waited outside Settwell's house, thinking I might take refuge there? However he had found me, he had set about the task with a single-minded determination, and that meant it was me he wanted to hurt, not my friends. So, let him hurt me. I was done hurting others.

"No," Inácio said. "I understand you too well, Sebastião. You care nothing if you live or die, but your friends—that is another matter." He stepped back slowly. "Everyone gets off the boat now, or someone dies. Maybe her." He gestured the gun toward Roberta. "You remember me, my sweet lady, don't you?"

Roberta rose and leapt awkwardly from the boat, walking to my side. None of the others moved.

Inácio grinned. "Ah, the lady. If there was but one I would have with me, it is you. Now, the rest of you, get out, or one of you dies."

"No one else leave the boat," I said. "I will manage this."

"How will you do that?" Inácio asked. "I have more pistols in my pockets, and I believe I can take two or three of you before you can reach me. You see, you are not the only one who does not fear death."

I studied him, his bandaged arm, his posture, the bulges in his pockets. It was possible he could do what he said, but he would be slow, uncertain. Even so, there were lives not my own in the balance, and if he was determined to hurt one of the others, I might not be able to stop him in time.

"Maybe instead of the pretty lady, I shall aim first for the child," Inácio said. "Or perhaps the Jewess. That would trouble our friend Sebastião, I think."

Roberta took a tentative step toward Inácio and swallowed hard.

"Roberta," I said. "Stay here."

She ignored me and took another step. She was pale, her lips almost white, but when she spoke, her voice was calm. "He says he loves me," she told Inácio. "So if you want to hurt him, take me."

Inácio studied her, trying to figure out the puzzle. "And what would I do with you once I had you?"

"I don't care," she said. "I have nothing left, but I know that if you take me, it will torment him. Even though I say this in front of him, it will still kill him to know you have me. That's enough."

"Perhaps you enjoyed my attentions more than you wish to admit," Inácio said.

"Believe what you like," Roberta returned.

Inácio was now laughing softly, shaking his head in wonder. Did he truly believe that after all he had done, Roberta felt some strange desire for him?

"We shall see," Inácio said to her. "I shall give you an opportunity to prove your loyalty, and if you do—"

"Careful, Inácio!" Roberta cried out. "Foxx has a knife."

Inácio, whose eyes had drifted toward Roberta, returned his gaze to me and raised the pistol. His eyes were narrow and intense, his muscles hard. Until that moment, I had not moved, but now I did. I had more than one knife, of course. I had many knives. I began to reach for one in my belt. Let him fire his pistol at me. Either he would hit me or he would not.

Neither of us saw Roberta coming. She lunged forward and thrust her own blade, the replica of the one that had once belonged to my father, into Inácio's thigh, all the way to the hilt, and then yanked it out in a single, fluid motion. Without stopping to see the damage she had inflicted, she leapt away and began to work at the ropes toward the aft of the boat. Understanding his role, Franklin moved to its front. I ran toward Inácio.

Inácio had been staggered by the wound, but only for a second. It must have been horribly painful, but he was not going to let it deter him. He took two steps back and then raised his pistol at me. I was now less than ten feet away from him. "One more step and you die."

I stopped and raised my hands, letting my blade drop. From the corner of my eye, I saw Franklin finish with the ropes and jump on the boat, wobbling and nearly falling in the water. It would have been comic under any other circumstances. Roberta was already on board. Inácio saw it too, but dared not react. He knew better than to take his eyes off me.

"Clever," Inácio said, trying not to grimace. "But your friends leave without you. She tricked you and escapes without you."

"It is what I want," I said. "And she knows it. She knows that I can be trapped here forever, so long as they are safe." I turned my head slightly. "All of you, go. *Go*, and do not stop. Do not look for me to catch up with you. I shall go another way and meet you in London."

I heard movement behind me. Settwell cried, "What are you doing? We can't leave him."

"It is what he wants," Roberta said.

"He is just saying that to deceive Inácio!" Settwell again. "We must wait."

"You don't know him. He wants us to make our escape. If we wait for him, and we fail, it will kill him. If you want to help him, then go!"

I did not turn to look at her, but I did not have to. I knew she understood. It wasn't callousness but tenderness that made her want to leave me behind, and I thought of my own departure ten years earlier. It was the one thing she could do for me, and for herself, and though I knew it was hard, she did not flinch. I kept my eyes on Inácio and listened to the sound of waves lapping, but there were no more voices. They were silent, I imagined, as they drifted out of the boathouse and toward the river. Were they watching me or had they turned away already? I hoped it was the latter.

Inácio scowled. Blood ran down his trouser leg, pooling about his boot, but he appeared unconcerned. "You want to be abandoned, despised by the people you protect?"

"This is how I protect them. You were right, you know. I could have endured anything but to see them harmed. Now I need not fear it."

We glowered at each other like two tomcats preparing for an inevitable fight, a conflict with no goal but victory. We kept our gazes locked while almost everything I cared about in the world slipped further away.

"Your friends left you," Inácio said. He grinned crookedly. "Just as you knew they always would. You are all alone. Abandoned."

"So it seems."

"How does it feel to be cast aside?"

"I am pleased," I said, utterly without inflection.

"You may pretend to be unaffected, but I know the truth. I was wrong. There is one thing harder for you than seeing your friends hurt. It is seeing how little they care for you."

"You know it is not so," I said. "I am content."

"Then be content to get on your knees." He flicked the pistol slightly downward.

"No," I said.

Inácio's face darkened. Perhaps he had expected that this would be easier. "If you do not, I shall shoot you."

"Then shoot me," I told him. "You said yourself that I care not if I die."

"Even such men as you will prefer to live."

"Perhaps so. I shall not be toyed with, however. If you mean to shoot me, then do so. If you think you, who have been beaten and stabbed so many times in the past few days, can do what a half dozen soldiers could not, then go ahead and defeat me in unfair combat. But I don't believe you have the courage. I believe you are a coward, Inácio. I believe you know that unless you drop your weapon and flee, you are going to die."

Inácio hesitated. Then he lowered the pistol. He quite clearly meant for the ball to strike me below the waist, a wound that would immobilize but not kill me. He did not want me dead yet. He had set out to hurt and betray me, and though he had caused me pain, it had gained him nothing. He had no gold for all his efforts, only wounds and humiliation, and he wanted me to suffer for it.

As Inácio prepared to fire, I dropped to my knees and leaned forward, throwing my arms wide and presenting my heart. So intent was Inácio not to kill me yet that by instinct he twitched to the right even as he pulled back on the hammer and fired the weapon. There was the pop of exploding gunpowder and the crack of the ball striking wood. Acrid smoke puffed out of the pistol in a diabolical belch. Inácio would know that this mishap was the best he would have to show for his efforts. I had defeated a half dozen soldiers, I had taken on the Inquisition in their own Palace, and I would be more than a match for this wreck of a man with but one good arm and one good leg.

Inácio was not prepared to surrender, however. He dropped the expended weapon and reached into his pocket for his second pistol. I was already there, ripping the weapon from his hand and tossing it into the water. It was now a fight of brute strength. I grinned, though I felt no pleasure.

I was tired. I was tired of death and suffering and misery. I was tired of Lisbon, and I was tired of attempting to do what was right and failing miserably time after time. I had come to Portugal because I believed it my obligation. I had no choice but to try to make things right, to restore order, to atone. Instead, I did nothing but leave a path of destruction behind me. I was weary, so weary, of trying and trying and destroying all I encountered. I was tired of disappointing the people who trusted me. I was tired of my own heart, which knew only broken love.

I leapt forward and grabbed Inácio by his left forearm, guessing where the worst of his wound was, and squeezed hard. At the same time, I kicked the flat of my foot brutally into the fresh wound on his thigh. His face went pale. His mouth slackened. Somehow, through force of will, he shook his head, keeping himself conscious, but it was not enough.

I took another step forward, and struck him in the side of the head. He stumbled backwards and fell to his knees. His face had gone white, and his eyes were wide, darting rapidly, as though he had forgotten where he was. This was not an honorable fight between equals, but I no longer cared about honor. I was angry and unafraid.

Inácio's gaze was unfocused, but he looked up, grinning with bloodstained teeth. "You should be thanking me. I killed the English-woman's husband. I have all but given her to you."

I felt the rage blossom afresh. Inácio must have seen it, because he managed to raise a hand in protest.

"Wait!" he cried. "I see I have been wrong. You and I are not to be enemies. We must be allies. We are alike. You know it is true. Think of what we could accomplish together. The old friendship!" His words were rapid and wheezing.

I hardly understood what he said. The anger was like a storm roaring in my ears. Even the priest had been less despicable than this man. Azinheiro, at least, operated within the rules of an institution, corrupt though it was. Inácio had killed Enéas, had betrayed me, had murdered Rutherford Carver and his servants. He had hurt Roberta. He had done it all for the pleasure of cruelty.

I saw Inácio's lips moving, and knew he was speaking, but I could not understand the words. I reached out once more and took his head in both my hands. "I found the priest," I said, "and I showed him mercy. You get none."

For a fleeting moment, looking into his face, I saw the boy as I'd first seen him, at the bottom of a staircase. Then, with a single, hard gesture, I twisted Inácio's neck sharply and heard the crack of his neck breaking. It was over. Quick and clean and without joy or flourish.

Before the dead man could begin to slump, I shoved him into the water, where he floated facedown, the waves lapping over his still form. I walked away, and looked out through the open door to the Tagus. There, in the distance, I saw the boat, farther away than I could have imagined. The tides or the winds were casting it away so swiftly. Perhaps if I ran, I might be able to signal them to return to shore and I could join them. I could sit with Franklin and Roberta and I could talk with Mariana. Even the thought of bickering with Eusebio seemed sweet to me.

It was foolishness. I could never catch them, and perhaps that was for the best. I would not have to face them every day. I would have given my life to save any one of those people—yes, even Eusebio— but each one of them was a scathing reminder of all my mistakes, all my broken vows.

I went back down the hallways and stepped outside the building and smelled the sooty air that stank of death and rot and a broken and burning city. I lowered myself upon the wet dirt of the road. Alone in this least broken quarter of a once-great capital, I opened the letter Luis Nobreza had given me. As I read, tears ran down my cheeks. I did not know I was weeping until I saw the drops of water plashing against the paper.

I put the letter away. There was still so much for which I had to atone.

Chapter 34

London, five months later

I lost track of how many weeks it took to cross into Spain. I traveled east, staying off the main roads, foraging and hunting, finding work along the way. The temperature dropped, and the snow began to fall, but I still walked, every day, as far as I could drag my legs, numb from fatigue and cold. There were incidents along the road, encounters with men who took me for an easy target, but those meetings were best forgotten.

Once in Spain, between my Portuguese, English, and a smattering of French, I was able to make myself understood. When I reached a town large enough to have an inn, I took the first in a series of long carriage rides. I hated them. I would rather have walked than sit all day, but I rode just the same. Eventually I made my way, perhaps ironically, to San Sebastian, where I remained until the spring. I found a small boardinghouse where no one asked me questions, and I lived off what back-breaking labor I could find and, from time to time, stealing from men who were themselves thieves.

When the weather warmed and the seas calmed, I took the first ship to England. I had hoped I might sail directly into London, but it was not to be. I traveled, instead, to Falmouth, but I would not allow myself to consider it symmetry. It was a port, and ports took ships. It was nothing more than that.

I remained in Falmouth until I could gather together enough funds, by fair means and foul, for a carriage to London. I had nothing but the clothes I wore. All the money I had saved in my life I had used for the venture in Lisbon, and the wealth I had taken from the Palace of the Inquisition had remained with my friends. When I was a boy of thirteen, I had come to England with little. Now I was a man of four-and-twenty, my birthday having come and gone on the long walk to Spain, and I had even less.

There had been time, so much time, to think about everything that I had done, and I was ashamed of having stolen out of London like a thief, saying goodbye to no one. Even so, I had been right to go, I decided, and all that had happened, all the harm I had done, was done with good intention and based upon sound choices. I regretted that people had been hurt, but I did not regret entering into the fray.

More than anything, I regretted leaving without speaking of my plans to Mr. Weaver.

I had begun my journey out of Lisbon determined never to see him again. It would be too painful for me to face what I had done. Somewhere on that long road, however, as I lay on cold dirt by weak fires, I decided that the pain meant nothing. What did humiliation amount to? Mr. Weaver had always been good to me. That was more important than my pride and hurt feelings.

So in April of 1756, having been gone for the better part of a year, I arrived in London. I was determined to set out at once to Dukes Place and Mr. Weaver's house. I was prepared to endure the shame.

I was not, however, prepared to see my foster father waiting for me as I disembarked from the coach. I felt like I had been gone so long, like I had endured so much, that I expected to find Mr. Weaver a decrepit old man. I soon realized that the time had not been as hard for my mentor as it had been for me. He was the same man, tall and muscular, imposing and composed, dignified in his advanced years without being defeated by time.

He smiled at me. "You did not think your whereabouts would be unknown to me."

I stood there in my ragged coat, my hair unkempt, stubble upon my face, and shook like a child. "You have been following my movements since Falmouth, I suppose."

"Since San Sebastian."

Caring nothing for the people who stared, I fell to my knees. "I beg your forgiveness for how I treated you."

Mr. Weaver raised me up by my elbow. "It is given," he said. "I understand why you did what you did. I can only hope you found what you were looking for."

"I saw the city of Lisbon destroyed," I said. "I saw the Palace of the Inquisition reduced to rubble. I killed priests, and I took their stolen money."

Mr. Weaver nodded. "That sounds like time well spent."

Back in his house, I realized Mr. Weaver already had heard a great deal of the story. "Your friends have been to see me. They told me most of what happened. I believe there were things left unsaid, but the accounting gave me much to be proud of."

"I made many mistakes."

"You cannot always be accountable for believing the lies of your friends," Mr. Weaver said.

Evidently, he had heard the truth about Settwell and Roberta. I did not know if I should be relieved or ashamed.

"Your friends set up an account for you at a local goldsmith's,"

Mr. Weaver explained. "Your share of the spoils of war. You'll not be wanting money for some time."

It did not occur to me to ask how much. I didn't care. "Do you know where they are settled? Are they all in London?"

"Not all," Mr. Weaver said. "Eusebio Nobreza and his wife have already departed for Rotterdam. I have given them a letter of introduction to my brother, and I have no doubt they shall do well there."

I said nothing. Was I saddened to hear she was gone? Was I disappointed? I did not think so. "And Luis Nobreza?"

"He remains here in London. He seemed eager to wait for you, but also apprehensive. Can you tell me why?"

I let out a long breath. "He destroyed my father."

The letter Luis left me had confessed everything. It was he, and not Kingsley Franklin, who had given my father to the Inquisition. He had done it not out of self-preservation, but because my father had given him several thousand pounds in negotiable notes, which he needed converted into gold. My father had set up a series of contacts, all of whom needed to be bribed for him to get himself, his family, and Gabriela and her father out of Lisbon.

"I had betrayed men before," Luis had written. "I had been inside the Palace of the Inquisition and made to call my friends and neighbors Judaizers, to swear by our Savior that I had witnessed crimes that had, in truth, never taken place. I had done this to save myself and my family. It excuses nothing, but perhaps it explains why betraying your father was not so difficult. Betrayal is a part of life in this city, and why should a man not betray for money as well as preservation? That your father stood poised to flee all of this angered me. It angered me that he could do what I could not.

"I told myself he would be caught with or without me, and better the money should be in my hands than the Inquisition's. Of course I was deceiving myself. Then, when I sensed you sought the truth of those events, I blamed a crass Englishman, already ruined. By that time, I had begun to suspect your true identity—you look so much like your father—that I thought it best to put you off my scent. I am embarrassed, but what truly shames me is that I clung to my lie, even to the point of asking you to abandon Mr. Franklin lest you discover my treachery. After you refused me, I decided you must know the truth. I was sick of the lies.

"On my behalf, I can only say that I am a product of this nation, this city which lies in ruins about me as I write these words. Lisbon has suffered as it deserves, and I will too."

"Where, precisely, can I find Luis Nobreza?"

Mr. Weaver's expression was impossible to read. "He has taken rooms not far from my house. He asked that I send word when you reached town, which I have done. And he has requested that you call upon him immediately."

I said nothing.

"What will you do?" Mr. Weaver asked.

"I don't know," I said. "He set in motion events that resulted in the destruction of my family, but it was ten years ago, and he is an old man. You must tell me what is the right thing."

Mr. Weaver shook his head. "You do me too much credit if you think I can answer a question such as that. But I have trained you for a long time, and I think you can read the signs as well as I can. What do you make of his decision to wait here for you?"

I considered this. "It is an impossible situation he puts me in, and he knows it. I think he has already decided what he will do. He wants only that I might witness his choice."

Weaver nodded. "I think so too."

"What of my other friends from Lisbon?" I asked after a moment.

Weaver smiled. "Mrs. Carver has set herself up with a fine townhouse near Grosvenor Square. She has become quite the talk of the town, you know. A beautiful and rich widow never wants for friends."

"Did she ask me to call on her too?"

"Not with words," Mr. Weaver said. "But I know she hopes to see you. As does your friend Franklin and his wife."

"His wife?"

"Yes. Apparently he met a Frenchwoman on the road, much younger than himself, and they took to each other."

For the first time in weeks, I laughed. Somehow, amid all the bodies and ashes, something good had managed to unfold.

I delayed for several days before revealing to any acquaintance that I had returned. I spent that time mostly sleeping and eating, but also inspecting the money left for me and using to it to obtain new clothes. I had my hair tended to, and I took pleasure in receiving a proper shave for the first time since—well, since Enéas had shaved me months before. Since then it had been all stubble and my own clumsy efforts with a dagger and cold water.

Mr. Weaver had made it clear that I might stay in his house as long as I wished. Soon I would find a place of my own, but I was not ready. Not quite yet. Once more I had come to London, a refugee of Lisbon by way of Falmouth. Once again, I stayed with Benjamin Weaver, a man as kind as he was intimidating. The last time I had been too frightened, too devastated, to appreciate the friendship offered me. This time I wanted it for its own sake. I wanted to savor such goodness as there was in the world, because I knew that goodness was real, and I knew it was rare.

On the morning of my fourth day in London, I wrote to Luis Nobreza and told him I would call on him at noon. I received a reply, but noon came and went. I had no intention of going. Luis needed to do what he thought best, but I did not want to witness it. I had no wish to gaze upon my friend with his throat cut or hanging from a rope or with a bullet to his head. I knew with absolute certainty that he intended self-murder. Perhaps I might have found the words to save him, but I had not the energy to look. Sometimes the transgressions between human beings cannot be forgiven. They can only fade with time.

Instead of waiting for the news of Luis's death to reach me, I hired a hackney coach and ordered it to take me to Grosvenor Square. I had already found Mrs. Carver's address in The London Magazine—she was indeed a most popular lady, and many men had made it clear that they would gratefully accept her hand in marriage. Thus far she had refused them all.

I knew better than to read anything into that. I knew better than to expect anything other than a slap in the face. However she chose to greet me, I would endure it.

I walked half a block from where the coach had dropped me. The streets were wide and tree-lined, and the sky was brilliant and nearly cloudless. Here and there strolled gentlemen and ladies in fine clothes and fashionable hats. Some had little dogs upon leashes. The spring air was beginning to warm but was still brisk, and the scent of flowers was everywhere. I admired the green lawns and the beautiful homes. In other quarters of the city, it was true, those little dogs would be stolen, slaughtered, and cooked within half an hour of making their appearance. Even so, I was in London and happy to be there. I was at liberty, free to walk the streets and bear my own name.

I found Mrs. Carver's stately new house—all red brick and square columns—and approached the front door. A liveried servant answered almost the moment I rang. I presented my card, and the servant studied it.

"Mr. Foxx," he said, "I have standing instructions to receive you."

I followed the servant to a sitting room where I was told to wait. I listened to the ticking of the clock and muted voices from outside, and the shuffle of servants' footsteps on the floor above me. Somewhere one of those fashionable little dogs barked. I waited, and it seemed to me that I also waited to find out what sort of man I was, what all the things I had done had wrought. I had saved lives and taken them. I had sought justice and delivered suffering. I had committed crimes and forgiven crimes and refused to forgive others. I did not know what all of that made me, but I so wanted to find out.

I stood facing the window, looking at nothing, listening for the sound of her footsteps, and I wondered what her first words would be. How would I find the strength to answer? I dared not wish for one outcome or another, but only for her happiness. That was what I wanted to see on her face. I wanted to see that all she had suffered, unbearable though it was, had not destroyed her. I wanted to see that Lisbon had not broken her as it had broken me so many years before.

I heard voices in the distance, a servant and a woman's voice. Roberta's. And still I waited. I thought of all the things I did not feel—anger and frustration and that wretched, tearing, unbearable impatience with the world as it was. Somehow I had let those things go. I thought of what I did feel: fear. For the first time in years, I was afraid, and I hugged myself with the pleasure of it.

From outside the room, a woman walked upon the floor, her shoes tapping the wooden planks as she approached. I listened to each step, and then the slight squeak of the slow twist of a doorknob.

Terrified and hopeful, I turned to look upon her face and to hear what she had to say.

Acknowledgments

All historical novels present their own challenges, but trying to recover eighteenth-century Lisbon, as it was before the earthquake, is one of the most difficult tasks I've undertaken as a writer. There were numerous books, both those from the time of the earthquake as well as more contemporary studies, that helped me get a sense of the time and place, but I never could have written *The Day of Atonement* without insight into the period from the fantastic historian Paolo Scheffer, who walked me through contemporary Lisbon and helped me to see the city as it was. I am grateful as well to my Portuguese editor and fellow comics fan Luis Corte Real for helping me navigate the city, and for the many insights from the brilliant Portuguese novelist Pedro Almeida Vieira. I am also grateful to the many historians at the Lisbon Museu da Cidade who answered my endless questions, and to the kind people at the Conceição dos Cardais. I owe much to Matt Richtel and Eileen Curtright, who labored through early drafts of the book and helped me to revise it, and for the many ideas and patient readings from Jennifer Hershey and Joey McGarvey at Random House. Again, I must thank my agent, Liz Darhansoff, for making all I do possible. Thanks, as always, to my wife, Claudia, for putting up with my crap, and for my children, Eleanor and Simon, for helping me keep things in perspective. And because I always like to mention my cats in my acknowledgments, I shall do so once again: cats!

About the Author

DAVID LISS is the author of *The Day of Atonement, The Twelfth Enchantment, The Devil's Company, The Whiskey Rebels, The Ethical Assassin, A Spectacle of Corruption, The Coffee Trader,* and *A Conspiracy of Paper,* winner of the 2000 Edgar Award for Best First Novel. He lives in San Antonio with his wife and children.

davidliss.com
@david_liss

About the Type

This book was set in Dante, a typeface designed by Giovanni Mardersteig (1892–1977). Conceived as a private type for the Officina Bodoni in Verona, Italy, Dante was originally cut only for hand composition by Charles Malin, the famous Parisian punch cutter, between 1946 and 1952. Its first use was in an edition of Boccaccio's *Trattatello in laude di Dante* that appeared in 1954. The Monotype Corporation's version of Dante followed in 1957. Though modeled on the Aldine type used for Pietro Cardinal Bembo's treatise *De Aetna* in 1495, Dante is a thoroughly modern interpretation of that venerable face.